Margaret Thornton was born in Blackpool and has lived there all her life. She is a qualified teacher but has retired in order to concentrate on her writing. She has two children and five grandchildren.

MARGARET
THORNTON

Cast the First Stone

CANELO

First published in the United Kingdom in 2012 by Severn House Publishers
Ltd

This edition published in the United Kingdom in 2021 by

Canelo
Unit 9, 5th Floor
Cargo Works, 1–2 Hatfields
London, SE1 9PG
United Kingdom

A CIP catalogue record for this book is available from the British Library.

Print ISBN 978 1 80032 721 4
Ebook ISBN 978 1 80032 389 6

Look for more great books at www.canelo.co

Printed and bound in Great Britain by Clays Ltd, Elcograf S.p.A.

One

'If you ask me it's far too soon, and he will live to regret it.' Mrs Ethel Bayliss stopped for a moment in her task of opening another packet of sandwiches. She looked towards her small team of helpers – all stalwart members of the church congregation and the Mothers' Union – for support and encouragement. 'Talk about marry in haste and repent at leisure! Poor Millicent! She must be turning in her grave.'

'Yes, and it's not all that long since he laid her to rest.' Mrs Blanche Fowler nodded in agreement, setting the bunch of artificial cherries on her hat bobbing as if in assent. 'A dreadful shock, wasn't it, her dying like that? Just as we were beginning to get to know her a little better. And to like her more as well. Do you remember, we weren't too sure about her at first?'

'Well, she was finding her feet, wasn't she?' replied Ethel Bayliss. 'Just like he was. And it had been a long time since we'd had a rector's wife at the helm. We'd got used to doing things in our own way.'

And you didn't like a newcomer telling you what to do, thought Mrs Ruth Makepeace, although she didn't voice her opinion. She was some fifteen or twenty years younger than most of the women and rather in awe of them. Besides, Ruth liked to keep her opinions to herself.

'But she turned out all right in the end,' Mrs Bayliss continued. 'She was a very determined woman, was Millicent, and very astute. Happen a bit straight-laced at times, mind.'

'No, not much sense of humour, had she?' added Mrs Joan Tweedale, another member of the little group. 'Not like the Reverend Simon. He's always ready for a laugh and a joke, isn't he?'

'A bit too much so at times if you ask me. Like chalk and cheese they were, the rector and Millicent.' Ethel Bayliss was arranging the contents from the next packet on to a large white plate. She lifted a corner of a sandwich to peer at the contents. 'Hmm... some more salmon. And it looks like that cheap salmon paste out of a jar.' She gave a derisory sniff. 'Tinned red salmon is much nicer. Who brought these? Does anybody know?'

'I think it was that young Mrs Jarvis,' replied Mrs Tweedale. 'You know, she's got three children in the Sunday school. I don't suppose she could afford anything else.'

'No, maybe not,' Ethel Bayliss agreed, a trifle grudgingly. 'We'll just have to make sure they don't go on the top table, that's all... As I was just saying, they didn't seem to have all that much in common, the rector and his wife – his first wife I mean, of course.' She nodded meaningfully. 'He seemed to be heartbroken at the funeral though. I remember he looked real grief-stricken. But she was taken from him so sudden like, wasn't she? It must have been an awful shock. She'd only been poorly for a week or so.'

'But it didn't take him long to find somebody else, did it?' The cherries on Mrs Fowler's hat were bobbing merrily again. 'Talk about off with the old and on with the new! And he couldn't have chosen anyone more different. I mean to say – honestly! – red painted nails… and that hair! Although I must admit that I've found her to be a very pleasant young woman…' Blanche Fowler tried to soften her criticism because she really did like the rector's new wife despite the fact that she was a very modern young woman.

'If you ask me a rector's wife should behave with a little more decorum; well, a lot more decorum actually.' Mrs Bayliss wiped her hands down the front of her floral apron. 'Pass me that basket, will you, Blanche, if you don't mind? I think that's Mrs Halliwell's offering. Her home-made gingerbread is always very popular. Oh yes… look. Gingerbread, and an iced sandwich cake. She's done us proud. Would you like to cut them up, please, Blanche, and arrange them on a plate? And there are some fancy doilies over there… Yes, as I was saying, our rector's new wife leaves a lot to be desired. Ah well, he's made his bed, and I reckon he'll have to lie on it. But if you ask me he'll soon live to regret it.'

But nobody is asking you, are they? thought Ruth Makepeace. She was quietly getting on with her task of setting out the cups and saucers. They were using the church's best crockery today – not china, to be sure, but a good quality earthenware with a willow pattern design – as it was a special occasion.

Ethel's remark was very apt under the circumstances, although Ruth doubted that the older woman was intending to refer to the newly married couple's honey-moon bed. It had been very much on Ruth's mind, however, over this past week whilst the Reverend Simon Norwood and his new bride were honeymooning in Scar-borough. At one time Ruth had nursed hopes that she might be the 'chosen one'. But it was not to be. As soon as Simon had met the newcomer to the small town, Miss Fiona Dalton, that had been it. He had had eyes for none of the others who might have had aspirations to become the rector's second wife. All in good time, of course; he had to be given time to grieve and to adapt to life on his own. But there had been quite a few helpful – and hopeful – young women who had made their way to the rectory door bearing a home-made fruit cake or a batch of scones.

Ruth had not been so blatant in her quest. She had, in fact, held back, believing that Simon might well turn to her in his own good time. They were friends already and had been so almost as long as Simon had been in the parish. As secretary to the church council Ruth had come to know him, and his wife, Millicent, quite well. She had never really taken to Millicent, though. A very humourless woman – as some of the others had just been remarking – but one who had held firm opinions and had known her own mind. At least she had done her best to keep Madam Bayliss and company in their place, and Ruth had admired her for that. Fiona, the new Mrs Norwood, would certainly have her work cut out there, she pondered.

In the months following his wife's sudden death Simon had turned to Ruth, who was more or less the same age as himself, for companionship and friendship. Nothing more than that, although she had fancied she had seen a look of admiration in his eyes that might well have turned to affection. And she had found herself growing more and more fond of him, believing that it was only a question of time before her feelings were reciprocated. Which was why it had been such a surprise to her, and to the other members of the congregation, when the rector was seen to be quite openly paying attention to the newcomer to the parish. And then, a few months ago, less than two years since his wife's death, he had announced that he and Miss Fiona Dalton were engaged to be married.

The wedding had taken place at his own church, St Peter's, in the small market town of Aberthwaite, in one of the northernmost Yorkshire Dales, on a Saturday in June, 1965. Simon's friend from his college days, the Reverend Timothy Marsden, had conducted the ceremony; then he and his wife had stayed for the weekend and he had taken the services on the Sunday, in Simon's absence.

The tea party that was presently being arranged in the church hall was by way of being a 'welcome home' celebration for the rector and his new wife. It was what was known as a 'Jacob's Join' meal, a northern tradition where each person brought their own contribution. The offerings would then be shared out amongst all the people who were present. Members of the congregation who intended to be at the tea party had been asked to bring their bags of goodies earlier in the afternoon; and the meal would then be prepared by a small team of helpers. They had also been asked to stipulate whether they would be bringing sandwiches or cakes, savouries or sweets, so that there would not be a glut of one thing and very little of another.

Each item had been carefully scrutinized, particularly by Mrs Ethel Bayliss, although it was agreed that all offerings must be gratefully received and all must be used. The system was seen to be working quite well, as was usually the case. There was a wide variety of sandwiches: salmon, some with the cheap pink paste sniffed at by Ethel, and others of the more appetizing red variety; egg and cress; boiled ham or tongue; chicken or sliced turkey; and grated cheese. There were sausage rolls and meat pies, and the more enterprising of the ladies had brought vol au vents and dainty morsels such as tiny sausages, cubes of cheese or pineapple chunks on sticks. The offerings that appeared to be rather less attractive were hidden beneath the more perfect culinary efforts, and care would be taken that they did not appear on the 'top table'.

And it was the same with the cakes. The badly iced buns or the pieces of fruitcake that had sagged in the middle were secreted beneath the luscious slices of gingerbread, coffee and walnut loaf, and sandwich cakes oozing with cream or topped with chocolate. There were large glass dishes of trifle, too, which would be spooned out into individual portions. These trifles were works of art created by Mesdames Bayliss and Fowler, who always tried to outdo each other in the contents and the presentation of these delicacies. The rivalry was never admitted or referred to, but the ladies of the congregation – at least those who considered themselves to be in the know – were well aware that it existed. They knew, too, that if anyone else should offer to bring a trifle they would find that it was politely declined.

Ruth glanced at the two huge dishes, covered carefully with the ever useful cling film, that stood on the working surface along with the sandwiches and cakes. They were also covered to guard against flies or wasps until the time came to unveil them. Mrs Bayliss's creation was topped with fresh cream skilfully piped in peaks, each topped with a glace cherry and morsels of angelica, whilst Mrs Fowler's effort, also covered in fresh cream, was sprinkled with flaked almonds and chocolate buttons. Handiwork that would be demolished as soon as a spoon went to work on them. It was not possible to see inside, but it was well known that neither of the ladies would have scrimped on the sherry to moisten the sponge cake. Most of the members of the congregation agreed that they reckoned nothing to 'Methodist trifle' flavoured with fruit juice! Mrs Bayliss was known to favour fresh raspberries and red jelly, whereas Mrs Fowler preferred tinned peaches and orange jelly. It was assumed, however, that both ladies used the well-known 'Ambrosia' custard that came out of a tin; but their efforts would be highly praised as the pièce de résistance of the meal.

Ruth and her friend, Heather Milner, did not really consider themselves to be part of the coterie of women who organized church teas and helped out at the social functions. Those were ladies of an older age group – late fifties, sixties or early seventies – whose children had long left home and had families of their own. They were retired ladies, too. Indeed, most of them had never worked outside of the home – whereas Ruth and Heather were both employed as teachers at the local school.

Ruth Makepeace was a widow. Her husband had been killed in the D-Day landings when he was twenty-two years of age, the same age as Ruth. They had been married for little more than a year, their wedding having taken place soon after Ruth had started her teaching career. Married women teachers were a rarity at that time, but the restriction about employing only single women had been lifted in recent years. The women, indeed, both married and single, had constituted the bulk of the teaching profession during the war years. The men who were employed in the schools were those who were too old or unfit for active service.

Ruth was now forty-three. Her marriage, though short, had been blissful, and she was sure, if Ralph had not

7

been killed, that they would still have been ideally happy together. She had concentrated upon her career, glad that she had such a satisfying job. She had been happy at home with her parents and younger sister, and so she had not sought a post elsewhere. She had moved, however, to a flat of her own, when she had been able to afford it. This had come about because, in her mid-thirties, she had been promoted to the post of head of the infant department.

She had remained a widow because she had never met anyone she could consider marrying, since Ralph; that was until her friendship with the Reverend Simon Norwood had shown signs of developing. Now, though, her hopes had been cruelly dashed; but she was trying to carry on as though she had never felt anything but feelings of friendship towards him.

The only person who knew her secret was her good friend and colleague, Heather Milner. Heather, aged thirty-eight, was happily married with two children who were now of secondary school age. Heather had resumed her teaching career that she had given up temporarily when the children were small. Her sensible outlook on life and her cheerful disposition had helped and were still helping Ruth to get over her disappointment and put it behind her.

She spoke confidentially to Ruth now as, together – at the request of the 'chief cook and bottle washer', Mrs Bayliss – they sorted out the glass dishes for the trifles. Each one had to be carefully checked to ensure they were clean and not cracked or chipped before being set out on the table top.

'How are you feeling, love?' she enquired. 'I must say you're looking very fetching in your new dress. Is that the one you got from M and S? The colour really suits you.'

'I'm feeling OK, thanks,' replied Ruth. 'Keeping myself well under control, I hope! Yes, this is the dress I bought at Marks and Sparks in Leeds. I liked the colour, but I wondered if it might be too short; in fact I'm still not sure about the length. What do you think, Heather, honestly?'

'Of course it's not too short,' answered Heather. 'They're all the rage now, these miniskirts. And you've got nice shapely legs, so why not show them off?'

'Thank you,' laughed Ruth. 'But at my age, I mean. Don't you think I might be too old? I saw Mrs Bayliss looking pointedly at my hemline when I came in.'

'Oh, be damned to her!' said Heather, rather too forcibly. 'Oops!' She put a hand to her mouth. 'Sorry; I was forgetting I'm on church premises. But who's bothered what she thinks? She's an old fuddy-duddy. Anyway, my skirt's just as short as yours.'

'Yes, but you're younger than me. You're not even forty yet.'

'I will be in a couple of years' time. And I never think of you as being any older than me. You're as young as you feel, that's what I say. And I think these new fashions are great.'

The length of skirts had been gradually rising since the start of the sixties, and now, in 1965, they were well above the knee. The dress that Ruth was wearing was a cherry red colour, what was known as a shift dress, in the new Terylene material, sleeveless, with a tie neckline in white and with a narrow white piping at the waist.

'As I was saying, that colour's just the right shade for you,' Heather continued, 'with your dark hair and eyes. And you're slim enough to get away with anything. I must say I envy you your trim figure. How on earth do you manage to keep so slim?'

'I don't know really.' Ruth gave a slight shrug. 'I don't watch what I eat, not particularly. I suppose I take after my mother; she's seventy now and still as slim as ever.'

'I started putting weight on after I had the children,' said Heather, 'and I've never been able to lose it. And of course this lot won't help today, will it?' She waved her hand towards the array of food that surrounded them. 'Gosh! What a spread! I can't wait to sample some of those cakes. That is if there are any left after we've served the VIPs.'

'Don't worry; there's enough to feed a regiment,' smiled Ruth. As she looked at her friend she couldn't help thinking that Heather maybe should lose a little weight. She, too, was wearing a dress with a short skirt, revealing plump thighs. The pale-blue colour suited her fair prettiness and her blue eyes. Her cheerful rounded face and her curvaceous figure were part of Heather's charm, though, and Ruth couldn't imagine her any other way.

'Ladies, will you listen, please?' Mrs Ethel Bayliss now called them all to order. 'It's time to carry the sandwiches and savouries through to the hall. A nice selection on each table, and make sure the top table is well served. Blanche and Joan – would you put the kettles on now, please? Our guests should be here in just a few moments.'

Two

Fiona, the new Mrs Norwood, looked round the room a little apprehensively. She didn't like being the centre of attention, although she supposed, as the rector's new wife, she would have to get used to the position. Simon had assured her that there was nothing to be anxious about. He had also assured her that she looked lovely – as she always did, he added – and she was quite pleased with her appearance as well. Simon had persuaded her to wear her 'going away' suit – a short-sleeved jacket with a peplum at the waist in a shade of buttercup yellow, over a slightly above the knee-length skirt with a scalloped hemline. He said she looked like a ray of sunshine. The suit had been a minor extravagance, purchased from Schofield's in Leeds rather than the M and S, or C and A stores where she usually shopped. She had decided, however, not to wear the small cap of artificial petals in a matching shade that she had worn on her wedding day, feeling that it might look a little too fancy for the occasion. Looking around she saw that it was mostly the older ladies who were wearing hats.

Fiona knew that some of those elderly ladies were inclined to look critically at her make-up and her painted nails, also at her blonde hair – which, contrary to what people might think, was her natural colour. She had always been conscious of her appearance and tried to look her best at all times. Her lips and her nails today were a coral colour, rather than a vivid red, which she felt was more in keeping with 'the rector's wife' image. Not that Simon cared two hoots, he said, about what the members of the congregation might think. He loved her just as she was and didn't want her to change at all.

She knew, though, that the position of rector's wife was regarded as one of importance in the parish and she couldn't help wondering how she would adapt to it. Simon had agreed that she should keep on with her job at the library for the time being. Fiona also knew it was Simon's hope that they would be blessed with a child in the not too distant future. 'Be blessed with…' That was Simon's way of looking at things. He regarded the good things that happened in life as God's blessings. Until she had met Simon, Fiona had attended church only spasmodically of late. She had not given much thought to spiritual matters; not since her teenage days, in fact, when circumstances had caused her to doubt all that she had been taught in Sunday school. Now, though, since her friendship with him had blossomed into love and then marriage, she had come to realize that there was a good deal more to life than the day-to-day routine with its ups and downs. She had found herself starting to believe more fully in this God who meant so much to Simon, and not only because it was her duty as the rector's wife to do so. She still had a great deal to learn, but with her beloved husband at her side she knew she would be all right.

Mrs Ethel Bayliss, whom she had soon learnt was one of the bigwigs in the church – the chief bigwig, in fact – had met them at the door and had led them, with a good deal of bowing and scraping, to their places at the table at the end of the church hall; the 'top table' she had called it. The assembled crowd – Fiona estimated at a glance that there might be about forty of them – had all clapped and smiled in a very welcoming manner as the rector and his wife took their places.

'What's it all in aid of, this tea party?' Fiona had asked Simon.

'Oh, it's just their way of welcoming us back,' said Simon. 'You especially, my love, as my new wife. But it's any excuse for a tea party, if you ask me. We have to humour them. Mrs Bayliss and Mrs Fowler are in their element when they're organizing church teas.'

Fiona had met both these ladies soon after she had started attending St Peter's church. She glanced across at Mrs Bayliss now, deep in conversation with Mrs Fowler, who was seated next to her. Ethel Bayliss was in her mid-sixties, Fiona guessed; a large-bosomed woman who moved in a stately manner like a ship in full sail, as though she considered herself to be of some importance. Fiona, in all fairness, had noticed that she always dressed well and in keeping with her age. The navy-blue dress with white spots was stylish but discreet, as was the small white straw hat above her newly permed hair. Ethel – although Fiona would not dream of calling her by her Christian name – was married to Arthur Bayliss, the church warden at St Peter's, a small unassuming man with a bald head and rimless glasses, whom Fiona rather liked.

'Yes, Mrs Halliwell's ginger cake is as delicious as ever,' Mrs Bayliss was saying, delicately licking her finger and picking up the crumbs that remained on the plate. 'I think it's the combination of a small amount of black treacle with the golden syrup that gives it that extra something. I'm just guessing though. She's very guarded about the recipe.'

'Yes, so I've noticed,' agreed Mrs Blanche Fowler. 'I did pluck up courage to ask her for the recipe once, but she was very evasive. Still, we all have our little secrets, haven't we?' She gave a tinkling laugh. 'I must confess I'm the same with my Christmas cake recipe. It's been handed down through our family for generations.'

Fiona was fascinated by the bunch of cherries on Mrs Fowler's straw hat. She assumed that this lady was roughly the same age as Mrs Bayliss, but the two were as different as could be. They were close friends, at least on the surface. Mrs Fowler was tall and slim and walked with a slight stoop. If one was to be unkind she might be described as 'mutton dressed as lamb'. Her full-skirted nylon dress was boldly patterned with pink and blue flowers that did not really match her headgear. However, Fiona found her not quite as intimidating as her friend, and of the two she much preferred Blanche Fowler. She was the wife of Jonas who was the other church warden. There were always two, known respectively as the rector's and the people's warden. Jonas was a large rotund man who was also in charge of the Sunday school.

'So you enjoyed your honeymoon, did you, Fiona?' asked Mrs Joan Tweedale who was sitting next to her. 'Well, you know what I mean,' she went on, colouring slightly. 'I didn't mean to be personal,' she added in a whisper. 'What I meant was did you enjoy Scarborough? You had lovely weather, didn't you?'

'Yes, we were very fortunate,' replied Fiona. 'There was only one day when it rained. And, yes, I love Scarborough, I've been several times before, and so has Simon. It's a favourite place for both of us.'

Fiona liked Joan Tweedale. She was the wife of Henry, the organist and choir master who was seated on the other side of her. Fiona put them both in their late forties, and they were rather more go-ahead in outlook than some of the other members of the congregation. Henry leaned forward to speak to Fiona.

'I have been wondering, Mrs Norwood, if you would be interested in joining the choir? I have noticed on a Sunday morning that you sing out with great gusto and I'm sure you would be an asset in the... soprano section, would it be?'

Fiona smiled. 'I should imagine so. I've never been in a choir, not since I was at school. But I can read music after a fashion and I enjoy singing, although I don't know whether I'm a soprano or a contralto! Yes – that would be a nice idea. Thank you for asking me. But why the formality? I would much rather you called me Fiona than Mrs Norwood.'

'Sorry... I was just giving you your full title as our rector's wife. I thought you would like it.'

'So I do, very much.' Fiona smiled. 'At least, I like being the rector's wife, but it's taking a bit of getting used to the new name.'

Simon had been listening to this exchange and he joined in the conversation now. 'I don't want Fiona to be known as "the rector's wife", although I'm delighted of course that she agreed to take me on! But she is a person in her own right, not just my wife.'

'Thank you, darling,' said Fiona. 'What do you think, Simon? Mr Tweedale – Henry – has just asked me if I would like to join the choir. Do you think I should?'

'Ra—ther!' replied her husband. 'That's a great idea. You have quite a few female voices now, haven't you, Henry? And they have certainly made a vast improvement to the choir.'

'I'm glad you think so,' said Henry Tweedale. He lowered his voice, speaking to Fiona in a confidential way. 'Our idea – Simon's and mine – to have women in the choir didn't go down too well at first, did it, Simon?'

'You can say that again!' laughed the rector. He glanced a little uneasily across the table, but the Fowlers and the Baylisses appeared not to be listening. 'Yes, that's right,' he went on, in a quieter voice. 'A certain amount of opposition, you might say, but we won through in the end. It's to be hoped we will do the same about Henry's idea for a Junior section, girls as well as boys.' He made a slight nod towards the other side of the table. 'But I think we're making headway. Rome wasn't built in a day, as they say. I've told Fiona about some of the – er – difficulties, haven't I, darling?'

'Yes!' she agreed. 'At some length.' She decided to change the conversation, though in case she might be overheard. 'I was just telling Joan how much we enjoyed Scarborough...'

Mrs Tweedale was one of the women with whom Fiona was on first name terms. They had got on well together right from the start. Joan had a small handicraft shop on the main street of the town which sold knitting wools, embroidery silks and tapestry sets, lace and ribbons, trimmings and buttons: everything in fact for those ladies who were good with their fingers. That was not really one of Fiona's talents, but she loved to go into the little shop for a chat with Joan and had been fascinated by the vast array of coloured wools. So much so that she had been encouraged to buy some wool in a shade that Joan called aquamarine – which Fiona had been assured was just right for her colouring – and a simple pattern for a jumper and the appropriate needles. Joan herself was usually seen in one of her own creations. Today it was a lacy jumper in a pale shade of green that went well with her auburn hair.

They chatted a little about Scarborough and the childhood holidays they had all spent there and also at Filey and Whitby. Simon moved to sit next to Henry as they were talking about the joys of fishing from the pier. 'Excuse me, darling,' he said, 'Henry and I are reminiscing. I'll leave you to chat with Joan.'

'How are you getting on with that jumper?' asked Joan. 'The pattern wasn't too difficult, was it?'

'No, it's fine,' replied Fiona. 'If I get stuck I'll come to you for help. I've done about six inches of the back, but it's been put aside for a while. I didn't take it on my honeymoon,' she grinned.

'No, I should think not,' laughed Joan. 'And I dare say you might find yourself too busy now to get back to it. I believe you're still carrying on with your job at the library? Good for you, I say. I approve of what Simon was saying about you being your own person.'

'Yes, he was quite insistent that I shouldn't be regarded as what he calls an unpaid curate. But I gather, reading between the lines, that his first wife was very active in the parish? Of course I don't enquire too closely, and he doesn't talk about her very much.'

'Yes, Millicent was quite a forceful woman and she did take over a lot of the duties. We hadn't had a rector's wife, you see, for ages. The Reverend Holdsworth was well into his seventies when he retired, and his wife had died some years before. Things had been allowed to lapse somewhat, so when Simon came along six years ago it was a big change for us.'

'A new broom, I suppose,' Fiona remarked.

'Yes, exactly. He reorganized the Sunday school and started a class for teenagers, as well as the Youth Club. And the choir too. I'm so pleased you've said you'll join us,' Joan went on. 'I joined when women were allowed into the hallowed ranks. It had been an all–male choir when the former rector had been with us. He wouldn't entertain the idea of women; I could never imagine why. I suppose he took too literally the view of St Paul that women should remain silent. And the diehards just went along with it.'

'I wonder what they will say when they hear about Simon introducing a guitar group?' smiled Fiona.

'Yes, Henry has been telling me about that,' said Joan. 'I was surprised really that Henry agreed so readily, but he's adopted a much more modern approach to music since Simon came along. Anyway, we shall see. And of course when Millicent took over the Mothers' Union and the catering arrangements that didn't go down very well with Mrs Bayliss and her cronies. They'd been running things their own way for ages.' Joan was talking more freely because Mesdames Bayliss and Fowler and their husbands had gone away from the table. 'They'll be starting the washing up now, I suppose. I'll go and help them in a little while, but I'm sure there'll be enough helpers in the kitchen… As I was saying, Mrs Bayliss and Co had their noses pushed out, so to speak, when Millicent took over. Mrs B had been acting as the enrolling member for the Mothers' Union – that's the one in charge – after the old rector's wife died, and then, of course, she had to give it up again when Millicent came on the scene. It's always done by the rector's wife, you see.'

'Yes, Simon was telling me something about it,' replied Fiona. 'He hasn't actually said so, but I think he wants me to take up the position. But I'm not a mother, am I?'

'Neither was Millicent for that matter,' said Joan. 'But that's how it's always been – the job of the rector's wife. You get in there, lass, and show them what you can do.'

'What about Mrs Bayliss, though? Won't she be annoyed? And I'm sure she can do it much better than I could.'

'Oh, be blowed to her!' said Joan. 'She has too much of her own way. Start as you mean to go on, that's what I say... Ooh, we'd best shut up now. Arthur's about to say a few words...'

Arthur Bayliss, the senior church warden, was standing near the stage at the far end of the hall, holding up his hand as a signal for everyone to listen. The ladies who had been in the kitchen came out, still wearing their aprons, and stood near the serving hatch.

'Ladies and gentlemen,' Arthur Bayliss began. 'I now have a very pleasant duty to perform. Will our rector and his lovely wife please come forward.'

'Come along, darling.' Simon came and took her hand as they went towards the stage, and once again everyone clapped and smiled.

'As you all know, Simon and Fiona were married recently,' Arthur continued, 'and we would all like to mark that occasion with a little gift. This is from the members of the church council and the congregation...' Arthur handed to Simon a small carriage clock made of brass. 'We hope that all your hours and days will be happy ones. God bless you both.' He shook hands with Simon, then, very gingerly, kissed Fiona's cheek.

'Thank you all very much,' said Simon. 'I'm sure you don't want to hear me sermonizing. I'll save that till tomorrow,' he added to a ripple of polite laughter. 'So... all I want to say is thank you for the lovely gift, which will have pride of place on our mantelpiece. Thank you all for coming and for the welcome home party, not forgetting the ladies in the kitchen who have worked extra hard today.' Fiona noticed how Mrs Bayliss smiled smugly as though she was preening her feathers. 'And thank you, all of you, for making my dear wife so welcome in the church,' Simon continued. 'Now, do stay and have a chat for a little while. There's no need to rush home. So long as we're gone by seven o'clock when the Youth Club starts.'

Fiona reflected on his remark about her welcome from the congregation. Some of them, indeed, had been very friendly towards her. But there were a few about whom she had reservations. Mrs Bayliss, of course, and there were others: in particular two women who were part of her clique: Miss Thorpe – a spinster of indeterminate age – and Mrs Parker, who Fiona believed was her sister. They had not yet passed the time of day with her.

There was another woman, too, rather younger, whom she felt she would like to get to know. That was Ruth Makepeace, who was a teacher at the local school. She was pleasant enough, and polite, and Fiona felt that on closer acquaintance she might well be a friend and ally. But so far Fiona had been unable to engender any reciprocal warmth from the woman. Her friend, however, Heather Milner, seemed altogether different, very amenable and outgoing. Maybe Ruth was the sort of person who preferred to have just one or two intimate friends; there were women like that.

Joan had gone into the kitchen, so Fiona decided she would start, as Joan had advised, as she meant to go on. She also went into the kitchen. 'Hello, ladies,' she began, 'you're all very busy. May I give you a hand? Pass me a tea towel and I'll wipe some of those pots. Goodness, what a mountain of washing up!'

Mrs Bayliss turned round from the cupboard where she was putting away the clean plates. Fiona noticed that she was not the one with her hands in the water; that was Mrs Fowler. 'No, thank you, dear,' said Ethel Bayliss. 'We've got quite enough helpers. If we get any more we won't have room to turn round in here.'

'There aren't any more tea towels,' said Miss Thorpe; it was the first time she had addressed any remark to Fiona. 'Anyway, we've nearly finished.' Which was obviously not true.

Mrs Fowler turned round from her position at the sink. 'Thank you very much, dear, for offering,' she said, smiling in what Fiona thought was a sincere and regretful manner, 'but it would be a shame to spoil your pretty dress. Another time, maybe.'

'Yes, another time...' echoed Fiona. She glanced round, smiling a little nervously at the six or seven ladies gathered there. It was probably true that they didn't need any more helpers. She caught the eye of Ruth Makepeace, and she fancied that the woman smiled back quite sympathetically.

She went back into the hall, and Joan quickly followed her. 'Be blowed to the lot of 'em!' said Joan. 'I flung my tea towel down, and I've left them to it. But don't let them upset you; it's only a few of them, and the rest of us are really glad to have you with us. You must be wanting to get home though, I'm sure. And here's Simon waiting for you. Bye for now, Fiona, see you in the morning.'

Three

'I'm afraid my offer to help in the kitchen didn't go down very well,' said Fiona when she and Simon had unpacked their suitcases and were taking their ease in the sitting room with a cup of tea.

'Oh dear,' said Simon. 'But I'm sure they were only trying to be thoughtful. They knew you were anxious to get home and unpack.'

'Hmm… maybe,' Fiona nodded. 'Some of them were quite nice about it. Mrs Fowler looked a bit sorry. I think she's a kindly soul, if she wasn't so much under the thumb of Mrs Bayliss.'

'Quite so!' Simon grinned.

'And Ruth Makepeace. I thought she gave me a sympathetic smile. She seems a nice woman. I'd like to get to know her better but she seems rather reluctant, or maybe she's just shy.'

'Yes… she's a nice person. Maybe, as you say, a little shy.' Simon sounded rather evasive. 'But you'll win them all over before long. Don't worry, darling.'

'I find that Joan Tweedale is the best of the bunch,' said Fiona. 'I feel she could be an ally, if ever I need one. She was telling me about Mrs Bayliss and how proud she is of her position as enrolling member of the Mothers' Union. She's the one that I find most… antagonistic. No, maybe that's a bit strong, but she's not very friendly. She soon gave me my marching orders from the kitchen. Her province, I gather, although I get the impression that she organizes the others to do the donkey work.'

Simon laughed. 'I think you've hit the nail on the head! You mustn't worry about her, darling. I admit she's had things her own way since... well, since Millicent died. But you are my wife now, and that's something she will have to get used to. I'm sure she has nothing against you; it's just that she's been kingpin – or should I say queenpin? – for the last couple of years.'

'Do you really want me to take on that enrolling member job? I'm sure it would be much better for Mrs B to carry on.'

'It's a position that is normally taken by the rector's – or the vicar's – wife, as the case may be. So it would be only right, my dear.'

'But I thought you didn't want me to be referred to as the rector's wife?'

'Nor do I. You have your own life to lead, irrespective of mine. But I think it would be right for you to take the lead in certain matters. We'll talk about it another time, shall we, love? Now, if you don't mind I had better adjourn to the study and finish off my sermon. You'll be all right, won't you, watching the television? Then we can have an early night. What do you say, Mrs Norwood?' He grinned at her.

'A good idea!' She smiled back at him, thrilled as always at the look of tenderness in his eyes. 'I won't watch the TV though. I'll finish reading my book.' She picked up the latest Ngaio Marsh mystery novel, with the familiar green Penguin cover, from the coffee table. Although she was a librarian she liked to have her own copies of books by favourite authors and had amassed quite a large library of her own. Her taste in literature was wide ranging but she had too much on her mind to settle to anything too profound at the moment.

'OK, but don't frighten yourself to death,' laughed Simon.

'No fear of that,' she told him. 'Anyway, you're only in the next room.'

Simon leaned over and kissed her gently on the lips. 'I'll leave you to it then, darling.'

Fiona sighed contentedly after he had gone, not starting to read immediately. This room, their sitting room, was pleasant and comfortable and she felt at home there already. The rectory, adjacent to the church, was a mid-Victorian dwelling but, fortunately, not one that was overlarge or labyrinthine in design as many rectories and vicarages were.

Upstairs there were three good-sized bedrooms and a box room, and a bathroom that had been added in the 1930s. Downstairs there was this quite large sitting room, a smaller dining room, Simon's study, a small cloakroom and toilet, and a fair-sized kitchen.

The sitting room was a mishmash of styles. The three-piece suite, in shades of brown and beige, dated from the 1930s. It was roomy and comfortable and the worn patches were disguised by chair back covers with crocheted edges. The cushions had embroidered covers that Fiona guessed might be Millicent's handiwork. The carpet, too, was of a similar nondescript pattern, but the curtains, in a bold fifties geometric design in yellow, orange and black added a more modern touch. Unfortunately they did not really harmonize with the rest of the room.

Simon had promised that Fiona could have a free hand with this room as soon as she had settled in. A new store called Habitat had recently opened in Leeds and she was intrigued by the modern furniture that was simple and functional in design, and the crockery and kitchen utensils in bold primary colours. They were planning a trip to Leeds quite soon. Simon had told her she could order whatever she wanted, within reason of course.

She knew that a clergyman's salary – they referred to it as a stipend – was not enormous, but she gathered that neither was it too stingy. And there was her own librarian's wage as well, which she intended to put towards their living expenses.

The one room in the house that was entirely to her liking was the kitchen. She had been agreeably pleased with the modern features in this room. There was a new material on the market called Formica, which hailed from the USA, as did many of the new inventions. It was a laminated plastic, tough and heat resistant, available in a range of bright colours, which could be used in many rooms but especially in the kitchen.

Another comparatively new idea was the fitted kitchen with built-in cupboards and working surfaces. Bright-yellow Formica – fortunately one of Fiona's favourite colours – covered every surface in the rectory kitchen and also the cupboard doors. There was a fairly modern electric cooker, a small refrigerator, a stainless steel sink, and a Bendix automatic washing machine. Fiona was thankful that Millicent had instigated these modern changes here, if not in the other rooms. She knew that she must tread carefully as the new wife, and not go rushing ahead with all the other plans she had in mind for the modernization of the rest of the rectory.

By and large, though, she was very contented with her lot and happier than she had ever been in her life. She had been amazed at the way their friendship had developed. Simon was not the sort of man she had ever dreamt she would marry. She had started to believe that marriage was not for her. 'Mister Right' had certainly been taking his time in coming along, or maybe she had been too choosy; she had definitely been too wary. Then she had met Simon. The attraction between them had been immediate; and the growth of their relationship inevitable, even though they might be considered – by others – to be poles apart. And the miracle in Fiona's eyes was that Simon felt the same way as she did and had had no doubts about marrying her. Neither did he seem to pay any heed to what might have happened in the past.

'I know you must have had friendships with other men,' he had told her. 'A lovely young woman like you. I'm sure you've had fellows queuing up to go out with you. I'm only surprised that you weren't married long ago. And it's my very good luck that you're not. Although I don't really believe in luck. This was destined to happen, Fiona, my darling. It's fate that we've found one another and I shall never stop giving thanks to God that we met. I love you so much, and I know we're going to be very, very happy.'

She felt very humbled, and a little guilty, too, when he spoke in that vein.

'I'm no angel,' she had told him. 'Far from it.'

'Same here,' he had answered. 'I've not always been a clergyman, you know. But whatever has happened to either of us in the past is over and done with. It's the present that is important… and the future.'

Fiona pondered on her new husband's words as she sat there quietly on her own. She found herself remembering the first time they had met…

Four

The two of them had met in the early spring of the previous year, 1964. Fiona had recently taken up her appointment as chief librarian at the library in the centre of Aberthwaite. It had been a promotion of sorts, following on from the time she had spent in a branch library in Leeds. It was only a small library in Aberthwaite, with one other full-time member of staff and a part-timer. But it was just what Fiona had wanted: chiefly to get away from Leeds with its many unhappy memories, especially now that her dearly loved grandmother had died. She would not have thought of leaving whilst the old lady was still living, and Gran had lived until she was ninety.

Now, though, Fiona was free to do as she pleased. It was fortunate that the vacancy had occurred in the North Yorkshire town so soon after her grandmother's death. There had been only one other applicant, and Fiona had been considered the more suitable one. Following her appointment she had had little difficulty in finding a flat that suited her. It was a rented flat, but she intended to save up and buy a place of her own – a flat or a small house – in the not too distant future.

It was a big change for her, living in the small market town of Aberthwaite after the large bustling city of Leeds. Fiona had been born there in 1934 and had lived in the district of Headingley with her parents. Then, after her parents had both been killed in an accident when she was twenty years of age, she had gone to live with her grandmother at the other side of Leeds.

She had visited the dales before, with her parents and then with her gran. She had always been charmed by the greystone houses, the numerous ruined abbeys, old churches and ancient castles. The rippling streams and waterfalls, the rivers spanned by humpbacked bridges, the village greens and cobbled market squares, she had found it all so fascinating. Her love of the area had increased a few years ago when she had accompanied a group of friends on a tour of Wharfedale and Wensleydale; cycling and fell walking, staying in small bed and breakfast places overnight.

Aberthwaite was a small market town that boasted many of the attractions that made the dales towns and villages so appealing. There was a cobbled market square, a twelfth-century ruined castle, and the squat greystone church of St Peter's with its square tower and ancient graveyard, parts of it dating back to the fifteenth century. Not far away, by the banks of the river, there was a picturesque ruined abbey and, all around, the limestone hills, criss-crossed by drystone walls.

It was during her second week at the library that Fiona looked up from her position at the counter to see a man browsing in the section that held the crime and mystery novels. He was what might be called 'a fine figure of a man', she mused, although his clothes were quite ordinary: grey flannel trousers and a tweed sports jacket. When he turned slightly she saw to her surprise that he was wearing a clerical collar, commonly referred to as a dog collar. She was not sure, though, why she should be surprised. Clergymen probably didn't spend all their time reading the Bible or other theological tomes. He was good-looking too, with fairish hair that waved back from a high forehead and well-defined features.

As if suddenly aware of her scrutiny he turned and looked at her. He smiled then, a smile which reached his eyes, creasing the laughter lines around his eyes and mouth. A little discomfited – Fiona could feel herself starting to blush – she asked, 'Can I help you, sir? Are you looking for something in particular?' She stepped out from behind the counter and went towards him.

'Yes, thank you,' he replied. 'As a matter of fact I was looking to see if you had the latest Ngaio Marsh in stock. At least I think it's one of her latest. It's called *Hand in Glove*.'

'Oh yes,' she replied. 'It is a recent one. She's a favourite author of mine as well. That is… I suppose you are wanting it for yourself?'

'Yes, I am,' he laughed. 'Don't look so amazed.' She hadn't been aware that her slight surprise was so obvious. 'We do relax from time to time, you know, we men of the cloth.' His bluey-grey eyes twinkled as he spoke. 'I read all sorts of books, but detective fiction is something that I especially enjoy.'

'Of course,' she answered. 'Why shouldn't you? I didn't mean… well, any disrespect. I'm sorry though. We don't have that one in at the moment. This is quite a small library and we're not as well stocked as some of the larger ones. But I can order it for you. They will probably have it at Skipton, or certainly at Leeds or Bradford.'

'Thank you, that will be most helpful. Do I have to fill in a form?'

'Yes, a card, sir.'

'I should introduce myself,' he said when he had completed the card. 'I'm Simon Norwood, the rector of St Peter's.' He held out his hand.

'Yes, I thought you might be,' said Fiona, shaking his hand. 'I'm very pleased to meet you. Of course you might have been a Methodist, or... something else.'

He laughed again. 'I'm pleased to meet you too. And you are...?'

'Oh, I'm Fiona. Fiona Dalton. I've only been here a couple of weeks. I moved here from Leeds.'

'Then that's why I haven't seen you before. But I shall look forward to seeing you again.'

'Yes... I'll phone you when your book comes in. Do you want to take out those other books? I'll stamp them for you.'

'Yes, thank you.' He had chosen a spy story and one of the Captain Horatio Hornblower books by C.S. Forester. A typical male choice, Fiona thought to herself. But then the rector of St Peter's seemed to be a very manly sort of man.

'Goodbye then,' he said, nodding and smiling at her, 'until we meet again.'

'I see you've met the dashing rector,' remarked Hilda, the part-time assistant. 'Quite a charmer, isn't he?'

'Yes, he does seem... very nice,' replied Fiona, with a show of nonchalance.

'He's set quite a few hearts a-flutter at his church, so I've heard,' said Hilda with a chuckle.

'Do you go to St Peter's then?' asked Fiona.

'No I'm a Methodist,' replied Hilda. 'Mind you, I did think of switching my allegiance at one time, I must admit. But you can't very well, can you?'

'Er, no... I suppose not.'

'It's OK. I'm only joking,' smiled Hilda. 'I'm happily married myself with a teenage son and daughter. But it must be nice to have someone so easy on the eye to look up to in the pulpit. Our minister's getting near retiring age. He's a jolly good preacher though, and we all like him.'

'What about the Reverend Norwood?' asked Fiona. 'I dare say he's well and truly married, isn't he, with a couple of kids?'

'No, as a matter of fact, he's not. He's a widower. His wife died a couple of years ago. It was very sad; she died quite suddenly after an attack of flu. There were no children. Mind you, she never seemed to be quite right for him somehow, although I believe she was a good help in the parish… Do you belong to a church, Fiona?'

'No, I don't. I used to, when I was younger, but I must admit I've not attended anywhere recently. I was brought up in the Church of England.' She might very well start attending services again, she mused. Maybe not just yet though; that might seem too obvious. Not that the rector meant anything to her, of course, apart from being a nice friendly sort of person.

Conversation came to an end as two ladies were waiting at the counter. Fiona was busy for the rest of the day and at home she was too occupied to spare any thought for the charismatic rector. She was doing a spot of painting to liven up the dull brown doors in her flat. She loved bright colours and the buttercup yellow she had chosen added a cheery note to the rather dark hallway.

However she was to see the reverend gentleman again much sooner than she had anticipated – in fact, the very next evening.

As she didn't yet know many people in the town, and because she wanted to earn some extra money to add to her savings for a place of her own, she had taken a job as a barmaid, three nights a week, at the Ring o' Bells, the pub just off the market square.

It was a somewhat quieter establishment than the Fox and Grapes, which was in the market square itself and was reputed to become quite rowdy later in the evenings, and it was also where the darts teams held their contests. The Ring o' Bells catered for the less hardened drinkers and had recently started serving bar snacks such as sandwiches, baked potatoes, scampi and chips, and chicken in a basket. The publican's wife, Ivy, now had her hands full with the catering, and so she had employed an experienced woman to assist with the cooking, and extra part-time barmaids, including Fiona.

She loved the ambience of the place, the chintz curtains at the small mullioned windows and the matching cushions on the oak chairs and settles. There were sepia photographs of Yorkshire scenes on the walls – the Shambles in York, the ruined Rievaulx Abbey, the harbour at Whitby – and on the delft rack that ran the length of the room there was an assortment of blue and white pottery, Toby jugs and copper and pewter tankards.

Fiona had just finished serving a middle-aged man and his wife who sometimes came in of an evening for a half of bitter and a port and lemon – as much for the company as the drinks, she guessed – and she glanced towards the next customer waiting at the bar. Her mouth dropped open a little in surprise and she heard herself give a tiny gasp, but she quickly recovered and smiled at the customer. It was the Reverend Simon Norwood, without his clerical collar now, she noticed. He was wearing a blue shirt with his tweed jacket and a colourful tie in a floral design.

'Hello there,' she greeted him. 'We meet again.' She didn't say that she was surprised to see him. After all, why shouldn't he visit a local public house if he wished to do so, just as he chose to read books that were not of a religious content?

'Yes,' he replied, smiling at her in a very friendly way. It was possibly he who looked the more surprised. 'I suppose I could ask you what you are doing here, but it's pretty obvious, isn't it?' He laughed. 'You're pulling pints! It's clear that you're a young lady of many talents. I expect you are just as surprised to see me here, aren't you?'

'No, not really,' she answered. 'It's none of my business anyway, is it? You have a right to socialize anywhere you wish, and I'm sure this is as good a way as any to get to know the local people.'

'Quite so,' he nodded. 'That's the main idea. I like them to realize that their rector is just an ordinary sort of bloke who can meet with them on their own ground. Mind you, not everyone sees it like that. There were a few raised eyebrows when it got round the parish that the rector was not averse to knocking back a pint.'

'So what?' Fiona laughed. 'Didn't Jesus change the water into wine? That's a cliché of course, I know, in defence of anyone who likes to have a drink. And didn't he also spend time with publicans and sinners? Not that I'm suggesting that the good people of this town are sinners!'

'Probably no more than anyone else,' remarked the rector. 'I see you are conversant with the Bible?'

'Well, sort of,' she answered, a trifle evasively. 'I remember it from Sunday school days and from when I was quite a lot younger. I must admit I haven't been to church much lately... Anyway, what are you drinking?'

'Just a half of bitter,' he replied. 'No, go on; I'll go mad. I'll have a pint of Tetley's, a good old Yorkshire brew. And what about you? Could you possibly join me for a drink? You're not stuck behind the bar all evening, are you?'

'No; actually I'm just about due for a break. I've been here since seven o'clock.' It was now half past nine. She called to Joe, the publican, at the other end of the bar. 'Is it OK if I take my break now, Joe? I'm just going to have a drink with... er, Mr Norwood.'

'That's fine, Fiona,' he replied. 'Hello there, Simon. Good to see you. Go and sit down and I'll fetch them over to you. What is it now?'

'A pint of Tetley's, and I'll have a gin and orange,' said Fiona. She glanced at Simon. 'Thank you very much.'

'The pleasure is all mine.' He smiled, getting out his money. He joined her a few moments later at a corner table.

'Please call me Simon,' he said. 'Most people do, except for a few diehards who seem to think it's disrespectful to call the vicar by his Christian name. And you won't mind, will you, if I call you Fiona?'

'Not at all,' she smiled. 'Thanks for the drink, and... well... cheers!' She lifted her small glass and clinked it gently against Simon's larger tankard. 'I'm just working here part-time,' she explained. 'Three nights a week, Tuesday, Friday and Saturday at the moment. As you can see we're not very busy tonight.' It was Tuesday. 'It's only my second week here so I'm still sort of finding my feet. Joe and Ivy are very good to work for and it's... well, a respectable sort of pub.'

'It's a good way of meeting people,' Simon remarked, 'although you meet quite a cross section of people in the library, don't you?'

'Yes, that's true, but a lot of the folk who come in are somewhat elderly. They get a younger crowd in here and married couples, and quite a few small parties now they've started doing bar snacks. I must admit though that my main reason is to earn some extra money. My librarian's salary is quite good – I can't complain – but I'm saving up to buy a place of my own, you see; a flat or a small house.'

'Where are you living now?' enquired Simon.

'I've got quite a nice flat in Cedar Avenue, the top storey of a house. It's fully furnished, so that was a help, although I do have some furniture in storage back in Leeds, bits and pieces that were in my gran's house. That's why I moved here, you see, after Gran died. There was nothing to keep me there any longer and I knew that I was ready for a change of scenery… and everything.'

'You don't have any other relations in Leeds then?' asked Simon.

'No, my parents both died in an accident ten years ago; that's when I went to live with my gran. We got on very well together and I was quite heartbroken when she died. She was ninety though, so I really couldn't have hoped to have her much longer.'

'It's always sad though, isn't it, when a loved one dies?' He smiled consolingly. 'So, as you say, you are having a fresh start?'

'That's right. Gran left me what little money she had – not a great deal – and the house she lived in was rented, as was my parents' house. Gran used to say to me, "Make sure you buy a little place of your own when you can. There's no sense in paying rent all your life like I've done." So that's what I intend to do eventually.'

'Good for you,' said Simon. 'My house is provided for me, of course, but most clergymen try to put something away for the future, when it becomes necessary to buy a place of one's own. I've heard some say that God will provide and that one shouldn't worry about the future. But I'm a great believer in the saying that God helps those who help themselves. A cliché, I know, but there's a good deal of sense in it.'

Fiona thought to herself that Simon was a very sensible sort of clergyman, a far cry from the vicar she remembered back in Leeds when she was in her teens, at the church where her sanctimonious parents had worshipped. She dismissed the unwelcome memory hurriedly as she heard Simon asking her if she would like to come along to St Peter's church.

'I don't believe in hounding people,' he said, 'although I must, of course encourage folk to give the church a try if they're so inclined. I think you would find that most members of the congregation would make you welcome. There are a few, though, I must admit, who are rather set in their ways; you get them in all churches. They don't like change. I met with quite a bit of opposition when I moved here six years ago. So did my wife when she took over some of the jobs that the ladies of the Mothers' Union had been doing... You knew that I'd been married, did you, Fiona?' he asked.

She nodded in assent. 'Yes, so I believe. Your wife died, didn't she? I'm sorry...'

'We'd been in the parish for about three years when Millicent developed bronchitis, which turned to pneumonia. It was very sudden. But she'd never been strong;

not in her body, I mean, although she could be quite a determined lady.' He smiled wryly. 'But life has to go on; another cliché but it's true. So… do you think you might give it a try at St Peter's?'

'Yes, I will. I'll come next Sunday morning,' agreed Fiona. 'I'm a confirmed member of the Church of England but, as I said, I'm afraid I've lapsed somewhat of late.'

'You're not alone in that,' said Simon.

She was thoughtful for a moment. 'I suppose, deep down, I do still believe,' she said. 'I've not always been a very good person, though.'

'Then join the club,' said Simon, laughing. 'We've all fallen short of God's standards at one time or another. None of us are perfect, but He's still there for us. As I've told you, though, I don't believe in preaching to people when I'm not in the pulpit. I'm glad you've said you'll come though, Fiona.' He reached out his hand and, very gently and fleetingly, covered her own.

And that was how it started, slowly at first. She attended the morning service at St Peter's the following Sunday, sitting near the back as unobtrusively as she could. The woman next to her in the pew introduced herself as Joan Tweedale and told her that her husband was the organist. A nice friendly woman, Fiona thought, so that was a good start.

Her eyes were drawn inevitably to the rector at the front of the chancel and then in the pulpit as he preached about the parable of the Good Samaritan.

Simon stood at the door to shake hands with the folk as they departed, and he introduced her to Arthur Bayliss, the church warden, who seemed quite jolly and friendly. His wife, Ethel, by contrast, appeared a little frosty and, possibly, a mite disapproving? Fiona reflected that perhaps her cherry red coat with the fur collar and the matching Cossack-style hat could be considered a little daring for Sunday morning worship, together with her knee-high boots with silver heels. And, of course, her lipstick and nail varnish matched her coat.

She was not surprised when Simon called in the library to see her towards the end of the week. He invited her out for an evening meal at a country inn a few miles away. They drove there in his Morris Minor car. It was the first of many outings. Simon's day off from his parish duties which he insisted on – all clergymen, he maintained, needed a day off from the job – was Wednesday, which was also Fiona's day off from the library.

They explored the countryside around Aberthwaite – the sleepy villages and the other market towns, ruined abbeys and castles – and they walked in the foothills and the wooded vales of the limestone fells.

Fiona stayed on the fringes of the congregation. Her work prevented her from taking part in the occasional social afternoon for ladies of the parish; neither was she eligible for the Mothers' Union, and the Youth group was rather too young. But she was contented as she was. She and Simon found themselves to be more and more compatible and, as time went by, very much in love.

Their love did not reach its fulfilment until their honeymoon, which was everything that Fiona could have wished for. Simon was a considerate lover, both tender and passionate in turn. He had, of course, been married before, although, reading between the lines, she had gathered that it had not been an ideal marriage. She had known, therefore, that he would not be lacking in experience. He must have realized that she, too, was not entirely lacking in the knowledge of sexual matters. But he had not commented on this – neither would she have expected him to do so – and to the joy of both of them they found that they were perfectly attuned to one another.

As far as Simon was concerned her past remained a closed book. She learnt week by week, as she attended the church, of God's forgiveness; and there were times when she felt His love and compassion surrounding her as she grew closer to the God she had disregarded for so long.

But what of Simon's forgiveness? she pondered. If he were to know about all that had happened to her so long ago – or so it seemed, although it was only fourteen years – would he be so ready to understand and to overlook the past?

Five

Mary Dalton was thirty-seven and Wilfred thirty-nine when their first and only child, Fiona, came along in the May of 1934, a child they had begun to despair of ever being born, as they had been married for ten years. They both loved her with a passion that was all consuming.

'She is all I've ever wanted,' Mary was often to remark. 'Such a precious gift, isn't she, Wilfred, given to us so late in life?'

'Aye, she is that!' Wilfred agreed. 'We must do everything we can for her, Mary. Our little treasure. She must have all the chances in life that we have never had. Just think; she might go to that training college near here.' There was a teachers' training college not far away in Beckett's Park.

'Or even to that university we pass on the tram every time we go to town,' added Mary. 'She might not want to be a teacher. She might be a doctor… No, p'raps not; I don't know as I'd be right keen on that idea. Or a solicitor or… what do they call 'em? – a chartered accountant.' Their dreams for her were manifold, the sort of careers they had never been able to aspire to themselves.

Mary and her brother, Eddie, had had no choice but to start work in their early teenage years, as their mother had been widowed at an early age. Mary had left school at fourteen and had gone to work in a shop, ending up, before she left to get married, in charge of a counter at the big Woolworths in Leeds. Her brother, Eddie, two years older, had started work at a woollen mill near the city centre as a 'bobbin ligger and taker off'. He had done quite well at the job and eventually became an overseer in charge of a number of looms. Their mother, Annie Jowett – Fiona's dearly loved grandmother – had worked there too, until the rheumatism in her hands had forced her to retire.

Likewise, Fiona's father had worked from an early age. He, too, was employed at one of the many woollen mills in the area, in the warehouse though, not on the factory floor.

Wilfred and Mary, on their marriage, had started to rent a small house in Headingley, just off the main road leading from the city centre. Wilfred insisted on Mary stopping work after they were married, as did many self-respecting husbands. He considered it was his job and his alone to be the breadwinner. Besides, they were hoping that before long they would have a family. This did not happen, but they were still contented with their simple life, then overjoyed when the longed-for baby arrived. Now their hopes and aspirations were all centred upon Fiona. Wilfred didn't seem to consider it ironic that he should want his daughter to have a career of her own, something he would never have wanted for his wife.

Their parish church was quite near to where they lived in Headingley, on the outskirts of Leeds. Mary and Wilfred attended spasmodically, but they had always insisted – as did most parents at the time – on Fiona going to Sunday school. She had attended regularly from being four years old.

It was around the time of Fiona's thirteenth birthday that a new vicar arrived in the parish. It was 1947 and the war had been over for two years. He was soon seen to be a 'new broom' if ever there was one. The state of affairs at the church – the services and the church life in general – had lapsed considerably during the last years of the previous vicar's incumbency. The numbers in the congregation at both morning and evening services were at times no more than twenty or so, and a general feeling of apathy had prevailed.

The Reverend Amos Cruikshank, therefore, was seen at first as a breath of fresh air. He was thirty-seven years old, by no means handsome – rather short of stature and portly, in fact, with wispy gingerish hair, a beaked nose and horn-rimmed spectacles – but his voice and manner were commanding. Mary and Wilfred had decided to go to hear him preach his first sermon and had to admit they were very impressed. The numbers in the congregation rose steadily; and it was the same in the Sunday school, which had previously been struck by a similar feeling of indifference.

The church, however, in the past had enjoyed quite an active social life – with whist drives, dances, concerts and the like – until members at these events had, likewise, dwindled. A monthly whist drive still took place, though, in the church hall, for anyone who enjoyed the game, and not just members of the congregation. There were also dances and social evenings from time to time for such occasions as Harvest, Hallowe'en, and Christmas.

That was until the Reverend Cruikshank came on the scene. Whist drives and dances, in fact almost all social occasions, were immediately stopped. Whist drives, he decreed, were a form of gambling, not to be countenanced in the house of God or anywhere near it. It was the same with dances, which he believed encouraged young people of the parish to get too close to one another. They were seen as the work of the devil, and once such goings-on were allowed on church premises one never knew where it might end. Especially so for the merrymaking at Hallowe'en; turnip lanterns and masks and dressing up as witches and ghosts, no matter that the children thought it was great fun, it was all taboo.

Fiona, who, along with her friend, Diane, liked to go along to the social evenings, asked her mother about this. 'Why has the vicar stopped the Hallowe'en party? It used to be good fun. I've made a turnip lantern every year since I was five. And you used to help me, didn't you, Mum?'

'That's true,' replied her mother. 'But the Reverend Cruikshank says that it's something that Christian people should not associate themselves with. It's a pagan festival, and that's why he's put an end to it.'

'Oh, that's just silly,' argued Fiona. 'It isn't as if we take it seriously. We don't go in for devil worship or casting spells on people. It was just jolly good fun. This vicar doesn't want anybody to have fun any more, does he, Mum?'

'I can see his point of view,' replied her mother. 'We should go to church to worship God and to learn about Jesus. All these other things, well... they are not what is important. That's all I want to say about it, Fiona.'

Fiona had noticed that both her parents were attending church regularly now. They never missed the morning service, which Fiona usually attended with them, and sometimes they went along in the evening as well.

Despite all the restrictions and reservations the congregation was growing week by week. There was no doubt about it, the Reverend Cruikshank was a force to be reckoned with: a dynamic preacher, and many were encouraged to follow his lead. He spoke of God's love and forgiveness, but above all of repentance – turning away from sin – and of a personal relationship with Jesus, something that had not been preached about so plainly in the days of the old vicar.

He started a midweek Bible class, and a Youth club. This was not intended to be a chance for the teenage boys and girls of the parish to get friendly and start 'pairing off' – although this did, inevitably happen – but to take part in such wholesome pursuits as tennis, rounders and five-a-side cricket in the summer, or table tennis and badminton in the winter, along with quizzes and discussions of a meaningful nature.

Fiona went along to the Youth Club, and she also joined the vicar's confirmation class, partly to please her parents – she had always been an obedient girl – and partly because her best friend, Diane, had agreed to go with her. They were both confirmed at the age of fourteen, wearing modest white dresses and with veils covering their hair. Fiona looked upon it all as seriously and reverently as she was able, but she could not in all honesty have said that she felt any different after the event.

Meanwhile, her parents were becoming more and more involved. The Tuesday evening Bible class soon became important to them, and Wilfred was proud and pleased when the Reverend Cruikshank asked him if he would become a sidesman. His duties included welcoming people to the services and going round with the collection plate. Within a year he had progressed from his position as sidesman to that of church warden.

For an ordinary man such as Wilfred, with no pretensions to wealth or eminence, it was a great honour. He insisted at first that he was not suitable or worthy – he was only a warehouse man in a local mill – but the vicar reminded him that Jesus himself had chosen his helpers from among the common people: the fishermen, the carpenters and the tax collectors.

Mary, also, had become a very active member of the congregation. She joined the Mothers' Union, which met once a month on a Wednesday afternoon for a devotional meeting, led by the vicar's wife, Hannah. The vicar's wife was a devout woman but she lacked the dynamism of her husband. She appeared to be very much in his shadow and followed his lead in everything. It was noticed that they were similar in appearance. Hannah had the same gingerish hair that she wore in a loose bun at the nape of her neck, and the same myopic blue eyes that peered out from behind rimless glasses. They were, in fact, second cousins who had known one another from childhood and it had always been taken for granted that they would marry. They had one son, Timothy, aged fifteen when they came to the parish, who was the apple of their eye.

Mary and Hannah found themselves drawn to one another. They were both of a quiet disposition and had not sought friendship or recreational pursuits outside the home or, in Hannah's case, the church. Mary's chief aim in life had been to make a comfortable home for her husband and, later, for their daughter. The only interest she had pursued was connected with Fiona's schools, firstly the primary school and then the grammar school for girls. (Fiona had passed her eleven plus exam with flying colours as they had always thought she would.) Mary was now serving on the committee of the girls' grammar school PTFA: a willing, self-effacing member who would take on any task allotted to her, usually making the tea and washing up, or looking after the home-made cake stall at the summer or Christmas fayres.

Now, at Hannah's persuasion, she had become a member of the church council, not a very vociferous one, to be sure, but she was becoming much more active in the life of the church.

Fiona was not too sure how she felt about the change in her mother – in fact, in both her parents. Her dad was quite cock-a-hoop about his position as church warden, and she was forced to suppress a smile when she watched him on a Sunday morning as he processed with the vicar and the choir down the centre aisle, proudly carrying his staff of office. And he was never seen at Sunday worship or at the midweek Bible meeting without his large black Bible. As far as Fiona knew it was a family heirloom that had been tucked away in a cupboard until the advent of the new vicar. Wilfred had become more forceful in manner, and his conversation was now peppered with references to God, and with the opinions of the Reverend Cruikshank.

Mary, on the other hand, was still her quiet unassuming self. She had used, though, to be a jolly, cheerful person, enjoying a laugh and a joke, in a gentle sort of way. Now she had become, to Fiona's way of thinking, a trifle boring, lacking the spurt of humour that had been the leaven of her shy disposition. Mary was a pretty woman with natural blonde hair that had darkened a shade or two as she grew older. She had not been averse, at one time, to brightening it up with a coloured rinse. But that was now a thing of the past. Moreover, she was now wearing her hair scraped back from her face in what Fiona thought was an unbecoming style, the one favoured by her friend, Hannah Cruikshank, whom Mary seemed to be emulating in all sorts of ways. She no longer used lipstick or face powder. Fiona longed to tell her that she looked dowdy, but she had always been a respectful girl, not given to bouts of disobedience and wilfulness like some of her contemporaries.

When she was fifteen, in the fifth form and preparing for her School Certificate Examination, Fiona started to use a little make-up – Coty Face powder and lipstick in a pretty coral colour that she had saved up for out of her weekly spending money. Most of the girls in her form were doing so, comparing the various brands – Coty, Max Factor, Yardley, and the far more expensive Helena Rubinstein (which none of them could afford) – and deciding which shade of lipstick went with their hair colour or the outfit they were wearing for best.

They were not allowed to wear make-up at school, of course, but they made up for it at weekends when they went out on a Saturday night to the pictures or to a local dance. These were usually at the church halls of the more broad-minded C of E churches, and at the Methodist Church in Fiona's neighbourhood. She was allowed to go on the understanding that she was home by ten o'clock, a stricture that was upheld by most of her friends' parents. The boys, however, were allowed a little more leeway.

Fiona had a shirtwaister dress in pink and white gingham with a large white collar and a full skirt which she wore at the dances in the summer, and a peasant style blouse worn with a full skirt of a bright floral design, which was made to stand out as far as possible by wearing two or more 'cancan' petticoats underneath it. These petticoats were made of nylon with numerous frills, and were made stiffer by dipping them in a sugar solution and then drip-drying them.

Fiona's mother did not seem to object to such frivolities – the fancy clothes or the make-up – although she did not comment, as she might have done at one time, telling her daughter that she looked nice and showing an interest in what she was wearing. Nor did Mary pass any comments about the dances or the films that she watched with her friends – light-hearted films such as *Annie Get Your Gun*, the 'Doctor' films starring Dirk Bogarde, or the Norman Wisdom comedies that were considered hilarious – although Fiona noticed that her parents no longer went to the cinema themselves. Mary and Wilfred had used to go to the local cinema at least once a fortnight. It had been their one indulgence and something that they had both enjoyed.

Fiona knew, of course, that she must dress circumspectly for church attendance on a Sunday morning. She was not forced to go along, but on the rare occasions when she had said she was staying at home – giving the excuse that she had homework to finish which, more often than not, was the truth – her mother's reproving glance made her feel that she was committing a heinous crime. It was easier, therefore, to comply rather than stage what was a minor rebellion.

There was one Sunday morning, however, when she felt she had to stick up for herself. Her mother had glanced at her suitable coat, and Fiona was also wearing a hat – a beret which she hated, but which her mother had declared suitable headgear, especially as there was a service of Holy Communion at the close of morning worship.

She was wearing make-up too, but only what she considered to be a modest amount; powder and lipstick and just the tiniest touch of green powder that highlighted the colour of her hazel eyes, making them appear more green than brown.

Her mother looked closely at her and shook her head reprovingly. 'Fiona…' she began, in the over patient voice that her daughter was getting to know only too well. It was not Mary's way to shout and be angry, but Fiona thought sometimes that it might be better if her mother did so, rather than assuming the long-suffering manner that was becoming so familiar. 'Fiona… I don't really think it's suitable to wear so much make-up to go to church. And I notice that you've started using eye make-up. I do wish you wouldn't. It makes you look… well… cheap and rather common. Not at all how a good Christian girl should appear when she's going to church.'

Fiona opened her mouth ready to protest vehemently, but she held her tongue for a moment. She had never been the sort of girl to give cheek to her parents, as she knew some of her friends were apt to do. She did, however, close her lips together in a stubborn line before opening them again to say, 'Well, I think it looks nice! And it certainly doesn't look common. How can you say that, Mum? You know how I always try to make the most of myself. You used to encourage me to dress nicely and to take pride in my appearance.'

If Fiona had one small vice it was that she was the teeniest bit vain about her looks. She knew that she was a pretty girl and that she had been blessed with attractive hair and pleasant features. And she had discovered lately that her looks could be enhanced by discreet make-up. It wasn't as if she was laying it on with a trowel, so to speak, as some of the girls in her form were doing, using what was known as pancake make-up of an odd-looking tan colour.

'You don't need make-up to help you to look attractive,' her mother replied, still with the same tone of forbearance. 'Anyway, it doesn't matter what we look like on the outside. It's what we're like inside that really counts… And that's what God will notice when you're in His house.'

'For goodness' sake, what's the matter with you, Mum?' Fiona couldn't help herself now. She had wanted to tackle her mother for ages about her own appearance and the way in which she had changed. 'You used to use lipstick yourself,' she went on. 'And you used to do your hair nicely, not all scraped back like you have it now. It looked lovely when you curled it and put a golden rinse on it. It seems as though you don't care any more about what you look like.'

Mary smiled, still not showing any sign of anger or impatience. 'That's the point, Fiona love,' she said. 'I've come to realize that these things don't matter – how we look and how we dress – although I still try to look clean and respectable, of course. You see, dear, since I've come to know more about Jesus I've tried to think about what He would want me to do and how He would want me to behave. And worldly things, such as make-up and clothes, they're not so important any more. And perhaps, in time, you will come to see it that way.'

Fiona didn't answer at first. She was annoyed, and hurt as well. She had always been an obedient daughter and had never had any arguments of any importance with either of her parents. She also felt it was embarrassing to talk about Jesus in such a familiar way. 'I do believe in God, and in Jesus,' she retorted. 'I always went to Sunday school, didn't I? And then I was confirmed because you wanted me to be. And I go to church with you, most of the time. And

I don't really believe that… that Jesus is bothered about me using make-up and trying to look nice. I just don't understand you, Mum.'

'Then we'll say no more about it just now,' replied Mary. 'But I would like you to go and rub off that eyeshadow and some of the lipstick in case the vicar notices. I don't think he would like it, especially for Communion. Go along now, Fiona, there's a good girl, and do as I say. We don't want to fall out about it, do we?'

Fiona was fuming inside. The thoughts that were forming in her mind were certainly not ones to be put into words. *To hell with the Reverend bloody Cruikshank! Why should I care what he thinks? And why does Mum let him influence her so much? Him and that mealy-mouthed wife of his!*

But Fiona never used swear words out loud, and neither of her parents had ever done so. She obeyed her mother then, like the respectful daughter she had always been. She knew, though, as she received the Communion bread and wine, that her thoughts were not as reverent as they should have been.

She had always been able to confide in her maternal grandmother, Annie Jowett, and she did so when she visited her the following Saturday afternoon. She took a tram to City Square and then a bus to where her gran lived in the district of Roundhay, on the outskirts of the city. She took a fruit cake that Mary had baked for her mother and a jar of marmalade from the batch she had made recently.

'Aye, she's always been a good daughter, has our Mary,' said the elderly woman appreciatively. 'And I know she's brought you up the same way, to be respectful and obedient. You're a good lass, Fiona.'

'Yes, I always try to be,' said Fiona, 'but I must admit, Gran, that they're trying my patience quite a lot recently, Mum and Dad – both of them.'

Annie nodded her head. 'Aye, I think I know what you mean, luv. I've noticed it meself. They've got real involved in that church you go to, haven't they, since that there new vicar came? What with your dad being church warden, and your mam getting herself on the church council. Mind you, there's far worse things. If your dad was to start drinking for instance, or gambling; or if your mam was gadding about all over the place. Like the woman next door to me. She's got herself a new feller – we all know about it – and her husband's the nicest chap you could ever wish to meet.'

'Yes, I know, Gran,' said Fiona. 'Mum and Dad are good people. But they're so pious, so strait-laced, and they never used to be like that.' She told her gran about the altercation she had had with her mother about make-up. 'Mum seems to think it's wrong now, to try to look nice – almost as though it's sinful. That's a word that's always cropping up. The vicar's always going on about sin and temptation.'

Annie nodded again. 'Aye, you're right. I must admit I had a few words with Mary myself when she started preaching at me, telling me about Jesus and how she'd become a Christian. I said to her, "Look here, lass, I've been going to church all me life, at least I did until this blessed arthritis took hold of me. I know all about God, and about Jesus an' all, and I reckon I'm as good a Christian as most folk. I know I might not read the Bible every day but I say me prayers and I'm a good living woman. So you don't need to start your preaching here, thank you very much!" All the same, they're not doing owt wrong; they're happen just a bit overzealous. But you'll have to respect their beliefs, even if you can't go along with them fully. You must remember the fifth commandment. You'll never go far wrong, lass, if you try to obey God's commandments.'

'Honour thy father and thy mother,' replied Fiona. 'That's the one you mean, isn't it, Gran? And I do try to, you know.'

'Yes, I know you do, luv.' Annie sighed. 'Well, ne'er mind. I expect it's done you good to talk about it. Now, go and put the kettle on, there's a good lass, and we'll have a cup of tea and some of your mam's fruit cake...'

Six

The Festival of Britain opened on the South Bank of the Thames in London, in May, 1951 when Fiona was seventeen years old. It came as a great surprise to many when the leaders of the Church Youth Club that Fiona attended decided to organize a trip during the school holidays to see this great exhibition for themselves. More surprisingly, the vicar gave his consent, agreeing that it would be a worthwhile experience for the young people to take part in such an event. Provided, of course, that the teenagers were supervised at all times and were kept well apart with regard to sleeping arrangements at the hotel.

Fiona and her best friend, Diane, were amongst the ones who wished to join the excursion. Her parents had raised no objection, and neither had Diane's, no doubt because the Reverend Cruikshank had given it his seal of approval. The arrangements were made for a group of eighteen teenagers – ten girls and eight boys – with three adults, to travel to London and back by coach, staying for three nights at a modest hotel – one that provided bed and breakfast and an evening meal – near to the South Bank festival site.

'I don't think my parents would have agreed so readily if they knew that Dave was going,' Fiona told Diane as they travelled home from school on the bus, one afternoon near the end of the summer term.

David Rathbone was Fiona's first boyfriend. He was a member of the Youth Club and had been in the same confirmation class. He was in the lower sixth form at the boy's grammar school, whilst Fiona and Diane were also in the lower sixth at the grammar school for girls. He walked home with her after the Youth Club meetings and she met him sometimes after school.

He kissed her goodnight quite chastely at first but she had realized that he was becoming a little more amorous just lately, and she knew she must be careful not to encourage him.

She was pleased, though, at the idea of having a boyfriend, like many of her sixth-form colleagues. She knew, however, from listening to their conversations that these friendships were not as innocent as hers and Dave's. That was if they were to be believed, however, which she guessed was doubtful! Dave was a secret, though, that she had kept from her parents.

'Actually, Mum and Dad don't even know about him yet,' she told Diane.

'Why not?' asked her friend. 'Why don't you tell them? You'll have to sooner or later, won't you?'

'Oh, you know what they're like,' said Fiona. 'I'd be put through the third degree about him and given a lecture on how to behave myself – you know, about sex and all that. At least I imagine I would… although it's something that Mum never talks about. I fully intend to, though – behave myself, I mean.'

'I don't suppose we'll get the chance to do anything other than behave ourselves,' replied Diane. 'You can be sure that Mr and Mrs Wilkes will keep an eagle eye on us or else they'll have old Cruikshank to answer to. I'm jolly glad he's not going, aren't you?'

'I'll say! He'd certainly put a damper on the proceedings. Dave says that Andy is going as well. So… you may well get lucky!'

'I can but hope,' said Diane with a sigh. She had been hoping for ages that Andy Mayhew, Dave's best friend, would look in her direction, but all he seemed to be interested in was football. 'All the same,' Diane went on, 'whatever happens – or doesn't happen – it'll be great going to London, won't it? I've never been before. In fact I've never been any further than Scarborough, or to my aunt's in Manchester.'

'Same here,' said Fiona. 'Scarborough and Blackpool; that's been the extent of my travelling. I'm getting real excited, aren't you? I can't stop thinking about it…'

-

The Festival of Britain had been planned to celebrate the achievements of the country and the Empire; also as a tonic to the nation after the years of wartime and the austerity that had followed. It had been, initially, the Labour government, led by Clement Attlee, that had instigated the idea, declaring that it was time for everyone to start enjoying themselves and shake off the post-war gloom. By the time the festival opened, though, the government had lost an election and was replaced by a Conservative government, led by Winston Churchill, back in power after his surprising – to many – defeat following the war. The present party was rather less enthusiastic about the event, as it had not been their idea. Nevertheless, it was formally opened by King George VI on May third, 1951.

The Youth Club group set off on their adventure on a Monday morning in mid-August. A small coach had been hired from a local travel firm, along with one of their drivers. It would be a long journey; they were expected to arrive in London at six o'clock or thereabouts, in time for their evening meal, so they were making an early start at eight o'clock in the morning.

It was an excited group that met outside the church gates. Most of the parents had come along, in some cases father as was well as mother, to bid farewell to their sons and daughters. The driver took charge of the luggage – they had each been restricted to one small case or travelling bag – storing it in the luggage compartment, then they all boarded the blue and cream coach. There was ample room and they could sit wherever they wished. Mrs Wilkes suggested, however, that anyone who was liable to suffer from travel sickness should sit near the front. No one owned up to this indignity, so Mr and Mrs Wilkes sat in the front seat with the other helper, a young woman called Rita, on the opposite seat.

The girls sat on one side of the coach and the boys on the other – not that they had been told to do so, but it seemed expedient at the start of the holiday. No doubt the situation might change as the week went on, Fiona thought to herself. She hadn't yet spoken to Dave or acknowledged that he was there, as both her parents were with her. The Reverend Cruikshank was there too, rather more jovial than usual; nevertheless, his presence did tend, somehow, to inhibit the merriment.

Fiona kissed her parents a little embarrassedly, but she knew it was expected of her; then she took her seat next to Diane, a few rows from the front. Dave, with his mate Andy, was opposite them; so that boded well for her friend, she mused.

The vicar boarded the coach at the last moment requesting that they should have a moment of prayer before they set off. He asked that the Lord would bless them all during the coming few days. 'Keep them safe, O Lord, from harm and temptation,' he intoned in his lugubrious voice, 'and grant them a safe journey there and back. May they enjoy, Lord, this time together for fellowship and fun with one another, and the opportunity to make new friendships and cement the old ones. Amen.'

'Amen to that!' echoed Diane with a giggle as she nudged her friend.

'Shut up!' shushed Fiona, aware of the vicar glancing around the coach.

Then they were off, waving goodbye to the parents standing on the pavement. They were all waving furiously as though their offspring were bound for a journey into the unknown. Some of the mothers were wiping away an odd tear. For many of them it was the first time they had been parted from their children. Others, though, had experienced a separation when their children had been evacuees, not all that long ago it seemed, and this parting brought back memories. Fiona had not been an evacuee. Mary and Wilfred could not have borne to part with her, she was so precious to them, and so, despite the anticipated dangers, they had kept her at home. As it happened their area did not suffer nearly so badly from the bombing raids as some cities had done.

The teenagers, though, were shedding no tears at the parting; they were too excited thinking of the pleasures that lay ahead. For the majority it was their first visit to the capital city.

They chattered excitedly, the noise increasing in volume until it sounded like the monkey house at the zoo, Mrs Wilkes – Sheila – remarked to her husband, Colin.

'Ne'er mind,' he replied. 'You can't blame 'em. It's a real adventure for most of them, I guess. They're good kids though, aren't they? I don't reckon we'll have much trouble with them.'

'We've had our instructions, though, haven't we?' said Sheila. 'You know that the reverend said they were to be supervised at all times. And we did promise.'

'I think we'll have to use our own discretion,' replied Colin. 'They'll need a bit of freedom, some time to themselves. It's not as though they're a class of infants.'

'Yes, we'll have to play it by ear,' agreed Sheila. 'We can't let them wander around London on their own, of course. But they should be alright going round the festival halls. We couldn't all keep together anyway. And there's a fun fair, isn't there, in Battersea Park? We'll have to let them loose there, Colin. So long as we make sure they're back in the hotel for... what would you say? Ten o'clock?'

'Oh, I think we could say half past ten,' Colin replied. 'Anyway, let's wait till we get there, then we can sort out rules and regulations with the young people, and with Rita. There'll have to be some rules to stick to, and I'm sure the kids will understand. But we must make sure it's a holiday as well as an educational experience. I must admit I'm as excited as any of 'em.'

'So am I,' his wife agreed.

Colin and Sheila Wilkes were a youngish married couple, both in their early thirties; childless as yet, but they had not given up hope. They were fond of children and got on well with young people, both of them being teachers at different primary schools in the area. They had volunteered to take charge of the Youth Club soon after the new vicar had arrived, and Amos Cruikshank had deemed them both eminently suitable. They respected the vicar, but they did not agree with all his rigid views. They were relieved that he had decided not to accompany them on this venture; he intended to visit the festival later in the year with his wife and son. Sheila and Colin had remarked to one another that there would have been fewer young people on the trip had he decided to go along.

The hubbub in the coach gradually lessened as they made their way south, out of Yorkshire, into Derbyshire and the Midlands. The driver used the main roads – the A roads – sometimes veering on to the B roads to bypass the busy towns. He was an experienced driver who knew the best stopping places. He knew of a roadside cafe just outside Birmingham where customers were allowed to eat their own sandwiches provided they bought a drink. They stopped there for nearly an hour to have some refreshment, to stretch their legs, and to allow Mike, the driver, to smoke a well-deserved cigarette. There had been what he called a 'comfort stop' mid-morning, and there would be two more short stops later on, he informed them, before they reached their destination.

The day was warm and sunny, and after the young people had purchased their drinks – sarsaparilla, lemonade or orange squash in the main, although tea and coffee were also available – they sat outside on the wooden benches alongside the rough wooden tables. Fiona nudged Diane as she saw Dave and Andy approaching their table. 'Seems as though your luck's in,' she whispered.

'May we join you?' asked Dave, as polite as always, as they sat down on the opposite bench.

'Hi, Fiona, hi there, Diane,' said Andy. 'Dave told me you were coming along. Perhaps we can spend some time together this week, the four of us. What d'you think?'

Diane must be thinking that all her Christmases have come at once, reflected Fiona. 'Yes, great,' she answered. 'But do you think we'll be let off the leash?' she added laughing.

'Oh, I don't see why not,' said Dave. 'It looks as though Rita might have other fish to fry anyway. Look over there. No... don't make it so obvious!'

Rita Johnson, the young woman who had come along as the third helper, was sitting at the table next but one to them talking animatedly to Mike, the driver. They were both smoking a cigarette, presumably before starting on their packed lunch. Rita was twenty years old, only a few years older than some of her charges, but she was considered a responsible adult. Several of her contemporaries were already married or engaged. It was believed that Rita had recently suffered a broken engagement – or near engagement – but it seemed now as though she was recovering nicely.

'Good for her,' said Diane. 'I've heard she's been quite upset just lately. I believe her boyfriend met someone else while he was doing his National Service.'

'It'll be our turn for National Service soon – well – quite soon, won't it, Dave?' remarked Andy.

'Suppose so,' answered Dave. 'Although I think you get deferred if you're going to university don't you? Anyway, let's not bother about that now, eh? What sort of sarnies have you got?'

'Sarnies!' laughed Diane. 'Goodness gracious! What sort of language is that? I get frowned on if I say sarnies in our house. My mum insists that we call them sandwiches and nothing else. Although I think sarnies was my dad's word in the first place. Mum's only joking though, trying to make out that we're posh.'

Dave grinned. 'Oh, well; perhaps we don't try to be as posh at our house. My dad's one that calls a spade a shovel, and a sandwich a sarnie.'

'We always call them butties,' added Andy. 'Anyroad, what's in a name, as someone once said. I'm ready for 'em, anyway, whatever they're called. Let's have a look then. What sort of sarnies have we all got?'

They opened their packets of sandwiches and spread them out on the table. Fiona pondered that there hadn't been a great deal of levity in her home just recently. She wished that her mum still laughed and joked in the way she had heard Diane's mum do. Her, Fiona's, mum had of course, made her a very appetizing packed lunch. Ham sandwiches on white bread and cheese ones on brown bread, with a tomato – there was even some salt in a screw of paper – an apple and two slices of her home-made fruit cake. There was also a Thermos flask of coffee that she had shared with Diane at an earlier break.

It turned out to be a veritable feast laid out in front of them. Salmon and cucumber, corned beef, sardine, and egg and cress sandwiches, as well as the more conventional cheese and ham; meat pies – each of the boys had one which they gallantly cut in half; packets of crisps; iced buns; gingerbread; and wrapped chocolate biscuits.

'Crikey! What a spread,' commented Andy. 'Let's share it, shall we? Come on; let's tuck in.'

'This should keep us going for a while,' Diane commented.

'It'll need to,' said Fiona. 'We won't get to London for ages yet, will we?'

'About six o'clock, so Mike said,' Dave remarked. 'I suppose it might have been quicker on the train, but the idea is that we'll have the coach to ride about on while we're there. Have any of you been to London before?'

The other three shook their heads.

'I went there once, ages ago,' Dave told them, 'but I don't remember much about it. I was only four years old, so it must have been just before the war started.' That, of course, had curtailed travelling for most folk. 'I seem to remember the soldiers in their red tunics and busbies – isn't that what they're called, those fur hats they wear? – but I can't recall much else.'

They all fell quiet as they started eating. There was very little left when they had finished, only a couple of chocolate biscuits which Dave handed to Fiona. They exchanged a smile and she felt a surge of happiness. The holiday was starting well. She decided that she must pluck up the courage to tell her parents about Dave when they returned home. That was if she and Dave were still 'going out' at the end of the week. Not that they had really been 'out' anywhere together as yet, but she was hopeful.

It seemed as though things were looking good for her friend as well. Diane was full of smiles as they boarded the coach again. 'That was a good start, wasn't it?' she remarked.

'Yes, I think Andy really likes you,' replied Fiona.

They all chatted less and less as the afternoon drew on, replete after a substantial lunch. Some of them tried to read or do a crossword puzzle, whilst others just nodded off. There were two short breaks to ensure that the driver didn't nod off himself. Then, at last, they began to notice signs that they were approaching London.

The roads were getting more and more busy with frequent stops for traffic lights and traffic jams. Then they noticed the underground signs which were appearing more often as they approached the city centre. West Hampstead; Swiss Cottage – although there was no sign of a Swiss chalet anywhere around; St John's Wood; Baker Street – wasn't that where Sherlock Holmes was supposed to live? Then they saw the sign for Marble Arch, and there it was, the familiar landmark that they had all seen pictures of.

Their route took them along Park Lane, skirting Hyde Park, then passing Buckingham Palace before heading towards the River Thames. There were excited shouts at the first view of the home of their king, George VI, with the Royal Standard flying, indicating that the king and queen were in residence. The driver tried to give them a running commentary whilst keeping his eye on the traffic.

'We'll see it all again tomorrow,' he assured them. The first full day of their visit, Tuesday, was to be a day's sightseeing tour.

There was more excitement as they crossed Westminster Bridge. The sight of the Houses of Parliament and 'Big Ben' was eclipsed by their first view of the Skylon, the slender tower resembling a futuristic silver rocket, soaring 300 feet into the air, the symbol of the festival that was the main reason for their visit.

The hotel was in a side street not far from the new Festival Hall. It was not a very prepossessing building, with dingy cream stucco walls and fading paintwork, but the sign over the door revealed that it went by the name of the Regency Hotel. They stood uncertainly on the pavement outside, tired after their day-long journey, but all with a happy anticipation of the pleasures ahead.

They carried their own suitcases and bags after Mike had unloaded them, waiting at the reception desk until Mr and Mrs Wilkes gave them their room keys. The hotel appeared brighter and more welcoming inside than out, with a bright-red carpet and highly polished woodwork and a large gilt-framed mirror on the wall. There was a faint odour of cabbage though, mixed with furniture polish and a vestigial aroma of cigarette smoke.

Fiona and Diane were sharing a room on the second floor. It was just about big enough for the two of them. There were twin beds covered with candlewick bedspreads in an odd shade of olive green, a small dressing table and wardrobe, and a wash basin with soap and towels provided. The bathroom and toilet were situated along the corridor.

There was just time for them to unpack their cases, which didn't take long as they hadn't been able to bring all they might have wanted to. It was probably just as well though, as it was a tight squeeze in the wardrobe. After a quick wash and tidy up it was time for the evening meal.

They were seated – twenty-two of them in all, including Mike, the driver – on two long tables. There were a few other guests in the hotel at smaller tables for two or four. Fiona and Diane were amongst the last to come down so they weren't able to sit near Dave and Andy, who were at the other table with the rest of the lads.

Mr Wilkes, who had said they could call him Colin if they wished, stood up and dutifully said the grace. Some of the other diners looked round in surprise, but it was noticed that most of them bowed their heads as well. The meal that followed was quite ordinary fare but very welcome to the hungry teenagers. Roast beef, but without the Yorkshire pudding that was a must back home; carrots and cabbage, which they had smelled cooking earlier; mashed potatoes and gravy; followed by apple crumble and custard.

Colin suggested that they should stay in that evening and make use of the visitors' lounge. He had brought along a selection of games – Snakes and Ladders, Ludo, dominoes, draughts, and even a chess set for those who had learnt the intricacies of the game. No playing cards, as those were taboo at their particular church, and he did not dare to disobey the orders of the Reverend Cruikshank in case word of his transgression should get back to the vicar.

Fiona and Diane were pleased when Dave suggested that the four of them should have a game of Ludo.

'Exciting stuff, this,' remarked Andy and they all laughed. They were having fun, though, the sort of fun that would meet with the approval of the church.

'We knew there would be no riotous living though, on this trip, didn't we?' said Dave.

'What do you know about riotous living, Dave?' asked Diane.

'Nothing… yet,' he grinned, 'but give me time.' He winked at Fiona and she felt herself blushing.

'There!' he cried a few moments later as he moved his last counter home. 'I've won! Now, what could be more exciting than that?'

Janet, who was in the sixth form with Fiona and Diane, was the pianist for the Youth Club. She sat down at the piano now and started to play the choruses that they sang at the close of their meetings. 'Cleanse me from my sin, Lord' they sang, followed by 'Christ Jesus lives today', and 'Trust and Obey'. But no one objected, not even the leaders, when Janet went on to play some of the popular tunes of the day. 'Singin' the Blues', 'Buttons and Bows' and 'Slow Boat to China'.

Before ten o'clock most of them were yawning with tiredness and so, by mutual agreement, they decided it was time to call it a day. They said goodnight to one another as they went upstairs, the girls on the first and second floors, and the boys, out of harm's way, on the third floor.

'That was good fun, wasn't it?' said Diane, flopping down on the bed.

'Yes… I suppose so,' replied Fiona.

'What's the matter?' asked her friend, eyeing her curiously. 'I enjoyed it. Like Dave said, it wasn't exactly riotous living, but it was good. Yes, it was fun. Oh, come on, what's up, Fee?'

Fiona, inexplicably, was suddenly feeling rather odd; a bit down in the dumps. She wondered if she might be homesick. It was the first time she had been parted from her parents. She had, actually, been looking forward to being away from them for a while, but she was finding the reality was rather different.

'Oh, I don't know. I'm just tired I suppose,' she replied. 'I expect I'll feel better after a night's sleep. That's what my mum always says.'

'I'm sure you will,' said Diane. 'Cheer up now. You're getting on well with Dave, aren't you? I've noticed the way he looks at you. And I think I might be getting somewhere with Andy.'

'Yes,' agreed Fiona. 'I think you are. I'm pleased about that. I shall have to watch it, though, with Dave. I really like him, Di, such a lot. But I know that we mustn't… well, you know what I mean, don't you?'

Diane nodded. 'Yes, I expect I do. Why? Has he tried…?'

'No, of course not. But he's been more – well – wanting more than just kissing, you know, lately. But I didn't let him go any further... Oh, Diane, I feel so muddled up. That's partly what's wrong with me, I think. I decided I would tell Mum and Dad about him when we get back home. But then I feel that I daren't; you know what they're like.'

'Yes, they've got quite involved with Mr Cruikshank and all that lot, haven't they?'

Fiona nodded. 'Your mum and dad haven't, have they?'

'No; they go to church, but not all the time. Just at special times like Christmas and Harvest and Easter. Mum always takes Communion at Easter, and they wanted me to be confirmed. I think they're just as good as the folk who go to church all the time. They're really kind, my mum and dad. Mum does the shopping for the old couple next door, and my dad does their garden. I call that being Christian, don't you?'

'Yes, of course I do,' agreed Fiona readily. 'But my mum and dad seem to think that they're special somehow; that they know Jesus in a special sort of way. I feel so confused sometimes. And Mum isn't any fun any more. I feel I can't talk to her about anything. Actually, I asked Mr Wilkes – Colin – about all this being a Christian business,' Fiona went on. 'And he said that it's God who judges us and knows what's in our hearts, not other people, and that I hadn't to worry. He said I just had to do what I knew was right. And that's what I try to do.'

'Yes, Colin's a good sort,' said Diane. 'Come on, Fee. Don't worry about it any more. Like you said, you'll feel better after a night's sleep.'

'I hope so,' said Fiona.

They undressed quickly, and after a quick visit along the corridor they got into bed without even bothering to wash. It had been an exhausting day.

'Goodnight, God bless,' they whispered to one another. And Fiona, despite the turmoil in her mind, fell asleep almost at once.

Seven

Fiona did, indeed, feel much better the next morning. As she opened her eyes the sun was shining through the curtains, which were not thick enough to keep out the light.

'Are you awake, Diane?' she called softly.

'Yes,' answered her friend. 'I've been awake for quite a while. I've just been lying here and listening to you snoring!'

'Oh, go on! I don't!' protested Fiona.

'Well, maybe just a bit,' said her friend. 'At least I know you've had a good sleep in spite of all your worries. Are you feeling better now?'

'Much better,' Fiona answered. 'Raring to go! Come on, let's get moving. I don't know about you but I feel rather grubby and in need of a bath. I'll nip along and see if the bathroom's free, or do you want to go first?'

'No, you go,' said Diane. 'Take one of those towels they've provided. Nice big fluffy ones, aren't they? All mod cons, eh?'

'They're making sure we don't pinch them though!' laughed Fiona. Printed on the towels in bold writing were the words Regency Hotel. She took a towel from the rail, picked up her toilet bag and donned her dressing gown. 'I won't be long,' she said, 'but we're quite early. It's only quarter past seven, and breakfast's at eight o'clock.'

They were ready in good time, both of them wearing their full-skirted summer dresses in bold floral designs. Fiona's had a dazzlingly white collar, and Diane's a sweetheart neckline. They had bought them together at their favourite C and A store, especially for the occasion.

They all tucked into a full English breakfast. It seemed that post-war restrictions were no longer rigidly adhered to, although ration books were still required. Bacon, sausage, fried egg, tomato and fried bread, with fragrant smelling coffee as a change from the tea they were all used to at home.

Then they all waited outside the hotel for Mike to bring the coach from his night time parking spot. At nine thirty the sun was shining brightly and warmly in a cloudless sky; there appeared to be no sign of rain. They had already noticed that the temperature was a degree or two higher here than in the somewhat chilly hills and vales of Yorkshire. Most of the girls carried a cardigan 'just in case', and several of the boys, dressed in grey flannel trousers and casual shirts, had decided to discard their sports jackets.

Their sightseeing tour took them across Westminster Bridge for a further look at the Houses of Parliament and Parliament Square. Mike, the driver, was very well informed – or, more likely, had been reading up about it – and he stopped the coach to pass on his words of wisdom. Big Ben he informed them, was not really the name of the clock as most people supposed, but the name of the bell, weighing fourteen tons that had been named after Sir Benjamin Hall, the chief commissioner of works when the bell was installed in 1858.

'We knew that already, didn't we?' said Fiona. Mrs Wilkes had given them an interesting talk at a Youth Club meeting about all the sights they would be seeing. 'But it's exciting, isn't it, seeing it all for ourselves?'

Then they were off along Whitehall with just a peek along Downing Street where the Prime Minister – Winston Churchill at the moment – resided at No 10. They saw the Cenotaph, the Banqueting Hall (from the window of which the ill-fated Charles the First had stepped out to his scaffold); Horse Guard's Parade where a soldier in a red tunic, high polished boots and a bearskin stood on guard, not moving a muscle. Along the Mall with Buckingham Palace, a mile away, coming gradually nearer, and then back to Parliament Square along Birdcage Walk, because the main visit of the morning was to be to Westminster Abbey. The Reverend Cruikshank had insisted on this, in spite of his adverse comment that the form of worship and all the pomp and ceremony practised there would not be to his liking. Nevertheless it was a must on the agenda.

Fiona, and indeed all the young people in the group, experienced a sense of awe and wonderment as they toured the abbey with the well-informed guide. The site of the original abbey dated from the time of Edward the Confessor who died in 1066. His tomb was there in St Edward's chapel which had become the focal point of the abbey. There were a myriad of other tombs of the great and the good. Queen Elizabeth the First; her sister Mary; Mary Queen of Scots; and other kings and queens from way back in the times when England was a Catholic country.

They were allowed a little time to wander around on their own. They remarked on how shabby and worn was the Coronation chair, the ancient throne of the Scottish kings with the stone of Scone beneath it, all a part of the age old tradition of the abbey. Of particular interest to most of them was Poet's Corner. They marvelled at the tombs, in some cases simple stone slabs let into the floor, commemorating poets such as Geoffrey Chaucer, Edward Spenser, Alfred Lord Tennyson, John Masefield, Robert Browning... Composers, writers and actors too; George Frederick Handel, Charles Dickens, Rudyard Kipling, Thomas Hardy, Henry Irving and Lawrence Olivier.

'What a wealth of talent,' observed Fiona.

'And how their memory lives on,' remarked Diane. Some of the names were very familiar as many of them had studied the various books and poems for their School Certificate Exam.

Most moving of all, though, was the tomb of the Unknown Warrior, surrounded by red poppies, commemorating the many thousands of soldiers who were killed in World War One and buried without being identified. They had all heard of the carnage of that dreadful war, but more poignant and meaningful to them were the memories of the more recent war. There were a few of the young people who had lost loved ones, an uncle or elder brother, and one of the lads had lost his father.

It was quite a sombre group who went out of the abbey into the glorious sunshine. Sad thoughts did not linger for long, though, as they boarded the coach again for Mike to take them to the place he had decided they would stop for lunch. This was St James's Park, which they had passed earlier on their way to Buckingham Palace.

'You can have an hour here,' Mike told them as he stopped the coach on Birdcage Walk. 'Make sure you're all back here at two o'clock. Try not to be late because I can't park for long. Off you go and enjoy yourselves.'

It was noticed that Rita stopped on the coach with Mike as he drove off to find a parking place. The two of them appeared to be getting on very well. Colin and Sheila, too, strode away quickly on their own, no doubt pleased to have some time to themselves.

St James's Park was a lovely place to spend an hour, one of the quiet oases of green to be found near to the centre of London, away from the noise and bustle of the city traffic and the crowds of people. It was not all that quiet, though, at lunchtime, as it was a popular place for the office workers to take their ease and eat their packed lunches. Most of the park benches were full with the business men and women and the families who, like the Youth Club group, were holidaying in the capital. Fiona and Diane, with Dave and Andy, who had joined them on leaving the coach, found a shady spot on the grass beneath a spreading sycamore tree, near to the lake.

The hotel had provided them with a packed lunch; there were two substantial sandwiches, one of ham and one of cheese; an apple; a chocolate Penguin biscuit; a packet of crisps; and an orange drink in a carton. They were all hungry despite the large breakfast they had consumed. The provisions were soon eaten and the waste deposited in a nearby bin.

'Come on, let's go and explore,' said Dave, reaching out a hand to Fiona and pulling her to her feet. 'You don't mind do you, you two?'

'Of course not,' replied Diane. She winked impercept-ibly at Fiona. Things were going just the way she wanted them.

As they wandered along the path that skirted the lake Dave took hold of Fiona's hand, and when she turned to look at him he smiled. 'I thought we'd sneak a little time on our own,' he said; and Fiona felt a stab of pure happiness. Her odd mood of the previous night – which she had put down to homesickness and the strangeness of being in an unfamiliar place – had completely vanished.

The park lake was the habitat of a great number of water birds. Some of them were easily recognized – the Canada geese, Mallard ducks and swans – and the more unusual ones could be identified by the recognition pictures fastened to the low iron railings that edged the lake. There was a notice saying that the birds could be fed, and Fiona threw them the morsels of bread she had saved in readiness. The swans were there first, amazingly large birds when you were close to them; probably fierce ones too, judging by the savage gleam in their eyes as they fought for their share of the bounty. Of course the cheeky London pigeons were there as well, and the little brown sparrows hoping for a crumb or two.

'Let's go and see the pelicans,' said Dave, 'that is if they'll condescend to show themselves.' They had been told that those elusive birds lived in an island at the end of the lake, near to the Horse Guard's Parade, the first brace having been a diplomatic gift from the Russian ambassador to King Charles II. This particular king had loved to walk in the park and to swim in the lake, a sport that was now strictly forbidden.

They stood by the railings, peering towards the island, and in a few moments their patience was rewarded. There, emerging from the bushes was one of the peculiar and exotic birds, then, almost at once it disappeared again. There was a notice stating that visitors were requested not to feed the pelicans, but it was doubtful that you could get near enough anyway.

They walked back along the path, then turned on to the elegant suspension bridge that spanned the lake. They stopped halfway across, leaning on the railings and looking south to the view of the Whitehall skyline. Seen from a distance, the white cupolas of the War Office and the spires and turreted roofs of the Whitehall buildings seemed like an enchanted vista of fairy-tale palaces. It was a magical view, right there in the very heart of the busy commercial city.

And it seemed like a magic moment to Fiona, one she believed she would never forget, as Dave put his arm round her shoulders, drawing her closer to him. He leaned towards her and kissed her cheek, then, as she turned towards him, he kissed her gently on the lips.

'I'm really glad I decided to come this week,' he said. 'Of course, it was because I knew you were coming that I made up my mind.'

'Yes… me too,' replied Fiona, suddenly feeling a little shy.

'D'you think, when we get back home, that we could start going out together properly?' he asked. 'You know, to the pictures or something, not just at Youth Club and meeting after school?'

Fiona nodded slowly, but a little uncertainly. 'Yes… I'd like that. I really would like to, Dave, but it'll mean that I'll have to tell my parents and…'

'And is that such a great problem?' he asked.

'Maybe, maybe not,' she replied. 'I'm not sure. They're so odd sometimes. Well, most of the time really now, not like they used to be.'

'They're part of Mr Cruikshank's inner circle, aren't they?' said Dave. 'The "holier than thou" brigade. I'm sorry, Fee, but that's how I think of them. It's as though the rest of us don't match up to them.'

'That's just how I feel,' she agreed. 'But they're my mum and dad, and I'm their only child, so I suppose they are rather too protective of me. They don't preach at me – well, not very much – but somehow I sense their disapproval. You know – about wearing too much make-up and staying out late. Not that I ever do,' she added 'stay out late, I mean.' Fiona knew that, deep down, she loved both of her parents and would never want to do anything to hurt or disappoint them.

'You're seventeen now, Fiona,' said Dave. 'You must learn to stick up for yourself.' He kissed her again. 'And I do want you to be my girlfriend. You must tell them – if you feel they have to know. And if you want to go out with me, that is?'

'Of course I do, Dave,' she said. 'And I promise I'll tell them. Anyway, we've got the rest of our time here, haven't we?' She didn't want to think yet about going home. And she knew it was going to be a fantastic time.

'Yes, sure,' he replied. 'And it seems as though we're being allowed more freedom than we expected. It's a good job that the Reverend Amos isn't here!'

'You're not kidding,' laughed Fiona. 'Come on; we'd better be heading back.'

They retraced their steps, walking quickly towards where the coach would be waiting.

'What wonderful sights have they in store for us this afternoon?' asked Dave.

'St Paul's Cathedral, isn't?' replied Fiona. 'Another church, you might know. But I must admit I was very impressed by Westminster Abbey.'

'Same here,' agreed Dave. 'Here we are, and we're not the last, thank goodness.'

In a few moments they were all assembled, chattering excitedly as the coach drew up with Mike at the wheel and Rita sitting on the seat next to him.

'All aboard,' he called and after a quick head count they were off again.

Christopher Wren's achievements had reached their peak in his plans for the rebuilding of St Paul's Cathedral. Following the Great Fire of London in 1666 the medieval cathedral had been left in ruins.

Standing near to the statue of Queen Anne they gazed in wonder at the great dome, one of the largest in the world, second only to St Peter's in Rome, and at the west front towers, one on each side that perfectly complemented the dome.

Once inside they could see that the dome was just as spectacular viewed from the nave of the church. Gilded arches led up to the dome with its carvings of apostles and painted scenes depicting the life of St Paul. Some of them climbed up to the Whispering Gallery with its strange acoustics that enabled you to hear a whisper from the other side of the dome, just as though the speaker were standing next to you. The young people were too intimidated, though, to whisper any more than, 'Hello, how are you?' or other such trite comments. After all they were inside a church!

There were monuments a–plenty; not so many, though, as in the smaller abbey. A bust of Lawrence of Arabia; the tomb of John Dunne, poet and a former dean of St Paul's; and memorials to the Duke of Wellington, Lord Nelson and Lord Kitchener. The most moving tribute was the tomb to Wren himself; a simple marble slab inscribed with the words, 'Reader, if you seek a memorial look all around you.'

They all agreed that St Paul's Cathedral was impressive, far more grand than Westminster Abbey, but it failed to move them in the way that the more intimate feel of the abbey had done.

Not far away was the stone column called the Monument. That, also, had been designed by Sir Christopher Wren to commemorate the Great Fire. It was 2005 feet high, said to be the tallest stone column in the world. They climbed, a few at a time, up the 311 steps that led to the viewing platform at the top. The views all around were splendid. The dome of St Paul's; the Tower of London and Tower Bridge; the Houses of Parliament and Buckingham Palace; in the distance the hills of Hampstead and Highgate; and winding through the city the silver ribbon of the River Thames.

Their way back led along Fleet Street, home of the newspaper giants; the Strand, Trafalgar Square, then back along the Embankment and across Westminster Bridge. Then there was time for a wash and brush-up before the evening meal.

That evening would be their first visit to the Battersea Pleasure Gardens. Sightseeing was enjoyable and informative, but tonight, they hoped, there would be a chance to let their hair down.

Eight

Battersea Park had originally been opened in 1858 on the site known as Battersea Fields, a swampy area notorious for every kind of vice, centred around a disreputable public house called the Old Red House.

It was soon considered necessary for Victorian Londoners to have somewhere to relax and enjoy themselves in a respectable setting; and, indeed, the new park soon became very popular. It boasted a man-made boating lake, rocks, waterfalls and laid-out gardens, and it became a very popular venue for the new craze of cycling, enjoyed by many Victorians, both young and older.

And in the summer of 1951 the park became the site for the Festival Funfair in what became known as the Battersea Pleasure Gardens. It afforded a spot of light relief from the more cultural and educational aspects of the festival itself on its site further down the river.

To Fiona and her friends their visit to the Pleasure Gardens promised to be one of the highlights of their visit to London, if not the best of all. After another satisfying evening meal of steak pie and chips followed by syrup sponge pudding, they all piled on to the coach again, ready for Mike to drive them to the park. After he had stopped the coach at the entrance he told them they must be back in the same spot by half past ten and no later. This was the directive given by Colin and Sheila, who considered they were being quite lenient. None of the young people disagreed. They all thought that their leaders were granting them far more freedom than they had been led to expect. They had, of course, been given a little pep talk about behaving themselves and acting in a responsible manner, '…because we trust you,' Colin had said, 'and we know that none of you will let us down.'

The funfair was all that they had expected, and more, no doubt because they were all in a happy and receptive frame of mind, determined to enjoy themselves to the full. It was all there; dodgem cars; roundabouts; coconut shies and sideshows; ice-cream and candyfloss; hot dogs and lemonade; and a switchback ride.

'Not as big as the Big Dipper at Blackpool Pleasure Beach,' Dave remarked, 'but it should be good fun all the same. Shall we go on it, Fiona?'

'Er… yes; perhaps in a little while,' she replied. She was feeling mesmerized, but very happy amidst all the dazzling sights and the mixed aromas of frying sausages, sweet candyfloss and pungent diesel oil, and all around the blaring sound of the mechanical music. She had never been on Blackpool's Big Dipper, and the truth was that she felt a little nervous. She was determined, though, not to let her fear be obvious. 'We've only just had our meal,' she said. 'Let's wait till it's settled; we don't want to be sick.'

'OK,' said Dave. He put an arm around her as they wandered around the fairground. He proved his prowess at the hoopla stall and won a tiny pink teddy bear which he presented to Fiona. Diane and Andy were not close behind, and the four of them had a turn on the dodgem cars, the two lads taking delight in racing around the rink and bumping one another's cars as hard as they could, to the excited squeals of the girls.

They wandered towards the lake where rowing boats could be hired, but decided they would leave that experience until the next night. They had been told that those who wished could make a second visit to the Pleasure Gardens, depending, of course, on whether their funds would allow it.

'No, we'll go on the Big Dipper instead,' said Dave. 'Come on, Fee; you said that you would.'

'I'm game if you are,' Diane said to her friend. 'It'll be fun. Anyway, you've got Dave to take care of you.'

Still feeling somewhat apprehensive, Fiona sat next to Dave, securely fastened into the little car and holding on to the rail in front of her like grim death. Then they were off... and it turned out to be not nearly as frightening as she had expected. Her heart was in her mouth as they slowly ascended towards the top of the first incline, then started on the rapid descent. There were screams from all the girls and whoops of delight from the boys. Fiona's stomach turned somersaults as she felt the wind rushing past, blowing her hair all over the place.

'Great, isn't it?' shouted Dave, pulling her closer to him and kissing her cheek. Then they were going up the next slope, and she was anticipating the scary delight of the whooshing of the wind in her ears and the crazy feeling of exhilaration. She felt her legs turn to jelly as she stood once more on terra firma, and her head was spinning round and round. But she agreed with the others that she wouldn't have missed it for anything.

'It's still only quarter past nine,' said Dave. 'We've got over an hour left. Shall we walk across to the other side of the river? We've plenty of time and we can do the rest of the funfair tomorrow. What do you think?'

They all agreed that they would do a little exploring. 'But we must keep an eye on the time,' said Fiona. 'We daren't be late back.'

'Stop worrying! We won't be,' said Diane. 'I say, aren't we having a good time?' she whispered to her friend as they loitered behind for a moment, letting the lads lead the way.

'Wonderful!' agreed Fiona. 'And you're getting on famously with Andy, aren't you?'

'So far, so good,' replied Diane. 'And so are you and Dave, aren't you?'

'Yes; he's asked me to go out with him; properly, I mean, as his girlfriend, when we get back home,' Fiona told her. 'I really like him ever so much, Diane. I don't want anything to spoil it.'

'Why should it?' said Diane. 'You're thinking about your parents, aren't you?' Fiona nodded. 'Well, don't! Just enjoy yourself while you can. Anyway, I'm sure it'll be alright. Come on, let's catch up with them…'

They crossed the river by the Albert Suspension Bridge which led to the part of the Embankment known as Cheyne Walk; an elegant road with medieval and eighteenth-century dwellings, as well as a few public houses. Dusk was falling and the view back across the river was an enchanting one. The delicate lines of the suspension bridge formed a filigree pattern against the darkening blue of the sky, and the lights strung amongst the trees in the park glimmered like jewels in the darkness. The only incongruous sight was that of the Battersea Power Station a little further upriver, looking like an upturned billiard table, the four chimneys, one at each corner, resembling the legs, black against the night sky.

As they passed one of the pubs on the waterfront they heard a shout. 'Hi there! Do you want to come and join us?'

Seated round one of the wooden tables at the outside drinking area were three of their fellow Youth Club members; Alison and Jean who were in the upper sixth form at the school that Fiona and Diane attended, and Paul, who was the same age as his two companions but who had left school at sixteen and was now working in his father's garage.

They all stopped and returned the greeting.

'Come and sit down,' said Alison. 'There's plenty of room. Paul, could you grab that stool from the next table, then we'll have enough seats.'

'Er... I don't think we should, really,' said Fiona. 'We're not old enough, are we? You lot are all eighteen, aren't you? But we're not...'

'You must be nearly eighteen though,' said Jean. 'You're only a year below us at school.'

'Next year actually,' replied Diane. 'My birthday's in April, and Fiona's is in May. I don't know about you two,' she said to the lads.

'We're almost there,' said Dave. 'I'll be eighteen next month, and Andy the month after.' He sat down on the bench. 'Come on, you lot. Don't be daft! Nobody'll know if we don't say anything. It's impossible to tell how old we are. And they're not going to ask for our birth certificates.'

'They might,' countered Fiona. 'And supposing Colin and Sheila walk past? They'd be really annoyed with us.'

'I doubt it,' replied Diane, sitting down on the stool at the end of the table. 'Stop worrying, Fee, it'll be alright.

Anyway, we look eighteen, if not more, when we're not in our school uniform. Come on now; sit down and shut up!'

'Oh, alright then,' said Fiona. But she was still feeling apprehensive. It was the first time she had ever been in a public house. Well, she wasn't really in one now, she told herself, just sitting outside, but it still amounted to the same thing. And she had scarcely ever drunk anything alcoholic. At one time her parents had used to buy a bottle of port or sherry at Christmas time and she had been allowed a little sip. But they no longer did so. It seemed that alcohol was one more thing that was taboo, like dancing or going to the cinema or wearing make-up.

'What are you having then?' asked Paul. 'It's my round.' As the only one of the group who was working he had a little more money than the rest of them to splash around. And they all knew that Whiteside's garage on the main road leading to Leeds was quite a prosperous one. 'Dave and Andy, what about you? A pint of Tetley's, eh?'

'Yes, why not?' replied Dave. 'That is if they sell our famous Yorkshire brew here?'

'Yes, of course they do,' said Paul. 'That's what I'm drinking. What about you girls?'

'Oh, an orange juice for me,' replied Fiona. 'Thank you very much, Paul.'

'Now come on,' said Paul. 'You want something a bit more exciting than that!'

'What are you drinking?' Fiona asked Alison and Jean.

'Lemonade shandies,' replied Jean. 'You should try one.' But Fiona was not too sure about that. She didn't think she would like the taste of beer, even if it was diluted with lemonade.

'Er, I don't think so,' she said. She was starting to feel a bit silly and immature next to these more sophisticated girls; they seemed to know so much more about what was considered 'cool' to drink.

'I know, I'll have a gin and lime,' announced Diane. 'Go on, Fee; you have the same. My mum drinks that and I've had a taste of it. It's nice; you'll like it.'

'Oh, alright then,' agreed Fiona, knowing she would look a fool if she hesitated much longer.

Paul, the man with the money, ordered their drinks from the barmaid who was hovering near. They arrived in a few moments; two pint glasses of frothy amber coloured beer, and two smaller glasses holding liquid of a most appealing shade of lime green.

Fiona tasted it warily, then decided it was not bad at all, in fact she liked it more than she had expected to. She drank it rather more quickly than she should have done. Diane, she noticed, was sipping hers more slowly. All around her there was chatter about what a good time they were having in London and what they had enjoyed the most.

'It's supposed to be the highlight of our visit tomorrow, when we go to the exhibition,' said Alison, 'but what's the betting we'll all be looking forward to another visit to the funfair tomorrow night?'

'Hear, hear,' agreed Dave, putting his arm around Fiona. 'We've had a great time, haven't we, Fee? Especially on the Big Dipper.'

'Yes, it was amazing,' said Fiona. 'I was a bit scared at first, but I don't know why, 'cause I really enjoyed it. I can't wait to have another ride.' She laughed out loud, and her voice, to her own ears, sounded louder and more shrill than usual. She was already halfway through her second gin and lime, which Dave had bought this time. She no longer felt worried about the fact that she was not eighteen, or about what Colin and Sheila might say if they walked past. In fact she felt very light-hearted, and light-headed as well.

Jean looked at her watch. 'Come on, you lot,' she said. 'We'd better be heading back. It's only ten o'clock but we'd better not risk being late.'

When they stood up Fiona felt rather unsteady on her feet, but everyone else appeared to be alright. The three older ones led the way as they went back over the Albert Bridge. Alison and Jean were both linking arms with Paul. It seemed as though they were all just good friends and that he was not 'going out' with either of the girls. Andy and Diane were walking hand in hand; Fiona was pleased that they were getting on so well.

As for herself and Dave, she felt as though she was walking on a cloud as they strolled along, their arms around one another. She knew that the slight dizziness she was feeling was the effect of the drink that she wasn't used to, but she didn't care because she felt so happy and as though she hadn't a care in the world. Now and again they stopped to kiss, not at all concerned if there was anyone to see them.

There was still fifteen minutes or so to spare when they reached the fringes of the park, near to where Mike had arranged to pick them up. Dave led Fiona into a secluded copse of trees, then he drew her into his arms, kissing her passionately. She did not demur when she felt his hands caressing her body. He had never done this before, although she knew that he had wanted to and that it had been up to her to say no. This time she did not want to stop him. She returned his kisses ardently… But after a few moments he broke away.

'We'd better go, Fiona,' he whispered. 'We daren't be late. But there's always tomorrow. Fiona… darling; you know how much I care about you, don't you?'

'Yes… I think so, Dave,' she whispered back. 'And… and so do I.'

He smiled at her, very lovingly and tenderly, then he kissed her lightly on the lips. They walked back hand in hand to where the coach was waiting. No one seemed to have noticed them, not even Diane and Andy, who were deep in conversation. Fiona decided that there were some things that it would be better not to tell her friend.

They all piled into the coach and when they were all seated Colin counted them. 'Good; all present and correct,' he said. 'That's what we like; keep up the good work, folks. You've all enjoyed yourselves, have you?'

There was a chorus of 'Rather!', 'You bet!' and 'Super duper!'.

'Smashing!' said Colin. 'Off we go then, Mike. Home, James, and don't spare the horses!'

Nine

Fiona had drunk only two gin and limes; not a huge amount but more than enough for someone as unaccustomed to it as she was. Her head was deliciously woozy and she felt that her inhibitions had taken flight.

She and Diane spoke very little as they got ready for bed. Diane had had the same amount to drink but seemed to be more in control of herself. Fiona was aware that her friend was looking at her rather oddly, but she did not ask any pertinent questions.

Thoughts of Dave and their growing intimacy floated around in Fiona's mind when she first laid her head on the pillow, but it was not long before sleep overcame her. She did not stir until the insistent clamour of the alarm clock woke her at seven thirty.

She found, to her relief, that she did not have a headache or any ill effects from the night before. Neither, it seemed, did Diane, but her friend was looking at her intently.

'Fiona,' she began tentatively. 'Be careful, won't you, with Dave? I know you might think it's none of my business but... well, you were a bit tipsy last night, weren't you and...'

'No more than you,' retorted Fiona. 'You had two gin and limes, the same as me. And what about you and Andy?

Maybe you should be careful too. It sounds like the pot calling the kettle black.'

Diane shook her head. 'There's nothing about me and Andy. We're only just getting to know one another. It's not like you and Dave. I've seen the way he looks at you.'

'I know what I'm doing, really I do,' replied Fiona quite offhandedly. 'Don't get your knickers in a twist, Di. I'm alright, honestly, and I can trust Dave.'

'Very well then, if you say so,' replied Diane. 'But just watch it, that's all.'

'OK, will do,' grinned Fiona.

If she were honest with herself she felt a tiny bit embarrassed when she saw Dave at breakfast time, but he greeted her quite normally. What had gone on between them the night before appeared to have been forgotten, or was not about to be mentioned in the light of day. They did, of course, have to act normally in front of Colin and Sheila and not appear to be too friendly with one another.

They set off soon after nine o'clock, on foot this time as the festival site was within easy walking distance. It was decided that the young people should be free to make their own way round the exhibition as they would each have their own particular interests. Fiona and Diane agreed to meet Dave and Andy later. They decided on a spot near to the Skylon where they would eat their packed lunches, once again provided by the hotel.

The lads were eager to visit the pavilions concerned with science and industry. There was the Dome of Discovery telling the story of British scientific and technological advances; the Production Pavilion, which housed craft workshops and a model coal mine; and the Land of Britain Pavilion which depicted the country's physical geography.

Fiona and Diane and several of the other girls were more interested in the Homes and Gardens Pavilion, so this was the place they visited first of all. It showed sample room settings in the modern style that was now becoming known as the 'contemporary look'. New shapes and brighter colours were being introduced to all rooms of the house, a contrast to the austerity and drabness of the war years and the years that followed.

Fiona and Diane had both grown up in houses with small kitchens that contained only the most essential requirements: a gas stove; a porcelain sink and wooden draining board; and a shelf above the cooker on which to keep pans. All the crockery and food items were kept in a tall free standing cupboard known as a kitchenette. At Fiona's home there was a meat safe that stood in the yard, just outside the back door. It was covered with a wire mesh to prevent flies and other insects from entering, and in it was kept meat, milk and dairy items. It was scarcely adequate, though, in the summer months; food was often less than fresh and sometimes, reluctantly, had to be thrown away. This had been looked on as a crime in the war years, and old habits still died hard.

They gazed in awe now at the modern refrigerator – what a boon that would be! – and the stainless steel sink and shining draining board; the electric cooker; and the built-in cupboards.

'Look at the bright colours!' exclaimed Fiona. 'Red and white; doesn't that look jolly? I thought kitchens were always painted cream and green. That's what ours is.'

'Ours as well,' agreed Diane. 'My mum would really love this.'

'I'm not so sure about mine though,' said Fiona. 'She'd think it was too modern. She's a great one for "making things do", as she says. Although, to be fair, I suppose there's never been too much money to spare for luxuries.'

There was another specimen kitchen in shades of blue, with a built-in breakfast bar and strip lighting on the ceiling. 'It'll be a long time, I suppose, before we all have kitchens like this,' said Diane. 'Perhaps by the time we're married, eh, Fiona? And just look at the automatic washing machine!'

They agreed that this would be the 'mod con' that would be of the most interest to women visiting the exhibition. There was a fully automatic one on display in one of the kitchens, and in the other one a model that was known as a 'twin-tub', with an electrically powered wringer. Fiona and Diane had seen for themselves what a trial the Monday washday was to the woman of the house. Fiona's mother was fortunate enough to have a small wash house outside the house. The clothes were washed in a dolly tub, then fed through a large mangle with wooden rollers to squeeze out the water. The back garden was large enough for the washing to be hung out to dry; but the bane of every housewife was a wet washday, when clothes were hung on an overhead rack or on a 'clothes maiden' round the fire.

The bathrooms, too, were luxurious to their eyes. Lavatories with low cisterns and a handle to flush, instead of a chain; baths and wash basins in pale colours – pink, blue, green and lemon – instead of the ordinary white that ended up a dingy grey. They were cased in as well, unlike the bath tubs that most of them were used to, and the walls were tiled from floor to ceiling, some highlighted with designs of flowers or birds.

'Very nice too,' said Fiona. 'I suppose we're quite lucky though, Diane, you and me. At least we don't have to go down the yard to the lav, do we?'

Fiona's home was a council house, but quite a modern one in that it had an indoor bathroom and toilet. Her grandmother still lived in a house with a WC at the end of the yard. Fortunately it was not one that was shared with neighbouring houses, as was the case, still, in many homes. Neither was there a bathroom, although the powers that be were supposed to be considering it, as they had been doing since the end of the war. Fiona's gran still bathed once a week in a zinc bath that hung on a hook in the wash house.

The furniture in the sample dining and living rooms was vastly different from the sort that most people were still living with in those post-war years. The cumbersome three-piece suites that took up most of the room in a small lounge were things of the past, as were the solid oak dining chairs and tables and glass-fronted display cabinets. The modern settees and armchairs – with wooden arms rather than the upholstered kind – were light and easy to move, with splayed tapering legs; far easier for a vacuum cleaner to get underneath. Dining chairs, too, were a new innovation, some made of laminated wood on spindly metal legs.

Gone was the wallpaper in the traditional colours of fawn, pale green and brown. The walls, instead, were painted – not papered – in bright colours or pastel shades of emulsion paint that could be wiped clean. Wallpaper, too, if it was used, could be wiped down.

Looking at the curtains and the rugs in bold designs of geometric shapes, Fiona pondered that it might be a long time before ideas such as these became popular in many homes. She could not see it ever happening in her parents' home.

Wandering round these 'ideal homes' took up most of the morning. After they had joined the lads for lunch they stayed together for a while, looking with interest and a certain amount of envy at the latest designs of radios and television sets. Only Andy's family, of the four of them, owned a television set. They were fascinated too by the latest record players, with something known as hi-fi and stereophonic sound. Fiona had a 'Dansette' portable record player, and being a sensible girl, aware that there was never too much money to spare, she knew she would have to be content with that, and with her small collection of records. At least her mother did not seem to object too much to her liking for Guy Mitchell and Doris Day.

By the end of the afternoon they were all feeling quite mesmerized by all the new sights and wonders they had seen. They all had a collection of leaflets about the latest inventions in design and technology to take home to show to their parents and friends. They were more of a souvenir, though, than anything else. It was doubtful that many of the innovations would be seen in the homes of ordinary folk until much later in the decade.

They were all looking forward to what would be their last evening in London. How quickly the three days had flown! And tomorrow, Thursday, they would be saying goodbye to the capital city, setting off quite early in the morning in order to arrive back in Leeds by the end of the afternoon.

They all opted to visit the funfair again although, for many of them, funds were running low. But they all agreed that they would help one another out financially if needs be, and make it a never to be forgotten last evening. Once again they all agreed to be back at the coach by ten thirty.

Fiona and Dave, and Diane and Andy stayed together for a while. They had a second ride on the Big Dipper. The girls found it not so scary this time, as they knew what to expect, but just as exciting and exhilarating. Then they wandered over to the boating lake and hired two rowing boats. The boys, of course, did the rowing whilst the girls sat lazily at the other end. Fiona listened to the distant sounds of the funfair; the laughter and shouts of excited visitors; and the somewhat discordant music from the roundabouts and mechanical rides. A little breeze drifted across the water and she felt chilly. She shivered as she fastened her cardigan, which she had been wearing loosely draped over her shoulders.

'Are you cold?' asked Dave.

'Just a bit,' she replied. 'I'll be alright when we get off the water.'

'We'll call it a day then, shall we?' he said. 'Shall we go across to the other side of the river again and have a drink? We'll feel warmer when we start walking.'

'Good idea,' she replied. 'We don't need to wait for Diane and Andy, do we? Look; they're over on the other side of the lake.' Fiona waved but her friend didn't appear to notice her.

'No, they're happy enough on their own,' said Dave. 'Anyway, we want to be alone together for a while, don't we?'

Fiona nodded, suddenly feeling a shade uneasy although she was not sure why. She and Dave had grown much closer to one another over the last couple of days. The more she had got to know him the more fond she had become of him; and she felt sure that she could trust him… couldn't she? Why then was she feeling a little bit afraid? She did not dare to examine her thoughts more closely. At the back of her mind, though, she knew she was a little bit scared of the growing intensity of her feelings towards him. If this was what it was like to fall in love, then maybe that was what she was experiencing, this heady feeling of delight mixed with anticipation and longing.

'You're very quiet,' remarked Dave, putting his arm more closely round her as they crossed the bridge to the other side of the river.

'Am I?' she answered. 'I'm a bit preoccupied, I suppose; thinking about the great time we've had, and that we've got to go home tomorrow.'

'Never mind,' said Dave. 'All good things come to an end, as they say. But it won't be the end for you and me, will it? Cheer up now! We've got the rest of the evening together, haven't we?'

There was an empty table outside the pub where they had stopped the previous night. There was no sign of the trio that they had met up with there, nor of Diane and Andy.

'Come on, let's have something to warm up,' said Dave. 'What about rum? My dad swears by that; to warm the cockles of your heart, he says, whatever that means. Parents say some odd things, don't they?'

'Yes; I've heard my gran say that,' smiled Fiona. 'She's a great one for these old-fashioned sayings. Yes, I think that might be rather warmer than gin and lime. You can't have rum on its own though, can you?'

'No; rum and coke, that's the thing to have,' said Dave, knowledgeably. 'I'll have that as well instead of beer.' He looked round for the barmaid to take their order.

Fiona no longer had any inhibitions about being too young to be there. There was another couple from the Youth Club that she knew vaguely, and Tim and Brenda, sitting further back. And near to them were – oh, my goodness! – Mike, the driver, with Rita. Fiona turned away hurriedly, but Rita had noticed them and she waved cheerily. She was obviously too interested in her budding friendship with Mike to bother too much about what her charges were up to.

Fiona soon found that the rum was making her feel a little warmer, just as Dave had said it would. It was a very pleasant taste, mixed with the Coca-Cola.

'I'll never forget these few days; they've been just great,' said Dave, holding her cold hand between his own. 'You're still feeling cold, aren't you? Let's have another of these.' He beckoned to the barmaid and placed their order. 'As I was saying,' he continued, 'these last few days have been wonderful, getting to know you so much better, Fiona. I wasn't sure that you liked me – you know, really liked me – until we came away.'

'Yes, I do, Dave,' she replied, looking at him intently. 'I really do.'

'And you won't be worried about going on seeing me after we get back home? You know, with your parents, an' all that?'

'No.' Fiona shook her head positively. She was feeling, again, rather light-headed – and with that came the feeling of light-heartedness that she had experienced the night before. 'I shall go on seeing you, and I don't really care what they say.'

'Good for you!' laughed Dave. He kissed her on the lips and she didn't care whether anyone saw them or not.

'Come on, sup up, as my dad would say, and we'll make our way back.'

It was still only ten o'clock and, as Fiona had guessed would happen, they made a detour into the copse where they had stopped on the previous night. They wandered a little further until the sounds from the fairground could be heard only faintly on the evening breeze. It had turned quite chilly now, but with Dave's arms around her she was scarcely aware of the cold, and the intensity of his kisses was making her breathless.

His hands were exploring her body, in all the more intimate places, and she was powerless to show any resistance, nor did she want to do so. Then they were lying on the ground on Dave's sports coat, which he had quickly removed. Her head felt woozy from the effects of the drink. She was carried away, too, on a surge of desire, hardly aware of what was happening… She heard herself cry out; she did not know whether it was from shock or the height of her passion. Then she lay passively in Dave's arms as he whispered to her that he loved her.

She felt, though, almost as though this was happening to someone else and not to her. It was like a dream; it was all so unreal, and soon she would wake up and find that she had imagined it all. When at last she rose to her feet her legs felt wobbly and her head was spinning. Dave brushed the leaves and bits of tree bark from their clothing before they set off back to the coach.

They were not late. They were, in fact, a few minutes early. Diane and Andy, hand in hand, joined them, both looking on top of the world.

'We've had a smashing time,' said Diane. 'Look what Andy's won on the shooting range.' It was a miniature model of the Skylon; Fiona thought it was rather ghastly but Diane seemed highly delighted. 'I shall keep it on my bookcase,' she said, 'and it'll always remind me of our trip to London. What's up, Fiona?' she added, looking anxiously at her friend. 'You're looking a bit peaky.'

'I'm alright,' said Fiona with a weak smile. In truth she was feeling a little bit unwell and it was not entirely the effect of the drink. She shivered, a tremor that went right through her. 'Actually I'm feeling rather chilly,' she said. 'I noticed it when we were on the lake. I hope I'm not starting a cold.'

'So do I,' said Dave concernedly. 'Look, the coach is here now. Let's get on and then maybe you'll warm up again.'

The two of them sat together on the way back. Dave took hold of her hand and smiled at her. She smiled back but neither of them said anything on the way to the hotel.

'See you all bright and early in the morning,' said Colin. 'We want to set off at half past eight. So breakfast at half past seven, OK? Goodnight everyone, and God bless.'

They all trooped off to their bedrooms, Dave and Andy saying a casual goodnight to the girls as they parted company, as Colin and Sheila were close behind them. Fiona was feeling far from well by now. She collapsed on to the bed as soon as they entered the room.

'Hey, what's the matter?' asked Diane. 'You're feeling rotten, aren't you? What is it? Too much to drink?' She sat down beside her and put an arm round her. 'Goodness! You're shivering. Come on now, get undressed and into bed. You'll perhaps feel better when you've had a good sleep.'

'Yes, I do feel peculiar,' said Fiona. 'We did have something to drink, but I don't think it's that. My throat hurts and I feel hot, somehow, as well as shivery. I'll just nip along the corridor, then I'll get straight to bed.'

She had never felt so relieved at slipping between the sheets. Her head spun round as it touched the pillow, a maelstrom of thoughts running through her mind. She couldn't sort them out or remember clearly what had happened. She just knew that she felt ill. The previous euphoria of the evening and the delight she had felt at being with Dave had vanished. All she wanted now was to sink into oblivion.

Ten

When she awoke the following morning at the strident call of the alarm clock Fiona knew almost at once that she had started a cold or something worse. Her head ached, her nose was blocked, her eyes were streaming and her throat was very sore. Of all the awful things to happen, after the good time they had been enjoying that week!

'Come on now, wakey!' called Diane, who was already up and dashing round the room. 'I set the alarm clock for quarter to seven seeing that you were in no fit state to do it. How are you? Feeling better this morning?'

'Not really,' answered Fiona, throwing back the bedclothes and staggering to her feet. 'I'm afraid I've got a cold; I feel really dreadful.' She looked and sounded a little tearful.

'Oh dear! Poor you!' Diane was at once full of sympathy and concern. 'I thought you might be starting one last night. Then I wondered if you were just a bit tipsy.'

'I didn't have all that much to drink,' Fiona mumbled miserably. 'Oh, Diane, I do feel ill. Everything's going wrong!'

'Of course it isn't!' said her friend. 'It's just because you're feeling lousy. You've not fallen out with Dave, have you? You seemed OK with him last night.'

'No, we're alright,' answered Fiona in a feeble sort of voice.

'Come on then, love.' Diane put an arm round her. 'You'll perhaps feel better when you've had something to eat. My mum always says you have to feed a cold.'

'Yes, feed a cold and starve a fever.' Fiona smiled weakly. 'My mum says that. The trouble is... I feel feverish as well. Hot as well as cold.'

'Well, you do sometimes at the start of a cold,' said Diane, trying to be as cheerful and optimistic as she could. She could see, though, that her friend really was far from well.

'Yes, that's true,' agreed Fiona. She tried to smile again. 'I'm sorry, Diane. I'm a right old weary Willie, aren't I?'

'It's not your fault,' said Diane. 'And you're managing a smile; that's better. It's not like you to be miserable, is it? You'll cheer up when you see Dave.'

'I suppose so,' said Fiona, then, as Diane was looking at her rather strangely, 'of course I will,' she added, trying to sound positive.

Her mind was still hazy, full of mixed-up thoughts and memories. What she had told Diane was true; she had not had all that much to drink. But because she was unused to any sort of alcohol it had gone straight to her head, affecting her thoughts and her actions. Now, in the cold light of day she knew – or thought she knew – that she had allowed Dave to do much more than she ought to have done. Had they? she wondered. Had they 'gone the whole way'? That was how she and her friends always referred to it. Yes, she feared now that they had. What on earth had she been thinking of? She realized now that she hadn't been thinking much at all. She'd been swept away on a tide of emotion, not giving any heed to what might happen. And it had, indeed, happened. She knew it must have done because, as well as the symptoms of an oncoming cold or whatever it was, she was feeling a little sore 'down there'.

She staggered along the corridor to the toilet, then had a quick wash and dressed in the first clothes that came to hand. Fortunately she and Diane had had the foresight to pack their suitcases before they left for the fairground the previous evening. So that was one less thing to worry about.

'You're very quiet,' said Diane, 'but I suppose I would be if I was feeling rotten like you are. Come on, let's go down to breakfast if you're ready.'

Fiona knew she was quiet, not just because she felt ill, but because of all that was on her mind. Diane hadn't asked any further pertinent questions about her and Dave, not since she had urged her to be careful. Well, it was too late now, and this was certainly not something she would be confiding to her best friend. Or to anyone. And it must never happen again. She wondered how Dave was feeling this morning and how he would react when he saw her.

He smiled cheerfully as she and Diane entered the dining room; he and Andy were already seated at a table. 'Come and sit here,' he called, standing up as the two girls went to the table. Dave really had very good manners for a young man of his age; many of his contemporaries were much more cavalier in their treatment of girls.

His smile faded though as he looked more closely at Fiona. 'Oh dear! Are you still feeling rough?' he asked. 'I was hoping you'd be better this morning.'

''Fraid not,' said Fiona, trying to smile and not be too much of a misery. 'I seem to have got a stinking cold.

Although it's my throat that hurts more than anything. Perhaps a hot drink will help.'

'Have you taken any tablets? Aspirins or anything?' asked Dave.

Fiona shook her head. 'No; I haven't got anything with me.'

'I'll see if Mrs Wilkes can help,' he said, going over to the next table.

Sheila Wilkes was pleased to oblige. 'Take a couple of these Anadin tablets, Fiona,' she called. 'I'm sorry you're feeling a bit under the weather. These summer colds are sometimes worse than the winter ones.'

'Thank you,' said Fiona. 'Don't worry about me; I'll be OK.'

She took the pills with a drink of coffee, but when she started to eat her cornflakes she realized that her throat was hurting dreadfully and it was painful to swallow. She struggled to eat most of the cereal, softened by the milk, but she knew she couldn't attempt to eat bacon and egg or toast. Dave was very concerned and she felt that he really cared about her. But no reference was made to what had happened the night before.

The journey home was by no means the joyful trip that the outward journey had been, at least not for Fiona. The young people went back to their original seats, and Diane was very mindful of her friend on the way home. She knew that Fiona was rather poorly. Her face was flushed and it was clearly very painful for her to swallow. When they stopped for lunch near to Birmingham she managed to eat a sandwich and two pieces of chocolate. The rest of her packed lunch was devoured by Dave and Andy, who tried to make a joke of it and cheer her up.

'We'll make short work of this, won't we, Dave?' laughed Andy. 'Come on; let's scoff these crisps before she changes her mind… I'm really sorry you're feeling poorly though, Fiona,' he added. 'We've all had such a good time together, haven't we?'

Fiona nodded. 'Yes, it's been terrific… until I've gone and put a damper on it all.'

'Don't worry,' said Dave, taking hold of her hand as they made their way back to the coach. 'We'll soon be home. You'll be glad to get back, won't you?'

Fiona nodded again. 'Yes, I certainly will. I'm sorry it's ended like this, Dave.'

'It's not ended,' he whispered, squeezing her hand. 'Not for you and me. Just try to get better soon, eh?'

She dozed on and off for a good part of the journey. She had never felt more relieved in her life when the coach, at long last, drew up outside the church back in Leeds. A crowd of parents waited outside the gates. Tears came into Fiona's eyes as she caught sight of her mother; her father, of course, would still be at work at four thirty in the afternoon. She hastily brushed her tears away – how silly she would look if she started to cry – but she felt a surge of affection for her mother, something she had not always felt of late. Mum would look after her now. She was, indeed, very glad to be home.

'I'm afraid Fiona's not feeling very well, Mrs Dalton,' Diane said to Fiona's mother as they got off the coach. Her own mother was further along the pavement. 'Hi, Mum,' she called. 'Be with you in a minute.'

'Oh deary me! Whatever's the matter?' Fiona felt her mother's arm around her shoulders, but she didn't want a big fuss making about her illness.

'I'll be alright, Mum,' she said dismissively, although she was feeling far from alright. 'Just a cold, I think. Don't get too close to me or you might catch it.'

'Never mind that,' said her mother. To Fiona's embarrassment she kissed her cheek. 'It's you I'm concerned about.'

'I'm sorry about this, Mrs Dalton,' said Sheila Wilkes, joining the little group. 'We've all had such a lovely time, haven't we Fiona? It's a pity this has happened, but I'm sure you'll soon be well again. Take care now, dear. See you soon, I hope.'

'Thank you for looking after her, Mrs Wilkes,' said Fiona's mum, 'and you as well, Diane. Come along now, love. Let's get you home.'

There was scarcely time for Fiona to exchange a fleeting glance and a half-smile with Dave before her mother led her away. Now was certainly not the time to effect an introduction. It passed through Fiona's mind that she would probably never do so, despite her brave words to Dave that she would tell her parents about him.

It was only five minutes' walk from the church to the terraced house where the Dalton family lived.

'Now, I think you'd better get straight to bed,' said her mother as they shut the front door. 'There's no place like home, is there, love? And no bed like your own bed. So off you go and get undressed and I'll bring you a hot drink. What would you like? A nice cup of tea?'

Fiona smiled. 'Yes, I think so. Your answer to all ailments, isn't it, Mum?'

'I'll have one with you,' said Mary. 'And you can tell me all about the exciting time you've had in London; that is, if you feel like talking. I could tell from the chattering going on that you've all had a good time. Such a shame that you're feeling poorly. Pop along then, love, and I'll be with you in a few minutes.'

Fiona undressed quickly and got into bed. The cool sheets felt very comforting as she slid between them. As Mum said, there was no bed like your own, and maybe a good sleep would work wonders.

First, though, she must try to talk a little to her mother. She was being so kind and caring that Fiona was almost forgetting the less than charitable thoughts that she sometimes harboured about both her parents. A spasm of guilt seized her as she realized that she could by no means tell her mother 'all' about the trip. She felt herself going hot, even hotter than she was already feeling, and there was a sickness in the pit of her stomach as she remembered what had happened.

She sat up and sipped at her tea as she told her mother a little about the Festival exhibition and all the wonderful new inventions, the sightseeing trip around London, and the Battersea Pleasure Gardens.

'They let you go round on your own, did they?' asked Mary with a touch of anxiety. 'You were with Diane, I expect?'

'Yes... there was a crowd of us all together,' answered Fiona evasively. 'Mr and Mrs Wilkes made sure we were back by half past ten, though.'

'That's what I would expect,' said Mary. 'I knew you would be in safe hands with Colin and Sheila. Now, you settle yourself down and try to have a sleep. I was wondering about calling the doctor, but we'll see how you are in the morning, shall we?'

'Yes; I'll probably be feeling much better by tomorrow,' said Fiona. 'I just want to go to sleep now.'

By the next morning, though, it was clear that she was no better. When she sat up in bed her throat was hurting more than ever and she could tell that her neck was swollen. She was unable to swallow anything apart from a drink of tea and a few mouthfuls of sweet creamy porridge that her mother insisted she try.

'You're burning up,' said Mary, feeling her forehead. 'We can't wait any longer; I must ring for the doctor. You snuggle down again and I'll go and call him. You'll be alright, won't you, love, while I just nip along to the phone box?'

Dr Mackintosh had known Fiona ever since she was a baby. He was a Scot, a kindly and sympathetic family practitioner. He was at the house in less than an hour.

'Now, let's have a wee look at you, young lady,' he said as Mary hovered in the background. Fiona sat up, coming round from another half sleep. She opened her mouth obediently and said 'ah' as requested. Dr Mackintosh frowned and nodded.

'Ah yes, I see. There's a nasty white coating over your tonsils. I expect your throat is very sore, isn't it?'

Fiona nodded. 'Dreadfully,' she agreed.

'What is it, doctor?' asked Mary. 'Is it tonsillitis? I wondered if she should have had her tonsils out when she was little. I know a lot of her friends did, but I didn't want her to have to go through that.'

'No, you were probably right,' answered the doctor. 'There was rather too much of that done at the time. But I don't think it's tonsillitis.' He felt at Fiona's neck and she winced a little. 'Sorry, my dear. That hurts, doesn't it? Your lymph glands are swollen. I suspect that what you have is glandular fever. No wonder you're feeling so poorly.'

'Glandular fever!' gasped Mary. 'Whatever is that? It sounds serious.'

'Probably not as drastic as it sounds, Mrs Dalton,' he replied. 'I'll just take a wee sample of blood to make sure I've got the diagnosis right… I would love a cup of tea, please, if you feel like making one,' he added as Mary continued to hover.

'Certainly doctor,' she said, leaving the room reluctantly.

'Best not to have Mum around, eh?' The doctor smiled understandingly at Fiona. 'Now, just hold your arm straight out, my dear; and I promise that this won't hurt, no more than a tiny bit.'

Nor did it, and Fiona felt herself relaxing a little. 'Now, tell me what you've been doing,' said the doctor. 'Your mum tells me you're just back from a little holiday.'

'Yes, I've been to London with a group from church to see the Festival of Britain,' she answered. She told him about it whilst her mother made the tea, and he listened with keen interest. He had what her gran called 'a good bedside manner'. She felt she would be able to trust him with anything, should the need arise.

'The only real cure is bed rest,' he told her mother as he drank his tea. 'The trouble is she seems to have a sniffly cold as well, which is not helping things. I'll prescribe some painkillers for your painful throat,' he told Fiona. 'You must have plenty of drinks, of course, and a little food that is easy to swallow when you feel like it. Soup or scrambled egg or porridge; your mum will know what to give you. And stay where you are for a few days. This fever is highly infectious, I'm afraid. So no visitors just yet. I'll come back in a day or two to see how you're going on. Cheerio for now, dear. I'm leaving you in good hands.'

He gave Mary a prescription to take to the chemist. 'Start her on these as soon as possible. I can see that she's in a good deal of pain, and these will ease it. But it will be a wee while before she feels really well again, and she'll be very tired.'

'But she will get better, won't she?' asked Mary. 'She's very precious to us, you know, doctor.'

'Yes, indeed.' Dr Mackintosh nodded. 'It will take a while, as I've said, but she will be fine again in a few weeks' time.' He had taken a blood sample, though. The symptoms could mean something more drastic, such as leukaemia. He did not think so but it was best to be sure.

—

Fiona was surprised at how much she slept. She was tired all the time and when she was out of bed for a visit to the bathroom she was relieved to get back. After a day or two she could manage foods such as soups, rice pudding, custard and ice-cream, which was very soothing to her still quite painful throat. The doctor called again confirming that is was, certainly, glandular fever that she had contracted. How or where was a mystery, and it was just a matter of time before she would be fully recovered.

Her mother told her that Diane had called. She had brought her some magazines and an Agatha Christie book, the sort that both girls enjoyed. 'But I couldn't let her see you,' said her mother. She cast a disparaging glance at the somewhat lurid covers of the *True Romance* and *Love Story* magazines, and at the murder mystery. 'She's sent you these, though they certainly wouldn't be my choice,' she added with a sniff of disapproval.

Mum's back to her old self, thought Fiona, *now that I'm feeling a bit better.* Out loud she said, 'Oh, Mum, I'd love to have seen her. It's miserable up here on my own. Why didn't you let her come up?'

'Because you're still infectious,' said her mother. 'Dr Mackintosh says so. Perhaps next time. We'll see how you go on.'

Fiona had now been in bed for almost a week. They had returned from London on Thursday and it was now the following Wednesday. She was feeling a little less tired and her throat did not hurt as much, but she was starting to feel very depressed. The doctor said it was one of the symptoms of her illness, and he assured her that it would pass.

She sat up in bed, leafing through the pages of *True Romance*; stories of unrequited love, or of couples reunited, or parents' opposition to teenage lovers. Her thoughts flew to Dave. She hoped he would have the good sense not to call and see how she was, but she was sure that Diane would have told him about her illness.

She was unable to concentrate on a love story, and she was not in the mood to start reading a murder mystery. Apart from feeling out of sorts and miserable there was something else that was worrying her. She should have started her period on Monday. She was now two days late...

Eleven

She tried to tell herself not to be so stupid. What was two days? It must be her imagination working overtime because of what she had done... what she and Dave had done. Her guilt and shame lay heavy on her conscience, and there was no one in whom she could confide. Her mother was refusing to let her see Diane, insisting that she was still infectious and must stay in bed for a few more days. And, besides, how could she possibly tell Diane? Her friend would be horrified. She had warned her to be careful, and she, Fiona, had taken no notice.

The days went by – Thursday, Friday, Saturday – and still there was no sign of what Fiona was longing to see. It was almost a full week, and she feared that by this time there really was cause for concern. She had started her periods at thirteen, and ever since that day she had been as regular as clockwork. She could time her monthly cycle to the exact day, almost the exact hour. And so could her mother...

Mary was the kind of mother who watched her daughter like a hawk. It was Mary who bought the necessary items each month and made sure that Fiona had an adequate supply in her dressing table drawer. Fiona wished that she wouldn't fuss so and would let her look after her own concerns a bit more. But it was Mary's way to interfere in this manner, although she saw it as helping.

Fiona doubted that she would ever change. She had often thought longingly of a time when she might escape from her mother's control. Maybe next year when she went away to training college. Fiona had decided that she would like to train to be a teacher – or was it really her mother who had made the decision? – and that meant she would be starting her training in just over a year's time. She had already made up her mind that she would stand firm and refuse to go to the training college in Headingley. Even if she were to live in there, it was far too near to her home.

But her future plans had become a little less important since she had become friendly with Dave. And now, with this great black cloud hanging over her she didn't dare to look into the future at all.

Her mother, of course, had noticed that she was a week late. Mary had come to the conclusion, however, that it was because Fiona was ill.

'Illness can play all sorts of tricks with your body,' she told her daughter. Fiona had no idea whether this was true or not, but her mother spoke with conviction. 'Maybe when you start you will feel better all round. You're certainly down in the dumps now, aren't you? I do wish you would try to cheer up a bit, love. I'm doing my best for you, you know, and I'm only doing what Dr Mackintosh advised. He said you must stay in bed for a while and not have any visitors. Perhaps next week you may be able to get up for part of the day. He did say, though, that the glandular fever might leave you feeling depressed.'

As, indeed, it had. But it was not just the effect of the illness that was making her feel so miserable. By this time Fiona was frantic with worry. She tried to tell herself that surely it couldn't have happened so easily. It just wasn't possible. She and Dave, they had only done it once, and she was not really sure about what, exactly, had happened. She tried to pray about it, to ask the God in whom she thought she believed to make everything alright. But in her heart she knew that it was too late for prayers if she was, indeed, pregnant. She hardly dared to think the word, let alone say it. The Reverend Cruikshank said that God was a God of miracles. But Fiona feared that her sin was too great for Him to work one on her behalf.

On Sunday her mother suggested that she should get up later in the morning and have some dinner. Mary and Wilfred went off to church, leaving a chicken in the oven to roast. Fiona was instructed to put the vegetables on at a certain time, but apart from that she would not be expected to help until she was feeling much better.

Fiona burst into tears as she heard the door close behind them. She felt so wretched and miserable, and frightened to death as well. And it could only get worse. She put on the immersion heater and soaked herself in a hot bath. She sat there for ten minutes or more until the water started to cool. She thought she had heard somewhere that that might do the trick. But it was to no avail. She dressed and put on a little face powder to cover up her tear-stained face and red eyes.

'I saw Diane at church,' said her mother as they started their dinner. 'She asked about you, and I said you were a little bit better, and that perhaps she could come and see you later in the week. That will cheer you up, won't it?'

Fiona smiled weakly and nodded. 'Yes, I hope so.' She managed to eat a couple of slices of chicken and a small amount of potatoes and vegetables. She was quite hungry really, after a diet of mushy food, and her throat didn't hurt as much now. Mary was a good cook of plain food, and she had made an easily digestible egg custard to follow.

The conversation over dinner was largely concerned with the church service and the vicar's sermon, and the forthcoming council meeting. Fiona took no part in it, except to nod her head in acquiescence when her mother suggested that she might be well enough to accompany them to church next Sunday.

The afternoon was warm, and Fiona sat in a deckchair in the small back garden, attempting to read the book that Diane had brought, but she was unable to concentrate. When her parents had gone off, once again, to the evening service she went to bed, hoping and praying that she would be able to sleep and that, by morning, her fears would prove to be groundless. Despite the torment in her mind she did sleep well, as her illness was still sapping away at her strength and vitality.

Strangely enough, her mother did not seem to be imagining that there might be another reason, apart from her illness, to prevent the onset of her period. Mary did not know, of course, about her friendship with Dave. If she had known, Fiona wondered if she would now be worried and wondering if her daughter had done some-thing that she shouldn't have, or did she believe that such a thing could never happen to her little girl? Fiona felt sick with fright at the thought of her parents finding out; but as the days went by – Monday, Tuesday, Wednesday – and still there was no sign, she tried to make herself face up to what she now felt certain had happened.

Should she pretend that she had 'started', she wondered. No; her mother was no fool and would soon discover that she was lying. Besides, it was only postponing the inevitable. She stayed in bed for most of the time although she was, in truth, quite a lot better. It would be best, though, to let her mother think that she was still feeling poorly. As, indeed, she was, but it was now a sickness of her mind rather than of her body.

Towards the end of the next week Mary sent for the doctor again, fearing that her daughter must have had a relapse. She was lethargic, complaining again that her throat was hurting, and so deep in a state of depression that she would scarcely speak to anyone. Neither did she want any visitors, which Mary thought was most unusual.

'Now, come along, love,' said her mother. 'You really must try to cheer up a bit. You're not helping yourself, you know.' Turning to the doctor she went on, 'I'm really worried about her. She's like this all the time. Her temperature is down now – I've checked – and I thought she'd be feeling better by now. I think there must be something seriously wrong.'

Dr Mackintosh smiled gravely. 'I told you, Mrs Dalton, that this illness can have a very debilitating effect on the mind as well as the body. Just leave me alone with her for a wee while, would you dear, then Fiona and I can have a chat?'

'I'll go and make a cup of tea then,' said Mary, nodding curtly.

When she had gone the doctor sat on the edge of the bed and took hold of Fiona's hand. 'Now, my dear,' he said. 'Try to tell me exactly how you feel.'

Fiona looked at his craggy face and beetling brows, and at the shrewd grey eyes observing her so concernedly. Typical Scottish features, she had always thought, and she felt that here was someone she could trust, someone who might well understand.

'Doctor,' she began, in a small voice. 'I've got something awful to tell you.' Her voice broke in a sob, then she took a deep breath before saying, 'I think I'm pregnant.'

'Oh, dearie me!' the doctor said, but quite calmly. 'No wonder you're in such a state. But try to calm down and tell me about it. You've missed a period, have you, or more than one?'

'No, only one, but I'm nearly a fortnight late now,' she replied. 'I know it's not all that long, but I've never been late before. And… well… I know what I've done.'

She told him about Dave, her first boyfriend, and how she had had too much to drink – although it wasn't really all that much – and how it had happened, just the once. 'And I know I'm pregnant; I must be, and I'm so scared of telling my mum and dad. They'll kill me!'

'Of course they won't,' said the doctor. 'They may well be surprised or even shocked, but loving parents like yours, they usually come to terms with it. But it's early days, Fiona. What you fear may not be so. You've been ill and you've been worrying about it, and that won't have helped.'

'I'm sure though,' she said. 'In my own mind, I'm sure. Can't you find out? Can't you tell me whether I am… or not?'

'It's too early to examine you,' he said. He looked at her gravely. 'I could take a urine test, and then we would know in a few days' time. Would you like me to do that?'

'Oh, yes, please,' she said. 'I shall have to know, won't I, and the sooner the better. But don't tell my mother, will you? Just in case, well, like you say, I may not be.'

'I promise you I won't breathe a word,' he replied. 'A doctor can't break a confidence, you know. It's just between you and me. I'll tell your mother that I'm taking a sample; that could be for all sorts of reasons. Here you are, lassie.' He took a small bottle out of his black bag. 'Off you go, and do what you can, and I'll be able to tell you in a little while. You've been a silly girl, but it's not the first time I've heard this kind of story, and it won't be the last. There's always a way round it, but you really must try not to worry too much. What's done is done, you know.' His smile was full of sympathy and understanding. 'And I'll do all I can to help you.'

'And… if I am,' said Fiona, 'will you be there with me when I have to tell my mother, please, Dr Mackintosh?'

'Of course,' he said. 'We'll face the music together. But we don't know yet, do we? Now off you go to the bathroom. I can hear your mother coming with the tea.'

Whilst Fiona was away he explained to Mary that her daughter was possibly having a 'wee complication', nothing to worry about, but he was taking a sample to see if he could get to the crux of the matter.

'Just look after your lassie,' he told her when Fiona returned. 'She's a grand girl. Maybe she's not recovering quite as well as I hoped, but it sometimes takes longer than expected.'

He drank his tea quickly then said goodbye. 'I'll call again in a few days' time,' he said. 'Chin up, Fiona. I've told you, sometimes it takes a wee while to get over what you've had.' He gave her a confidential wink when her mother was not watching. 'But you're going to be fine, I'm sure. Don't worry now. We'll look after you… Goodbye for now, Mrs Dalton. Keep up the good work; plenty of drinks and a little food when she feels like it.'

'Oh dear!' said Mary after the doctor had gone. 'I do hope there's nothing else wrong with you, with the doctor taking that sample, I mean. I can't help worrying.' Fiona was sure, though, that the most probable reason for taking a sample had not occurred to her mother.

'There's no point in worrying,' said Fiona. Knowing that Dr Mackintosh was sympathetic and would be there to support her was helping her to feel a little bit easier about everything. 'It's just taking longer than we expected for me to get right again, that's all.' She knew that until the doctor came again she must exaggerate how poorly she was feeling.

'Oh dear!' said Mary again. 'I was hoping you would be able to go to church with us on Sunday.'

'Oh no, Mum. I don't feel well enough for church just yet,' she replied quickly. 'Maybe the week after.'

'I hope so,' said Mary. 'I can think of no better place for you to go to help you to get well… I can't help thinking that a lot of it is in your mind, Fiona,' she added a trifle sharply.

Fiona knew that it was, indeed, in her mind. She was nearly out of her mind with worry, but for a very different reason. She feigned illness for the next few days and her mother did not appear overly suspicious.

'There's a letter here for you from Diane,' Mary said when they returned from church on Sunday morning. 'She sends her love, and I told her that maybe she could see you soon.'

She opened the envelope in the privacy of her bedroom. There was a cheery letter from Diane saying how much she missed her and how sorry she was that the holiday had ended with her being ill. She also wrote that she was now going out with Andy, that they had been to the pictures together and were getting on really well. There was also a note from Dave.

*My dear Fiona, I can't tell you how sorry I am
that you are ill. We had a great time together in
London, didn't we? Please get better soon. I'm
longing to see you again. I know I mustn't call
at your house. I don't suppose you've told your
parents about me yet, have you? Love you lots.
Dave.*

She felt a lump on her throat, then the tears started.
Whatever was she going to do? She shoved the letter
away at the bottom of her underwear drawer and tried
to contain herself before going down to make an attempt
to eat the Sunday dinner.

When the doctor came on Wednesday morning Fiona
was still in bed.

'Here's Dr Mackintosh,' said her mother brightly.
'Come along now, Fiona, and tell the doctor how you're
feeling. I think she's rather better, Dr Mackintosh.'

'Good,' he said, nodding briefly. 'Could you leave us
for a few minutes, please, Mrs Dalton? Fiona and I need
to have a wee chat.'

'I'll be downstairs then,' said Mary. She appeared not
to like being summarily dismissed.

The doctor sat at the edge of the bed and took hold
of Fiona's hand. She looked at him appealingly, but she
could tell by the grave look in his eyes that it was not
good news. 'Yes, my dear,' he said. 'It is as you feared.
You are pregnant.'

She took an intake of breath and gave a long shud-
dering sigh. 'Oh… no! Whatever am I going to do?'

'As I told you, we're going to face this together,' he
said. 'Straight away. We'll have to tell your mother. You
know that, don't you?'

She nodded. 'I'm really frightened. She'll go absolutely mad.'

'Maybe,' he replied. 'Maybe not. But we'd better find out.' He squeezed her shoulder gently. 'Just try to calm down as much as you can, my dear.' He went out on to the landing and called for her mother. 'Mrs Dalton, could you come up here, please.'

She arrived very quickly and the doctor motioned to the bedroom chair. 'Sit down, would you, dear. We have something to tell you.' He glanced reassuringly at Fiona, then went on quickly to break the news to her mother. 'I have discovered that Fiona is pregnant.'

'What!' Mary's cry could have been heard out in the street. 'She can't be. She's not got a boyfriend. No, no, you're wrong, doctor.'

'You do realize, though, that she has missed a period?' he asked.

'Well, yes, but it's because she's been ill. It's not that… It can't be!' Mary looked at her daughter, her expression changing from indignation to one of shock and horror as Fiona nodded slowly.

'Yes, I am, Mum,' she said. 'I'm sorry…'

Mary stared at her as though she didn't understand, her mouth open in sheer amazement. 'But why… how could it have happened?'

Even though she was still scared to death Fiona was tempted to say, 'In the usual way, Mum,' but it was no time for levity. Her mother would not appreciate it at all.

'It was… while we were in London,' she said. 'I'm afraid that – I'm really sorry, Mum – I had too much to drink one night and… well… it happened.'

'On a church holiday!' Mary gasped. 'I only let you go because I thought you were in good hands with Colin and Sheila. What on earth were they thinking of, letting something like this happen? And you'd been drinking, you say? But you don't drink, Fiona. Somebody took advantage of you, didn't they? It wasn't him, was it? Colin Wilkes?'

'No… no, of course it wasn't.'

'Well, who was it then?'

Fiona shook her head. 'I'm not going to tell you.'

'Oh yes you are, young lady!' stormed her mother. Anger was taking the place of shock and horror now as the awful truth dawned on Mary. 'You're going to tell me who has done this. I shall be down at that youth club and I'll tear him limb from limb, whoever he is. And I can't believe that you would do… that… willingly. Somebody forced you, didn't they? Come along, Fiona, tell me. They're not going to get away with this.'

Fiona shook her head again as she felt tears start to prick at her eyes. 'No,' she said. 'I wasn't forced. I told you; I'd had a drink, and I'm not used to it. And it just happened. But I wasn't…' She took a breath. 'I wasn't raped.'

'Then that makes it worse,' cried Mary. 'You're a wicked deceitful girl, Fiona. You're nothing more than… than a trollop! This is just terrible… terrible!' She clenched her trembling hands tightly together. 'I would never have believed it of you, Fiona. I'm ashamed of you, thoroughly ashamed. I shall never forgive you.'

Dr Mackintosh had been standing there helplessly. He moved across the room now to the distraught woman and laid a hand on her shoulder. 'Now, come along, Mrs Dalton. This won't do any good, you know. You've had a shock and I know you're upset. But Fiona is not a wicked girl and I'm sure you don't mean that. I've known her since she was a tiny wee lassie, and I know how much you and your husband love her. Maybe she's been a silly lass, but these things happen sometimes. I've seen the same thing time and time again. And what Fiona needs now is your support.'

Mary didn't answer. Both mother and daughter sat in silence for several moments, Mary still shaking her head as if in disbelief. Then she spoke. 'I don't know how we're going to get through this. There's never been anything like it in my family, nor in Wilfred's. It's shameful... shameful. Whatever are people going to think? I shall be ashamed to face anybody.' She looked angrily at her daughter. 'How could you, Fiona? How could you disgrace us like this?'

The doctor sighed. 'Your reaction is, I suppose... predictable. You're upset and angry and maybe you've a right to be. But it does happen, all the time, even in the best of families. And these situations often resolve themselves quite happily. There's always a way through, you know.'

Mary looked at him indignantly. 'If you mean what I think you mean then that is out of the question. I wouldn't dream of letting you... put an end to the pregnancy. My husband and I are Christians, and it would be against our principles. No, Fiona has done wrong and she will have to face up to what is ahead... somehow.'

'You don't know me very well, Mrs Dalton, if you think that,' said the doctor sounding sad as well as a trifle vexed. 'That — what you were inferring — is illegal, apart from in exceptional cases; and I, too, abide by Christian principles and by the oaths I made as a doctor. If, as you say, you are Christians, then maybe you should try to show some Christian love and forgiveness, now, to your daughter. What I meant was that matters can be resolved, especially in a family such as yours. I know how well you have brought Fiona up… and how much you love her?' His last words were said in a questioning way, rather than as a statement of fact.

'Anyway, it's early days,' he continued, 'but you can be sure that I'll be here to take care of Fiona's progress, and to help you in any way I can.' He stepped towards the door. 'I'll leave you now. I'm sure you will have things to talk about.' He smiled at Fiona, a sympathetic smile which made her feel slightly better about the mess she was in. Here, at any rate, was someone who understood.

'Goodbye for now, Fiona, my dear; goodbye, Mrs Dalton. I'll let myself out.'

As soon as she heard the door close behind the doctor Mary started again, but a shade less aggressively. 'Come along now, Fiona; you're going to tell me. I insist. Who is responsible for… this?'

Again Fiona shook her head. 'I won't tell you. I've already said… I was partly responsible. And I wasn't… forced. Yes, I'd had a drink, and maybe, well… I know I let things go too far. But I can't tell you. I won't tell you.' She was not sure why she did not want to incriminate Dave. She was not sure, in fact, what she wanted to do at all. But the last thing she wanted was her mother seeking out Dave and attacking him verbally, if not physically; she was in such a rage.

'Alright then, madam. Have it your own way. But I'll find out. You can be sure of that. I shall be there at that youth club the first chance I get, and Colin Wilkes will have to tell me what's been going on. Such disgraceful behaviour, and on a church outing!'

All that Fiona could think of saying was, 'I'm sorry, Mum, really I am.'

She fancied that there was just a trace of sympathy there in her mother's half-smile. 'Well, what's done is done, I suppose. We'll say no more about it at the moment. I can't imagine what you father is going to say though. And you'd better get up and dressed. There'll be no more lounging in bed pretending you're ill. I know you've been poorly, Fiona, but there's nothing wrong with you now except what you've brought upon yourself. You'd best come down and have a spot of dinner when you're ready, not that I feel much like eating, I can tell you.'

The rest of the morning and afternoon passed by quietly as neither Fiona or her mother felt like talking. Fiona went up to her bedroom again after she had eaten her meal – a hastily made shepherd's pie – and helped her mother, in near silence, to wash the pots. She tried to settle to reading a magazine but her thoughts were all over the place. She felt a little easier now that the worst hurdle – telling her mother – was over. There was still her father, though; she couldn't imagine what his reaction would be. Both her parents were quiet, reserved sort of people, although Mary could get angry when roused, as Fiona had just seen. It was really the one and only time that Fiona had seen her so outraged. She felt that her father would be more able to keep a check on his anger... but time would tell.

Mary always had her husband's cooked meal ready for him as soon as he came in from work at around six o'clock, she and Fiona having had their main meal at midday and a lighter meal at teatime.

'Leave me to tell your dad,' she said to Fiona. 'I'd best wait till he's had his dinner, or else he may not feel like eating at all.' She sighed deeply. 'You've got a lot to answer for, young lady. I never thought I'd have to tell him that our daughter has got into trouble.'

'Leave it, Mum,' said Fiona wearily. 'I've said I'm sorry, haven't I? Don't keep reminding me.'

'You'll be reminded of it for the next nine months,' retorted Mary. 'Just think on that, and ask God to forgive you.'

I thought God would come into it sooner or later, Fiona thought as her mother left her alone.

She didn't hear what went on between her parents. She stayed in her room for what seemed hours and hours. It was half past seven when her mother came to tell her to come down and see her father. 'He's had the shock of his life,' she said. 'It's a wonder he didn't have a heart attack. He's very disappointed with you, Fiona. Anyway, you'd best come and explain yourself to him if you can. Come along now; shape yourself.' Fiona had actually fallen asleep on the bed, mentally exhausted with all the trauma of the day.

Her father appeared more sad than angry. Fiona was distressed to see the look of anguish in his eyes, but she felt there was more compassion there than her mother had so far shown.

'I'm sorry, Dad,' she said, before he spoke to her. He did something that her mother had not yet done. He put his arms round her, holding her gently.

'I can't pretend I'm not shocked at your behaviour, Fiona,' he said. 'Your mother and I are both very disappointed. But it's done now, and it has to be faced. Sit down, and we'll tell you what we've decided to do.'

Twelve

Fiona's parents had decided that no one was to know about her condition, no one at all. Wilfred had vetoed Mary's intention to go to the youth club to find out who had done this dreadful thing to their daughter.

'No… we shall tell no one,' he said. 'Everyone knows that Fiona has been ill, and maybe that's a blessing in disguise. We must go on pretending now that she's still poorly and can't see anyone. We could say, maybe, that she's had a nervous breakdown.'

'And has to go away somewhere,' said Mary. She was starting to think that her husband's idea of secrecy was the best – the only way – to get over this problem. 'Yes, I think you're right, Wilfred. I'm so ashamed… I would never be able to hold my head up in that church again if they knew the truth. Just imagine what the Reverend Cruikshank would think! He would be appalled.'

'Quite so,' agreed Wilfred. 'We will need to confide in someone though… Perhaps she could go and stay with our Beattie for a while. That's far enough away.' Wilfred had a sister, Beatrice, who was married to a man called Donald Slater who owned a farm in Northumberland. They were in their late fifties and their children were married and living elsewhere. 'It's a long while since I heard from Beattie but we always got on well enough. We could make it worth their while, although they're not short of a bob or two. The last I heard the farm was doing quite well.'

'And what about… the baby?' said Mary. 'She mustn't be allowed to keep it?'

'No, of course not,' said Wilfred. 'You weren't thinking that she could, were you?'

'No, there's no question of that,' replied Mary. 'And I couldn't pass it off as mine, like some do.' They both knew of instances where a child had been brought up by the grandmother, not knowing that the supposed elder sister was really the mother. Such happenings were not uncommon. 'There are places, aren't there, where unmarried girls can go, and then when the baby is born it's adopted?'

'It would be the best solution,' agreed Wilfred. 'But I can't believe this is really happening to our precious little girl. I would never have believed it of her.'

'She can be wilful at times,' said Mary, shaking her head. 'She's never learnt to ask for God's guidance in her life, has she? Not like you and I.'

Wilfred nodded. 'That's true, my dear. Maybe this will make her realize that this is what can happen when you stray away from the straight and narrow pathway.'

When Fiona came to listen to what they had to say it seemed to her that it was all cut and dried. They had made a peremptory decision without even asking her how she felt about anything. She was so stunned by her father's words – it was Wilfred who was doing most of the talking – that she did not hesitate to tell them what she thought, forgetting for a moment that she was in deep disgrace.

'So you have decided, have you?' she said. 'What about how I might feel, or what I might want to do? And have neither of you realized how deceitful all this is? You're prepared to tell lies so that your precious vicar and all his cronies don't find out that I've… well, I suppose I've sinned, haven't I, in your eyes?'

'How dare you speak to us like that?' said her mother. 'Yes, you have… done wrong, and it's up to your father and me now to sort it out. You will never go near that youth club or that church again. You will stay in this house until we've made arrangements about what can be done for you.'

'What do you mean?' countered Fiona. 'That I can't go out at all? You can't keep me a prisoner here. Are you really so ashamed of me that you have to hide me away as though I'm a leper or something?'

'Yes, I'm afraid we are… deeply ashamed,' answered her mother. 'Ashamed that a daughter of ours should disgrace us like this.'

'Yes, that's all you're bothered about, isn't it? The disgrace – as though you'll be blamed for not bringing me up properly?' She looked at her mother imploringly. 'But it's not your fault, Mum. You and Dad have brought me up well, to be obedient and truthful. I'm sorry about what has happened. I can't say any more except that I'm sorry. But you heard what Dr Mackintosh said. It happens all the time. I'm not the first and I certainly won't be the last girl to find out she's having a baby.'

'You've got a great deal to say all of a sudden, young lady,' said her mother. 'All I know is that it's never happened in our family. And *you're* not being truthful now, are you? You won't tell us who's responsible for this, apart from you, of course!'

'No, I won't,' said Fiona as defiantly as ever. 'Perhaps you might be more understanding if I told you it was a gift from God, that it had been conceived by the Holy Ghost?'

'Fiona! You wicked girl!' screamed her mother. 'That's blasphemous, taking God's name in vain! How could you?'

'Aye, that's going a bit far, love,' said her father, more gently. 'There's no need to be irreverent.'

'I know, I'm sorry,' said Fiona meekly. 'But I don't suppose they believed Mary at first, did they?' she added, almost to herself. Suddenly she burst into tears. 'I'm sorry, I'm sorry… But I did expect a bit more sympathy, once you got over the shock. You're supposed to be Christians, aren't you? Shouldn't Christians be able to understand… and forgive?'

Again it was her father who put his arm around her shoulders. 'There, there, don't take on so,' he muttered, glancing uneasily at his wife. 'We're trying to help you, you know.'

'That's quite enough of that,' said Mary, 'throwing our faith back in our faces. We're trying to do what's best for you.'

'So it doesn't matter to God if you're telling lies?' Fiona sniffed, trying to fight back her tears; she was not easily driven to them. 'Pretending that I'm ill and making me hide away.'

'It's for the best,' said her father quietly. Her mother remained silent.

'I won't be kept a prisoner,' said Fiona again. 'I want to go and see my gran. I will go and see her, and you can't stop me.'

Mary and Wilfred looked at one another. Wilfred nodded. 'Yes, we'd best tell your mother,' he said to his wife. 'It wouldn't be right to keep it from her.'

'No, I've been thinking about that,' agreed Mary. 'We'd best go and see her one night and tell her what's happened. Although it'll give her the shock of her life, especially at her age.' She cast a reproachful glance at her daughter.

At least she'll be more sympathetic than you are being, Fiona reflected, but she wisely kept the thought to herself.

'I shouldn't worry; she's a tough old bird,' replied Wilfred with a wry smile. 'I dare say your mam'll take it in her stride.'

'Yes, I'll allow you to go and see your grandmother,' said Mary. 'But I can't imagine how she's going to react to all this.' She shook her head sorrowfully. 'Many a time your gran's said to me, "That little girl is the light of my life." She'd waited a long time for a granddaughter – our Eddie had three lads – and she made such a fuss of you. She's going to be bitterly disappointed in you, Fiona.'

'I think we've said enough, Mary,' said Wilfred quietly. 'Off you go now, Fiona love.' He smiled at his daughter. 'Go up to your room and read a book, or listen to some records or summat… We'll get through it somehow,' he added in a whisper.

–

Annie Jowett listened almost in silence to the tale that her daughter, Mary, was telling her about how Fiona had 'got into trouble' and the disgrace that she was bringing to the family.

'Wilfred and I are mortified,' said Mary, 'and so ashamed. To think that our daughter should behave like that! And she's even admitted that she was partly to blame. Maybe there might have been some excuse if she'd been forced, been taken advantage of, but she says not. And she refuses to tell us who it is. I was all for going to that youth club and finding out, but Wilfred convinced me that we must keep it to ourselves. Nobody has to know.'

Annie nodded thoughtfully. 'Aye, I can see how you might be thinking you've to hush it up… but I'll tell you what I think. It seems to me that you're more worried about how this is going to affect you, than showing concern for that poor lass.'

'Of course we're concerned, Mother,' retorted Mary. 'We're just trying to do what's best for her.'

'By pretending it's not happening, eh? By sweeping it under the carpet?' Annie gave a wry chuckle. 'Oh aye, I can see that you're worried about what the folks at church would say, and your precious vicar.'

'Yes… I'll admit that we don't want them to know,' replied Mary, a trifle grudgingly. 'We're ashamed, like I've told you. This sort of thing doesn't happen in respectable families like ours.'

'Huh! That's what you think!' replied Annie. 'I'll tell you something then. My young sister, your aunt Gertie, she "had to get married", if you want to put it that way. But nobody made a song and dance about it from what I can remember, and our mam and dad didn't go on at her like she'd committed a crime. Her and Wally, they just got married a bit earlier, that's all, and your cousin Fred was born five months later.'

'I never knew that,' said Mary.

'No, why should you?'

'But that was different,' Mary went on. 'They were engaged, weren't they? Not like this with our Fiona, carrying on with some lad from church.'

'At least he goes to that church that you're always on about,' said her mother. 'He's probably a very decent sort of lad.'

'How can he be?' retorted Mary. 'To behave like that! We didn't even know she had a boyfriend. It's all been going on behind our backs.'

'Aye, maybe it has.' Annie nodded sagely. 'You're so self-righteous these days that she probably didn't dare to tell you. And I don't suppose there's been much going on at all. It sounds to me as though they just got carried away, with being on holiday and away from home an' all that. Aye, she's been a silly girl and she's made a mistake. But can't you show a bit of that there Christian love and forgiveness that you're always harping on about? She's going to need her mam and dad, you know, whatever happens.'

Mary did look a bit abashed. 'We do love her, don't we, Wilfred?' She looked at her husband and he nodded.

'Aye, of course we do. But we think this would be best, Ma. To get her right away from here where everybody knows her.'

'And pack her off to a load of strangers?'

'Our Beattie and Donald aren't strangers,' replied Wilfred. 'I know Fiona hasn't seen them much lately, but we had a couple of holidays at their farm when she was little. I remember how she loved the animals. Beattie offered to have her during the war – as an evacuee, like – but we couldn't bear to part with her.'

'But you're prepared to make use of 'em now, eh?'

'It's rather different now,' said Wilfred, looking a little uneasy. 'Anyroad, we've still to contact them and make arrangements.'

'And what does Fiona think about it all?' asked Annie.

'She's got no choice, Mother,' said Mary, sounding just as intransigent as before. 'I'm afraid she will have to abide by what her dad and I decide is best for her.'

'Well, I suppose it's got nowt to do with me,' said Annie. 'You're her parents and I suppose you're doing what you think is best. I don't like all the deceit though… Anyroad, I'll go and make us a cup of tea.'

Annie's living room had hardly changed at all since Mary had lived there as a child. The same brown chenille table cover with a bobbled fringe – many of the bobbles missing now – was shabby and worn in places, as was the brown patterned carpet and the easy chairs. The huge Victorian sideboard still dominated the room. A myriad of framed photographs stood on top of it, together with the pair of Staffordshire dogs and the imitation Crown Derby fruit bowl, a long ago wedding present. A photo of Fiona stood in pride of place, an enlargement of a snap taken by Wilfred's box Brownie camera on a holiday in Scarborough a few years ago. Wedding photos too; of Mary and Wilfred; of her brother, Eddie and his wife, Elsie; and one of Annie and Frank on their long ago wedding day, towards the end of Queen Victoria's reign. Mary's father had died when she was ten years old, so her memories of him had grown hazy over the years. She remembered how her mother had always done her very best for them after she was widowed. Annie had always been brusque though, the gentler side of her nature showing itself more in her dealings with her grandchildren, particularly with Fiona. Mary admitted to herself that she was still, even now, a little in awe of her mother and didn't want to do anything to displease her.

'You'll let her come to see me, won't you?' asked Annie as they drank their tea. 'Before she disappears to... wherever she's going.'

'Of course we will, Mother,' said Mary. 'She said she wanted to see you. Don't be too soft with her, mind. She takes notice of what you say, and I don't want her to think you're condoning her behaviour.'

'I think she's had enough harsh words thrown at her, don't you?' replied Annie. 'I shall say what I think fit. When all's said and done, she's the one who has to go through it, poor lass.'

–

'They're packing me off to Northumberland, Gran, to Aunty Beattie's,' said Fiona.

It was Saturday afternoon and she had travelled to her gran's house by tram and bus, as she usually did. It was the first time she had been out since the news had broken on Wednesday. She hadn't seen anyone she knew on the journey, something that her mother had feared might happen.

'And how do you feel about going there, luv?' asked her grandmother.

'I don't really mind,' she replied. 'But it all depends on what Aunty Beattie and Uncle Donald say; Mum's waiting for a letter. It'll be a relief to get away, really. It's been awful at home. They've calmed down a bit now – actually, Dad's been a lot better about it than Mum – but they won't let me go out in case I see somebody I know. And tomorrow they're going to tell the folk at church that I've had a relapse or something, and that I'm going away to recuperate. It's all lies, Gran.'

'Well, happen it is for the best, luv,' said Annie, 'although I told your mam I didn't like the deceit. But what else could they do, eh? I believe you won't tell them who the lad is? And I take it you don't want him to know either? I'm not going to ask you who it is, seeing as you haven't told your mam and dad.'

Fiona shook her head. 'I can't tell him, can I? It would cause such an uproar. We didn't mean it to happen. I didn't think it could happen so easily, Gran. I mean, I didn't really know what we were doing. It just… happened.'

'Aye, I know it can happen more easily than you think,' said Annie. 'That's Mother Nature for you, and you're young and… well… fertile, I suppose. But you'll still be young, you know, when it's all over. Still not quite eighteen. Young enough to put it all behind you and start again. This lad though, was he your boyfriend, luv?'

'Sort of,' said Fiona. 'He's at the boys' grammar school, like I'm at the girls', and we've been seeing one another at church and youth club an' all that. But it was only when we went to London that we started to… well, you know. And he asked me if I'd be his girlfriend when we got back home. But then I was ill and now…' She shook her head. 'I won't be able to see him. Anyway, he'll be going to university next year. He was – is – a very clever lad, far cleverer than I am. He'll be studying Chemistry. No, I couldn't mess all that up for him. Oh, Gran! What a mess it all is! I really liked him. He wouldn't have wanted this to happen. It probably never occurred to him that it might.'

'No, I don't suppose it did,' said Annie wryly. 'I can see that the last thing he'd want is to be saddled with a wife and a baby. That's what some parents would do, you know; insist on the pair of you getting married.'

'That's not possible, Gran,' said Fiona pensively. 'That's why I can't tell him. I suppose Mum and Dad are right there, wanting to keep it a secret. But Mum went mad at first, you know, for me to tell her who it was.'

'And I suppose it's put paid to your plans an' all, hasn't it?' said her grandmother. 'Going to college next year, like, and training to be a teacher.'

'I think that was always Mum's idea rather than mine,' said Fiona with a half-smile. 'She liked the idea, you know, of her daughter being a teacher. And I sort of went along with it. I thought it would be nice to get away, you see, and have a bit of freedom. But now... well, I can't go back to school in September. I'll have to find something else to do when... when it's all over.' She looked at her grandmother in some alarm. Now and again a feeling of fear and panic seized hold of her.

'Oh, Gran, it's all so awful! I can't believe it's really happening. But you'll be here for me, won't you? You're not terribly ashamed of me, are you? I'm really sorry about it all.'

'No, lovey, I'm not ashamed of you. Like I told you, you've been a silly girl and you've made a mistake.' Annie moved across the room to sit next to her on the settee. She put an arm around Fiona, drawing her head on to the pillow of her comfortable bosom. 'But we're all here for you. Your mam and dad love you very much, you know, in spite of everything. You'll get through this. It's not going to be easy, but it'll sort out, you'll see. We all find out sooner or later that life isn't always a bed of roses. You're finding out a bit sooner than some of us, but there'll be good times ahead for you, Fiona love, I feel sure of that.'

Thirteen

Fiona felt slightly less apprehensive after her talk with her grandmother. She knew that she had an ally in her gran. She would have liked to stay there, away from her parents' reproachful glances – her mother's at least. Her father did appear a mite more sympathetic; but it seemed as though he did not dare to show too much understanding for fear of what his wife might say. It was Mary, now, who was taking the lead in what was to happen to Fiona.

'Your aunt and uncle have agreed to take you in for a few months,' she told her daughter on the Wednesday of the following week. 'You are a very lucky girl, Fiona.'

Fiona did not think that the adjective was very well chosen. On the other hand, she was starting to think that the sooner she got away from home the better it would be. Mary had said very little since her and Wilfred's visit to church on Sunday morning. She had told Fiona, in quite a matter-of-fact way, that she had informed Colin Wilkes, the youth club leader, that her daughter was suffering from a breakdown following the attack of glandular fever and was going away to recuperate.

'He sends his best wishes,' she had added curtly, 'and says he hopes you will soon be better. But I've made it clear that you're not well enough to see anybody. I don't want anyone coming round here, so you stay put until we've heard from Beattie and Donald.'

Now, following the arrival of the letter, she told Fiona that she was to go to Northumberland the following weekend. 'Your uncle has offered to come down and take you back in his Land Rover,' she said. 'It's very kind of him to go to all this trouble.' Fiona was left in no doubt that she was the cause of the trouble. 'He'll stay here on Saturday night, then you'll be off early Sunday morning. Beattie says you're welcome to stay for the first few months. So, like I say, think yourself lucky that somebody is willing to take you in.'

'And… what's going to happen after that?' asked Fiona.

Mary pressed her lips together in a tight line before answering. 'We're going to make arrangements for you to stay at a home for unmarried girls,' she answered briefly. 'I don't know where yet. Somewhere up there, probably. Dr Mackintosh may know of a place.' Fiona deduced from her mother's tone of voice that it would be as far away as possible, which was where she was going now, to the wilds of Northumberland.

Her uncle arrived on Saturday, towards teatime. He greeted Fiona as though everything was normal. 'Hello there, young lady. My goodness! You certainly are a young lady now, aren't you? But then I've not seen you since you were knee high to a grasshopper. You're a pretty lass, just like your mother.'

Mary simpered and blushed a little as Donald kissed her cheek. 'Have you had a good journey, Donald?' she asked.

'Aye, not so bad. I reckon it's about a hundred and fifty miles, so I've made quite good time. I set off at ten o'clock and stopped off to eat my sandwiches somewhere near Durham.'

'We're very grateful to you, Donald,' said Wilfred, 'coming all this way.' He looked and sounded somewhat apologetic.

'Think nothing of it,' said Donald. 'We'll be delighted to have Fiona to stay with us. It's been far too long since we saw any of you.'

No mention was made of the real reason he was here, and Fiona dared to believe that her uncle would not be one to condemn her. He seemed to her to be the very archetype of a farmer; like the farmer, Old Lob, that she recalled from her Beacon reading book in the infant school. Uncle Donald was portly with ruddy cheeks and kindly but shrewd blue eyes. Beneath his pork pie hat, which he took off on arrival, his faded gingerish hair stood up in tufts. All he needed was a straw in his mouth to make the image complete.

'Well, you'll be ready for a meal now,' said Mary. 'There's a steak and kidney pie in the oven, and I've made a bed up in the spare room for you.'

'Champion!' replied Donald, with a beaming smile.

Fiona made herself scarce that evening, guessing that her parents would have plenty to say to her uncle. She completed her packing, including, at the last minute, the little pink teddy bear that Dave had won for her at the hoopla stall. It still all seemed very unreal to her. She had wondered whether to write, secretly, to Diane; her friend would be thinking that it was all very mysterious. But she had decided it might be better to leave things as they were.

She looked pensively at the little teddy bear. What a happy and memorable time they had shared, she and Dave, Diane and Andy, at the funfair. And how disastrously it had ended. She wondered if she would ever see Dave again. She doubted it. And what must he be thinking about her disappearance? She would probably never know.

She put into her case some of her well-loved books from childhood and her early teenage years: *Anne of Green Gables* and *Anne of Avonlea*. How she had loved to read of the budding romance of Anne Shirley and Gilbert Blythe on Prince Edward Island. Dave had reminded her of Gilbert, Anne's first love; he turned out to be her one and only love as the books progressed. But Fiona knew that such a happy ending was not for her. She included *Little Women*, *Rebecca*, JB Priestley's *The Good Companions* – a host of lively characters there who became like friends as she read about them – and two of Thomas Hardy's Wessex novels, *The Mayor of Casterbridge* and *The Return of the Native*.

During her time in the lower sixth form Fiona had become acquainted with the works of Thomas Hardy – they were studying them as part of the advanced English course – and she was now an avid reader of his books. She regretted that she would be unable to complete the English course. The excellent teacher of the group, however, had awakened in her a love for literature, and she felt that this could be a solace to her in the months that lay ahead.

Her case felt as though it weighed a ton, but it would only have to be carried as far as her uncle's vehicle.

She went downstairs at half past nine to make herself a drink of cocoa. Her parents and uncle were deep in conversation which stopped when she entered the room.

'I'm going to have an early night,' she said. She placed a perfunctory kiss on the cheeks of her mother and father; they still seemed to expect it.

'Don't I get a kiss?' joked her uncle. It was he who kissed her cheek affectionately. 'Goodnight, luv, and God bless,' he whispered.

'Make sure you're up bright and early in the morning, Fiona,' said her mother. 'Set your alarm for seven o'clock. You uncle will want to be on his way pretty sharpish.'

'OK, Mum, will do,' she answered, disappearing upstairs with her cocoa.

She had her drink in bed, then tried to settle herself for sleep. It would be her last night in this bed for... how long? Sleep was a long time coming as she tossed about, anxious as to what the future might hold for her. The baby – how incredible to imagine that – what about the baby? 'It' would have to be adopted, given to someone else. The shame of a fatherless child would be too great for her mother to ever contemplate. Eventually her restless mind was stilled and she slept until the alarm clock broke into her slumber.

Her mother had cooked bacon and eggs, no doubt in honour of their guest, but Fiona could only eat cereal and one piece of toast. She knew it was too early for the morning sickness that she had heard expectant mothers suffered; nevertheless her stomach had tied itself into knots.

She had dreaded the goodbyes to her mother and father, but her mother's uncompromising attitude towards her had lessened considerably as she put her arms round her and kissed her fondly. 'Goodbye, Fiona love; God bless,' she said. 'Your dad and I will be saying our prayers for you.' There was even the glimmer of a tear in the corner of Mary's eye.

She felt her father give a slight sob as he held her close to him for a moment. 'Be a brave girl,' he said. 'It's for the best, you know. Your mum'll write to you, and we'll come and see you... sometime soon, I hope.'

'OK, Dad. Take care of yourself and Mum,' she said. 'I'll write soon. Cheerio then.' There was really nothing else to say.

What a relief it was to be on the way at last. Fiona and her uncle spoke very little as they made their way northwards out of the urban sprawl of the city of Leeds and on to the North York Moors. She had scarcely ever seen the moors in all their late summer glory even though she lived so near to them. They were at their loveliest in late August with the heather at the height of its flowering. The distant hills were a haze of purple, broken by outcrops of white limestone and solitary sheep grazing here and there. Nearer to the road were bushes of golden gorse and fronds of bracken, shading from copper to a rich bronze hue.

Despite her anxiety about the traumas that lay ahead of her Fiona felt an uplifting of her spirits at the sight of the beautiful countryside, and the churned-up feeling in her stomach began to ease a little.

'It's a lovely sight, isn't it?' she said. 'I can't remember the last time I came up this way. I'd forgotten how beautiful it is.'

'Aye, it's all reet,' said her uncle, in an understatement typical of a true Yorkshireman. He had been Yorkshire born and bred before moving north to Northumberland. 'It's a bonny sight, I'll admit, and you'll find it's not so bad where we live an' all. Bloomin' cold in t'winter, mind.'

'That won't bother me, Uncle Donald,' said Fiona. 'We get our fair share of cold weather in Leeds. I'm... I'm looking forward to seeing the farm... and everything,' she added, rather diffidently. 'Thank you very much for saying I could stay with you.'

'Aye, well… Beattie and me, we'll be only too glad to have a bit of company.' He glanced sideways at Fiona, nodding understandingly. 'Seems you've got yerself in a spot of bother, eh, lass?'

'That's right, Uncle Donald,' she replied. 'I'm in the bad books at the moment. Mum and Dad went mad at me, at least Mum did. I can't blame them though. I know I've been very silly and caused a lot of trouble. I never meant this to happen. I can't really believe it has.'

'Aye, we never do,' answered her uncle. 'A moment's madness and you're up the creek without a paddle. I know you're a good lass though; I can see that. Not one o' them flibbertigibbets. We'll not say much about it, your aunt and me, and we'll look after you.' He smiled at her. 'I don't suppose you'll mind earning your keep, though, will you?'

'Not at all,' she replied. 'Helping on the farm, you mean?'

'Aye, summat like that. Your aunt and me, we were talking about it. We had a couple of land girls during the war, you know. Two grand lasses they were. Our two farm lads were called up, but only one of 'em came back. Young Jimmy, he were lost on D-Day. Barry's back working with us, but we could do with another pair of hands. We won't expect you to do owt too heavy, mind. I reckon you could learn how to milk our cows. We've got machines now instead of doing it by hand. And I remember how you took a fancy to our little piglets when you were a nipper. Mind you, it's a bit of a mucky job, looking after t'pigs.'

'I don't mind a bit of muck, Uncle,' she replied, eager to prove that she was willing to work.

'Aye, well then, we'll get you sorted out with the right tackle. There's some wellies that the girls left behind and dungarees. Like I say, though, we won't expect you to do owt too strenuous seeing how you're… well, you know.'

'I don't feel any different,' said Fiona. 'Maybe I will, soon, but just now it feels, sometimes, as though I've dreamt it all… I wish it was only a dream,' she added pensively.

'Ne'er mind, luv,' said her uncle. 'Your Aunt Beattie'll look after you. We've had two lasses of our own; we've got grandchildren an' all now, so we know what it's all about. Summat else that you might like to do is go to market with your aunt. We have a stall at Alnwick market and one at Rothbury. Our farm's midway between 'em, so we can do both of 'em.'

'And what do you sell?' asked Fiona.

'Oh, all sorts o'stuff. Our home-grown produce; spuds and carrots, Brussel sprouts, cabbage; whatever's in season. We're a mixed farm, you see, part arable and part live-stock. And Beattie makes jams and marmalades, chutney, pickles… There's nowt she won't have a shot at. Happen you could help her in the kitchen.'

'Yes, I'd like that,' agreed Fiona. 'My mum makes marmalade and jam, only in a small way, just for us, and I used to help her sometimes. Lately, though, she's started making it to sell at church, at coffee mornings and sales of work and that sort of thing.'

'Aye, I've been hearing about their obsession wi' t'church.' Her uncle nodded. 'Sorry, luv, but that's what it sounds like to me. I never thought of yer mam and dad as being keen churchgoers.'

'No, they weren't until… well, it's a few years ago now that they got so wrapped up in it all.'

'Your aunt and me, we don't have too much time to go to church, happen two or three times a year. We try to go at Easter if we can. Of course we all went to Sunday school when we were nippers. That's where I met Beattie, at summat to do wi' church. And I remember Wilfred, your dad; he were there an' all. He were about five years younger than Beattie. It were quite a lot later that he met your mother. Aye, we had happy times in Sunday school, and it stands you in good stead. You never really forget what you learnt there. So I'm not saying that there's owt wrong with yer mam and dad being so keen, like. But Beattie and me, I reckon we're pretty good law-abiding folk, and we try to lead Christian lives. We don't need to be at church every Sunday.'

'No, I know what you mean, Uncle Donald,' said Fiona. 'They've just got a bit carried away with it all, and it made it harder for me when... well, when all this happened.'

'Aye, I can understand, lass,' said Donald.

They were silent for a while after that interchange of thoughts as they passed through the lovely countryside of Wensleydale and Swaledale. They stopped to eat the sandwiches and to drink from the flask of coffee that Mary had prepared for them, just north of Richmond. Then after what Donald called a 'comfort stop' behind a drystone wall, they set off again.

Leaving Yorkshire behind, they bypassed Darlington and Durham, travelling north towards Northumberland. Their route took them through the Cheviot Hills, catching a glimpse now and again of the River Coquet. This was sheep country of flat moorland and wide dales. Donald pointed out the Blackface and the Cheviot sheep roaming on the hills, remarking that they owned a small flock of Cheviots.

'Not far now,' he said as they passed through an area of forest and then a gorge of sandstone rocks. 'I can see you're getting a bit weary, like.' Fiona, indeed, had felt her eyes beginning to close.

The scenery was more rugged now. Her uncle told her they were near to the sites where the English and Scottish armies once went to war, and there was a wildness about the landscape that appealed to Fiona.

Eventually they turned off down a narrow lane, pulling up after a mile or so at a farm with solid greystone buildings grouped round a cobbled yard. It appeared forbidding at first glance, like a fortress from medieval times, which might well be how it had started out; but there was a column of smoke arising from the chimney of the farmhouse and the door was propped open with a large stone as if in welcome. As Fiona looked at her new home a ginger and white cat came through the door and made its way towards them, its tail held high in the air.

'Here we are then,' said Uncle Donald. 'This is Cragside Farm, and here's Felix coming to say hello.'

Fourteen

Fiona stayed at Cragside Farm for more than four months, until the January of 1952. Looking back on it she realized that it had been one of the happiest times of her young life, despite the fears and misgivings she had about the future. Her aunt and uncle were kind to her and very understanding.

Aunt Beattie was her father's sister but did not resemble him in looks. Wilfred was of a wiry build, but Beattie was undeniably plump. She and her husband, Donald, had grown alike over the years as many happily married couples tended to do, both being of a similar corpulent build. But that was also due, no doubt, to the good food they produced – and enjoyed themselves – on the farm.

From Fiona's bedroom window there was a superb view across to the distant hills, and in the nearer fields, criss-crossed by drystone walls, her uncle's flock of Cheviot sheep grazed. Just to look at the vista evoked in Fiona a feeling of calm and contentment, and she dared to hope that in the end all would be well, sometime, somehow...

Her mother wrote to her once a week, rather stilted letters – Mary had never had much call to correspond with anyone – telling her mainly of church matters and of the people there. She wrote that some of Fiona's friends – she did not say which ones – had been asking about her, but that she had not told them of her whereabouts. 'Best if they know as little as possible. As far as they are concerned you are suffering from a breakdown following your illness.'

In the third letter she received her mother told her that she and her father had applied for a transfer from their present council house to one on the other side of Leeds. 'It would be a good idea for us to be nearer to your grandma,' she wrote. 'Her arthritis troubles her a lot now and I will be able to help her with her shopping and housework. Also, of course, I want you to have a fresh start when you come home.'

Fiona knew that this was the real reason. When she returned to Leeds it was to be to a place where she knew nobody and where she would be far away from her former undesirable friends, one in particular, of course. What lengths they were prepared to go to, she pondered, to keep her shameful behaviour a secret, and to safeguard their own pride. To move away, even to distance themselves from the church they had become so attached to, and their precious vicar and his wife!

Fiona told Aunt Beattie what her parents had in mind. 'It seems as though I'm to have no contact with my old friends,' she said. 'I do worry about Diane – she was my best friend. She must be thinking that it's all very strange that I haven't written to her. And Dave… Goodness knows what he must be thinking. Mum didn't even know his name, because I wouldn't tell her. It doesn't matter if I'm telling you, though, because that's all you know about him, his first name.'

'And… did you love him?' asked her aunt, tentatively.

'I thought so,' replied Fiona. 'He was my first boyfriend. I was his first girlfriend too, I think… Yes, I'm sure I was. It all got out of hand, with us being away from home… and everything. And now… this.' She put a hand to her stomach.

Beattie smiled and put an arm round her where they stood in the homely farm kitchen. 'It will pass, Fiona love,' she said. 'All things pass. In less than a year from now it will all be over. It's just a year out of your young life; try to look at it like that. But you should think about what you'd like to do next. You were going to train to be a teacher, weren't you? There's no reason why you couldn't go to college later. It would be a shame to give up on the career you'd planned.'

Fiona gave a wry smile. 'I rather think it was Mum's idea more than it was mine. I said to my gran that she liked the idea of me being a teacher. With Mum, you see, it's a question of what people will think. And they'd be impressed by that, wouldn't they? But now – well – I've let her down, haven't I, and she's ashamed of me.'

Beattie nodded thoughtfully. 'Maybe, at the moment, but she'll never stop loving you, you know. Mothers never do.'

'I should've been taking my A-levels next year,' Fiona went on. 'I couldn't go to college without at least two A-levels. Anyway, I know that I really have no desperate desire to be a teacher.' She paused. 'I've been thinking, though; I got a good School Certificate: distinctions in English Language and Literature – they were always my best subjects – and credits in all the rest. I'd rather like to be a librarian. Yes, I think that's what I shall aim for… when all this is over.'

'Good!' said her aunt. 'That sounds like a grand idea. And it's good for you to have something to look forward to… Now, let's get on with this jam, shall we?'

One of Fiona's favourite tasks that she had been allotted at the farm was helping her aunt in the kitchen, especially with the marmalade and jam making. Today it was strawberry jam. It had been boiled in the huge copper pan and now, sufficiently cooled, it was ready to be poured into the jars. It was Fiona's job to do the finishing off. A circle of greaseproof paper was placed on top of the jam, then a larger circle of fancy paper – red and white check – covered the top of the jar, secured with a rubber band. Then she wrote 'Cragside Strawberry Jam' on a gummed label, in her best italic script, and stuck it on to the jar.

Before that, though, she had prepared the fruit ready for boiling. Hulling the strawberries was quite a simple job once you got the hang of it. Topping and tailing gooseberries and blackcurrants was more arduous, but Fiona was determined to do her very best at whatever job she was given.

It was great fun to go to market – Tuesdays and Fridays – with her Aunt Beattie. Fiona set out the stall with an array of jams and marmalades; jewel bright colours glistened in the jars, ranging from yellow to orange, red, deep crimson and purple, and the rich burgundy hue of the damsons and blackcurrants. There were pickles and chutneys too, and vegetables in season attractively arranged in their boxes and baskets. Potatoes; garden peas, full and almost bursting from their pods; runner beans, carrots and onions; and some vegetables that Fiona had never come across before, such as broccoli and asparagus. Her mother was a reasonable cook but by no means adventurous. Her accompaniment to a meal would be peas – often from a tin – carrots or cabbage, with Brussel sprouts at Christmas as a treat. Fiona had never even seen broccoli or asparagus, let alone tasted them.

One of her tasks was to cut the tender young shoots of asparagus, then arrange them in bundles of twenty and tie them with string, ready for sale at the market. The broccoli too – both the purple sprouting and the green varieties – were popular at the stall, arranged in shallow trays and covered with cellophane wrapping.

Fiona soon became popular at the market, both with the other stallholders and the customers. They welcomed her youthful prettiness and her cheerful face, a change from the middle-aged farmers' wives whom they were accustomed to seeing week by week. Her aunt often left her in charge whilst she went to do her own shopping. There were stalls selling all manner of things apart from farm produce: fishmongers; confectionery; sweet stalls; haberdashery and ironmongers' stalls, in fact almost anything and everything could be obtained there.

On the farm itself she lent a hand wherever she was required to do so. She became fond of the little piglets, as she had done when she was a little girl. She tried not to think ahead to what would ultimately be the fate of these dear little creatures. The calves, too, were lovable; but she knew that by the time the baby lambs were born in the early spring of 1952 she would no longer be at the farm.

As late summer turned into autumn, there was a decided nip in the air, more noticeable up there in the north, especially in the early mornings. She had been suffering from the dreaded morning sickness, but fortunately it had been of short duration. By the end of October, a month into her stay, she was feeling quite well again.

The family doctor had seen her a couple of times. He, of course, had been told of her predicament. She found the initial examination embarrassing and slightly painful, never before having experienced anything like it. The doctor tried to be gentle, and like Dr Mackintosh at home he was a kindly middle-aged man. It was this, though, that brought it home to her, more than anything else, that in another six months or so she would give birth to a child. Her breasts started to feel fuller and there was a slight thickening around her waist and tummy. It was not possible to tell, though, if one did not know, that she was pregnant.

Her parents had not been to see her despite their promise to do so. Admittedly, it was a long way up to Northumberland and they would need to travel by train and stay overnight. But Fiona guessed that they were closing their eyes and their minds to her condition, as much as they possibly could. She doubted that she would see them again until next May when she returned to Leeds. Then they would try to behave as though nothing had happened.

In December, her mother wrote that they had been allotted a council house in the district of Harehills. This was several miles away from their present home in Headingley, and much nearer to her grandmother's house. They would be moving there in January and, of course, they were very busy at the moment. Mary assured her that they missed her and that Christmas would not be the same without her; they would be thinking about her and remembering her in their prayers.

Fiona shed a few quiet tears. Despite everything she loved her parents, but she feared that the disgrace she had brought to them was such that things would never be quite the same between the three of them. Her mother also informed her that they had made arrangements, with the assistance of Dr Mackintosh, for her, Fiona, to go to a home for unmarried expectant mothers at the end of January. It was situated on the outskirts of Newcastle upon Tyne, not too far from Donald and Beattie's farm, and was run by the Methodist churches in the area.

'They will take good care of you,' wrote her mother, 'both before and after the birth and will make all the necessary arrangements. And then, we hope and pray that this unfortunate incident can be put behind us.'

Fiona wept a little more at this news. Her baby was to be dismissed as though it was of no consequence. It was, in fact, an embarrassment. Beattie had also received a letter with the relevant information, and she assured Fiona that they would take her there to the home when the time came, and would visit her as often as they were able. They knew the whereabouts of the place, north of Newcastle and near to the coal mining area, but also near to green hills and pasture land and within easy reach of the pleasant sandy beaches of the Northumberland coast.

–

Christmas was a strange time for Fiona that year, both happy and sad. She still did not dare to make contact with any of her friends in Leeds, so there were very few Christmas cards for her to send. Her Aunt Beattie took her shopping in the town of Alnwick. She had a little money saved from the wages that her uncle insisted on giving her. It wasn't a great sum but her needs were few at the moment.

As the new year, 1952, started and January drew on, she felt a definite change in her figure. It was obvious now that she was pregnant, and in the middle of the month she felt an odd little fluttering in her abdomen, very slight at first and then it came again. She realized that the child inside her was stirring. She did not know whether to feel happy or sad, but more than anything she felt bewildered, desperately wishing for the next few months to be over.

On the last Sunday in January her uncle drove her to the place where she was to stay for the next four months. Her aunt sat with her on the back seat, holding her hand and talking in a friendly and comforting way.

'We'll come and see you at weekends, whenever we can,' said Beattie. 'From what I've heard of this place, it's not so bad. They look after you very well; and you know, of course, that the other lasses'll all be in the same boat as you. I dare say you'll make some nice friends there, girls you can get along with well enough at any rate. So cheer up, love. Like I've told you before, it's only a few months out of your young life, then it'll all be over.'

'Looks as though we're here,' said Donald as they came to a sign at the end of a narrow lane stating that this was Burnside House. 'Ready then, Fiona love? Let's get your baggage out and tell them you've arrived.'

Fifteen

Burnside House was situated a few miles from Newcastle upon Tyne, midway between that industrial city and the more rural town of Hexham; the nearest village was Bywell. It was a large house built of greystone, standing in its own grounds. Aunt Beattie had told Fiona that it had once belonged to a wealthy family until the line had died out, and it was then taken over by the nearby Methodist churches as a home for girls such as Fiona.

On first impressions it did not look too intimidating. There was a lawn in front of the house surrounded by a border which in the summer would be bright with roses. The bushes, now, resembled dead sticks, looking as though they would never bloom again. Likewise the tall trees – Fiona guessed that they might be beech trees – that partly hid the house from the road. It had snowed earlier that morning and traces of it still lingered on the bare branches and on the garden soil.

Beattie rang the bell, and the door was opened almost at once by a middle-aged woman wearing a blue overall. 'Hello,' she said in a friendly manner. 'You must be Fiona. We've been expecting you. And… Mr and Mrs Dalton?'

'No, we're not her parents,' Beattie explained. 'We're her aunt and uncle, Beattie and Donald Slater. Fiona's been staying with us for a while.'

'Very good,' said the woman. 'I'm Mrs Armstrong, one of the assistants. I'll take you along to Miss Copeland; she's our superintendent.'

They followed Mrs Armstrong into the hallway. It was rather dark and gloomy, with just a faint light filtering through the stained-glass panels on the door. The hall and stairs carpet was a nondescript design of brown and green leaves, toning with the dark-brown woodwork and the faded beige and brown wallpaper. The place looked a little shabby and in need of decorating, but at least the oaken banister gleamed with recent polishing. A faint aroma of lavender floor polish lingered on the air, together with the less appetizing smell of cabbage.

The superintendent's office was more welcoming, with a cherry red carpet and curtains, two armchairs, and pleasing pictures of country scenes on the walls. Miss Copeland rose from behind a large mahogany desk, a woman of indeterminate age – late fifties, or sixties? – with iron-grey hair cut short, and rimless spectacles from behind which her piercing brown eyes looked out search-ingly. She was dressed in a tweed suit with a cameo brooch at the neck of her cream-coloured blouse. She stepped forward to greet them.

'Fiona Dalton, I presume?' She held out a hand, and Fiona felt hers caught in a firm grasp. 'I am pleased to welcome you to our home. And… your parents?'

Beattie explained again who they were, and when the introductions had been made Beattie and Donald sat in the armchairs with Fiona on one of the hard-backed chairs.

'You will be here until late May or early June; that is correct, isn't it?' said Miss Copeland.

Fiona nodded. 'Yes, that's right.'

The woman went on to explain about the rules and the running of the home. Visitors were allowed on Saturday and Sunday afternoons. The girls were expected to help with all the work in the house, apart from the actual cooking of the meals which was done by Mrs Walker, the housekeeper and cook. There were two non-medical assistants, Mrs Armstrong, whom they had already met, and Mrs Wagstaff. The nursing staff consisted of Sister Travers and Nurse Grant, both very experienced nurses and midwives. A doctor called every week to check the girls' health and was ready to help out should there be an emergency. The girls were allowed to go out each afternoon, but not on their own – they must go in twos or threes – and outings were arranged from time to time to the nearby seaside towns or to Hexham or Morpeth. No girl was allowed out in the evening, and 'lights out' was at ten thirty. Morning prayers took place each day at nine o'clock, after breakfast, and there was a devotional service in the home each Sunday morning.

Fiona listened attentively; there seemed to be such a lot to take in. She was beginning to feel mesmerized by it all, but when she glanced now and again at her aunt, Beattie smiled encouragingly.

'We like to think that we are strict but fair,' said Miss Copeland as her discourse drew to a close. She gave a half-smile and her eyes softened just a little. 'You will be well looked after, Fiona, and we hope you will be contented here. You should be if you don't step out of line. We occasionally get young women who are wilful and don't appreciate what we are trying to do for them, but on the whole we don't have much trouble. Now… say goodbye to your aunt and uncle and I'll show you where you will be sleeping. You will be sharing a room with three other

young women. We have twelve residents at the moment…
and we usually find that as one leaves there is another one
to take her place,' she added wryly.

'Take care of yourself, love, and God bless you,' said her
aunt, putting her arms around her and kissing her cheek.
'You'll be alright here; I know you will. And we'll come
and see you soon.'

Her uncle seemed too choked to speak. He just hugged
her and whispered, 'Chin up now, luv.'

It was clear that Miss Copeland did not want them to
linger over their goodbyes. She picked up Fiona's large
suitcase as though it weighed very little, and Fiona took
the other bag and followed her up the stairs.

'We have four dormitories,' Miss Copeland told her,
when they stopped at the first floor, 'two on this floor
and two higher up, although we don't usually call them
dormitories. It sounds too much like boarding school,
doesn't it?'

'Yes, like Enid Blyton and Angela Brazil,' Fiona dared
to say.

'Quite.' A hint of a smile moved the woman's lips. 'Enid
Blyton is more your era than mine, but I do remember
reading the school stories by Angela Brazil.' It seemed
that the superintendent might be quite human, not the
martinet that Fiona had feared at a first glance.

'However, as I was saying, we can accommodate up
to sixteen young women, four in each room. We have
only twelve at the moment but the vacancies will soon be
filled. You will be in here, Fiona, so this room will have its
full quota again.' She opened the door leading into a large
room. A girl sitting on the bed nearest to the window
looked up in some surprise. She stood up immediately.

'Oh, hello there, Ginny,' said Miss Copeland. 'I didn't realize there was anyone here. This is Fiona Dalton, your new room-mate. So you can look after her and bring her down for lunch.' She glanced at a fob watch pinned to the lapel of her suit. 'That will be in about twenty minutes. You've finished your chores for this morning, have you, Ginny?'

'Yes, Miss Copeland,' replied the girl deferentially. 'I've cleaned the baths and toilets. I was just going to write a letter home.'

'Well, leave that now. You'll have plenty of time later. You can show Fiona where to put her belongings.' The woman turned to Fiona. 'Come and see me in my room at two o'clock, when lunch is over, and we'll have a little chat.' She nodded briefly at the two girls as she left the room.

'Hello, Fiona,' said the girl called Ginny as the door closed. 'I expect you're feeling a bit lost and frightened, aren't you? But you don't need to be, honestly. We all felt like that at first, but it's not all that bad here, and we do manage to have some fun.'

'Hello... Ginny, isn't it?' said Fiona. She smiled at the girl. 'Do you know, you are making me feel better already.' She guessed that the girl might be about the same age as herself. She appeared to be a little further on in her pregnancy. She had ginger hair and freckles and bright blue eyes. It looked as though she might always have been on the plump side, notwithstanding her condition. She laughed easily.

'Yes, I'm Ginny. Virginia, actually, but you might say that my name's not very appropriate.' She grinned as she glanced down at her spreading waistline. 'Virginia Adams, that's me.' Fiona was not sure how to answer the girl's comment, but there was no need because Ginny went on talking.

'Not a bad room, is it? Come on, let's get your case on to the bed. You'll be in this one, here.' Together they hauled the heavy case on to one of the iron-framed beds, resembling a hospital bed.

Glancing round Fiona noticed two large wardrobes, a little cupboard at the side of each bed, and just one large dressing table with a somewhat speckled mirror by the window. The candlewick bedspreads were green, as were the curtains and the rather worn carpet. In one corner of the room there was a wash basin and a towel rail.

'The view's not bad,' said Ginny, pointing to the window. The room was at the front of the house over-looking the garden, and through the skeletal branches of the tall trees one could just make out the distant hills, their tops now covered in snow.

'Where are you from then, Fiona?' asked Ginny. 'I'm from South Shields, but I expect you guessed that from my accent.' Indeed, Fiona had realized from her sing-song way of talking that the girl was what was known as a Geordie.

'My parents live in Leeds,' replied Fiona, 'but I've been staying with my aunt and uncle near Alnwick. They brought me here, and they've said they'll come and see me.'

'That'll be nice,' said Ginny, 'that is, if you want to see them?'

'Oh yes, I do,' said Fiona eagerly. 'They've been very good to me, far more understanding than my parents.'

'Yeah, same here,' said Ginny. 'My parents are pretty annoyed with me, especially me da. It's me gran who's sticking up for me, and she's the one who comes to see me.'

'Yes, my gran's the same,' agreed Fiona, 'but it's too far for her to visit. She lives in Leeds as well.'

'I'm just a nuisance, y'see,' said Ginny. 'I'm the eldest of five, and me da hit the roof when he found out about this.' She patted her tummy. 'I'm supposed to help me mam to look after the kids as well as going out to work. I got a job at Woolie's when I left school, and my wage has come in very handy. The rest of 'em are still at school, so now they've got to manage on what me da earns.'

'And what does your father do?' asked Fiona.

'Oh, he's a coal miner, like most of the fellers round our way,' said Ginny. 'It's not bad money, with overtime, but they'll be waiting for me to get back home and start helping out again.'

'So… will you keep the baby?' asked Fiona tentatively, wondering if it was permissible to ask the question.

'No,' Ginny replied briefly. 'It'd just be another mouth to feed, wouldn't it?' She shook her head sadly. 'But… well, these things happen, don't they?'

'I suppose so,' said Fiona. She didn't know yet whether the girls spoke openly to one another about their circumstances, or whether it was a question of the least said the better.

'Anyway, this is where you can put your belongings,' said Ginny, opening the door of a huge wardrobe. 'I've shoved my stuff up to make room. And the bottom drawer of the chest of drawers will be yours as well. We haven't got much time though, now.' She glanced at a clock on a bedside cupboard. 'Oh crikey! It's five to one already. We'd best get moving. Do you want to spend a penny or anything?'

'Yes, actually I think I do,' said Fiona.

'The lav's along the corridor, and the bathroom's next door,' said Ginny. 'And this towel is yours.' She handed her a pink towel from off the rail. 'We have different colours so we don't get mixed up. Off you go now – the door at the end – and I'll wait for you.'

–

Interested faces looked up as Ginny and Fiona entered the dining room. Most of the girls were already there, awaiting the arrival of the members of staff who would sit at a table at the end of the room.

'This is Fiona,' said Ginny, going to a table where four young women were seated. 'Mandy, Judith, Hazel and Bridget.' She pointed to each girl in turn and Fiona smiled at them.

'Hello,' she said. 'Pleased to meet you.' They all smiled and nodded in return, with a chorus of 'hellos'.

'Hazel and Bridget are our room-mates,' Ginny was just starting to explain when the members of staff entered the room. All the girls stood up and bowed their heads as Miss Copeland said grace.

'For what we are about to receive, may we be truly thankful and ever mindful of the needs of others.'

Fiona realized she was quite hungry. It seemed a long time since she had had her breakfast at the farmhouse. The meal consisted of steak and kidney pie with mashed potatoes and – as she had already guessed – cabbage. It was followed by rice pudding; a good nourishing meal, far better than she had expected.

'So how far gone are you?' asked the girl called Hazel, who was sitting next to her.

'Er… I'm due at the end of May,' replied Fiona, a little taken aback at the blunt remark. 'And… what about you?'

'End of March, two months to go,' said Hazel. 'Can't wait to get rid, I can tell you. I was going to have an abortion. It was all arranged, and then – well – I chickened out. So now I've got to go through the whole damned business. I shall keep my legs crossed in future, believe me!'

Fiona was embarrassed at hearing such revelations from a complete stranger. She wasn't used to such plain speaking, but she guessed that in such a place as this there would be girls from all sorts of backgrounds and with differing personalities. She realized that this girl, Hazel, fitted into the category that her mother would call 'common', and her gran might say 'was no better than she should be', whatever such a silly expression might mean. She was a full-bosomed girl with blonde hair that was dark at the roots, growing out to its normal shade, it seemed. She wore a good deal of blue eyeshadow and bright-red lipstick, and was wearing a tight sweater with stripes of pink and black. Fiona had been pleased to learn that the girls were allowed to wear their own clothes and not some sort of uniform resembling prison garb, which might have been the norm not all that long ago. She was determined, though, not to make a hasty judgement about Hazel. The girl might turn out to be quite likeable on further acquaintance.

'Now, you've got your tête-à-tête with Connie at two o'clock,' said Ginny as they cleared away their pots at the end of the meal.

'Connie?' queried Fiona.

'Connie Copeland,' said Ginny. 'We call her Connie behind her back, of course. She's called Constance. We all get the same pep talk when we arrive. She's alright though, provided you keep your nose clean. Off you go then. Some of us have to help with the washing up, so I'll see you in our room afterwards. OK?'

–

Fiona was pleasantly surprised to be invited to drink coffee with Miss Copeland.

'As I said before, I hope you will settle down here, Fiona,' she began. 'It is not our business to pass judgement on any of you, or to seek to punish you in any way. I know that may have happened in homes such as this, and not all that long ago either. And, regrettably, sometimes done in the name of religion. This is a home run by Christians who try to live up to that name. We know that you have all been foolish and have made a mistake, and most of you realize that; but we are here to help you and to try to offer you some guidance for the future, if we can… Now, is there anything you would like to ask, Fiona?'

She couldn't think of anything, so she shook her head and answered, 'No, thank you, Miss Copeland.'

The woman went on to enquire about her general health and whether she had suffered any complications so far in her pregnancy. She explained that the doctor would see her in the morning, and she would soon get to know Sister Travers and Nurse Grant who would take care of her at the birth. 'You are not worried about giving birth, are you?' she asked.

'A little apprehensive, maybe,' Fiona began. Then, 'Well, yes, I suppose I am rather anxious about it,' she admitted.

'Try not to be,' said Miss Copeland. 'Our nursing staff make it as easy as they can for you. We don't regard it as your punishment for wrongdoing, which I am afraid used to be the case in some homes. I am sure you will find that there's nothing to fear.'

It's all very well for you to talk, Fiona thought to herself, looking at the woman whom she guessed to be in her mid-fifties. She was manly in appearance, tall and angular and, seemingly, lacking in feminine character- istics. It was pretty certain that she had never given birth... But maybe she had regretted that fact, who could tell? Fiona always tried to see both sides of a question, and Miss Copeland, despite her forbidding looks, seemed to be an understanding person.

'And... the baby is to be adopted?' Miss Copeland asked. Fiona nodded. 'We will make all the arrangements,' she continued. 'We try to make sure that parting from your baby is as painless as possible for you. We find it is best if this is dealt with as soon as it can be arranged, so that you don't form too much of an attachment to the child. You are young, Fiona, and there is no reason why you should not give birth again at a later date, in a happy and stable relationship.'

'Thank you, Miss Copeland,' Fiona murmured. It was the first time that the birth of her baby had been referred to so openly, and she experienced a pang of fear and of doubt. How would she feel when her baby was taken away from her?

'Off you go then, my dear,' said Miss Copeland, bringing the interview to a close. 'Ginny's a good girl; she'll look after you. But if you have any problems please don't hesitate to tell me or any of the other members of staff. Goodbye for now, Fiona... God bless you.'

Sixteen

Fiona soon found that Ginny was a great person to have around. She was sensible and practical, able to look on the bright side of life and ready to have a laugh, though not at the expense of others; unlike Hazel Docherty whose jesting was often thoughtless, even cruel at times, directed at those who were of a more timid disposition.

The fourth occupant of the room was Bridget O'Connor, a small dark-haired girl whose accent and Celtic features betrayed that she was of Irish descent. She was often the butt of Hazel's unkind humour, being referred to as Paddy or Mick or 'our little friend from the potato fields'.

Bridget's home, now, was in Sunderland. Like Ginny, she was the eldest of a large family. She, too, was seventeen years old, the same age as both Fiona and Ginny, and had five younger siblings. Beyond that, however, she had divulged very little of her circumstances. Her mother sometimes came to visit her, a shabbily dressed, tired-looking little woman who was probably not yet forty, but who appeared much older. She resembled Bridget, with the same sad, dark eyes. The father was never to be seen, and when asked, Bridget had replied briefly that he worked on the docks.

Hazel, at twenty, was the eldest of the four room-mates. She stated, quite unashamedly, that the father of her baby was married and that there was no chance of him leaving his wife, nor did she want him to do so. 'We dropped a clanger, that's all,' she shrugged.

Ginny had told Fiona how she had come to be 'in the family way'. 'It was the lad next door,' she said. 'He's a few years older than me, more of a mate, really, than a boyfriend. We went to the pub one night, and I had too much to drink, and so did he. He didn't mean this to happen, but… well, it did! Actually, he said he'd marry me, but me mam and me da won't hear of it.' Fiona thought she sounded a little regretful, but Ginny was never downhearted for long.

She confided in her new friend about Dave, and how she had been quickly removed from the scene and not allowed to see him or any of her friends again.

'Oh, poor you!' said Ginny. 'And you really loved him? I don't think I love Arthur, but he's a real nice sort of lad and we've always got on very well.'

'Well, I thought I loved him,' said Fiona, 'but I know I've just got to try and forget him.'

Bridget, however, did not say how she had become pregnant. Hazel frequently tormented her about it. 'It was one of them leprechauns, so it was!' she jeered. 'A little green man who crept into your bedroom at dead of night, didn't he, Bridget?'

'Leave her alone, can't you?' Fiona snapped one afternoon when the older girl had gone too far, leaving Bridget in tears.

'Oh, shurrup, you!' retorted Hazel. 'Don't start telling me what to do! You've only been here five minutes, and you think you're the bee's knees just because you've been to a posh school.' She flounced out leaving the other two girls to comfort Bridget. It was then that she told them her sorry tale.

'Don't tell anyone else, please,' she begged, her voice scarcely audible through her sobs. 'It was my dad... It's my dad that did it.'

'Your dad? What do you mean?' asked Fiona, looking puzzled.

Ginny frowned at her, shaking her head. She understood what Bridget was saying, even if Fiona didn't. 'Oh, you poor love!' she said to Bridget, putting her arms around her. 'I thought it might be something like that.' Ginny had heard of such instances before, where a father or sometimes a brother was involved. She knew, though, that Fiona was far more naive. Despite the fact that Fiona was cleverer than the other three and had stayed longer at school, she was unused to the darker side of life. 'Does your mam know about it?' she asked Bridget gently.

'Yes, it's been going on for ages,' said Bridget, sounding a little calmer now. 'But she can't do anything about it.'

'But you won't be going back to live there, will you?' asked Ginny. 'Bridget, you can't!'

'No, I'm going to my grandma's – that's my mam's mother – back in Dublin.'

'But... couldn't your mother leave him, and go as well, to your grandma's?' asked Fiona, feeling very bewildered, and horrified, too, at the situation.

'She'd like to, but there's the rest of the kids, y'see. She can't afford it, not to take them all. But maybe when I've gone it might be better... Thanks, you two, for listening. I don't know what I'd do without you, honest to God! Miss Copeland knows, and she's been grand, so she has.'

'We'll look after you,' said Fiona with a show of confidence. 'We'll tell that Hazel where to get off, you see if we don't.'

'P'raps the least said the better,' warned Ginny. 'Hazel's a nasty piece of work. We don't want to make an enemy of her. She'd stab you in the back soon as look at you, that one.'

Fiona nodded. 'Yes, I can see that.' In point of fact, she was flabbergasted at Bridget's revelation. She had never heard of anything like that in her life. The girl's own father! It was beyond belief. She was realizing there were many things in life of which she was totally unaware.

'I had no idea about anything like that,' she said to Ginny when they were on their own. 'It's monstrous, isn't it? Her own father! And you say that sometimes it might be a brother who's involved?'

'I'm afraid so, yes,' replied Ginny. 'It's my guess that there may be one or two here that that has happened to. You've never heard of it?'

'Er… no,' said Fiona hesitantly. She didn't want to appear so innocent – stupid, in fact – in front of her more worldly-wise friend. Fiona realized that she had led a comparatively sheltered life, despite being brought up on a housing estate. It was an area where most of the people were law abiding and not given to extremes of behaviour, but not able to afford to buy their own homes. She supposed that Ginny might have been reared in a very different environment. The girl was intelligent and quick thinking, just as much so as Fiona herself was, but circumstances had forced her to leave school at an early age and find employment to help with the family's finances.

'It's what is called incest,' explained Ginny. 'Sexual relationships with a close family member, like your father or brother. It can happen in large families like Bridget's. I guess that her mother was pregnant a good deal of the time, and that the father sought his pleasures elsewhere.'

'That's horrible!' Fiona shuddered.

'Yes, so it is,' agreed Ginny. 'Thank goodness I've never experienced anything of the sort. Me da can be handy with his fists at times but he's quite… well… normal in most respects. We'll have to try to look out for Bridget now that we know about it, but Hazel must never find out.'

'No, of course not,' said Fiona. She had a good deal to mull over in her mind, but the following day they all had something else to think about.

It was at the end of the midday meal on Wednesday, February sixth, that Miss Copeland stood to make an announcement. 'Girls, will you all listen, please. I have some very sad news to tell you. Our beloved king has passed away. He died peacefully in his sleep early this morning.'

There were gasps of shock and murmurs of 'Oh dear!' and 'How dreadful!' King George the Sixth was only fifty-six years of age. He had had an operation for lung cancer the previous September.

The girls, on the whole, were subdued for the rest of the day.

'So Princess Elizabeth'll be the queen now,' said Fiona as she and her room-mates did the washing up; it was their turn for the whole of the week. 'How strange it'll seem. She's in Africa, isn't she, with her husband? They'll have to come back, won't they?'

'We'll have to sing "God save the Queen" now instead of "God save the King",' said Bridget. 'That'll sound funny, won't it?'

'I never sing it anyway,' retorted Hazel. 'Why should we? They're only folk like us, our precious royal family, except that they've got a bit more brass.'

'Don't be so awful!' said Fiona with an angry look at the girl. 'The poor man's dead, isn't he?' She had been determined not to get upset by her, but Hazel was so lacking in respect that Fiona couldn't help retaliating.

'Oh, get down off yer bloody high horse!' retorted Hazel. 'It don't make any difference to me that the king's popped his clogs.'

'I think he's been ill for a long time,' said Ginny, ignoring the older girl's remark. 'Of course, he did smoke a lot, didn't he? It must have affected his lungs.'

'Well, it won't stop me from having a fag when I want one,' said Hazel. She flung down her pot towel. 'That's where I'm going now. So long, you lot.' She flounced out of the kitchen. The girls were not supposed to smoke, but Hazel, and probably some of the others, did so secretly, in the bedrooms near to an open window.

'Good riddance!' said Fiona. 'She's insufferable, isn't she?'

'Yes, but perhaps it's better not to rise to her bait,' said Ginny. 'That's what she wants you to do. Shall we go for a walk when we've finished this lot?'

Burnside House was on the fringe of the coal mining area, and slag heaps and winding gear all around formed part of the landscape. But there were stretches of green pasture land as well, and pleasant farms and villages. The three of them wandered along the country lanes to the pretty village of Bywell. All that remained now of the former iron-working centre were a few houses, a market cross and two large churches. Dusk came early and there was a decided chill in the air as they made their way back. Spring still seemed a long way off.

There was a sombre feeling throughout the country. The BBC was broadcasting nothing but serious music until the king was finally laid to rest. And then, gradually, things returned to normal.

The days and the weeks passed, brightened by visits of family members and excursions for the young women to the market town of Morpeth, the cathedral city of Durham, and in March, when the cold weather had given way to sunshine, for a short time at least, to the seaside resort of Whitley Bay.

Hazel was due to give birth at the end of March, Ginny at the end of April, and Fiona and Bridget both in May. Hazel's baby – a boy – was born a week early and there were no tears shed at her departure. She had not been popular with the other girls or with the members of staff.

Fiona was delighted to see her aunt and uncle again on a Sunday afternoon early in April. She couldn't help noticing that Ginny had a visitor too, a young man whom she had not seen before, deep in conversation with her friend. Visitors were entertained in the lounge, which was large enough to afford them all the privacy they needed. Fiona had guessed before Ginny told her that this might be Arthur. He was a well-built young man with rugged features and, she noticed from time to time, a broad smile and a hearty laugh.

Ginny broke the news later that afternoon. 'Guess what? Arthur's asked me again if I'll marry him. And I've said yes! So I can keep the baby. Isn't that wonderful?'

'Oh… I'm so pleased for you, Ginny,' said Fiona, hugging her friend. She could not help, however, the sinking feeling in her stomach as she thought about her own plight, but she had to try to be happy for Ginny. 'If that's what you want?' she queried. 'What about your parents? They were dead against it, weren't they?'

'My gran's been talking to them,' Ginny replied, 'trying to persuade them to let me keep it. The twins'll be leaving school soon and starting work, so there'll be some more money coming in.' That was Ginny s fourteen-year-old twin brother and sister. 'And Arthur went to see me mam and me da as well. He can be very persuasive,' she smiled. 'And they said yes, he could marry me, if I agreed.'

'And then he had to persuade you?' said Fiona.

'Oh, I didn't need much convincing. He's steady and reliable, and he's got a good job, not down the mine, thank goodness; he works at the docks. And a mate of his knows of some rooms we can rent. I do like him such a lot. I told you we were real good pals.' Ginny was quite cock-a-hoop with excitement.

'Well, that's a good start,' said Fiona. 'I hope it all works out for you, Ginny.' And so she did, sincerely, but it also increased the sadness she was feeling. There could be no happy ending such as this for her.

Ginny's baby was born at the end of April as expected; a boy weighing eight pounds, with bright ginger hair inherited from his mother. He really was a bonny baby and Fiona could feel only happiness for her friend when she saw her nursing him, her freckled face alight with joy.

'Arthur's thrilled with him,' she said. He had visited her earlier on that Saturday afternoon. 'And guess what? Me mam and me da are coming to see me tomorrow. That's a turn up for the book, isn't it? Seems as though they're coming round to the idea.'

Fiona shed a few tears when her friend left two weeks later. Ginny was tearful as well. The two of them had formed a close bond.

'It won't be long for you now,' said Ginny. 'And it's not too bad, honest. You mustn't worry about it. It'll soon be over. Oh, Fiona… we must keep in touch, whatever happens. Promise me you'll write, won't you? And when you get back to Leeds, let me know how you go on.' Fiona, fighting back her tears, promised that she would.

There were only two of them left in the room now. There seemed to be a temporary dearth of unmarried mothers. Bridget was very quiet, but happier now that Hazel had gone. She was actually due to give birth the week before Fiona, but it didn't turn out that way.

–

It was at about nine o'clock on the Saturday evening, May seventeenth, when Fiona became aware of a sharp pain in her abdomen. She was in the lounge with some of the other girls, listening to favourite records on the Dansette record player.

'They try to tell us we're too young,' sang Jimmy Young as Fiona's pains grew worse. She had tried to ignore them at first – she was more than a week early – but after about twenty minutes they were recurring regularly and she knew she must be in labour.

'I think I've started,' she whispered to Bridget.

'Do you, really?' said the other girl. 'I'll go and tell somebody.'

She came back in a few moments with Nurse Grant. 'Now, what's the problem?' she asked a trifle brusquely.

'I think I might have started in labour,' said Fiona. 'But it's early.'

'Oh, babies are a law unto themselves,' said the nurse. 'Come on then; let's be having you. We'll go and find out what's happening.'

It was when Fiona entered the labour room that her waters broke. 'Oh, oh!' she cried. 'Oh dear! How awful!'

'It's just part of the process,' said the nurse briskly. 'Get undressed, there's a good girl, and put this gown on.'

It was all a blur in her mind from then on, when she looked back at it. She was subjected to the indignity of an enema, something she had heard of but never experienced before. Then she was left on her own for what seemed ages, to cope with the pains as well as she could. The nurse was within calling distance but Fiona didn't want to make a fuss, so she tried to grin and bear it. The pains went on until the early hours of Sunday morning, and then Sister Travers was there to assist with the birth. Fiona was given access to the gas and air machine and she clung to it like a lifeline. As one pain receded and she awaited the next she reflected that she was paying dearly for those few passionate moments in Battersea Pleasure Gardens.

When she was told to 'Push… push like mad, Fiona, there's a good girl,' she did as she was told. And then, suddenly, it was all over. There was a moment when she felt that she was being ripped apart, and then she heard Sister Travers say, 'It's a girl! You have a lovely little girl, Fiona.'

There was a faint cry, like a kitten mewing, then a louder wail as the nurse cleaned the baby and wrapped her in a blanket.

'Can I see her?' asked Fiona.

'In a minute,' said the sister, 'when we've dealt with the afterbirth.'

A few moments later the baby, cocooned in a soft woollen blanket was placed in her arms. 'Just for a little while now. You understand, don't you, Fiona?' said Sister Travers, firmly but not unkindly.

Fiona looked down at the tiny infant in her arms, her eyes misted with tears. She blinked them away, then wiped them with a corner of the sheet. She had known that this moment would come, and she must try to be brave. The baby seemed to be staring up at her with misty blue-grey eyes, but Fiona knew that she couldn't really see her; her eyes were unfocused as yet. Her hair was dark brown – like Dave's, Fiona remembered; her own hair was blonde – a downy covering of curls clinging damply to her scalp. She had the tiniest little rosebud mouth and a pink and white complexion. It was not true, then, that all babies were red and wrinkled. She really was an exquisite little thing. Fiona felt a sob in her throat as she gently pulled back the blanket to reveal a tiny hand like a miniature starfish. She placed a finger in the palm and the baby's fingers instinctively curled round it, grasping it for a moment.

'Hello, little girl,' she whispered. 'You're beautiful, aren't you?' At that moment she felt as though she would do anything to keep her baby. She would put up with the shame, the ostracism; she would live in one room; she would be poor and lonely and friendless if need be, if only she could keep her. And if her parents were to see this lovely little child, surely they would relent? No one could be so hard-hearted as to reject a little baby such as this, one of God's children, when all was said and done.

They left her alone with the baby for a little while, then Sister Travers returned. 'Come along now, Fiona. I know it's hard for you, but it's the best way, really it is. And you signed the form, didn't you, agreeing to give up your baby for adoption?'

'But how can I?' pleaded Fiona. 'Not now that I've seen her; she's so lovely. If I managed to persuade my parents?'

'No, I'm afraid that won't happen,' said the sister firmly. 'Your baby will be going to a good home, it's already been arranged, and it really is for the best, Fiona. You made a mistake, like hundreds of girls have done – you're not alone in this, you know – and it could have been much worse. The birth was straightforward and there is no reason why you shouldn't conceive again, in happier circumstances. So... give her to me, there's a good girl.'

Fiona hesitated for a moment, unwilling to let go of her baby. Then she had a sudden thought. 'Sister Travers,' she said, 'would you pass me that little pink teddy bear, please? It's sitting on the cupboard.' The Sister did so, and Fiona tucked it under the blanket that was around the baby. 'It'll be nice to think of her holding this when she's older,' she said, her voice choking with tears.

Sister Travers held out her arms. 'Come along now, dear.' Fiona kissed the baby's forehead. 'Goodbye, little one,' she said, then she handed the baby over. She felt as though her heart would break...

–

Fiona had formed an attachment with the auxiliary helper, Claire Wagstaff, during her stay at the home. It was not exactly a friendship; the members of staff were warned not to become too involved with the girls. But Claire was sympathetic, and at only thirty was much closer in age to the girls. She had gone off duty when Fiona had started in labour, but was back there the next morning after she had given birth. She popped into the room to see Fiona, who had been left on her own for a time, to come to terms with everything.

'Hello, love,' she said in her usual cheerful way. 'So it's all over now?' Her smile was full of understanding.

Fiona nodded. 'They keep trying to tell me it's for the best. Claire… you don't know where she'll be going, do you, my baby?'

The young woman shook her head but she didn't actually say no. 'We're not allowed to say,' she answered. 'You know that, Fiona. The fewer people that know, the better. You just concentrate on yourself now, and try to look forward, not back. You'll be going home soon, won't you, and you can have a fresh start? It'll get easier as time goes on, and you're still very young, aren't you?'

'I shall be eighteen next Thursday,' replied Fiona. 'Then I'll be going home soon afterwards, I suppose.' She knew she didn't sound very enthusiastic about the prospect, and nor was she. She couldn't imagine what sort of a reception would await her back in Leeds.

'Cheer up then, love,' said Claire. 'You'll feel better when you get back with your friends. There's a new girl coming into your room today.'

But Ginny had gone, and Bridget was not very chatty; and Fiona had not formed a close attachment to any of the other girls. She went back to her room later that day, where she would need to stay in bed for a week to make sure that all was well. She was given tablets to deal with the problem of her milk, which would not be needed. Her breasts were sore for a while but the ache passed. She knew it would take longer for the ache in her heart to subside.

Her aunt and uncle were surprised, when they visited her on the Sunday afternoon, to learn that it was all over. They behaved in a cheerful and practical way, and Fiona tried hard not to break down and cry. It was decided that she would be allowed to go home in a fortnight's time, on the last day of May, provided all was well. Once again, her Uncle Donald agreed to take her.

'I'll write and tell your parents about the baby,' said her aunt, 'so you don't need to worry about that. We're relieved that everything went well, Fiona love. I know it's sad for you, but don't forget that Donald and I will always be there for you whenever you need us. You feel like another daughter to us now, so some good has come out of all this, hasn't it? Every cloud has a silver lining, as they say.'

–

The new house that her parents had moved to during her absence felt strange at first, and she did not know the area at all well. It was much nearer to her gran's home, though, and she became a frequent visitor to the elderly lady.

As she had anticipated, her parents made no reference to the baby; it was just as though nothing had happened. They had welcomed her in a friendly enough way when she arrived back with Donald, her father appearing more touched at seeing her again than was her mother. Mary, however, had baked a cake for Fiona's birthday that had taken place the previous week, and Donald, as usual, added a touch of lightness to the little celebration. She was sorry to see him depart the next day.

Her parents had found a new church to attend. 'Not quite the same sort of worship as we've been used to,' said her mother. Nevertheless they went there regularly each Sunday morning and evening, and Fiona was left to her own devices.

It was not long before she saw an advert in the local paper, for an assistant librarian at one of the branch libraries in Leeds. She applied, and was fortunate enough to be appointed to the post. Things were looking up, she reflected; and she made up her mind to concentrate wholeheartedly on her work, and not to look back.

Seventeen

Simon had known right from the start of their relationship that he did not know everything about Fiona. She was keeping something back from him, but he did not enquire too closely about the details of her past life. He considered himself to be a good judge of character and he knew that Fiona was an admirable person. She was kind and sympathetic, concerned for the needs of others, and made friends very easily. He had been attracted by her looks as soon as he had met her, as any normal red-blooded man would be. And on further acquaintance he had realized that she was as good as she was beautiful. He counted himself fortunate that she had been equally attracted to him; not just fortunate but blessed indeed.

He believed that a happy marriage was one of God's richest blessings. His first marriage to Millicent had not been ideally happy, but when Millicent had died suddenly and unexpectedly his grief had been genuine. It was regret, though, as much as sadness; regret that he had not been a better husband.

Simon's parents had taken to Fiona at once when he introduced her to them at their home in Bradford, the house in which Simon and his sister had been born and brought up. They had never really warmed to Millicent, feeling that she was too strait-laced and humourless for their go-ahead, energetic and fun-loving son.

'You've got yourself a real bobby-dazzler this time, lad,' his father said to him when Simon's mother and fiancée were busy in the kitchen. 'She's a pretty lass and no mistake. Not my idea of a vicar's wife, mind – no, sorry, you're a rector, aren't you, not a vicar? – but I reckon you know what you're doing. I hope so, anyroad. She does go to church, doesn't she? There'll be some raised eyebrows if she doesn't.'

'Yes, she attends church regularly, Dad,' replied Simon. 'She's sincere in what she believes, and I'm hoping she'll take a more active part when we're married. I'm determined, though, that she won't be known as "the rector's wife" like Millicent was. Fiona has her own career, and I want her to carry on with it, for a little while at any rate, if she wants to.'

'Yes, no doubt you'll be wanting to start a family though, won't you? Don't leave it too long, lad. Your mother and I would like some more grandchildren. You've met Fiona's folks, I suppose? I guess she's Yorkshire born and bred, same as we are?'

'Yes, she was born in Leeds,' replied Simon, 'and she lived there until she moved to Aberthwaite. She has no parents now. She's not told me a great deal about them. Apparently they were both killed in a coach crash, about nine years ago, I think. She went to live with her grandmother, and when the old lady died she decided to make a fresh start at the library in Aberthwaite. And I'm delighted that she did. She's a wonderful girl, Dad. I'm glad you both like her.'

'Yes, we'll be looking forward to the wedding, quite soon we hope,' said his father. 'Have you fixed a date yet?'

'No, not exactly,' replied Simon. 'Sometime in June, we think. As you say, we don't want to wait too long.'

'No, why should you? Especially as you've got the girl that you really want, and I can see that you have this time… Sorry, maybe I shouldn't have said that, but Millicent was never exactly right for you, was she?'

'No, not at all, Dad. But I've been given another chance and I know it will be right this time.'

'And we're very pleased for you, an' all. I reckon your mother'll be off to Brown Muffs before long to buy a new outfit. You'll be inviting your Aunt Gladys and Uncle Herbert, won't you? And our Chrissie and Tom, of course, and their kids?'

'Yes, Dad,' Simon smiled. 'We'll try not to forget anybody. It's quite a problem knowing who to invite, especially from the congregation. We have to be so careful not to offend anyone.'

–

Simon asked Fiona, soon after the meeting with his parents, about her family and whom she would want to invite to the wedding.

'I don't have many relations,' she said, 'with me being an only child. There's my Aunt Beattie and Uncle Donald up in Northumberland; Beattie is my father's sister. But they're quite elderly now, and it might be too far for them to travel. They were so pleased to hear about our engagement though, so we must invite them. They used to have a farm near Alnwick, but they're retired now… I spent some time with them there once.' She looked pensive for a moment, her eyes misty as she stared unseeingly across the room. 'They were very good to me; in fact, I don't know what I'd have done without them at that time.' There was a moment's silence, then she seemed to become aware of Simon's curious glance. 'I'd been ill, you see,' she explained, 'and… and they looked after me for quite a while whilst I recuperated.'

'So when was that?' asked Simon. 'A long time ago?'

'Yes… It was – let me see – 1951. I was seventeen, and I'd had glandular fever. I was quite poorly actually, but it did me a world of good, staying on the farm. I hope they'll be able to come, because I don't have any more relations, only cousins that I've not kept in touch with. My mother's brother, my Uncle Eddie, and his wife, both died a few years ago.'

'And what about friends?' asked Simon. 'Girls that you knew in Leeds perhaps?'

'I lost touch with most of the girls that I knew at school,' replied Fiona, 'except for my best friend, Diane… and I didn't see her for quite a few years either.'

'Why was that?' asked Simon. He was aware that Fiona was looking a little ill at ease. 'Did you fall out with her, or something like that? You don't need to tell me, though if you don't want to.'

'No… we never fell out,' said Fiona. 'It was when I was ill, you see. Well… whilst I was up there my parents decided to leave the council house we had in Headingley, and they got a transfer to one in Harehills.'

'Oh, I see,' said Simon. 'Why did they decide to move just then?'

'Well… my gran's arthritis was getting worse, so Mum decided she wanted to live nearer to her, to help her with shopping and… and everything. She was a tough old lady though, really, was Gran. She lived till she was ninety.'

'Yes; you were very fond of her, weren't you?' said Simon. Fiona had spoken far more about her grandmother that she had about her parents. He sensed that there might have been a rift between them, but maybe she would tell him about it in her own good time.

'Yes, I loved my gran very much,' she said with a sad smile. 'I suppose I was lucky though, to have her until she was ninety. Anyway, as I was saying… when I went back home to Leeds it was to this new council house… and so I didn't see any of my old friends again.'

Simon nodded. 'I see.' It crossed his mind that it seemed to be an odd thing for Fiona's parents to do, to move house whilst their daughter was away. Not very considerate of them, especially as she had been so ill. It must have been strange for her, going back to a different home, nowhere near to the homes of her former friends. But there were trams and buses in Leeds; why couldn't she have got in touch with them again? There was something here that he didn't understand, but again he kept quiet. He knew that Fiona would tell him just as much as she wanted to, and there was no reason for him to make a mystery of it when maybe there wasn't one.

'I got a job quite soon at a branch library, not too far from our new home in Leeds,' she went on to explain, 'on the strength of my good School Certificate results. I was in the sixth form, you see, the lower sixth, when… when I became ill, and so I missed a lot of schooling. I'd been studying for A-levels; I was supposed to be going to college to train to be a teacher, but I decided to get a job as a librarian instead. And I never regretted it.'

'You could have gone to college later, though, couldn't you?' asked Simon.

Fiona shook her head. 'I'm not sure that I ever really wanted to. It was more my mother's idea than mine, for me to be a teacher. Anyway, it was what Diane did… I was telling you about my best friend, Diane; we were inseparable when we were in the fifth form and the lower sixth. She went to the training college in Bingley and trained to be an infant teacher. She didn't teach for long, though – only about five years – because she married Andy, the lad she'd been going out with when we were at school, and they soon started a family. She's thinking of going back to teaching though, when her children are at school.'

'So you did get in touch with her again then, eventually?'

'Yes… it was when my parents were killed,' said Fiona. 'She read about it in the paper. They were on a church outing in the dales, and the coach collided with a lorry somewhere near Leyburn. A few passengers were killed, including my parents who were sitting near the front, and a lot were injured. It made headlines, of course, at the time. And Diane recognized the names and got in touch with me. She went round to my gran's house because she didn't know our new address. And so… well, that's how we met up again, and we decided to keep in touch.'

'You would have a lot of catching up to do, no doubt,' said Simon.

'Yes, quite a lot,' agreed Fiona. 'It had been about four years since I'd last seen her. And in the meantime she'd done her two years at college and got a teaching post in Leeds. I was surprised to hear that she was still going out with Andy.'

'Yes, I should imagine you would be,' said Simon. 'These boy and girl romances don't always come to anything, do they?'

'Er… no,' said Fiona. 'No, they don't.'

Again he noticed that she looked a little bit uncomfortable. He wondered if Fiona, also, had had a boyfriend whilst she was at school, a friendship, perhaps, that had come to a disappointing end.

She seemed to recover quite quickly though, going on to say, 'Actually, I'm thinking of asking Diane to be my bridesmaid. Well, she'll be matron of honour, won't she, seeing that she's married? I still think of her as my best friend even though I don't see her all that often. Then there's Ginny, another friend who lives up in South Shields. I'd like to invite her and her husband.'

'Is she an old school friend as well?' asked Simon.

'Oh no; she's a girl that I met when I was... when I was staying up in Northumberland. I told you, didn't I, that I stayed with my aunt and uncle when I was ill? Well, Ginny was... she was somebody that they knew, and we got quite friendly because we were about the same age. Ginny's married as well. In fact she's been married to Arthur for ages, since she was eighteen. Their little boy, Ryan – well, he's not little any more, he'll be thirteen – and they've got two daughters as well.' Simon noticed that Fiona seemed to be talking quickly, her words falling over one another, as she told him about her friends from the past, details that she had not mentioned before.

'So there will be quite a few people that you want to invite, won't there? You must invite as many friends as you like, as you don't have many relations. There are quite a few relatives on my side who will have to be invited. Then there are the church folk. That's going to be quite a problem, knowing who to ask and who to leave out. I've told my parents that there'll probably be about fifty guests, all told.'

'It's very good of your parents to offer to pay for the reception and everything,' said Fiona. 'It's usually the bride's parents who foot the bill, isn't it? That's not possible, of course, in my case, but I thought that we might pay for it ourselves. I know some couples do, these days.'

'Let's not talk about money,' said Simon, laughing. 'It's vulgar. Actually, my parents are delighted to do it. They're really charmed with you, my darling, as I knew they would be, and they can see how happy we are together. So… we'll fix the date and get on with the arrangements. I shall ask my friend Timothy, who I met at college, to officiate. Seeing that I can't conduct my own service!' He laughed. 'So you can go ahead and choose your wedding dress. You'll want a traditional white wedding, won't you? A flowing veil and all the trimmings, and perhaps more than one bridesmaid?'

'Oh no, I don't think so,' Fiona replied quickly. 'I was thinking of something more simple, perhaps, and not white. Maybe cream, or pale blue or pink, but not white.'

'Why ever not?' asked Simon. 'You do surprise me. I know you're a very modern sort of girl, but I thought that you'd want a traditional white wedding dress.'

'Oh… well, I'm not twenty-one, am I?' said Fiona, with a shrug and a little laugh. 'I'm thirty-one; I'll be thirty-two by the time we get married. I think I ought to go for something a little simpler perhaps. I'm not bothered about a lot of fuss and palaver. I'm just so happy that you want to marry me, Simon. Sometimes I can scarcely believe it.'

'Well, it's true,' he replied, putting his arms around her and kissing her tenderly, 'and you'd better believe it. But it's your choice, of course. You must wear just what you like. Whatever you choose I know you'll look radiant and beautiful, and I shall be so proud of you.'

Fiona smiled at him. 'Thank you,' she said simply. 'And I shall try my best to be a perfect wife for you. Well, maybe not perfect because none of us are, but I promise that I will try to make you happy and... and be worthy of you.'

Simon shook his head. 'On the contrary, I sometimes wonder if I am worthy of you, my darling.'

–

Simon was, indeed, proud of his new wife on their wedding day. It was as perfect a day as they could have wished for. A cliché of a day, with the sun shining from a cloudless blue sky on to a beautiful radiant bride.

The church was almost full. Nearly every member of the congregation was there whether they had received an invitation or not, to wish their rector and his new wife every happiness and God's richest blessings.

Everyone agreed that Fiona looked lovely in her simply styled dress of deep cream-coloured moiré silk. It was mid-calf length, with a boat-shaped neckline, elbow-length sleeves and a fitted waist with a pleated cummerbund. She wore a tiny matching pillbox hat with a short veil that reached to her shoulders. Her small bouquet was of roses in shades of apricot and gold. Her one bridesmaid, Diane, wore a dress of a similar style in apricot silk, and carried a posy of cream-coloured roses. Fiona's golden hair and fair complexion were a contrast to Diane's dark-brown hair and her slightly olive-tinted skin. Everyone agreed that they were a most attractive pair of young women.

Around fifty people gathered at a country inn on the outskirts of Aberthwaite for the wedding 'breakfast' at two o'clock. Simon was pleased that Fiona's elderly aunt and uncle had managed to make the journey. He noticed that they treated her as a dearly loved daughter, and he decided that they must keep in touch with the couple.

Then there were Diane and Andy and their two children; Ginny and Arthur, the couple from Tyneside, but without their family of three; and the three other members of staff, Fiona's colleagues from the library at Aberthwaite, with their husbands. So Fiona's 'side' was quite well represented despite her lack of close relatives. Simon's friend, Timothy Marsden, made an admirable best man, full of fun and wisecracks despite being 'a man of the cloth'. There was unrestrained banter and high spirits, and showers of confetti as the newly-weds set off for their honeymoon in Simon's Morris Minor car.

'Happy, my darling?' he asked as they drove away from the market town, following the road eastwards across the North York moors to Scarborough.

'Happier than I've ever been in my life,' Fiona told him.

'Same here,' he replied, reaching across and holding her hand for a moment. He felt a deep contentment, knowing that he was truly blessed in this marriage.

–

Simon was not surprised to discover that his new wife was not totally innocent with regard to sexual matters. He knew it was unlikely that an attractive young woman such as Fiona could have reached the age of thirty-two without having had some experience. He wondered if that was the reason she had decided not to wear a conventional white dress – supposedly a sign of virginity – but something, as she had said, 'more fitting'. He was aware, though, that not everyone bothered now about a virginal white dress being a sign of purity. He had conducted several marriages where it was quite obviously not the case.

Their love-making was tender and beautiful, and he knew that they would find fulfilment in that side of their marriage, just as they had each found a soulmate in one another.

He did not yet know everything about Fiona. He guessed that there was something deeply hidden in her past life that she did not feel ready to talk about. But who was he, Simon Norwood – now the Reverend Simon Norwood – to question what might have happened to her? His own past had been far from exemplary. There were incidents that he had not talked about for years, things that he had had cause to regret...

Eighteen

Simon was a clever boy, but he had left school at sixteen, contrary to the advice of his parents, because he liked the idea of an office job and money in his pocket rather than a lengthy course at college or university. He was eighteen when World War Two started, and he joined the RAF almost immediately. He had not been sure of his path in life, but now he could see his way ahead, at least for the immediate future, maybe longer; who could tell?

His first billet as an RAF recruit – an AC2 – was in Blackpool, a resort of which he had fond memories of seaside holidays with his family. It was at the Tower Ballroom where he met the girl, a member of the WAAF, who gave him his first real sexual experience. But she was soon forgotten. He had been immature and gullible, but he knew it was just a fleeting physical attraction.

He decided he must concentrate on his career – for as long as it might last – in the RAF. He had very soon decided that he wanted to train as a navigator. He passed all the relevant tests and interviews, rising quickly through the ranks to AC1, corporal, then sergeant. He was eager to put his new-found knowledge and skills to the test, to be responsible for plotting routes and guiding aircraft to targets in Germany.

His second posting after his initial training was to a camp on the Lincolnshire plain, quite near to the city of

Lincoln. He was to remain there for the duration of the war.

As a vital member of an aircrew he was doing the job for which he had been trained. But as the years went by – 1941, 1942, into 1943 – he, like his colleagues, some of whom were now close friends, wondered how much longer it could go on.

Simon found it hard to dismiss from his mind the horrific sights he had seen. A damaged plane sinking in the dark water of the North Sea with all the crew on board; a bomber and its occupants reduced to a ball of flame by high explosives. The worst of all, to him, was the sight of German cities burning below, knowing that he was, in part, responsible for their destruction.

Each operational tour consisted of thirty missions, then the men were granted a period of rest and recuperation before starting on the next tour. They were all relieved when flight number thirteen was safely over; a superstition, but one to which many of them would admit, insisting on carrying lucky mascots or charms, or St Christopher medals.

Simon had no such lucky charms. He was starting to believe that he must put his trust in a much higher power. His belief in the God and Jesus of his Sunday school days had waned over the years, and he had not said any prayers for a long time, but he was starting to do so quite regularly now as the war droned on with no end in sight.

One afternoon he had spent a while on his own in Lincoln cathedral. It was a place where he felt close to the God who was becoming more real to him day by day, month by month, as the war droned on relentlessly. Leaving the cathedral he stood for a while in contemplation, looking up at the west front where the honey-coloured limestone glowed with a golden light in the afternoon sun.

'A penny for them,' said a voice next to him. He looked round to see one of the WAAFs from the camp standing near to him. He knew her by sight, as he knew many of the young women, but he had never been in her company before. She was an attractive dark-haired girl with rosy cheeks and a pleasant smile.

'Oh, hello there,' he said. 'Yes, I was miles away, wasn't I? I'm always awestruck by the beauty of this place. I've been inside for a little while. I find it helps to clear my mind… and try to make sense of it all.'

'Yes, you sometimes wonder what it's all about, don't you?' said the young woman. 'We haven't been introduced, but you're called Simon, aren't you?'

'Yes, that's right, Simon Norwood. How did you know my name?'

'I heard one of your pals address you,' she explained.

'Oh, I see. And you are…?'

'I'm Yvonne, Yvonne Stevenson.'

By mutual consent, it seemed, they walked away from the cathedral precinct to the cobbled street that led to the town. 'Do you fancy a cup of tea?' asked Simon. 'There's a little cafe I've been to not far from here. They do a good pot of tea and nice cream cakes, too. Well, "mock" cream, I suppose, but it's as good as you can get.'

'Yes, thank you,' said Yvonne. 'Why not?'

They set off, chatting in a companionable manner. The tea shop was an old-fashioned sort of place, one of the town's quaint medieval buildings. The room was small and rather busy but they found an empty table for two at the back of the shop. The round table was covered with a pristine white cloth edged with lace, and the wheel-backed chairs held chintzy cushions. The polished floor was uneven in places, there was a delft rack which held blue and white pottery plates and pewter tankards, and on the walls were pictures of Lincoln in days gone by.

'It's the sort of place that the Yanks think of as "little old England",' Simon remarked as they squeezed themselves into the corner. 'I've seen several GIs here from time to time.'

'Old England indeed,' remarked Yvonne. She sighed. 'It almost makes you believe everything is quite normal, doesn't it?'

'Yes,' agreed Simon. 'That's why I come here. A touch of normality in a world that's gone mad.' They looked at one another, nodding in agreement and understanding.

'So how long have you been at this camp, Yvonne?' asked Simon.

'Just a few weeks,' she replied. 'I was transferred from a camp near to Norwich. I joined up last year when it became compulsory for women of my age... I don't mean that I didn't want to enlist,' she added. 'I'd been thinking of it for a while, but my parents and my boyfriend were not all that keen. Anyway, when they brought in conscription for women I was twenty, so I had no choice.'

'I see,' said Simon. He guessed she would be twenty-one by now, the same age as himself. 'And I guess you're a northerner like me,' said Simon. 'I'm from Bradford, Baildon, to be exact.'

Yvonne told him she came from Manchester. 'You're part of an aircrew, aren't you?' she asked.

'Yes, I'm a navigator,' he replied. 'It's what I wanted to do when I joined up, and I was proud of myself when I got my stripes. But now I find myself hating what we're doing. I guess that a lot of us do really, but we don't talk about it very much. What about you, Yvonne? What job are you doing?'

She told him she was doing clerical work, as she had done back home. She was a shorthand typist, now in charge of her office since her transfer to Lincolnshire.

'Good for you,' said Simon. He had noticed that she had two stripes on her arm.

They stopped talking for a while to concentrate on eating the cream cakes. The cream tasted almost like the fresh variety with melt-in-the-mouth sponge and pastry.

'We'd better be making tracks, hadn't we?' said Simon when they had finished.

'Yes... thank you, Simon,' said Yvonne. 'That was delicious. I shall tell my friends about this place.'

'Maybe we could come again... sometime?' he asked tentatively. He had enjoyed being with her very much; it was a refreshing change to have some feminine company after the time he had spent almost solely with his male companions.

'Yes, I'd like that,' Yvonne agreed, smiling at him in a friendly way.

They made their way down the steep hill that led to the main part of the town. Buses ran from the square to just outside the camp.

'I'm so pleased to have met you,' Simon told her as they sat side by side on the bone-shaking bus. 'I'm glad you stopped to speak to me instead of walking past.'

'You didn't think it was too forward of me?' she asked a little teasingly.

'No, not at all. As I said before; do you think we could meet up again? No strings attached,' he added. 'You said you have a boyfriend, didn't you? I mean just to spend some time together... as friends?'

'Yes, I have a boyfriend,' she replied. 'He's in the Merchant Navy, so I don't see him very often. We've been going out together for a year or so, but we haven't got engaged or anything. We decided to wait until this lot comes to an end. What about you, Simon? Do you have a girlfriend?'

'No, not me.' He smiled. 'I don't really think it's the right time to be making commitments, although I know lots of couples are doing so... Would you like us to meet again, then?'

'Yes, I would, Simon,' she agreed. 'I've made some good friends since I came here, like I did at the last camp. The girls in the hut with me, we all get on well together. But it'll be nice to have a change of company now and again.'

They alighted from the bus and he said goodbye to her just inside the main gates. Their huts were on different sides of the camp. They agreed to meet in the NAAFI in a few days' time.

Simon whistled as he made his way to his hut, feeling more cheerful than he had for ages. What a very nice girl she was, like a breath of fresh air. He told himself, though, that he must make his head rule his heart and not get involved in a romantic entanglement. Yvonne knew the score, though; he guessed she was not the sort of girl to play around when she already had a boyfriend.

As Simon's friendship with Yvonne continued he began to look forward to seeing her more and more. During their times together he was able to forget, if only for a short time, the fears he still encountered with every flight, and the gruesome memories that haunted him in the night when he was unable to sleep.

Yvonne was a good listener, and he was able to talk to her about anything and everything. They met in the NAAFI, and went to dances in the sergeants' mess. Sometimes they walked the mile or so along the country lane to the pub in the village or went into Lincoln to the cinema. Sometimes they were on their own, and other times with a small group of friends.

As the weeks went by, however, Simon began to realize that it was difficult to have a purely platonic relationship with a member of the opposite sex, especially one as attractive and friendly as Yvonne; but he knew it was what he must try to do. He did hold her hand, though, when they walked back from the village late at night. The darkness was a little scary when owls hooted, bats flittered to and fro and small creatures of the night scampered into the bushes.

One night as he said goodbye to her near to her hut he plucked up courage and kissed her gently on the lips. To his surprise she put up her hand and drew his face down to hers. 'Kiss me properly, Simon,' she whispered. He did so, feeling her warmth and eagerness as she responded to him.

'There,' she said. 'There's no harm in that, is there?'

'No, none at all,' he agreed. 'Thanks for tonight, Yvonne. It was just what I needed – the film, I mean – to take my mind off everything.' They had been to see a light-hearted musical starring Fred Astaire and Ginger Rogers. 'I'll see you in a day or two. There's a big op coming up, so I'd better catch up on my beauty sleep,' he grinned.

She smiled at him, very fondly, he thought. 'Yes, see you soon, Simon. I'll be thinking of you; I'll say a little prayer for you. TTFN!' She waved cheerily as she left him.

He knew it would be very easy to fall in love with Yvonne. That kiss had certainly made the earth move for him, but they had agreed 'no strings', and he knew he must try to keep to that.

Nineteen

The next time he saw Yvonne it was a couple of days after the next op – one that had turned out to be the most disastrous yet, for Simon. On returning to base after a raid on Germany the damaged plane had burst into flames and their pilot had been killed.

'What a waste of life! He was such a bloody good skipper,' Simon told her. 'I don't think I shall ever make sense of it all.'

He found it helped, if only a little, to go over the happenings of that dreadful night, and Yvonne was always ready to listen. There had been assistance at the scene almost immediately. An ambulance and fire engine had soon arrived, whilst several of his colleagues were trying to beat back the flames engulfing their pilot, but his burns had been too severe and he had died in hospital the following day. The plane, of course, was completely destroyed. The mid gunner was still in hospital, following concussion, but was expected to make a good recovery.

'Were you very close to your pilot?' asked Yvonne. 'You hadn't known him long, had you?'

'No, it was only our fourth op together. No, we weren't close mates with him. He was a commissioned officer, and the rest of us are just sergeants.' The wastage amongst commissioned officers was so great that many of the non-commissioned men were promoted to what were known as sergeant pilots. 'But he was so calm and level-headed, you couldn't imagine him making a mistake. He must have let his guard slip for a moment. It had all been going so well, then the enemy plane appeared out of the blue. I couldn't believe it when I heard that bloody great bang...'

Dusk was falling as they walked round the airfield arm in arm. 'Shall we go down to the pub and have a drink?' asked Yvonne. 'Or do you want to keep a clear head?'

'The next op isn't for a few more days,' he replied, 'unless there's an emergency. Yes, maybe that's a good idea. And I'll try to talk about something else. No amount of talking can make any difference.'

They met a few friends in the village pub and Simon managed to join in the banter and not to let his sadness and anger show. On the way back to the camp he felt more relaxed than ever in Yvonne's company.

'Feeling better now?' she asked.

'Yes,' he replied. 'A little better... I must admit I'm scared, though, Yvonne. I can't say that to the others, but I can tell you, can't I? The thought of boarding that plane again scares the pants off me. Not the same plane, of course, nor with the same skipper...'

'How many more ops have you to do this time?'

'Oh, four or five, I'm not sure. I've lost count. Then I'll be grounded for a while, thank God.'

'It'll pass,' Yvonne said gently. 'All things pass. Who knows; one big push and then it might be all over?'

'Let's hope so,' said Simon. 'I don't think I can stand much more.'

Neither of them spoke for the next few moments, but as if by mutual agreement they walked towards the shrubbery at the edge of the camp, near to the perimeter fence. They had exchanged a few kisses since that first time, and Simon knew that Yvonne was feeling the same as he did. They were falling in love. He knew now that he could hold back no longer.

They stopped by an oak tree. Yvonne leaned back against it and opened her arms to him. 'Come along, Simon,' she said gently. 'I think you're in need of a spot of comfort, don't you?'

He nodded silently before putting his arms around her and kissing her in the way he had wanted to for so long. It was October and the leaves had fallen from the trees making a soft carpet on the ground. It was a balmy evening, not at all cold for the time of the year. Simon took off his greatcoat that he was wearing and laid it on the ground. He didn't feel guilty that they were breaking their promise to one another to remain just good friends as they made love for the first time. It was a tender and gentle consummation of what they felt, more a quiet need in both of them than a raging passion.

He sighed as he buried his head on her shoulder, stroking her hair and kissing the softness of her neck. 'I know we said we wouldn't... but thank you, Yvonne. I suppose it was bound to happen, wasn't it?'

She smiled at him. 'It was what we both needed. Come along, Simon. We'd better get a move on.' She laughed easily. 'Brush yourself down, or there'll be some comments made.'

They brushed the dry leaves from their clothing, emerging a little sheepishly from the coppice, but there was no one to see them. The camp seemed deserted, but there was more sign of life as they came near to the huts and the main buildings; couples walking arm in arm, as they were, and a group of AC2s returning rowdily from wherever they had been.

He said goodnight to her at the corner of her hut, kissing her gently on the lips. 'Goodnight, love,' he said, using an endearment common to all northerners, but one he had not used before in speaking to Yvonne. 'Sleep tight.'

'Dear Simon,' she said, stroking his cheek. 'You sleep well, too.'

–

Simon felt lighter in spirit as he went to bed that night, not brooding so much about the ill-fated flight that had killed one of his comrades and wounded another. It wasn't as if this had not happened before, but it had affected him more deeply this time. He was realizing more than ever the futility of it all, and wondering how much longer he could continue. How he wished – and prayed – for an end to it all, but there was no sign of a swift end in sight.

He felt, though, as he lay there that he was not alone. 'Thank you, Lord,' he whispered, daring to believe that there really was someone watching over him. He did not dwell on what had happened with Yvonne. He would think about that another time.

–

The next op, two days later, was completed satisfactorily, but the op that took place the following night was to prove fateful for Simon. Again, it was on the homeward flight that they ran into trouble. This time they were aware of the enemy plane suddenly appearing, and after a brief skirmish it was shot down. But Simon had been wounded. The bullet entered his left shoulder, but as he doubled up with the pain and felt the blood start to flow he found himself breathing a sigh of blessed relief that he would be out of it for a while.

Fortunately they were in sight of home. The plane had not been damaged and there were no more casualties amongst the crew. His comrades staunched the flow of blood from what was not a life-threatening wound. It was enough, though, to put him in the camp hospital for the next few days.

It was good to see his mates, and Yvonne, who all came to visit him.

'You jammy devil!' said Steve. 'That's you grounded for a while… Seriously, though, you're due for a respite from it all, aren't you?'

'True enough,' Simon agreed. 'Only two more ops and then I would be due for some leave, but I can't say I'm sorry to be missing them.'

'Poor old Simon,' said Yvonne, kissing his cheek. 'Does it hurt very much?'

'Yes, it's bloody painful,' he answered truthfully. 'But it could have been much worse. There'll be a scar where they got the bullet out, but what does that matter? Thanks for coming to see me. It's strange to be lying here and being waited on.'

'Make the most of it,' said Yvonne. 'You deserve it.'

She didn't stay long, nor did she say 'See you soon,' or any such words; but Simon was quite sure he would see her again.

A few days later, when he was discharged from the hospital, he was asked to report to the Wing Commander. He was told that after his leave, which was due immediately, he was to be taken off flying duties. When he returned to the camp in two weeks' time he was to be an instructor, teaching new recruits who were aiming to be navigators. He felt as though it was an answer to his prayers.

There was hardly time to say goodbye to his mates and to Yvonne. He caught up with her in the NAAFI to tell her his good news, but they were unable to spend much time together as she had promised to go out with some of her friends later that evening and she did not want to let them down.

'Good luck, Simon,' she said. 'You deserve a break if anyone does. Enjoy your leave... and I'll be seeing you.' She kissed him fondly but without a great deal of passion, giving a cheery wave as she went out of the door with her friends.

He felt a little deflated. It would have been good to spend the evening with her, but they were not beholden to one another, and there was the boyfriend in the Merchant Navy that she never mentioned any more.

He spent a little more time with his mates before going back to his hut and packing his kitbag ready for departure the next morning. His parents did not know he was coming home so soon, although they knew about his injury. It would be a nice surprise for them when he arrived, and he was looking forward very much to seeing them again.

–

Simon enjoyed his leave and the welcome rest and relaxation. It was good to see his parents again, and his sister, who came home from the farm where she was working as a land girl. He found, though, as the time drew near for him to return to camp that he was looking forward immensely to seeing Yvonne again.

On his return he was relocated to a different hut where he would be in charge of a group of AC2s, several of whom would be amongst the trainee navigators that he would instruct each day. He met his new room-mates, unpacked his bags and settled in, and after the evening meal he made his way to the NAAFI, hoping to see Yvonne again. He could not see her when he entered the room, so he sat and chatted with a group of his old flying mates, catching up on what had happened during his absence. His eyes kept straying towards the door, looking out for the young woman he was now thinking of as his girlfriend. In a little while a group of Yvonne's friends came in; Phyllis, Mavis and Eileen, all of whom he had met before. He was expecting Yvonne to follow, but she did not appear.

The trio of girls sat at a table, then Mavis got up and went to the counter. 'Excuse me,' Simon said to his pals. 'I'll just go and see if Yvonne is around.'

He expected a few meaningful guffaws or sly remarks, but the men were silent and he saw Steve and Andy glance warily at each other. He crossed the room and sat down next to Phyllis and Eileen. They greeted him in a friendly way, but he noticed a glance pass between them, as he had with the men.

'Hi there, Simon. Enjoyed your leave?'

'We've missed your smiling face. It's not the same without you.'

'Hello there,' he said. 'Yes, I've had a good rest more than anything, but it's nice to be back. Er… is Yvonne around? I thought she would be with you.'

They seemed ill at ease as they looked at one another. 'As a matter of fact… Yvonne isn't here now,' said Phyllis.

Simon frowned. 'What do you mean, not here? Has she gone on leave? Or… she's not ill, is she?'

'No, she's been transferred to another camp,' said Eileen. 'She went a few days ago, but we don't know where she's gone. She didn't say, or maybe she didn't know.'

'But she's only been here – what? – five months or so. I don't understand.'

'No, neither do we,' said Phyllis. 'She was rather cagey about it, I must admit.'

Mavis returned with a tray holding three mugs of coffee and three Kit-Kat biscuits. 'Hello, Simon,' she said. 'Oh dear! I should have got a drink for you. Sorry, I hadn't seen you there.'

'No, thanks,' said Simon. 'I won't be stopping. They've just been telling me about Yvonne.'

'Oh… yes, I see.' Mavis gave him a sympathetic smile. 'I'm sorry, Simon. Actually… I did ask her if she had a message for you, but she said no.'

'Is that all she said?' asked Simon, feeling very puzzled and disappointed.

'Well… what she actually said was, "No, I don't think so. It's probably best this way." And the next day she'd gone. It was a shock to us as well.'

'I suppose that's that then,' Simon shrugged. He paused before saying, 'We were just good friends, you know, Yvonne and me. We never intended to get serious, but I must admit I was getting very fond of her.' He stopped then; there was no need to give any explanation to Yvonne's friends. They were looking at him with concern. He smiled wryly. 'It's just one of those things,

I suppose. Thanks for telling me anyway. I'll see you around.'

He didn't feel like returning to his mates. It was November, and the night was cold and still with just a faint glow from the moon. He made his way along the country lane that led to the village pub. He didn't want any company save his own, and there was no one there that he recognized.

The whisky he ordered soon disappeared, followed by his usual pint of bitter, then another in quick succession. He was brooding about how much he would miss Yvonne. What had gone wrong? Had her sudden departure got something to do with him? Maybe she was regretting what they had done, although she had been just as willing as he was to take that step. Maybe she had heard from her boyfriend and was feeling guilty about him, Simon. Had she asked for another transfer, to get herself out of a difficult situation? He would probably never know, or ever see her again.

He could not remember ever feeling so bewildered and dejected. He was about to order a third pint. Why not drink himself into oblivion? What the hell did it matter? Then something brought him to a halt. He closed his eyes; he felt decidedly woozy, but the commonsensical part of his brain told him he would be unable to get back to camp if he drank any more. This was not the answer to his problem. What was it all about, anyway? A young woman with whom he had had a wartime friendship. Yvonne had simply brought it to an end, and he had to get over it.

Twenty

Simon was twenty-four when the war came to an end. He was demobbed from the RAF in the late summer of 1945.

His position at the estate agency in Bradford was still open for him, should he want to return to it. He felt somewhat guilty in doing so as he had already made a decision about his future career. He saw it as more of a 'calling', though, than a career that he had actively chosen. Simon knew that he wanted to enrol at a theological college and train to be what was known as a 'Clerk in Holy Orders'; in other words a parish priest or a vicar, as they were more commonly called in the Church of England, starting initially as a curate. He made it clear to his employers that he was working there only on a temporary basis.

It was too late for the admission of 1945, but in 1946 he was pleased to learn that he had been successful in his application and interview and was to start his training in September at a college in North Yorkshire.

No one was more surprised than the members of his own family.

'By heck, lad, that's a turn up for the book!' his father said in his usual forthright way. 'I must confess I've never seen you as a "Holy Joe".'

'And nor will I ever be, Dad,' replied Simon. 'I've had a change of heart. Some might call it a conversion, but it wasn't a sudden thing with me. I've come to realize, though, that I had no real aim in life before I joined the RAF. I was just… drifting.'

'You were only young though, Simon,' said his father. 'You were no different from many young men of your age. I knew you would settle down eventually and make something of your life. It's just rather a surprise, that's all, to think of you being a vicar.'

'I'm sure he'll be a very good vicar,' said his mother loyally as they drank their customary cup of tea when they had finished their Sunday dinner. 'He knows how to talk to people, and how to listen to them as well, as though he's really interested. My friends at the Mothers' Union were thrilled to bits when I told them, Simon. It's not every young man who goes out of his way to talk to his mother's friends the way you do.'

'Thanks for the vote of confidence, Mum.' Simon smiled. 'That's part of it, of course. Learning to get on well with folk.'

'Aye, I know you've got the gift of the gab,' laughed his father. 'Our parson's not without it neither. I must say it was a damned good sermon he preached this morning. Oh… sorry! A jolly good sermon I should have said. I reckon I'd best watch my language now, hadn't I?'

'Don't be so damned silly, Dad,' said Simon laughing.

–

Simon was twenty-seven when he had finished his training. He had kept in touch with Mike Sedgewick, his padre friend from his RAF days. Mike had been very pleased at the choice of career Simon had made. He was still in the same parish in Sheffield, and by a stroke of good fortune – or maybe it was fate – he was in need of a curate just at the time that Simon was seeking his first placement.

Simon found suitable 'digs' with a family in the parish and settled down well in his new surroundings and his new profession. He was popular in the parish – as good-looking young curates always tended to be – with the older as well as the younger women; and with the men, too, who found him down-to-earth and approachable.

Millicent Hogarth was the daughter of the family in whose home he had found lodgings. At twenty-eight she was a year older than Simon and she worked as chief buyer at a bookshop in the city. It was inevitable that they should become friendly. They shared a love of literature and they worked quite closely together in the church where Millicent was a Sunday school teacher and a keen and active member of the parochial church council.

After he had been in the parish for several months it seemed to be a foregone conclusion to everyone – the members of the congregation, Millicent's parents and, of course, Millicent herself – that the couple would discover that they were right for one another. Simon, indeed, had found that the liking he had for her had turned into fondness, and then to what he supposed might be love. They got on well together, they had interests in common, their commitment to the church being the one of primary importance. She would make, he thought, a most suitable wife. Although he might not have been aware of it, he was attempting to make up for his past indiscretions, proving to himself and his parishioners that he intended to live an exemplary life.

Mr and Mrs Hogarth had taken to Simon right from the start and saw him as an ideal husband for their daughter; a far better and more suitable match than they had dared to wish for. The young women of the parish, many of whom had harboured their own hopes of gaining the attention and affection of the new young curate, were to be doomed to disappointment. In the autumn of 1948, a year after he had moved to the parish, the engagement of the couple was announced. They were married in the summer of the following year.

If the vicar, the Reverend Mike Sedgewick, had any doubts or reservations about the match he felt it was not his place to say so. He knew that Simon was not without experience as far as the fair sex was concerned; and there was no doubt that Millicent Hogarth would make him an admirable wife. An ideal vicar's wife when the time came for him to have a parish of his own.

The couple moved to a small house provided for them by the church and they stayed there in Sheffield for the next three years. It was rather a long time for a curacy but Mike and Simon worked well together and neither of them really wanted to break up the partnership.

Simon knew, though, that the time would come when he had to move on. In 1951 they moved to Hull where Simon started his second curacy. By this time he was thirty years of age, and Millicent was thirty-one. They had hoped that she would conceive and bear a child, but time after time they were disappointed. Then, in 1952, they were delighted when, at last, Millicent discovered that she was pregnant.

Their joy, alas, was short-lived as she suffered a miscarriage five months later. They were told that the child would have been a boy. It was a bitter disappointment to Simon. He had badly wanted this child for both their sakes. He was aware that cracks were beginning to appear in the fabric of their marriage, and he had hoped that a baby might bring them closer together again. There was more disillusionment ahead, however. Millicent had suffered greatly with the miscarriage, and they were told that it would not be advisable for her to have any more children.

Simon was disappointed, not only because of his hope that a child would bring some purpose back to their marriage, but also because like most men he wanted children of his own. He would have been overjoyed to be the father of a son. What man didn't want to have a son? Or a daughter, of course; that would be great, too. One of each eventually he had hoped, or more. Now his wishes were not to be fulfilled.

Millicent, too, was disappointed, but not as much as he had expected her to be. After the first sadness and bitterness that she showed on hearing the doctor's advice, she then seemed to accept it as inevitable, 'just one of those things'.

Simon continued as a curate until 1959 when he was appointed as rector of St Peter's church in Aberthwaite. There was a certain mellowing in his relationship with Millicent at that time. Simon was pleased at his promotion, determined to do all he could to be a good leader of his new flock. He understood that the previous rector had been old and rather set in his ways. He knew that Millicent was pleased for him too, and she seemed happier at the move to North Yorkshire than she had been for several years.

They proved popular as a couple in the parish. Millicent stood her ground with the somewhat implacable ladies of the congregation who had had all their own way in the running of the church activities for too long. The two of them worked well together and the church started to develop and prosper under their leadership. New innovations that he introduced, such as women in the church choir, and a Youth Group, were accepted after an initial resistance. He was gratified when people told him that they had noticed a revival in the church after a period of stagnation.

On a personal level Simon knew that his marriage was not all that he would like it to be; but Millicent seemed happier than she had been at any time since their very early days together. He realized that they must try to appear to others as a devoted couple. He was, however, still a young man and he regretted deeply the lack of any real spontaneous love within their marriage.

It was a great shock when Millicent was taken ill, very suddenly, in the winter of 1962. There had been an outbreak of flu in the town and she had succumbed to it more severely than many others. It was an even greater shock when it developed into pneumonia and she died as a result.

The people of the congregation were very sympathetic and helpful. They had liked Millicent well enough, but she had never evoked the same respect and affection that they had felt for their rector. Simon was touched by their concern for him. He did not need to put on an act as he was genuinely sad at Millicent's death. He had been very fond of her; he had believed at first that he truly loved her. They had been married for thirteen years and her death would leave a void in his life, mainly because he was so used to her being there.

He noticed with wry amusement the attention of the women of the parish, especially the younger unmarried ones. He accepted their offers of help and their more material offerings of cakes, pies and home-made scones gratefully but impartially. He had worked closely, even before Millicent's death, with a nice young widow called Ruth Makepeace. She was secretary to the church council, and they had come to know one another quite well. He had wondered for a while whether he might take their friendship a stage further. He suspected that she would not be unwilling, and because of this he knew he must be very careful not to encourage any reciprocal feelings she might have until he was quite sure of his own.

He came to the conclusion that although he liked her very much it would never develop into anything more than a friendship. Admittedly, she would be an ideal clergyman's wife; the church, together with her work as a schoolteacher, was her main interest in life. She was attractive in a quiet way, friendly and homely, and she was the same age as himself. He knew, though, that the vital spark that should attract him to her was missing. He knew now that it had never really been there in his relationship with Millicent either, and he must not make the same mistake again. He sensed her disappointment and a certain coolness towards him as she began to realize his feelings – or lack of them – towards her.

Fiona Dalton came on the scene unexpectedly, miraculously, like a burst of sunshine on a dull day. And Simon knew at once that this was the young woman for whom he had been waiting for so long.

Twenty-One

Fiona had made up her mind to be a good wife to Simon in every way. She was a reasonable cook as she had lived on her own for quite a while, and before that she had done the shopping, cooking and household chores for herself and her grandmother.

She and Simon had decided that it might be better if she worked only part-time at the library. She did not mind forfeiting her post as chief librarian as she now had far more responsibilities. She found she was able to manage the part-time work quite easily after the long hours she had been used to working. And this, of course, left her with time to help Simon with his church work.

Fiona knew that this was expected of her, not so much by her husband as by the members of the congregation. St Peter's was not a large enough parish to warrant the extra help of a curate, and so the new rector's wife was seen by many to provide the ideal solution. She was eager to help in any way she could, but Simon had told her right from the start that she was not to be regarded as an unpaid curate, which was the lot of many clergy wives.

She volunteered to be a Sunday school teacher. The attendance on Sunday afternoons in 1965 was still encouraging. Between fifty and sixty boys and girls met in the church hall at 2.30 each Sunday, dividing into small groups of six or eight, each with their own teacher.

The groups were strictly segregated; it had never been considered ideal to have boys and girls together although that was the norm at day schools. Fiona – somewhat cowardly she felt – opted for a group of eight- and nine-year-old girls, thinking that they might be easier to control.

She had also joined the choir at the suggestion of Henry Tweedale, the organist and choir master. She enjoyed the Friday-night meetings when they practised the hymns for the following Sunday, and often an anthem for inclusion in one of the services, either Matins or Evensong.

Simon had also suggested – although he had not insisted – that she should take over the position of enrolling member of the Mothers' Union.

'It's usually held by the rector's wife,' he told her. 'Mrs Bayliss and her cronies will have to recognize you as the leader whether they like it or not. I suggest that you attend a couple of meetings and see how things are run. You may have ideas of your own about changes you might like to make. Then you could take over in a month or so, perhaps?'

Fiona was very unsure. She reluctantly attended the next meeting. It was the first meeting of the autumn session as they had a break during the month of August.

Mrs Ethel Bayliss was in charge of proceedings and she welcomed the rector's wife in quite a cordial manner, although Fiona still felt that the woman was looking critically at her short skirt and bare legs. It was a warm early September day and Fiona was making the most of the summer, still wearing her light dresses and fashionable sandals which showed her painted toenails. Most of the women, though, she noticed, were clad as though it was already autumn, in tweed suits or in coats and the inevitable hats.

'We are pleased to welcome Mrs Norwood, our new rector's wife, at the meeting this afternoon,' said Mrs Bayliss. 'Pardon me! I should, of course, have said our rector's new wife.' She gave a little laugh. 'Simon, if I may be so bold as to use his Christian name, has been with us for quite a long time, but Mrs Norwood is still a relative newcomer to the parish. Anyway, we welcome you, Mrs Norwood, and hope that you will enjoy our fellowship this afternoon.'

'Thank you… and please call me Fiona,' she replied. Mrs Bayliss's condescending smile seemed to suggest that her request would fall on stony ground, at least in some quarters.

They started with a hymn, 'Fight the Good Fight with all thy Might', which Fiona hoped was not to be a prediction of her future dealings with the Mothers' Union. Mrs Blanche Fowler played the piano, the cherries on her hat bobbing merrily in time to the music.

There was a short prayer led by Mrs Bayliss, then the ladies all joined in saying the Mothers' Union prayer which Fiona, to her embarrassment, did not know. Mrs Bayliss pointedly handed her a card with the prayer printed on it. She vowed that she would learn it before the next meeting.

Mrs Bayliss then introduced the speaker for the afternoon, a lady from a local flower-arranging club, who showed them how to make an attractive display with just the minimum of flowers, enhanced with the use of ferns and any greenery that might be available in one's own garden. She made it all look very easy. The most important item, Fiona gathered, was the block of oasis.

She decided that she would purchase some and have a go when she had the time.

After a final hymn they all adjourned to the other end of the hall where cups of tea and biscuits were being handed out from the kitchen behind the serving hatch. A couple of the ladies had tiptoed out during the singing of the final hymn to prepare the refreshments.

Fiona sat with Joan Tweedale at one of the little tables dotted around the room. 'Well now, how are you enjoying it?' asked Joan with a grin.

Fiona sighed. 'I feel so-o-o intimidated,' she replied. 'For a start I didn't know the prayer and I felt such a fool! Why didn't someone warn me?'

'Sorry!' said Joan. 'I never thought about it.'

'It's not your fault,' said Fiona, 'Simon should have told me; on the other hand I don't suppose he has much to do with the Mothers' Union. I enjoyed the flower arranging though. What happens? Do they have a different speaker each time?'

'More or less, on a variety of topics. Or occasionally one of the members might give a talk. Millicent used to speak, now and again. It's more or less expected of the rector's wife. Oh... sorry! Does that frighten you a bit?'

Fiona knew that the horror must have shown on her face. 'Quite frankly, it scares the pants off me!' she admitted. 'Actually, I've already decided, Joan, that I can't take this job on – the enrolling member thing. I'm going to tell Simon. From what I can see, Mrs Bayliss is in her element, and woe betide anyone who tries to oust her from her position! I don't want to make an enemy for life.'

'Well, if that's how you feel then I do understand,' said Joan. 'I know old Ma Bayliss can be rather overpowering, but some of us don't like to think that she's getting all her own way. To be honest, I only come because I feel it's expected of me as the organist's wife, although I shall enjoy coming a lot more now that you're here. The shop is closed on a Wednesday afternoon, of course – half day closing in Aberthwaite – so I've no excuse not to come.'

'Yes, I've noticed that you are the youngest one here,' said Fiona. The majority of the women seemed to be in their sixties or seventies, with one or two exceptions. Apart from Mrs Bayliss and Mrs Fowler, the older contingent consisted of Mrs Halliwell – renowned for her home-made cakes; the two sisters, Miss Mabel Thorpe and Mrs Gladys Parker, who both seemed to be giving Fiona the cold shoulder; and several others, some of whose names she knew but by no means all of them. She knew that it was one of her requirements, as the rector's wife, to know everyone's name. What a daunting task! To Fiona they all tended to look alike; of a 'certain age', grey-haired, many of them bespectacled, and wearing tweed coats and hats. 'Don't any of the younger women come?' she asked.

'They're not able to attend in the afternoons,' Joan replied. 'Most of the younger age group – well, forties and fifties – are working. Ruth and Heather are teachers, and most of the others who might come have jobs. Then there are the much younger ones, of course, but they're looking after their children or meeting them from school. Anyway, I dare say they would find the idea of the Mothers' Union a bit off-putting.'

Fiona nodded in agreement. She was remembering that in the church she had attended in Leeds there had been a Young Wives' group. She had never known much about it except that it was there. It hadn't concerned her as she was a teenager, and neither had her mother been part of it. Mary had been well into her fifties by that time, and had probably considered herself too old; she recalled that her mother had joined the Mothers' Union. A Young Wives' group… now there was a thought…

She decided to broach the idea, tentatively, to Joan before mentioning it to her husband. 'There's nothing really for the younger women, is there?' she began.

'No, not really,' said Joan, 'but as I've told you, they're too busy in other ways, especially those with children. There's a crèche, though, on Sunday mornings, so that they can attend the morning service if they wish to. The young mothers take it in turns to look after the kiddies in the church hall. It seems to work quite well. We've actually had a few husbands coming along to the services as well, since your Simon came on the scene. Before that I'm afraid it was a mainly elderly congregation, and mostly women, apart from the few men who were actively involved.'

'Like Mr Bayliss and Mr Fowler, and your husband, of course?'

'Yes, and a few more who were on the church council. But we've got several younger men now who are very helpful. There's Graham Heap; he works in a bank and he volunteered to be our treasurer. And jolly good one he is as well. Now, he's the exception to the rule; he attends church regularly but we don't see his wife very much. She's called Gillian, and he brings her along on special occasions, but apart from that she seems to keep herself to herself.'

Fiona was thoughtful for a moment. 'There may be others as well, like her, who would come along if there was something to interest them.' She laughed a little uneasily. 'I mustn't say that to Simon! I know he makes the services as interesting as he can but – well, you know what I mean – something else, a more social occasion where younger women could get to know one another, then they might be encouraged to come along to Sunday services. Those who don't already attend, I mean! This Gillian – she's quite young, I take it? I know who Graham is, and Simon thinks very highly of him as the treasurer.'

'Yes; Gillian's in her late thirties I would say, the same as Graham. She works at the hospital, in the office. There again, afternoons would be out for her.'

'Actually, I was thinking more of an evening meeting,' said Fiona. 'Has no one ever thought of forming a Young Wives' group? I'm surprised Simon hasn't mooted the idea. Or his first wife… er… Millicent?'

'Oh, she was heart and soul in the Mothers' Union,' said Joan. 'I don't suppose it occurred to her. Yes… it might not be a bad idea. Have you mentioned it to Simon?'

'No, I've only just thought of it. I told you, I'm scared to death of treading on Mrs B's toes, and this would be something different, just for the younger women. She couldn't get her claws into that, could she?'

Joan laughed. 'She might well try! No, quite seriously I don't think she would dare. I think it's a brilliant idea. There's just one snag though… The word "wives". We don't want to exclude the young women who are not married, do we?'

'No, of course not,' said Fiona. 'But it doesn't need to be a problem, does it? The Mothers' Union doesn't exclude women who aren't mothers does it? Millicent wasn't one, and neither is Miss Parker, and there must be others. Perhaps we could call it the Young Wives and Friends' group, like they do at the schools. It's usually called the PTFA now isn't it – parents, teachers and friends – instead of PTA as it used to be?'

'Actually, it was a teacher I was thinking of,' said Joan. 'Ruth Makepeace; she's a widow now, so she has been a wife; but I wouldn't want her to feel she wasn't welcome, especially as her friend, Heather, would no doubt come along.'

'Ruth… yes,' said Fiona thoughtfully. 'I've not got to know her very well. She seems rather shy, although I don't see why she should be. She has an important post at the school, hasn't she?'

'Yes, she's in charge of the infant department. It doesn't follow though that she should be just as confident in the company of older people. Yes, Ruth is rather reticent at times. It will be a good chance for you to get to know her better; for us all to get to know one another better.' Joan clasped her hand. 'You go for it, girl! I'm sure Simon will be delighted that you've come up with such a good idea.'

Their conversation was interrupted by Mrs Bayliss appearing at their table. She sat down, leaning towards Fiona and smiling in a friendly but still rather condescending way. 'We're so pleased you've come along to our little meeting today, dear,' she said. 'Have you enjoyed it?'

'Very much so, Mrs Bayliss,' said Fiona. 'I was rather ignorant about the Mothers' Union, I must admit. I can see now what a worthwhile organization it is for the possibly… more mature women; mature in age, I mean. I noticed it doesn't seem to attract the younger element.'

'Oh, they could come along if they wished to; they would be made welcome just as you have been, my dear,' said Mrs Bayliss airily. 'But they're mainly tied up with other concerns – looking after their children, of course –

and they might well find us a little too... er... traditional in outlook, but that's how the members like it.'

'Perhaps so,' replied Fiona. 'Maybe if I could persuade some of the younger women to come along we could start to look at some things differently. Liven the meetings up a bit. More modern hymns perhaps, for a start?' Fiona really had little intention of doing so. She knew she was being rather naughty, but she had felt herself bristling at the way the older woman had so condescendingly called her 'dear'. It wouldn't do any harm for her to wonder if she was about to be ousted from her position of authority. 'I understand that my predecessor, Millicent, was in charge until she died so suddenly,' she continued. 'I know that Simon was very grateful to you for taking over in the absence of a rector's wife.'

'Oh, I was no stranger to the job,' replied Mrs Bayliss hurriedly. 'I'd done it for several years after the old rector's wife passed away, until Millicent came. Of course she was much older than you are, dear, and she very quickly got into the way of how we run things. You will find that the ladies will not want to go along with newfangled ideas... But we do hope that you will join us again sometime, Mrs Norwood.'

'Yes, I certainly will.' Fiona smiled agreeably. 'And I shall make sure I know the prayer next time.'

'Oh yes; I'm so sorry, dear. I didn't mean to put you in a spot. I felt sure your husband would have put you in the picture.'

'Well, he didn't,' smiled Fiona. 'I shall have words with him when I get home.'

'Don't be too cross with him, dear.' Mrs Bayliss looked at her reprovingly. 'He is a very busy man, you know.'

'Yes, I do know,' countered Fiona. 'Don't worry, I was only joking.'

'Well, you took the wind out of her sails, all right,' commented Joan as Mrs Bayliss left them.

'I had my tongue in my cheek,' said Fiona, grinning. 'I shall be as nice as pie the next time I see her to make up for it. I just wanted to give her something to think about. I say… do you think I should give them a hand in the kitchen with the washing and all that?'

'No, why should you?' said Joan. 'You're an honoured guest today. Besides, they have a rota; it's my turn next time. Mrs B is always there though, to make sure that things are done properly. You could go and have a word with the speaker, though. I'm sure she would be delighted to meet the rector's wife.'

'Oh, glory be!' Fiona laughed. 'I still haven't got used to my official role. To tell you the truth, I haven't really known many clergy wives, and I feel that I don't quite fit the bill.' She was remembering, suddenly, the vicar's wife back in Leeds, Hannah Cruikshank, her mother's great friend and mentor. She hastily pushed the unwelcome thought to the back of her mind.

'Don't talk daft!' said Joan. 'You're great; just what we needed. Off you go and do your duty.'

The lady from the local flower club, aptly named Mrs Gardner, was, indeed, delighted to talk with Fiona. She was sitting with Mrs Fowler and Mrs Halliwell; and they all smiled welcomingly as Fiona sat down at their table.

'What a refreshing change to meet such a young and pretty vicar's wife,' said Mrs Gardner. 'I've done quite a few talks in the area, and at all the churches and chapels I've visited the clergy are near retiring age, and their wives too, of course. That's not meant as a criticism – we all get older eventually, don't we? – but I'm sure the congregation here must be delighted with you.'

'Yes, so we are,' said Blanche Fowler, patting Fiona's hand. 'We're very pleased you've come along today... Fiona.' Her smile and her comments were obviously sincere, and Fiona felt a lump in her throat at such unexpected praise.

'Yes, you're doing very well, my dear,' said Mrs Halliwell, and this time Fiona did not find the use of the word at all patronizing. After all, these women, on the whole, were thirty years older than she was, even more, and she must seem like a schoolgirl to many of them. It was up to her to prove that it was not so; that she was a mature woman with her own ideas.

–

'Well, how did you get on, darling?' asked Simon, greeting her with a kiss as she came through the door.

'All right, I think,' she replied. 'Most of the women made me welcome, and I enjoyed the flower demonstration. But I didn't know the Mothers' Union prayer, and I felt such a fool, Simon.'

'Oh dear! Sorry...' he said. 'I forgot all about it. I don't go to the meetings all that often. Sometimes I'm invited to give a talk, but apart from that I leave them alone. How did you get on with Mrs B?'

Fiona didn't answer for a moment. Then, 'Listen, Simon,' she began. 'It would never work, me taking over that enrolling member thing. She resents me, I know she does.'

'Oh, come on now, love. I'm sure she doesn't resent you. She doesn't like change, that's all. She was the same when Millicent took over, but she very soon realized it was the way it had to be.'

'But it's different now, Simon. She's already pointed out to me that Millicent was a lot older than I am, and presumably much more capable. No, I could never get her to give up her position for me, nor do I want to. Look, come and sit down. I'll make us a cup of tea, then I'll tell you all about it. I've had an idea…'

Simon listened as she told him about the idea she had already discussed with Joan. 'Provided you agree, of course,' she said. 'You're the boss! I'm afraid I was rather naughty, though. I may have given the impression to Mrs B that I would like to see a few changes. Honestly, Simon; those hymns! "Fight the good fight" and "Jesus shall reign where e're the sun". They came out of the ark! We used to sing "Jesus shall reign" at day school; every Monday, I seem to remember.'

'That's probably why they choose these old hymns,' answered Simon. 'They're familiar and easy to sing, never mind that the words might be rather archaic. Good old "Ancient and Modern".'

'Ancient and stodgy, more like!' retorted Fiona. 'Sorry, Simon. I'm being contrary, aren't I? It wasn't all that bad. I told you, I quite enjoyed it. Mrs Fowler and Mrs Halliwell were really nice to me. Blanche actually called me Fiona. I feel I've made a breakthrough there. But it's Mrs Bayliss; she rubs me up the wrong way and I don't want to make things worse. She'll have to stay in charge… please, Simon.'

'Of course, darling; I understand. I would never make you do anything you're not sure about. And this idea of yours about a Young Wives' group; I think it's really great. I can't think why nobody's thought of it before.'

228

'Probably because they're all too busy, that's why. And they would have needed somebody to take the lead, which I'm willing to do. I feel it would be something new and different, and it might attract some of the younger women who are not really involved at the moment.'

'You mean we should include those who are not regular church attenders? I'm all for that. My one quarrel with the Mothers' Union – although I would never dare to say so – is that it's rather a closed shop, for church members only. There's just one little problem though, Fiona. The word "wives"; that would be making it too exclusive, wouldn't it? We don't want anybody to feel that they're not wanted.'

'We've already thought of that, Joan and I,' said Fiona. 'We thought it could be Young Wives and Friends. That would include anyone, single ladies or widows. Joan mentioned Ruth Makepeace. She would probably come along with Heather Milner; I've noticed they're very good friends.'

'Yes, we must certainly include Ruth,' said Simon. 'She's such a good worker for the church. I don't know how she manages to cope with being secretary to the church council as well as her job at the school.'

'She has no husband to look after; maybe that's why,' observed Fiona. 'She's a war widow, isn't she?'

'Yes, her husband was killed in the D-Day landings; it was very tragic; they hadn't been married very long. I didn't know her then, of course. It was after we came to the parish that she took on the secretary's job, so I... well, Millicent and I... got to know her quite well.'

Fiona noticed that Simon always seemed a little ill at ease when Ruth Makepeace was mentioned. She wondered now, not for the first time, if there had been something between her husband and Ruth before she, Fiona, came on the scene. But she decided not to enquire. After all, she had not been entirely truthful about her past life – far from truthful, in fact. She had never told any out and out lies, but she had been guilty of keeping silent about a great deal. Even now, when she knew Simon so much better and believed that he might understand, she could not bring herself to tell him her shameful secret. That was how her parents had made her feel, that it was a shameful thing, so much so that they had moved away from their church rather than admit it to anyone. That was what held her back. What would the church members here at St Peter's think about it, even if her husband might understand? These feelings came upon her from time to time, quite unexpectedly, as they had done now as she thought about her husband and Ruth Makepeace.

Simon, however, didn't seem to notice her preoccupation. It had only been of a few seconds' duration as the memories raced through her mind. She went on quickly to say that the meetings would, of course, have to be in the evening so that those with children and those who went out to work could attend.

'And to make it more of a social occasion – not too formal – what about meeting here at the rectory?' suggested Simon. 'You could use the lounge; it's plenty big enough. And I really feel that we don't make enough use of the rectory. We have an occasional business meeting here, but most of the time it's just the two of us. Of course I'm hoping that it won't always be just the two of us...' He smiled at her lovingly, questioningly, with his head on one side.

'So do I, Simon,' she smiled back. 'But first things first, eh? Let's see if we can get this Young Wives – and Friends

– group off the ground. What a brilliant idea to meet here instead of the church hall. It will be so much more homely and comfortable. I'll make a list of all the young – well, youngish – women that I know, and perhaps we could get some leaflets printed to advertise it...' She was beginning to feel quite excited at the project, at getting to grips with something that was all her own idea.

Twenty-Two

In just over a month's time the new Young Wives and Friends' group was up and running. The first meeting took place in the spacious lounge of the rectory towards the end of October. There were ten young women present, which Fiona felt was quite a good number to start with, and there might be others as time went on. The ten who were there all had some connection with St Peter's church. There were, of course, many other young women in the area, but it was felt that it would not be fair to encroach upon the other churches in the district, such as the Methodists and the Roman Catholics.

Fiona was pleased to see that Gillian Heap, the church treasurer's wife, had come along. Fiona, after having had a word with Graham, had gone along to their home to talk to Gillian and to invite her to join the new group. She had learnt the reason for Gillian's reticence regarding the church, something that Graham had not divulged.

Gillian had made Fiona very welcome in their sitting room whilst Graham and their two teenage children were doing the washing up after their evening meal.

'You've got them well trained,' Fiona observed with a laugh. 'I didn't realize you had any children. I know Graham, of course, and we would like to know you better, Gillian, if you would consider joining us.'

'Yes…' said Gillian. 'I would like to, really I would. You see, the reason I don't come to church with Graham…'

'That's not necessary,' Fiona interrupted. 'We don't want the group to be what my husband calls a closed shop. Whether you attend church or not you are still welcome.'

'Let me explain,' said Gillian. 'I was a Roman Catholic, you see, before I married Graham. I suppose that's how I still think of myself, although I don't go to Mass or anything any more. When Graham and I got married – we lived in Barnsley then – I'm afraid we had reached what you might call an impasse. My family were devout Roman Catholics – they still are – and they didn't like it at all when I wanted to marry a Protestant, although they had nothing against Graham as a person. He'd always attended the Church of England; he was church treasurer in Barnsley at quite an early age, just as he is here. He wouldn't "turn", as they call it, and why should he have to do so, I wondered. And my parents were dead against me getting married in his church, so we got married in a registry office, something neither of us really wanted, but it seemed like the only solution. So I don't go to church – to St Peter's, I mean – because I have this hang-up about it that I would be doing wrong to attend when I'm still technically a Catholic. I'm afraid that's what my parents would still think. And because I don't go, our children don't attend church either.'

'You're happy though, aren't you, you and Graham?' asked Fiona. 'Forgive me for asking, but you do seem to be on the occasions I've seen you together.'

'Very happy,' replied Gillian. 'So long as we don't talk about religion. I've been to social occasions with Graham, but that's all. He's always kept very quiet about our situation, and your husband has never enquired about it.'

'No, Simon doesn't believe in hounding people, unless they ask for advice.'

'I've felt like talking to him – your husband, I mean – many a time, but I've never done so. That's why I'm pleased to be able to talk to you now, Fiona. You don't mind if I call you Fiona, do you?'

'Not at all; that's what I want everyone to do, but some of the older ladies still seem unsure about me.' Fiona was pleased that they were getting on so well together and especially that Gillian felt that she could confide in her. She had taken a liking to her as soon as they got talking together. Until then she had not known the young woman except just to say a brief word to her, and had got the impression that she preferred not to become involved. Gillian was tall and dark-haired, quite a striking looking woman, and she always dressed very smartly. Even now, in the comfort of her own home, she looked elegant in a stylish green blouse and a just above the knee-length woollen skirt in muted shades of blue and green.

'Yes, I must admit that a few of the ladies in your congregation tend to intimidate me,' said Gillian. 'You get them in all churches, of course. I suppose there will always be those who think that their way is right and that everyone else is out of step. That's how I was made to feel when I married Graham, and so I've never gone anywhere at all.'

Fiona nodded. 'I do understand. You see… I didn't attend church for several years either. A different reason from yours, but I felt that there were those who would disapprove of me. It wasn't till I met Simon that I started going again. He's taught me that it's how you stand in the eyes of God that's important, not the opinion of other people… and that there's room for everyone in

God's church, every sort of church. Anyway, I mustn't preach, Gillian.' She smiled. 'That's my husband's job. But I do hope I can persuade you to come along to our first meeting.'

And there she was, a few weeks later, with her next-door neighbour, a woman called Vera who was about the same age as Gillian and who attended St Peter's church from time to time. Simon had been delighted that Fiona had made a breakthrough with Gillian. The woman, at Fiona's suggestion, had gone along to the rectory to have a chat with him. She had wanted so much to belong to St Peter's along with her husband, she told him, but having been confirmed into the Roman Catholic faith at an early age she had felt that she could not do so, especially when it came to taking part in the Communion service, which the Roman Catholics referred to as Mass.

'We welcome everyone to our Communion service,' Simon told her, 'irrespective of which church you belong to. But if you would feel happier about it you could attend confirmation classes, and become a full member of the Church of England.'

Not only had Gillian agreed to do this, but she had persuaded her teenage son and daughter to go along to the youth club, a first step, she hoped, to their involvement in the church.

Simon made a brief appearance at the first meeting of the new group. He made everyone welcome at his and Fiona's home, and wished them every success and blessing on their new venture. 'But this is my wife's project,' he added, 'so I shall make myself scarce. I know she has all sorts of ideas. So... cheerio for now, everyone.'

Fiona felt nervous to be in charge, even though it was only a small group. She had never done anything like it before, but all the ladies were smiling at her encouragingly. Her friend, Joan, winked at her as she began to speak.

'So… as my husband has said, welcome to our home. Now… where shall we begin?'

'Let's start at the very beginning,' said Joan.

'A very good place to start!' added Heather Milner. They all laughed and the ice was broken.

'What we need to decide is how we want to proceed – what sort of meetings we would like – and how often we want to meet…'

It was decided that they should meet fortnightly on a Tuesday evening, which was not the same day as the Mothers' Union, although that was an afternoon meeting. It was decided, also, that there was to be no restriction as to age, even though the word 'young' featured in the name.

'You're as young as you feel,' said Joan Tweedale. She looked round at the group of women. 'Oh dear! I think I must be the oldest one here.'

'Then we can all benefit from the wisdom of your age,' smiled Fiona. 'We can't stipulate a cut-off point – say fifty or fifty-five – can we? I'm sure we all know women in their sixties or seventies who are young at heart, but I think they will have the common sense to realize that they might be a little too… elderly.' She was imagining Mrs Bayliss or Mrs Fowler coming along and she smiled to herself. It was not very likely though. Even Mrs B would know that this was a pie into which she could not put her finger.

Fiona was to be the chairman, for want of a better word. They agreed to stick to the traditional term rather than say 'chairwoman' or the ridiculous name of 'chair'. They needed a treasurer, too, as they agreed to pay the nominal sum of a shilling each meeting. The money could be used to pay visiting speakers, or maybe help towards a Christmas treat – a meal out or a theatre visit. Joan agreed to do that, and when it was suggested that Gillian should be the secretary she agreed that she would try.

'Does that mean I have to take minutes of the meeting and all that?' she asked.

'Well, I think we must act in a businesslike way,' said Fiona. 'But we'll make it all quite informal. And perhaps you could write the invitations to visiting speakers, Gillian?'

Fiona was delighted that Gillian was willing to be actively involved. It was agreed, however, that they could make use of the talents of the members themselves to give some of the talks. Gillian admitted that she was quite good at dressmaking and that she had made the outfit that she was wearing that evening, a simple shift dress in a soft woollen material in a lovely shade of deep pink. Fiona enquired if she had also made the green skirt and blouse she had been wearing at home, and she agreed that she had. She said that she would be willing to pass on a few tips about dressmaking, 'which is not all that difficult once you know how', and lend a hand to the ladies who required one.

Her offer was greeted with enthusiasm, as was that of her next-door neighbour, Vera, who went to flower-arranging classes and offered to do a Christmas demonstration.

Joan offered to help with simple arts and crafts, another lady said she was quite good at cake icing, and another offered to show slides of her recent holiday in Switzerland. And Fiona thought, *Oh help! What can I do? I really ought to offer to do something.*

She wasn't much good at handicrafts, and she hadn't been on any exotic holidays, but as the rector's wife she would be expected to give a talk occasionally. The thing she enjoyed above all in her leisure time was reading, and she was a librarian. She suggested that she might talk about the new trends in books and what women in their age group were currently borrowing from the library. She also offered, very bravely, to be the first speaker at the meeting in a fortnight's time. Gillian agreed to plan a programme to take them as far as the spring of the following year and to see about having it printed.

Fiona had been busy in the kitchen all afternoon, and when the business part of the meeting ended they all enjoyed a cup of tea or coffee and sampled her fruit loaf and Victoria sponge cake. To her relief they all pronounced it delicious, and she felt that their comments were sincere. They agreed, however, to take it in turns to bring the refreshments and not leave it all to Fiona.

She looked round at the group of happily chatting young women and felt that this first meeting was proving successful. She knew she must have a word with each of the members; Sandra Jarvis, for instance and her friend Karen Wilde. They were both in their mid-twenties, the youngest two there tonight. They lived on the housing estate on the outskirts of Aberthwaite that had been built just after the war. Fiona knew that Sandra had three children and Karen had two, and that the ones who were old enough attended the Sunday school. She guessed that a rectory was not the sort of place they normally visited and that she must make them feel welcome. They both said how much they were enjoying themselves.

'It's a real treat to be rid of the kids for a while, isn't it, Karen?' said Sandra. 'Our hubbies are babysitting tonight. It'll do 'em good, won't it?'

Fiona agreed that it would. 'You'll come again then, will you?' she asked.

'We sure will,' said Karen. 'Talking about us using our talents, I don't know as I've got any, but Sandra's a lovely singer. She used to do a bit of entertaining round and about, before she had the kids, didn't you, Sandy?'

'Hey, shut up, you!' retorted Sandra. 'I've not done any for ages. I did used to like singing though...' she added wistfully.

'That's great,' said Fiona. 'I wonder if you would like to join the church choir?'

'Oh no, nothing like that,' Sandra replied hurriedly. 'I don't sing anything churchy like. But I wouldn't mind singing at a concert, perhaps... sometime. Something a bit... well, you know... popular stuff.'

'Wonderful!' said Fiona. 'There hasn't been a church concert lately. I remember going to one soon after I met Simon, and it wasn't too churchy, as you put it.' She laughed. 'I know just what you mean. I enjoy all sorts of music. I'll talk to Simon and see if we can arrange one before too long. I'm so pleased to have had a chat with you two. Excuse me now; I must go and have a word with some of the others.'

She was pleased at everyone's enthusiasm; they all promised to come again, next and every time.

Heather spoke for herself and her friend, Ruth. 'Well done, Fiona. You've got us off to a flying start. It's just what we needed; something for us young – well, youngish – women. We've enjoyed it, haven't we, Ruth?'

Her friend replied quietly, 'Yes; very much so.'

'I'm really glad you've come,' said Fiona. 'I know you're both very busy people with your teaching jobs and… everything. And I know that Simon appreciates your work with the church council, Ruth.'

'I enjoy doing it,' said Ruth, a little curtly, Fiona felt. But then she smiled, albeit a trifle warily, at Fiona. 'I'm glad I came. I'm very busy, as you say, but Heather persuaded me. And… I wish you and Simon every happiness,' she added.

'Thank you,' said Fiona. She felt that Ruth's remark was sincere. 'That's very kind of you. Yes, we are… very happy. I'm trying to be a good wife to him; a good rector's wife.'

Ruth nodded. 'Yes… I'm sure you are.'

As Fiona moved away her sharp ears overheard Heather's remark. 'There; that wasn't too bad, was it?'

And Ruth's reply. 'No… She's very pleasant, isn't she?'

Fiona felt a little guilty. She knew she had been straining to hear what they said, and she was convinced now that Ruth must have had quite strong feelings for Simon, whether or not he had felt the same about her.

Most of the ladies were making moves to depart now as it was getting on for ten o'clock. Fiona knew that it was time for her to bring the meeting to a close. Simon had told her that it was customary to close all meetings with a prayer, and she felt nervous about something that she had never done before.

'What shall I say?' she asked him. 'It's alright praying on my own, or with you… as we do sometimes. But with everyone else… I'm not used to it.'

'You soon will be,' Simon assured her. 'Just say the evening collect. You can't go wrong with that. And it will be easier the next time, I promise.'

She took a deep breath and said, 'Shall we have a short prayer before we go home, ladies?' They all bowed their heads and Fiona began, 'Lighten our darkness, we beseech Thee, O Lord...' They all joined in with the familiar words that they recited at the Sunday evening service, and Fiona breathed a sigh of relief. That wasn't too bad, she thought, and she knew she would not feel nervous the next time.

Joan stayed behind when all the others had gone. 'I'll give you a hand with the washing up,' she said. 'Maybe that's something else we should have a rota for. It's not fair to leave it all to you.'

'I don't mind,' replied Fiona. 'I've never minded washing up. They've all got to get back to their homes and families. I'm really pleased it's gone so well.'

'So you should be,' said Joan. 'Well done. I think you did a wonderful job. You were really confident and in charge of things.'

'I was nervous,' Fiona admitted, 'but they all wanted to help, didn't they? And what a lot of different talents they have. Simon's always saying that we should make full use of our talents. I'm not really sure what mine are though,' she laughed. 'I was so impressed at Gillian Heap making all those lovely clothes she wears.'

'Yes; she's very good at dressmaking. She knits as well; she comes in the shop for wool and patterns for jumpers that she makes for all the family. I'm glad you got her to come along. Don't say that you don't know what your talents are, Fiona. You've proved that you're good at welcoming people and making them feel at ease. Look at Gillian, and those two young women, Sandra and Karen; they just needed a bit of encouragement, and that's what you gave them. And you can sing, and bake; that cake and fruit loaf were delicious. You're turning into a first-class clergy wife, you know.'

'Thank you,' said Fiona with a smile. 'I'm glad you think so. I am trying…' She paused, looking round from the sink. 'Can I ask you something, Joan?'

'Yes, of course; what is it?'

'Ruth Makepeace… Did she have… er… a fancy for Simon?'

Joan smiled. 'Well, yes. To be truthful, she did. She wasn't the only one though. Just think about it. A young charismatic clergyman who's just lost his wife. Ripe for the picking, wasn't he?'

'And what about Simon? Was he interested in Ruth?'

Joan hesitated. Then, 'I don't think he ever was,' she said, 'not in the way you mean. They worked together, of course, so I suppose it was inevitable that she should get fond – perhaps too fond – of him. But he never gave her any real reason to hope, I feel sure of that. And then you came along. It was love at first sight, wasn't it, for both of you?'

'Almost,' said Fiona, 'if you can believe in such a thing. I was attracted to him straightaway, and I could hardly believe it when I realized he felt the same way about me. I'd almost given up hope, you see, of finding somebody that I could really care about. I was thirty-one; most of the girls – well, women I should say – that I knew were married, and I felt that I was being left on the shelf, as they used to say.' She laughed. 'So I was concentrating on my career; I'd just got the job as chief librarian, and I was saving up to buy a place of my own. Then Simon came along, and that was that!'

'You're a beautiful girl, though, Fiona. Lovely looking, as I'm sure you must know, and so personable. You must have had lots of admirers. Sorry; I'm being nosy, aren't I?' said Joan. Fiona was looking a little fazed. 'But I couldn't help wondering.'

'Not all that many admirers!' smiled Fiona. 'Let's say I was being extra cautious. I'd had one or two friendships that showed signs of developing, but nothing significant. I knew I had to be really sure.' She was tempted, for a moment, to confide in Joan about what had happened fourteen years ago, about Dave and the consequences… She had a strong feeling sometimes that she must confide in someone, but she hadn't plucked up the courage to tell her husband. And Simon would be appearing soon to see how she had gone on with the meeting.

He popped his head round the kitchen door at that moment. 'Hello, love. Hello there, Joan. Well, how did it go?'

It was Joan who answered. 'She did marvellously, Simon. You should be proud of her.'

'As indeed I am,' agreed Simon. 'I was coming to help with the washing up, and then the phone rang. It seems that I'm too late.'

'That's a good excuse,' laughed Joan. 'We've finished now. So I'll be on my way. It's been a lovely evening…'

'Now, tell me all about it,' said Simon when they had said goodnight to Joan. 'I always knew, though, that you'd make a go of it. I am very proud of you, my darling.'

Fiona felt a pang of conscience. She hoped her husband would never have a reason to feel disappointed in her.

Twenty-Three

The Young Wives and Friends' group proved to be a successful venture, and several new members joined during the autumn. By the early spring of 1966 the number would grow to sixteen, which was just about right for the size of the rectory lounge.

Elsewhere in the church community the organizations were continuing to thrive. It had been agreed by the church council that children should be admitted to the choir; not young ones, though; boys – and girls – over the age of eleven. Six youngsters had joined, three boys and three girls, and had proved to be an asset to the choir. And a guitar group for teenagers had been started. Graham Heap, the church treasurer had, it seemed, been hiding his light under a bushel. He was a competent guitarist and had agreed to take charge of the new group. There were six members, seven including Graham, two of them being his own children, Nigel and Jennifer, plus two more boys and two girls, all aged from fourteen to sixteen.

The carol service, held on the Sunday evening before Christmas in 1965, included several new items, appreciated by most, but not all, members of the congregation. One of the new choristers, a twelve-year-old boy called Kevin, was found to have quite an exceptional voice. It was decided that he should sing the first verse of 'Once in Royal David's City' as the choir processed round the church, the choir joining in with the second verse, and the rest of the verses being sung by the congregation. It was the way it was done in all the big churches and cathedrals, and Fiona, herself a member of the choir, found she was moved almost to tears by the feeling of reverence and quiet joy engendered by this opening hymn.

Later in the service there was an anthem sung by the choir, 'Tomorrow shall be my Dancing Day'.

'It's rather challenging,' Henry Tweedale, the choir master had told them, 'and no doubt there will be some who don't appreciate it. But we must try to stretch ourselves; we can't do the same old things year after year.'

There were a few puzzled faces in the congregation as the choir sang the unfamiliar words:

Tomorrow shall be my dancing day;
I would my true love did so chance,
To see the legend of my play;
To call my true love to my dance!

Going on then to sing of the virgin pure and the babe laid in a manger, '*betwixt an ox and a silly poor ass*'. Strange words, to be sure, dating from as early as the seventeenth century, Henry had told them, and based on the idea of associating religion with the dance of life.

Fiona had found it strange at first, but it had a haunting melody and the four-part harmony enhanced the music and made it a joy to sing. But maybe not to listen to, at least not to everyone, she pondered as she saw Mrs Bayliss, sitting near the front of the church, turn to her neighbour Mrs Fowler at the end of the song, clearly making what was a derogatory remark.

The congregation was all smiles later though as the six new young choristers sang 'How far is it to Bethlehem?'. Some had objected to children joining the choir, but now Simon's and Henry's decision to allow this seemed to have been vindicated.

The item by the guitar group, however, a simple modern setting of the popular carol 'O Little Town of Bethlehem', met with a mixed response. To use guitars in a church service was a very new idea, one that was not universally popular. This was made clear when the church members met together in the hall after the service for a cup of tea and a biscuit.

Ethel Bayliss very soon voiced her objections to Henry Tweedale. 'We used to have a very good choir, Henry, when you sang things that we could understand. Mind you, I'm not saying anything about the quality of the singing. They still make a pleasant sound, and the children have fitted in quite well, though I must admit I had my doubts about them at the beginning.'

'So what exactly are you objecting to, Mrs Bayliss?' asked Henry.

'That silly anthem,' she replied. 'What on earth has dancing got to do with baby Jesus and the Christmas story? Why can't you stick to nice carols that we know, like "The First Noel" and "Away in a Manger"? Never mind your newfangled nonsense. The traditional ones are the best, and I'm sure most people would agree with me.'

Henry smiled, a trifle pompously. 'You couldn't get anything more traditional than "Dancing Day". It dates from the seventeenth century and it's sung in all the cathedrals. You probably don't understand it, Mrs Bayliss, that's all.'

He could see the lady positively bristling. 'Nor do I want to,' she replied. 'And what about the guitars? It's coming to something when we've got a pop group performing in church!'

'Then you'll have to take that up with Graham Heap,' Henry replied. 'It's his project, not mine; but one that I approve of wholeheartedly. Surely if it will encourage more young people to join us it is all to the good, isn't it, Mrs Bayliss?'

The lady turned away with a derisory snort that sounded like a horse harrumphing. She did not find, though, that all her minions agreed with her.

'This place is getting out of hand since she came on the scene,' Mrs Bayliss remarked to anyone who would listen; she was at the centre of a group of Mothers' Union stalwarts. 'Guitar groups and silly anthems that no one can understand! Whatever next, I wonder?'

'If by "she" you mean our rector's wife, then I'm sure it's none of her doing,' said Blanche Fowler, bravely. 'You can't blame Fiona. She's not responsible for what the choir sings.'

'She's in it though, isn't she?' retorted Ethel. 'She probably had a lot to do with it.'

'Actually, I quite liked that anthem,' said Blanche. 'It was different, and a lovely tune. Personally, I think Fiona's doing very well. That new group she's formed is very popular with the younger women, and she's teaching in Sunday school. If you ask me she's working very hard.'

'But nobody asked you, did they?' mumbled Ethel Bayliss, almost inaudibly. But Blanche overheard her, and so did Joan Tweedale who had listened to the whole of the interchange.

Oh, dearie me! she thought. This was one item of gossip she would not be repeating to Fiona. She knew that what was affecting Ethel Bayliss was pure and simple jealousy. The rector's young wife was proving very popular in the parish. The more people got to know her the more they liked her, especially since she had started the new group in which Ethel, to her annoyance, could have no part.

Fiona was pleased at the way the carol service had gone. Everyone she had spoken to had said how much they had enjoyed it, particularly the new items. She had noticed, however, that Mrs Bayliss was at the centre of a group of women, laying the law down about something or other. It was Mrs B who was doing most of the talking, and it appeared that she was not getting a great deal of encouragement from the others. Fiona turned away. As Simon often said, you couldn't please all the people all the time. So long as his decisions regarding church matters squared with his conscience and what he felt was right with God, then he had no qualms about going ahead. Simon, too, had been gratified at the way the 'new look' service had been received.

Christmas Day fell on a Saturday that year. Boxing Day, therefore, was on a Sunday, which was, in truth, an awkward time for the clergymen. After consultation with the church council it had been agreed that there would be only a short service on the Sunday morning, after which Simon would be free for the next few days so that he could spend time with his family.

There was, of course, the customary Midnight service on Christmas Eve, and Simon had agreed that this should be very traditional; no guitar groups or anything that might be termed 'mod' or 'way out'.

Fiona had never felt so happy as she did on that occasion, sitting with the rest of the choir and singing the well-loved old hymns, 'Hark the Herald Angels Sing' and 'It came upon the Midnight Clear'; listening to Simon's short address about the love brought to the world by the Babe of Bethlehem, love we should feel for one another, or try to feel for the ones we might find it difficult to love; smelling the fragrance of the pine needles from the tall tree that stood at the side of the chancel. It had been decorated by members of the Youth Club the previous week, and the nativity scene on the straw-strewn table beneath it had been added to, week by week, during Advent by the Sunday school children; Mary and Joseph, shepherds, angels and wise men, and the baby would be placed in the manger the following morning at the Toy service.

It was a cold still night with a sprinkling of snow on the ground and the branches of the trees silvered with hoar frost as Simon and Fiona walked home to the rectory hand in hand. There was no need for words as they smiled at one another. Fiona knew that Simon was filled with the same delight as she was. The warmth in his eyes spoke of his love for her as they celebrated their first Christmas together as husband and wife.

The Toy service on Christmas morning provided an opportunity for the children to bring along a toy that Father Christmas had brought. As Fiona watched the bright-eyed boys and girls chatting to Simon about a new baby doll, a fire engine, racing car or cuddly panda, she hoped that soon she might have some special news for her husband. She knew that he wanted a child, and they were doing nothing to prevent this happening.

He would – or will – make a wonderful father, she pondered as they spent the rest of the day quietly together.

She hoped that she, too, would be a good mother. And this thought gave rise to another one… Somewhere there was a thirteen – almost fourteen – year-old girl who was unaware of her, Fiona's, existence. Unless, of course, she had been told of her adoption… She tried to banish the thought, as she knew she must.

'What's the matter, darling?' asked Simon coming upon her in the kitchen, staring into space.

'Nothing, Simon.' She smiled, shaking her head. 'I'm just waiting for these roast potatoes to brown. They're taking ages.'

'Never mind,' he replied. 'We've got all day. The chicken looks delicious.'

They were having what Fiona called a 'mini' Christmas dinner as they would be celebrating on the following day with Simon's family. She had bought just a small chicken which had cooked to perfection whilst they had been at church, and a minute Christmas pudding, big enough for the two of them, which was steaming away on top of the stove. They had decorated a small tree and strung their myriad Christmas cards on ribbons across the walls of the lounge. They would be away from home until the Wednesday of the following week, giving Simon a well-earned rest from his parish duties.

After the short service on Boxing Day morning – Fiona felt that she had spent nearly all her time at church recently – they set off southwards across the hills and dales of North Yorkshire. It was not a long journey 'as the crow flies', but some of the roads meandered between the steep hills and alongside the rivers. The scenery was familiar to both of them but neither of them ever tired of the beauty of their home county. The day was perfect for travelling, the roads clear of the snow that had fallen before Christmas, now lying in drifts at either side of country lanes.

They arrived in Baildon mid-afternoon to an enthusiastic welcome by Simon's parents, his sister, Christine, and her husband, Tom, and their two teenage children Susan and Michael. It was a happy few days with lots of fun and laughter. Fiona had met Christine a few times, but came to know her much better during this Christmas period. They found that they got on amazingly well together, and Fiona also enjoyed the company of Tom, a dales farmer who had left the farm in the capable hands of his second in command.

This was family life at its best, Fiona thought, and she felt that she was experiencing it for almost the first time. She had been happy enough with her mother and father, she recalled, until 'that' happened, and then it had never been the same again. Even as a child, though, she had known nothing of this camaraderie and affection, along with the good-humoured bickering from time to time that made it all the more realistic and wholesome. Only once before had she known a similar kind of family love, she remembered; that was the time that she had spent with her aunt and uncle and her cousin and the children, when she had been sent, in disgrace, to the wilds of Northumberland.

Christine and Tom had been married in 1945, when the war had ended. Christine had been twenty-five then, and Tom, she guessed, a year or so older. Their children were now fourteen and sixteen. She and Simon, especially Simon, would be older parents, but she hoped that she too, some day, would experience the sort of happiness and unity that this family shared.

The rectory felt cold after their few days' absence but, fortunately, there were no burst pipes, a continual fear during the winter months. They warmed the house with roaring fires in the lounge and dining room, plus electric fires to take the chill off the bedroom and study. It had been agreed, however, by the church council that the rectory should now be centrally heated, and this work was to begin in the early spring. There was ample room in the kitchen for a boiler to be installed. Fiona was looking forward to instant heat at the touch of a switch instead of the arduous ritual of laying and lighting fires each day, although Simon often undertook this task.

The 'Watchnight' service on New Year's Eve, to celebrate the start of the New Year, 1966, was well attended. Fiona was beginning to feel that she was surrounded by friends, and as they all embraced and exchanged good wishes for a 'Happy New Year' she had a feeling that it would be a momentous year for herself and Simon.

The next event on the social calendar at St Peter's was to be a springtime concert featuring the various talents of the members of the congregation. The choir was to sing songs of a secular, rather than a religious, nature. Ivor Novello and Jerome Kern were found to be the favourite choices of the older members of the choir, so Henry Tweedale had arranged two medleys featuring the songs of these two popular composers. The younger choir members were to sing a selection of traditional songs, such as 'Hearts of Oak', 'The British Grenadiers', and 'Strawberry Fair'. They had learnt them at school and enjoyed singing them, and they would, no doubt, be popular with the audience.

There were, inevitably, amongst the congregation, a man who recited humorous monologues such as 'Albert and the Lion'; another who was something of a stand-up comic; a conjuror; a very competent lady pianist; and a man who played the ukulele in the style of George Formby.

Fiona had been asked to sing a solo, but she had demurred, not feeling confident enough to sing on her own. She had agreed, though, to take part in a trio with two other young women. One was Sandra Jarvis, the young mother of three who had come along to the first meeting of the Young Wives' group and was still a keen member, and Denise who was an alto in the church choir.

They had opted to sing 'Three Little Maids from School' from *The Mikado*. Fiona was a keen fan of the music of Gilbert and Sullivan. She had seen several of their comic operas when she lived in Leeds, and had even suggested to Simon that they might consider starting a G and S group at the church.

'Er… maybe sometime in the future,' he had said, warily. 'It's a good idea, but we have rather a lot going on at the moment. Let's not run before we can walk, eh? I'm pleased you're singing in the concert though. That's great, darling. Good for you!'

The concert was planned for the last Saturday in March, the week in which spring officially started, according to the calendar. It was on the Friday morning that Fiona told Simon that, 'One of the three little maids from school is in danger of being expelled.'

'What do you mean, love?' he asked.

'Well, it seems that she's in an interesting condition,' she answered. 'It's sure to be frowned upon by the "genius tutelary".' She smiled roguishly at him.

'You mean… you? You're telling me that you're…' Simon's mouth stayed open in astonishment.

'Yes… I'm pregnant,' she replied. 'We're having a baby, Simon. At least… well, yes, I'm almost certain.'

'Oh, my darling!' He got up from where he was sitting at the breakfast table and went over to her. 'That's the most wonderful news. When… do you know?'

'As I said, Simon, I can't be absolutely certain, not yet. But I'm pretty sure, and I have a feeling that I am.' She was only just over a week late, but that was unusual for her; besides, she felt confident in her mind that it was so. 'Sometime in December, I think.'

'A Christmas baby! Better than ever,' Simon exclaimed. He kissed her soundly on the lips.

'Rather earlier than that, I think,' she replied. 'I shall have to find out definitely. I'll wait a week or so, then I'll go and see Dr Entwistle and make sure.'

'It's wonderful news,' said Simon again. 'I feel as though I want to go and tell everybody, to shout it from the roof tops.'

Fiona laughed. 'Hold your horses, darling. We'll know for sure in a little while. Until then it's our secret, isn't it?'

Twenty-Four

Three little maids who all unwary,
Come from a ladies' seminary,
Free from a genius tutelary,
Three little maids from school,
Three little maids from school.

Simon and Fiona exchanged a fleeting glance and a secret smile as the trio of Japanese schoolgirls sang the popular chorus. Simon was seated in the centre of the front row, while his wife performed. He was taking no part in the concert apart from doing the welcome speech, and he would give the appropriate word of thanks at the end. Nor had he had much to do with the arrangements. They had been done by a committee chaired by Henry, the organist, who, with Fiona and four others, had planned the programme. Fiona, however, had asked Mrs Bayliss if she would take charge of the refreshments, as she usually did; a sop, in truth, because the said lady had no part in the organization of the concert itself. Fiona had told Simon that she had graciously inclined her head and agreed to do so, adding, a trifle grudgingly, that she was looking forward to the event although, for her part, she preferred music of a more serious nature.

Fiona looked very different in her black wig with the pink lotus flower, wearing her brightly flowered pink and blue kimono and fluttering a gaily painted fan. He was proud of her. She had a lovely singing voice along with her many other attributes.

This was the last act before the interval; Simon then mingled with the members of the audience who all agreed that it was a superb performance. It had attracted a goodly number of folk who didn't normally attend the church services; but he would invite them, at the end of the evening, to join in the worship at St Peter's the following day if they wished to do so. He was pleased that the new guitar group, playing and singing a medley of Beatles' numbers, had been well received. Most people, he believed, even if they insisted it was not to their liking, found themselves humming or singing quietly along to such numbers as 'She Loves you', 'Eleanor Rigby', or 'When I'm Sixty-four'. Simon had done so and had been unable to stop his feet from tapping in time to the rhythm.

He did not see his wife as she was changing out of her Japanese costume into the choir 'uniform' for the final act of the show. On a Sunday they wore their traditional robes and the ladies wore a sort of mortar-board hat. Tonight, though, they had agreed to dress in black and white – black trousers or long skirts, white tops or shirts – with red ties for the men or red scarves for the ladies.

Simon enjoyed the second half just as much as the first. It didn't matter that a couple of the conjuror's tricks were transparently obvious, or that some of the comedian's jokes 'came out of the ark'. The lady pianist's performance of 'Clair de Lune' was note perfect, and the monologue 'Albert and the Lion' was still as amusing no matter how many times one heard it.

The choir's selection of songs by Jerome Kern was a splendid ending to the show. The audience clapped and cheered as the last notes of 'Old Man River' died away, and Simon waited several moments until the applause died down.

'Yes, that was superb, wasn't it?' he said. 'As, indeed, all the acts have been.' He expressed his thanks to all concerned, and after his invitation to everyone to 'join us again tomorrow', he closed the evening with a short prayer. It was Simon's belief that in all church activities, religious or of a secular nature, God should be seen as the main reason for everything in which they took part.

'It's been a huge success, darling,' he told Fiona as they sat by the fireside enjoying their bedtime drink of chocolate. They were appreciating the advantage of the newly installed gas fire which had replaced that coal fire, and the radiators in each room. The workmen had finished the job earlier that week, and what a difference it had made to the normally chilly rectory.

'And a good deal of the success was due to you,' he went on. 'Henry has told me what a help you have been to him. I don't believe he would have considered putting on such a diverse show without your assistance. He used to be rather reserved – well, a bit "old hat" you might say – in his choice of music. He's certainly moving with the times, now.'

'It was a team effort,' Fiona insisted. 'I've done no more than anyone else. We worked well together because we enjoyed it, Simon.'

'And so did the audience,' he said. 'Well done anyway, to all of you.' He had noticed that evening that his wife now seemed completely at home amongst the members of the congregation. She had worried at first that there was some resentment from a few of the parishioners, and she had not found it easy, he knew, in her position as the new wife of the rector. Now, though, they all seemed to like and respect her. He silently gave thanks again for the joy and satisfaction, the completeness that she had brought to his life.

–

Fiona waited another week before she went to see the doctor, by which time she was certain in her own mind that she was pregnant. Dr Entwistle had been Simon's doctor and Fiona had signed up with him on their marriage, although she had not had any occasion, until now, to call on his services. She knew him reasonably well; he and his wife attended St Peter's, although not every week. She guessed that he was nearing retirement age, and she knew that he was well liked by his patients.

'Mrs Norwood, how nice to see you,' he greeted her. 'May I say how much I enjoyed your performance the other night – all of the show, in fact. My wife and I were very impressed.'

'Oh, the concert,' she replied. 'I didn't know you were there.'

'Yes, Doris and I enjoy these social occasions. Now… what can I do for you? Actually, I think I can guess…?' His kind grey eyes twinkled as he smiled at her.

'Yes, perhaps you can,' she said, smiling back at him, though a little unsurely. She was rather concerned about what she felt she ought to tell him. 'Yes, Dr Entwistle, I think I might be pregnant.'

'Well, that's great news,' he said. 'Hop up on to the couch and we'll take a look, shall we?'

He felt her stomach and examined her breasts which were already a little tender, and asked her the relevant questions about her periods. 'Yes,' he said. 'It's as you thought. You're expecting a baby, Fiona… I may call you, Fiona, may I?' She nodded. 'What wonderful news for your husband. By my reckoning it should be around mid-December, give or take a few days, of course. Well done! I'm sure Simon will be delighted. Now, we must see about booking you into hospital, as it's your first child…'

She interrupted him then. 'Dr Entwistle… there's something I must tell you. It isn't, you see. It's not my first baby.' He looked at her a little concernedly, but not at all reproachfully. She went on. 'I had a baby when I was seventeen. It was fourteen years ago, and my parents made me give it up for adoption – it was a little girl. I had to go into one of those homes, you know, for unmarried mothers up in Northumberland and… the thing is, you see, that I haven't told Simon. I know I should, but I haven't, and I suppose he'll find out, won't he?'

He shook his head. 'He won't find out from me. There is such a thing as patient confidentiality. We can't discuss anything we're told in the surgery. But… you really should tell him, my dear. I can see, by what you've told me, that you went through an unhappy time. But it happens; it's happening all the time. And I'm sure your husband would understand. Do tell him, Fiona, before someone else does. These things have a habit of leaking out…' He raised his bushy eyebrows, looking questioningly at her.

She nodded. 'I'll try,' she said. 'Yes, I will… tell him.'

'Good girl.' He nodded. 'Now, I'll see about booking you into the Queen Elizabeth hospital in mid-December.' This was on the outskirts of Aberthwaite and had been opened in 1938 by the queen, the wife of King George the Sixth, who was now known as the Queen Mother. 'They will want you to attend their clinic each month to make sure all is going well. Now, remember what I've said, Fiona, and I'm sure it will be fine. Goodbye for now, my dear.'

But she didn't tell Simon. The more she thought about it the more afraid she became, although she felt in her heart that it would be alright; Simon would understand.

Her first appointment at the clinic was in two weeks' time. Simon drove her there, dropping her off outside the hospital. He had offered to come in with her and wait whilst she had her examination, but she had insisted she would be alright on her own.

The truth was that she didn't want Simon with her. She was sure that the other women would not be accompanied by their husbands. Besides, she was very jittery about the forthcoming appointment with a doctor that she didn't know. She was intimidated by hospitals in general, although she knew it was unreasonable of her; rather childish, in fact. Also she was in a quandary because she hadn't yet told Simon, and the more she thought about it the larger it loomed in her mind. She knew she was playing games with herself; she would tell him tomorrow, or the day after. Now she had decided she would tell him today when she got home after the consultation.

She gave her name at the reception desk and then sat along with several other women awaiting her turn. She couldn't remember ever feeling so worked up about anything, not since her first pregnancy. Her stomach was churning and she could feel the tension in her neck muscles. She did not look at any of the other women in the waiting room, so full was she of her own concerns.

Quite soon her name was called by a nurse who emerged from one of the doors. 'Fiona Norwood, please.'

As she walked across the room she noticed, out of the corner of her eye, someone who looked vaguely familiar. She only caught a glimpse of her; a buxom blonde, dark at the roots, somewhat older than herself, and heavily pregnant. Then she forgot about her as she went into the surgery.

He was a doctor who was actually a surgeon and was therefore known as Mr Bellingham. He nodded curtly at her, and she decided at once that he didn't have what was known as a bedside manner. He glanced at the form he had been given, confirming the details with her. 'Fiona Norwood, age thirty-one. Your baby is due on or around the fifteenth of December according to your doctor. Not your first pregnancy; you had a child in May, 1952?'

'Er… yes, that's right,' she replied. Already, it seemed, the secret was leaking out.

'Very well, Mrs Norwood. Let's take a look at you.' Thankfully there was a nurse present, and she helped Fiona to prepare herself and climb up on to the couch. She knew it would be an internal examination, and she felt herself growing tense at the thought. She hated the indignity of it; she remembered from the first time what an ordeal it had been for her as a terrified seventeen-year-old. It ought not to be so this time. She and Simon were delighted about the baby, but she was still cringing at the surgeon's touch.

'Relax, Mrs Norwood,' he said, quite sharply. 'I have to make sure that all is well, and it will be worse if you don't keep still.'

The nurse smiled understandingly at her and took hold of her hand. It was soon over. 'Everything is in order,' said

Mr Bellingham. 'Make an appointment for a month's time from now, Mrs Norwood. It will most likely be one of the midwives who sees you next time.'

Thank God for that! she thought. Fiona didn't speak the heartfelt words out loud. She dressed as quickly as she could and went to book her next appointment. She left the hospital, still not looking at any of the other women. She felt a little sore, but decided not to wait for the bus. The day was cold, but clear and bright. A brisk walk would perhaps clear her mind in readiness for what she knew she must tell Simon.

–

The blonde-haired woman, whose name was Hazel, turned to speak to the young woman sitting next to her as she watched Fiona walk across the room. 'Do you know that person, by any chance?' she asked. 'Fiona Norwood... I'm sure it's the same girl that I knew, but she was Fiona... Dalton, I think it was back then.'

'I only know her by sight,' replied the other woman. 'Actually, she's married to the rector at St Peter's church, the Reverend Simon Norwood. I don't go to church myself, but my next-door neighbour's a big noise in the Mothers' Union there, and she's told me about her. You say that you used to know her?'

'I did indeed! So she's the rector's wife now? That's very interesting.' Hazel gave a knowing little chuckle. 'When I came across her she was in a home for unmarried girls up in Northumberland.'

Her neighbour gave her a curious glance.

'Aye, I was there meself,' she said. 'I don't mind admit-ting it. We were all in't same boat, up the duff, you might say. I had a little lad; he's fourteen now. I was supposed to be having him adopted, then at the last minute they decided to let me keep him. And then I find I'm preggers again after all this time. Would you believe it? I'm married though now. Oh aye, I'm quite respectable now. My hubby's a builder, and we've just moved down here from Newcastle, only a month ago.'

'You live in Aberthwaite then, do you?' asked her confidante, who was agog with curiosity.

'Just outside,' said Hazel. 'Just round the corner from here, so it'll be handy when I start. Next month I'm due, an' it can't come soon enough, I can tell you... Anyway, like I was saying, I had young Gary in March, and Lady Fiona was still there when I left. I never knew what happened to her, and neither did I care, until now. She didn't half fancy herself; thought she was a cut above the rest of us 'cause she'd been to a grammar school. The other lasses we shared with seemed to like her well enough but I never had much time for her, snooty little madam! How does she get on with t'church folk?'

'I don't really know,' answered the younger woman. 'My neighbour says she's started a new Young Wives' group, and some of the Mothers' Union ladies are a bit jealous, like, from what I can gather. She likes things her own way.'

'Aye, that figures.' Hazel nodded. 'I wonder if her husband knows about her fall from grace?'

'I really couldn't say. They've no children, I do know that. The rector was married before but his first wife died, and he married Fiona last summer. I believe they're very happy... It's not really any business of ours, is it? I mean to say...'

'Happen it isn't… or happen it is. At any rate, it's food for thought.'

'Hazel Cartwright, please,' called the nurse, a different one this time, and Hazel stood up.

'That's us then. Been nice chatting to you. See you again, maybe.' She gave a cheery wave as she followed the nurse across the room.

Her new acquaintance was astounded at all those revelations. As she had said, it was really none of their business. All the same she was only human, and it was too exciting a piece of gossip not to pass on to her next-door neighbour.

-

'How did you go on, darling?' asked Simon when he saw her at lunchtime.

'It was rather an ordeal, to be honest,' she said. 'The examination… you know.' She didn't want to go into details. 'But I won't have to go through that again. I'll be seeing the midwife next time.'

'My poor love,' he said. 'I should imagine it's not very pleasant, especially with it being your first baby. It's all new to you, isn't it? Never mind, it's over now, and we've got such a lot to look forward to.'

'Yes… we have, haven't we?' she agreed, without a great deal of enthusiasm, but he didn't seem to notice. She knew she had an ideal opportunity then to tell him everything. But once again her courage failed her.

Two days later she was unable to evade the truth any longer.

Twenty-Five

Simon picked up the small pile of letters from behind the door and leafed through them. 'There's one for you, darling,' he said, coming into the kitchen where they had just finished their breakfast.

'That makes a change,' said Fiona, 'They're usually all for you. I wonder who it's from? I wasn't expecting anything.'

'Well, you won't know until you open it, will you?' teased Simon.

'True,' she agreed, looking at the unfamiliar writing on the envelope. It was addressed to Fiona Norwood, in block capitals, with no courtesy title. She slit open the envelope and quickly scanned the message inside, just a few lines which she read with increasing horror. There was no 'Dear Fiona' or any such greeting, just the bald statement:

> Does your husband, the rector, know about the illegitimate child you gave birth to in 1952? If he doesn't, then you had better tell him, hadn't you, before someone else does so.

She gave a gasp of panic and terror, and her hands started to shake as she held the shocking missive tightly in her grasp.

'Darling, whatever's the matter?' asked Simon, his voice and his look full of concern.

She knew she could prevaricate no longer. She thrust the crumpled piece of paper at him across the table, then she sat looking down at her hands as he read it.

He was silent for a moment, then he spoke, just one word, 'Fiona...' She looked across at him, fearful as to what his reaction would be. 'Is this true?' he asked.

She nodded numbly. 'Yes, I'm afraid so,' she replied. 'Oh, Simon... I'm so sorry.'

He didn't speak at first, then he jumped up from his seat and came across to her. He knelt down, putting his arms around her. 'Oh, my darling,' he muttered, holding her closely to him. 'Why ever didn't you tell me? You should have said. Surely you didn't think I would...?'

She didn't let him finish. 'I didn't know what to think, Simon. I know I should have told you, straightaway, before we were married. But I couldn't, and then time went on and...' At this stage she burst into tears, unable to contain her anxiety any longer, and her relief that it was, at last, out in the open.

'Come along, love,' he said. 'Let's go and sit down, and you can tell me all about it... that is if you want to.'

'Of course I do,' she replied. 'I've been bottling it up for so long.'

They went into the sitting room and as they sat together on the settee she, at last, opened her heart to him. It all poured out of her, about her first boyfriend Dave Rathbone – 'He was a nice boy, he really was, Simon...' – and how on their visit to the Festival of Britain they had let their feelings get out of control. 'But I didn't think anything like that would happen, and I know Dave didn't mean it to.'

Above all, though, she told him about the reaction of her parents when they found out, and her banishment to Northumberland so that no one would know about it. 'They were ashamed of me, Simon, so ashamed that they didn't want anybody at the church to find out, especially not their precious vicar.'

'Yes…' said Simon. 'I remember you telling me that you stayed with your aunt and uncle – I met them at our wedding, didn't I? – because you were ill.'

'That was true,' she said. 'I was ill, but I was also pregnant, and they had me put in this home until it was all over. My aunt and uncle were so kind, though. And the home was OK, all things considered. That's where I met Ginny; you met her at the wedding as well.'

'Oh yes; Ginny and Arthur… I remember.'

'Ginny was allowed to keep her baby at the last minute. It was a little boy, and then she and Arthur got married. And then in May – it was May eighteenth; I'll never forget the date – I had a baby girl. She was the loveliest little baby, but they took her away from me almost at once…' She felt her eyes misting over again at the thought of it, but Simon was holding her close.

'My poor love…' he whispered. 'How dreadful for you. But we're going to have a baby, Fiona, you and me, and it'll be wonderful, won't it?'

'Of course it will, Simon,' she answered, smiling at him through her tears. 'It will make up for everything. Thank you, darling, for being so understanding.'

'What else could I be?' he said. 'Of course I would understand. I remember saying to you once that I've not always been a clergyman. I've done things that I now regret – sowed a few wild oats, you might say – but it's all in the past. What I don't understand, though, is how your parents could have been so... so self-righteous about it all. It seems to me that the church they attended was lacking in compassion and forgiveness. The sort of religion that dwells on what is sinful – in their eyes at least – instead of focusing upon the love of God, his love for all of us, saints and sinners alike. A doctrine of "Thou shalt not..." is a very negative outlook, in my view.'

'Yes; the Reverend Amos Cruikshank – that was his name, can you believe it? – was always preaching about turning away from sin and following Jesus. Diane and me, we used to get so confused about it all.'

'Diane... she was your bridesmaid, wasn't she? Your best friend? And you lost touch with her until the time when your parents died?'

'Yes, that's right. Like I told you, Mum and Dad had moved to another part of Leeds, supposedly to look after my grandmother, but I knew it was really so that I wouldn't be near any of my old friends when I came back from Northumberland. Cutting off their nose to spite their face, really, because it meant that they had to go to another church, and they had to keep quiet there, too, about their daughter who had strayed from the straight and narrow.'

'Your parents were influenced by this vicar then, were they, this... Reverend Cruikshank?'

'Oh yes; they changed completely when he came on the scene. Things that they used to do before – like going to the pictures, or my mum using make-up – they stopped doing them, as though they were sinful things. Like I said before, Diane and I couldn't understand it.'

'To be honest, neither can I,' said Simon. 'It seems that this vicar had a great effect upon the congregation, but one that was far too judgemental. It is the duty of the vicar – or rector, minister, priest or whatever – to try to lead his flock, but not to put the fear of God into them. I remember when I was at college there were a few chaps there who seemed to think they had a special relationship with God, something that the rest of us were lacking. They used to talk about the exact moment when they came to know the Lord; a sort of road to Damascus experience. You know... like what happened to St Paul?'

'Yes, I know,' said Fiona. 'That was how my parents behaved. I was made to feel... not quite good enough. And then, when they found out I was pregnant... well, you can imagine, can't you?'

'Yes, indeed,' said Simon. He took hold of both her hands in his. 'I can see that it was a very traumatic time for you, and I'm so pleased that you've told me, at last. It seems to me that your parents were more concerned about how it would reflect on them, rather than showing you the love and understanding that you needed.'

'I suppose they did eventually,' said Fiona, 'as much as they were able to; my father rather than my mother. But they never really forgave me; it was never mentioned again after I came home.'

'And that was why you stayed away from church for so long?'

'Exactly. I felt I was too great a sinner for God to be bothered with me. I still believed in God, deep down, but it was only when I met you that I realized He would forgive me, and so I came back to church. I'm so glad I did.'

'But you were not sure that *I* would be able to forgive you? Was that it?'

'Maybe,' she replied. 'It was very wrong of me not to tell you. And it's such a relief now that I have.' She leaned her head against his shoulder, feeling the comfort of his arms around her.

'There's room for everyone in God's kingdom,' said Simon. 'That's what I try to get across to the congregation. I could never go along with the way your vicar preached. He was well meaning, I'm sure, but not everyone comes to know the Lord in a sudden burst of light. It can take years of steady growth sometimes. I couldn't tell you the exact time that I became aware of God's love, but I do know now that He is always there for me. And who am I? – who is the Reverend Cruikshank? – to make judgements about others. Only God can do that, and I truly believe He has room for us all. Anyway, that's quite enough sermonizing, my love.' He kissed her cheek. 'Tell me, though; I'm rather confused. Your friend, Diane; did she know about what happened to you, about… the baby?'

'Not at first,' said Fiona. 'No one had any idea what had become of me. I didn't see Diane again until after my parents died. She read about it in the paper and contacted me through my gran. We met up again, and it was so wonderful to see her. She told me that when I disappeared they came to the conclusion that I'd had some sort of breakdown. I rather think they imagined it was a mental breakdown, there was so much secrecy about it. Maybe that's what my parents let them believe. Anyway, Diane was relieved to see that I was still of a sound mind. Strangely enough, no one had guessed at the truth.'

'And… what about Dave?' asked Simon, gently. 'Did she tell you anything about him?'

'Yes, she did. He was at university in London then, nearing the end of his training. He had been as baffled as everyone else at my disappearance, especially as I hadn't written to him. Well, I couldn't, could I? Diane told me, rather apologetically, that he had a girlfriend in London – he still kept in touch with Andy, you see – and also that he wouldn't be returning to Leeds when he had finished his course. His parents had emigrated to America, and he was going to join them there and, hopefully, get a position there as an industrial chemist; he was studying for a science degree. So… that was that. She had to tell Andy, of course, but we agreed that there was no point in Dave ever knowing anything about the baby… bless her! She was the most darling little thing, Simon. It's no use saying that I don't think about her, because I do. But it's been much, much easier since I met you, and especially now that we're going to have a baby of our own. I haven't told Diane yet. I know she'll be thrilled, just as she was when I told her about meeting you.'

'It's rather early to be telling anyone just yet, darling,' said Simon, 'although we must tell my parents, and your aunt and uncle. It'll be hot news on the parish grapevine, though, when the news gets out.' He paused. 'Just one thing, though. Who wrote this letter? Have you any idea?'

Fiona nodded. 'Yes, as a matter of fact, I have. It just came to me when I mentioned the home. I caught a glimpse of this woman, you see, the other day at the clinic. I thought she looked familiar, but then it went right out of my mind – I was so worked up about the examination and everything – until just now. I've remembered who she was. It was Hazel; Hazel Docherty, that was her name. We were room-mates, along with Ginny and another girl called Bridget. She – Bridget – was a little Irish girl, and Hazel used to be really unkind to her, always taunting her and making fun of her. I tried to stick up for her, and Hazel turned on me. She said I was a stuck-up bitch, or words to that effect, because I'd been to what she called a posh school. She and I never got on; well, Hazel didn't really get on with anyone. Yes… it must have been Hazel.' She screwed up the offending letter she was still holding. 'She must be living round here now. Oh dear! I hope I don't come across her again. She looked very pregnant, though, so she may well have had her baby before I go to the clinic again.'

'Don't worry, darling. She's had her say now, and she can't do any more harm. She's done you a good turn in a way, although I know it wasn't her intention. You can hold your head up high, Fiona, and you know I'll be with you every step of the way.'

In spite of his encouraging words to his wife, Simon was concerned about her. This woman, Hazel, must have found out from somebody the information she wanted about Fiona; her married name, where she lived, and above all the fact that she was now married to the rector of St Peter's. She was obviously out for some sort of petty revenge against a girl that she hadn't liked very much. Simon could imagine how such feelings of resentment and bitterness might occur in a closed community such as the home where Fiona had been made to stay, usually without any real reason for rancour or enmity.

From whom had she got her information? he wondered. From a member of the congregation, or from someone who knew Fiona only by sight? He felt, human nature being as it was, that the matter wouldn't stop there. There would be repercussions, he was sure, possibly sooner rather than later. Why else would this Hazel have set the ball rolling by writing to Fiona? The last thing he wanted to do, though, was to give his wife anything more to worry about.

Poor Fiona! What a quandary she must have been in, and for so long. She must have known, surely, that he, Simon, would not have condemned her for something that had happened when she was a teenager? At the same time, he could understand her unwillingness to tell him. He felt angry at the way she had been treated by her parents. He had guessed by the way she had spoken about them – or, more tellingly, had not spoken about them – that the relationship had not been an ideally happy one. What a sanctimonious, unforgiving couple they must have been. His fear, now, was that there might be others in his own congregation who, likewise, would set themselves up as judge and jury, should the facts about Fiona's past come to light.

He would be there with her, though, as he had promised, all the way.

Twenty-Six

The woman to whom Hazel Docherty – now Cartwright – had spoken was called Dora Cookson. She did not attend St Peter's church except on special occasions, but she had always made sure that her children went to Sunday school. Her daughter, Susan, was actually in the class that Mrs Norwood was teaching.

Mrs Cookson's next-door neighbour, the one she had mentioned to her new acquaintance as being 'a big noise in the Mothers' Union' – was Miss Mabel Thorpe. She, along with her sister, Mrs Gladys Parker, prided themselves as being amongst the 'chosen few' who formed the committee of the MU, deciding on such matters as procedure and protocol. Dora Cookson knew that Mabel would be delighted to hear the titbit of gossip that she had gleaned whilst she was at the clinic. She called on her the next morning, on the pretext of returning a knitting pattern, although there was no need for such urgency.

Mabel, who was in her early seventies, lived alone in the house where she had been brought up with her sister, Gladys, and her two brothers. She was the only one who had not married, although she liked to hint that she had had her moments and had once been engaged. Dora guessed that she was one of the many thousands of women who had been bereaved as a result of the First World War.

She invited Dora into the living room at the back of the house; she was wearing the flowered apron and the turban that indicated that she was busy with housework. 'I was just about to tackle the bedrooms, with it being Thursday,' she said, looking a little flustered. She had a set pattern for her cleaning, Thursday being bedroom day. 'But I can put it off for ten minutes or so.'

'I'm sorry, I didn't mean to hinder you, but I've got something to tell you. I was at the clinic yesterday and...'

'Oh yes, how did you go on?' enquired Mabel. 'Is everything all right?'

'Yes, all in order,' said Dora. 'Only another three months to go, thank God.'

'I expect you'll be wanting a little girl, will you, this time, after your two boys?'

'Well, our Susan's dying for a little sister, but I've told her not to set her heart on it. Anyroad, like I said, I've got something to tell you. You'll never guess who I saw at the clinic!'

'I'm not much good at guessing games,' said Mabel with a sniff, 'but I can see you won't rest till you've told me. I reckon I'd best put the kettle on and make us a pot of tea, seeing as I've been interrupted... Sit yourself down. I won't be long.'

'Well, who did you see then?' asked Mabel a few moments later, when they were both seated with a drink of tea, in Mabel's second-best china, and a digestive biscuit.

'I only saw your rector's wife!' replied Dora, as though she was pulling a rabbit from a hat. 'Going in to see that important chap, Doctor – no, they call him Mister, don't they? – Mr Bellingham, the one I saw the first time.'

'You mean she's...?' Mabel's eyes behind her small wire-framed spectacles were wide with curiosity.

'Pregnant? Aye, I suppose she must be. But you won't believe this!' Dora leaned forward, holding tightly to her cup. 'It's not her first baby! Oh no, would you believe... she had a baby fourteen years ago!'

'What!' Mabel's tea spilled over into her saucer, and she hastily put it down on the stool at her side. 'You mean... before she was married? Or... perhaps she was married before... Hang on a minute, Dora... How do you know all this?'

Dora embarked on the tale of the woman who had sat next to her. 'Rather a common sort of woman, actually; definitely not "out of the top drawer" if you know what I mean – dyed blonde hair, and a bit tarty looking. But what she told me was God's honest truth, I'm sure of that. She wouldn't make it up, would she? She recognized her alright, knew her name and everything, and you don't come across women called Fiona all that often, do you? How old is she anyroad, your rector's wife? Do you know?'

'Oh, a good bit younger than he is. I've heard tell she's in her early thirties. So she must have been – what? – only seventeen or so when she had the first one. The little madam! Of course, some of us have had reservations about her all along. She can be as nice as pie, but this shows her in her true colours, doesn't it? And human nature doesn't change.'

'I wonder if he knows about it, the rector?' mused Dora.

'I doubt it,' replied Mabel. 'Surely he wouldn't have married her if he'd known about it. I mean to say, a girl like that! You never know though. Love is blind, so they say, and he fusses around after her as though she's the Queen of Sheba. He's had his head turned all right, I know that.'

'Not the first one, nor will he be the last to have his head turned by a pretty face,' observed Dora. 'And she's a pretty lass, I'll give her that.'

'Handsome is as handsome does,' countered Mabel. 'And have you noticed the length of her skirts? Honestly, it's disgraceful! I tell you what; if the rector doesn't know about it, then I think it's our duty to make sure he does, as soon as possible.'

'And how do you intend to do that?' asked Dora. She was feeling a little fearful now that she might have opened a whole can of worms. 'I mean… is it really any of our business?' She knew she had made it her business, though, hadn't she, by gossiping about it? And it was too late now to start feeling guilty about what she had done.

'Of course it's our business,' retorted Mabel. 'He's our rector, and we think a lot about him. I'll tell my sister and see what she thinks. And Mrs Bayliss – Ethel – she'll know what to do if anybody does. But I'll go and see our Gladys first, this afternoon.'

Mabel Thorpe's bedrooms didn't get done that day. Dora stayed too long as she often tended to do, but this time Mabel didn't fidget and keep watching the clock as the rector's wife's reputation was torn to shreds. She had an early makeshift lunch, then set off to see her sister, Gladys Parker, who lived about five minutes' walk away.

'Hello; what brings you here?' asked Gladys, opening the door in her pinny and with a pot towel in her hand. 'We've only just finished our dinner, Wally and me. Anyroad, come on in. There's nothing wrong, is there?'

'It depends on how you look at it,' said Mabel darkly. 'You'll never guess what I heard this morning!'

'No, I don't suppose I will, but you're dying to tell me. What's up? You've not had a win on the pools, have you?'

'Don't be ridiculous, Gladys. You know I don't hold with gambling.' Mabel was very strait-laced; neither did she have much sense of humour.

'Just joking, dear,' said Gladys, who had only said it to rile her. Gladys's husband, Wally, did the 'pools' religiously every week, far more religiously than he attended church. It was a bone of contention between the sisters, as it had been between Gladys and Wally at one time. But she tended now to live and let live; Wally was not a bad husband all things considered, and she had learnt to count her blessings. She had watched her sister grow more and more embittered over the years since she had lost her Cyril in the first war.

'Here, help me dry these pots.' Gladys thrust a pot towel into her sister's hand. 'Then you can spill the beans.'

Wally left his fireside chair when he saw that the sisters were getting ready for a fair old chinwag. 'I'll go and take a toddle round t'garden,' he said, lighting up his pipe, 'then I'll not be stinking t'place out, eh, Mabel?' Another of her bugbears was how the air in her sister's house was often blue with tobacco smoke.

'So what's eating at you then?' asked Gladys when they were both furnished with a cup of tea, a necessity when there was serious gossiping to be done.

Gladys's expression changed from interest to surprise, then to shock almost verging on horror as she listened to the tale her sister was telling. 'Well, I never did!' she said at last. 'Little Miss "Butter wouldn't melt in her mouth"! A child born out of wedlock! Well, I've heard everything now. Do you suppose he knows about it, our Simon?'

'I've no idea. I wouldn't think so. A Church of England clergyman! They have to be careful, don't they, about who they ask to marry them? I mean to say, Millicent was the perfect vicar's wife, wasn't she? What a pity she died!'

'In some ways she was,' replied Gladys. 'But I got the impression that they weren't all that happy together, her and Simon. And he and Fiona do seem to be happy, don't they?'

'It looks as though he's just the same as all fellows, though,' said Mabel with a sniff. 'Taken in by a pretty face and blonde hair. Well, he's burnt his bridges now, hasn't he, whether he knows about it or not.'

'To be honest, I was getting to like her a bit more now,' said Gladys. 'She's always so nice and friendly, and it must be hard for her sometimes, with us older ladies. She must know there are some who resent her.' Gladys, in fact, was feeling a pang of guilt after her initial outburst. They didn't really know all the facts, did they? And there must have been thousands of girls over the years who had made the same mistake as Fiona had done. Gladys recalled now, with a stab of conscience, that their own brother, Bert, had 'had to be married' way back in 1920. She was remembering, fleetingly, her own courting days, too. Almost impossible to think of Wally in that guise now... She pulled her thoughts back to the present.

'She's tried hard, hasn't she?' she continued. 'To pull her weight in the church, I mean. She teaches in Sunday school, she's in the choir, and she's started that Young Wives' group. And that concert not long ago, that was lovely; Fiona had a lot to do with that.'

'Hmm... you're changing your tune,' snapped Mabel. 'Should she really be teaching innocent children in Sunday school, and be in charge of a group when her morals are obviously not what they ought to be?'

'And what are you suggesting we should do about it?' enquired Gladys. 'I think that maybe we should just... leave well alone.'

'At least we should go and talk it over with Ethel Bayliss,' said Mabel. 'She's the one we always look to for a lead, isn't she? And she really ought to know about this. Ethel will decide what needs to be done.'

Gladys decided to take the line of least resistance. She was in a quandary. In one way, she wished she hadn't heard about all this and that the woman, Hazel, whoever she was, had kept her mouth shut. But they did know, and she could see that it wouldn't be right to keep it to themselves. And it was true that Ethel Bayliss was always regarded as the fount of all wisdom as far as the womenfolk of the congregation were concerned.

–

Ethel's reaction was predictable. 'I'm not a bit surprised,' she declared, even though the others knew that she was, in truth, just as surprised as they were. 'Didn't I say he would live to regret it? Marry in haste and repent at leisure; that's what I said. And you can be sure he'll be regretting it now!'

'That is... if he knows about it,' ventured Gladys, a mite fearfully. Ethel, in high dudgeon, was a force to be reckoned with.

'You think that Simon might still be unaware, then, about the trollop he's married?' countered Ethel.

'Oh, come on now! That's a bit harsh,' said Gladys. She was not feeling quite so sure now about this scheme, this vendetta or whatever it was, that they were embarking upon.

'I speak as I find,' retorted Ethel. 'And you know that I've had my doubts about her right from the start. Well, if Simon doesn't know, then it's up to us to make sure that he does, and as quickly as possible.'

'And how do you think we should do that?' queried Mabel. 'Should we write to him, perhaps? What about an anonymous letter?'

'You've been reading too much Agatha Christie!' snapped Ethel. 'No; I don't approve of anonymous letters.'

'You don't propose telling him to his face, do you?' asked Gladys. Rather you than me, she thought, fervently wishing at that moment that she were anywhere but in Ethel Bayliss's house drinking yet another cup of tea. They would all be drowning in it soon.

'No… but there are more subtle ways of going about it,' replied Ethel. 'Word will soon get round about our dear Fiona, you can be sure of that. And some folk may well decide that she is not a fit person to be teaching their children in Sunday school. Or they may decide to boycott her precious Young Wives' group. Do you see what I mean?'

What Gladys could see, in fact, was that Ethel Bayliss did not have the courage of her convictions. It was all very well talking about what must be done, but Ethel was not brave enough to beard the lion in his den. What she was proposing seemed, to Gladys, to be somewhat underhand and invidious.

'I wonder if Joan Tweedale knows anything about this?' said Mabel. 'They've become very pally, haven't they, Joan and… Fiona?'

'Yes, so I've noticed,' replied Ethel. 'But I don't intend to tell Joan Tweedale. She and I have crossed swords more than once, so I steer clear of her now, if I can. She'll find out though, soon enough, then we'll see what she thinks about her bosom pal, won't we? Just leave it to me, and I'll drop the word into a few ears...'

–

Miss Mabel Thorpe, however, could not resist calling into Joan Tweedale's shop on the High Street the following morning.

'Hello, Joan,' she said brightly as the doorbell jingled its welcome. 'Lovely morning, isn't it?'

'Good morning, Mabel,' replied Joan, rather less cheerily. Mabel was not one of her favourite people, but she reminded herself that the woman was a customer, and it was her policy to treat all her clients with respect and friendliness. 'Yes, it looks as though it'll be a fine day. Now, what can I do for you this morning?'

'Well... actually, dear, I haven't come to buy anything, not just now,' replied Mabel. 'I've come to see if you've heard the news?'

A titbit of gossip, no doubt, thought Joan. Out loud she said, 'I don't know, do I, until you tell me what it is?'

'Well, fancy that! I felt sure you would know, with her being such a good friend of yours...'

'And which good friend of mine is it that you're talking about?' asked Joan. She had an inkling as to who it might be and wondered what Fiona might have been doing now to set Mabel Thorpe's tongue wagging.

'Well... it's the rector's wife, Fiona,' whispered Mabel, leaning across the counter in a conspiratorial way. 'I have heard – from a very reliable source – that she's... pregnant!' The last word was spoken in a hushed tone.

Joan, admittedly, was a little taken aback that this inveterate busybody should know before she did – and no doubt half the parish would know as well – but she did not let her slight feeling of pique show. 'Well, that is very good news,' she said. 'I'm sure they must be thrilled to bits.'

'Ah, but that's not all,' said Mabel. 'It seems that it isn't her first child.' Joan's puzzled frown caused Mabel to pause for a moment before going on. 'Oh no – and I've heard this on very good authority – she had a baby when she was only seventeen years old! In one of those homes for unmarried mothers, up north somewhere. And we were all wondering, Gladys and Ethel and me...'

'What?' asked Joan abruptly. 'What are you wondering?'

'Well, we're wondering if the rector knows about it. I mean, he's such a good living man, isn't he, the Reverend Simon?'

'And you mean to make sure he finds out, is that it? It is really none of our business is it – Miss Thorpe – and you would be well advised to keep your mouth shut, if you can manage that, just for once.'

'Well really! There is no need to take that tone with me.' Mabel's face was turning a bright shade of puce which matched the woollen hat she was wearing. 'I don't go around saying things that are not true. My next-door neighbour told me. She saw her – Fiona – at the clinic, and the woman sitting next to her told her all about it, how she had been in the same home as her and...'

'I don't want to hear any more, thank you,' said Joan. 'Now, if you don't want to buy anything I think you had better go. Good morning, Miss Thorpe.' She strode across the shop floor and opened the door; and Mabel departed without another word.

Joan was taken aback to say the least. She felt, in spite of wanting to disbelieve it, that what the busybodies had got hold of was most probably true, as these tales often were. Should she tell Fiona about the story that was already hot gossip? She said nothing to her husband, trying to disguise her preoccupation. Henry, preparing for his choir practice, did not seem to notice.

She did not have long to deliberate about the problem, as on Saturday morning Fiona came into the shop. She looked happy, blissfully so in fact, and Joan knew at once that the young woman must be pregnant, but certainly not aware of the gossip that was circulating.

'Hello, Fiona,' Joan greeted her cheerfully. 'You're looking very bright and bushy-tailed this morning. Have you come to shop, or is this just a social call?'

'A bit of both, actually,' replied Fiona. She smiled, radiantly, rather than coyly. 'As a matter of fact, I've come to buy some wool – pale blue or lemon, I think – and... I want to have a look at your patterns for baby wear!'

'You're pregnant!' cried Joan. She came round the counter and kissed her friend on the cheek. 'Well, that's wonderful news! I expect Simon is pleased, isn't he?'

'Tickled pink!' replied Fiona. 'We haven't known for very long; it's not due till December. And you are almost the first to know.'

'I'm really delighted for you,' said Joan. She knew, though, that however reluctant she was to burst Fiona's bubble of elation, she really must warn her friend that the gossip-mongers were already at work. 'There's something I must tell you, though, Fiona.' She walked across to the door and turned the notice round to 'Closed'. 'Come through to the back and we'll have a little chat.'

'What about the customers?' asked Fiona.

'Oh, they'll come back later,' replied Joan. 'This is rather important.'

Fiona sat down on a chair in the stockroom, surrounded by the merchandise that was piled high on the shelves; balls of knitting wool in what appeared to be hundreds of shades; tapestry sets; embroidery silks; ribbons and lace; buttons and bows. Joan pulled up a chair near to her.

'I'll come straight to the point,' she said. 'I'd already heard about the baby... because the story is on the parish grapevine. And... I'm afraid that's not all.'

'What do you mean?' Joan saw the look of elation die away from her friend's face to be replaced by one of fear. Then Fiona gave a deep sigh. 'I can guess what it is,' she said. 'Are they talking about...? Are they saying that I had a baby when I was seventeen? Because... it's true. I'm sorry, Joan.' She lowered her head, shaking it from side to side. 'I'm... so very sorry.'

'Why are you apologizing?' asked Joan. 'You don't need to apologize to me, or to anyone, for what happened ages ago. Good gracious! I know you well enough, Fiona, to understand that it must have been a dreadful time for you, whatever happened.'

'I thought it would be all right,' said Fiona in a small voice. 'Once I'd told Simon I felt safe. He said he'd take care of it all for me, and that she couldn't do any more harm. But she has, hasn't she? She's told somebody, and now it's all round the parish.'

'Fiona...' said Joan, very calmly. She leaned forward and took hold of her hand. 'Who are you talking about?'

'Hazel Docherty,' replied Fiona; but the name didn't mean anything to Joan. 'I guessed it must have been her who sent the anonymous letter. But Simon said she's had her say now and that would be the end of it. But she must have told somebody else and...'

'But who is Hazel?' asked Joan. 'I haven't heard anything about an anonymous letter. It was Mabel Thorpe who told me; her next-door neighbour saw you at the clinic.'

'Oh yes; Miss Thorpe's an old busybody, isn't she? So all the Mothers' Union clique know, do they?'

'I gave her short shrift, I can assure you,' said Joan. 'In fact I was quite rude to her. But I knew I had to come and tell you what is happening... Do you want to tell me about it, love?'

Fiona told her how she had caught sight of a familiar face at the clinic, and so when the anonymous letter had arrived she had realized who must be the culprit; Hazel Docherty, the girl with whom she had crossed swords in the home for unmarried mothers. 'What a fool I am!' she cried. 'I might've known she would cause trouble. She was noted for it when we were in the home.'

She embarked, then, on the story of how she, Fiona, had come to be in the home; all about Dave, and the church holiday; her unsympathetic parents; her banishment to Northumberland; and the subsequent adoption of her dear little baby girl. Joan listened with growing sympathy and a desire to help her young friend.

'You poor love!' she said. 'What an awful time you must have had. So... I gather you didn't tell Simon until you received the letter?'

'That's right.' Fiona nodded. 'I know I should have done, but I was scared I might lose him. But he was

286

wonderful about it, Joan, so understanding… I do love him so much.' Her eyes were brimming over with tears.

'As he loves you,' said Joan. 'I think I'm getting the picture now. These busybodies – I gather Ethel Bayliss is one of the number, as usual – they think that Simon might still be in the dark about it all, and they want to make it their business that he finds out. Just how… I'm not sure about that. As I said, I shut Mabel up as quickly as I could.'

'So what shall I do?' asked Fiona, looking quite lost and helpless.

'Nothing,' said Joan. 'Just carry on as usual. After all, it's wonderful news that you and Simon are expecting a baby, and I'm sure that most people will be delighted to hear about it, when you feel ready to tell them.'

'They probably know already,' said Fiona gloomily, 'and the rest of it.'

'Then leave it to Simon,' said Joan with conviction. 'He'll know how to deal with the problem, as he always does. Now, you came in to choose some patterns and wool, didn't you? Let's see what we can find. Think positively, Fiona. You are expecting Simon's baby, and that's terrific news. Put everything else to the back of your mind. It'll all sort out; I feel sure it will.'

Twenty-Seven

The first sign that something was amiss was on the following Sunday when two of the girls in Fiona's class were not there.

'Where's Susan,' she asked, 'and Tracey? It's not like them to be missing.' Well, not like Susan Cookson at least, she thought to herself. Tracey, whom Susan called her 'best friend' had not been attending Sunday school very long, but she had seemed quite keen, and Susan had never been known to miss it.

'Please, Mrs Norwood, Susan says she's not coming any more,' answered Shirley, who was usually the one with the most to say. 'And Tracey won't come if Susan doesn't.'

'Oh dear! That's a shame,' said Fiona. 'Have you any idea why they're not here?'

'Susan says her mum's told her she hasn't to come no more,' said Shirley.

'Oh, I see.' Fiona was surprised but didn't think any more about it just then. 'Well, never mind,' she said. 'We'll have a look at our story for today. It's about what happened when Jesus went to a wedding.'

'Please, Mrs Norwood, I'm going to a wedding soon,' said Wendy. 'My aunty's getting married – here, at this church – and I'm going to be a bridesmaid.'

'Well, that's very exciting, isn't it, Wendy?' The girls were always ready to chat to her with titbits of family news. 'You can tell me all about it later, all about the dress you'll be wearing. Let's listen to the story now...'

The girls listened attentively as they always did. Fiona enjoyed her time with them on a Sunday.

She mentioned to Simon, though, whilst they were having their tea, that two of her class had been missing that afternoon. 'It's very strange,' she said. 'Susan is such a friendly little girl. She loves to chat; well, they all do.'

'Like all women!' laughed Simon.

'Yes, maybe so,' smiled Fiona. 'Susan told me her mum's having a baby; quite soon, I think. I know she was very excited about it. Oh, I wonder...' A thought had suddenly occurred to her. The maternity clinic, Hazel Docherty...

'Simon,' she went on, a little fearfully, 'I've just thought of something. Susan's mum would go to the clinic, wouldn't she? I wonder if she met that woman that I told you about. You know... Hazel, the one that knew...'

'The woman that knew you in the home,' said Simon. 'Well, I suppose it's possible. But try not to worry about it, darling. You didn't notice Susan's mother there, at the clinic, did you?'

'No, but I don't really know her,' said Fiona. 'I might have seen her once or twice, but I didn't notice anybody that day; I was so het up about the examination and everything. It was only Hazel that I caught a glimpse of, and then I put two and two together.'

Simon would have loved to say to her, 'Yes, and made five!' But he was afraid that what she had said about the little girls being missing might be the start of something. He knew though that he mustn't worry her unduly, especially at the beginning of her pregnancy. She was keeping very fit; no signs of any sickness so far, and she looked positively radiant.

He knew she was delighted at finding out she was pregnant, as he was. It should be a joyful time in their lives, one of expectancy and hope with nothing to mar their happiness as they looked forward to the birth of their child. Instead of which he knew there was a dark cloud looming on the horizon. A small one as yet, but he knew how the smallest rumours could grow and grow even within a church community. Possibly as much in a church congregation as anywhere, he reflected a trifle cynically. There were always those who regarded themselves as the upholders of morality, ready to condemn any who, in their eyes, had fallen by the wayside, however small the misdemeanour. Self-righteousness was something he had always abhorred. It was, unfortunately, a trait sometimes found in the most hard-working members in the church, those who believed themselves to be the very backbone of the place and thought that their services were indispensable.

A proverb came into his mind, an overused cliché about the pot calling the kettle black. Then, more aptly, a verse from scripture; 'Why do you see the mote that is in your brother's eye but do not notice the beam that is in your own?' Matthew's gospel, he thought; he must look it up. It would be a good text for next Sunday's sermon. He had just told Fiona not to worry, but he knew that she would be sure to do so. He had to be there to support and protect her, and he felt that he must quell these rumours before they got out of hand. Fiona had told him that already some of the Mothers' Union members had got hold of the story, and that Joan Tweedale was refusing to have any part in it. Joan was a good person and a loyal friend; one of the best.

Simon understood perfectly why his wife had kept the truth from him for so long. It was up to him now to persuade her to hold her head up high and show the gossip-mongers that she was not afraid of them.

'You've gone very quiet, Simon,' Fiona said now. 'You do think there's a reason for Susan and Tracey staying away this afternoon, don't you?'

'Well… there might be,' he admitted, 'if I'm honest. And I'm going to be honest with you, darling… This story seems to have got around the parish already, and nothing spreads more quickly than gossip. I think you are right in assuming that it stems from this woman you call Hazel. And she told the woman who lives next door to Mabel Thorpe. Is that right?'

'Yes, that's right. And I'm thinking now that she may well be Susan's mother. It all fits, doesn't it?'

'Whoever she is, she couldn't have chosen anybody worse than Mabel Thorpe,' said Simon. 'She's a real nosy old… so and so! And she would tell her sister – Gladys Parker's a much nicer person than Mabel Thorpe, though, in my opinion – and no doubt Ethel Bayliss would be the next to know…' He shook his head in bewilderment. 'I know I've told you not to worry, and you really must try not to let it get to you too much, my love. But I'm wondering what their game is?'

'Joan says they – this Mothers' Union crowd, I mean – think that you don't know anything about it, and that they believe it's their duty to make sure that you find out about your… sinful wife!' Simon was pleased to see that Fiona managed a weak smile despite her worries. 'But they're going about it in an underhand way, that's what

Joan thinks. Perhaps they believe that if they snub me, and people start avoiding me – and it's started already hasn't it, with those two little girls? – then you'll want to know why. And then the truth will come out.'

'But what they don't realize is that I already know about it,' said Simon. 'I believe there's an answer to all this, Fiona, my love. God always provides an answer, one way or another. When you think about it, this woman, Hazel, has been an answer to your problem in a funny sort of way, hasn't she? You've had to unburden yourself to me at last. And believe me, darling, I know what a burden it must have been to you all this time.'

'Yes, so it has,' agreed Fiona. 'And it's such a relief that you know all about it now. I must admit, though, that I'm scared, Simon. I don't feel like going to church tonight – singing in the choir and feeling that everyone's looking at me – but I suppose I'll have to go, won't I?'

This conversation was taking place at the tea table. They always had an early tea at half past four on a Sunday to give Simon time to prepare himself for the Evensong and for Fiona, also, to get ready to sing in the choir.

'Yes, you must go, my love,' said Simon. 'You have nothing at all to be ashamed of. I really mean that, and let them see you're not ashamed. Why should you be? You made a mistake, one that thousands of girls have made over the years and will continue to do. You can't deny it because it's true, and I know that you would not want to deny it. "Speak the truth and shame the devil." I don't think that's a biblical quotation, but it's what my mother always used to say, and it's a valuable maxim. Do you agree, darling?' Fiona smiled faintly at him. 'Come along then,' he said. 'Let's get these pots washed, then we'll face the music together.'

The evening service passed without any noticeable difference in the attitude of the congregation. Fiona suspected that one or two members of the choir seemed a little embarrassed at seeing her, but she decided it might well be her imagination playing tricks. There was a visiting preacher that evening; a clergyman who had been a missionary in Africa. Mrs Bayliss and some of her minions from the MU were not there. They did not always attend both services of the day, and Fiona guessed that the way of life in far-flung Africa might not be of interest to Ethel Bayliss. She and her coterie were very parochially minded.

The preacher was interesting and inspiring, speaking movingly of his work overseas. Fiona noticed that there were more than a few pound notes in the plate for the retiring collection in aid of missionary work; this was in addition to the usual offertory for week-by-week church expenses. Fiona reflected that it was good sometimes to think of God's wider world and of the millions of folk who were not so fortunate of those at home in our own comfortable little existence. She was forced, not to forget, but to lay aside her own problems for a short while as they prayed, at Simon's lead, for people of other nations.

She was determined to be brave and to do as Simon had urged that she should, to hold her head up high and refuse to be intimidated by her critics. She was starting to feel a little unwell, which she knew was only to be expected. She could scarcely remember how she had felt fourteen years ago; her feeling of sickness then had been brought about more by anxiety and sheer terror rather than by her condition. Now she felt a little queasy in the mornings, but it was, fortunately, of short duration and by the afternoon and evening she felt quite well again.

It was the Tuesday that week for the fortnightly meeting of the Young Wives and Friends' group. Fiona put on a smiling face as she greeted them, although she felt a little apprehensive. How would they react on seeing her face to face? Had the story reached the younger women of the congregation yet? She glanced round at the women gathered in the rectory sitting room as she prepared to make her little speech of welcome. Joan Tweedale was there of course, her great friend and ally. So was Gillian Heap who had proved to be a most efficient secretary. Ruth Makepeace and Heather Milner were there too, and the two younger women, Sandra and Karen. Their number had risen and remained at a steady sixteen; a quick count of heads showed that there were only twelve members there that night. The ones who were missing appeared to be those who had joined most recently, although they had all seemed keen to continue. Fiona decided to enquire if anyone knew of their whereabouts. Maybe it was just coincidence that they were all missing together, but she had a feeling that the four of them were near neighbours. They had all joined at the same time and seemed, somehow, to keep themselves apart from the rest of the group.

Fiona welcomed everyone without drawing attention to the smaller number, then she helped Sylvia to set up her projector and screen to show the slides of her holiday. It had been a coach tour of Switzerland, Austria and Germany. They all marvelled at the stunning views of Lake Lucerne, the Austrian Tyrol and the pretty villages of the Black Forest; Sylvia's husband was a talented photographer. Fiona wondered if she and Simon, one day, might embark on such a journey. Foreign travel was becoming more popular now, for those who could afford it. Sylvia was one of the older members, whose two children were both grown up and married. This type of holiday was out of the question for most of the young women, but Sylvia was by no means boastful, and the rest of them showed no envy, only interest and appreciation to Sylvia for her interesting talk.

It turned out to be a happy evening, but Fiona was still aware of a few curious, although not unpleasant, glances in her direction… Or was it, once again, her imagination?

Joan had baked the cakes for that evening – the members took it in turns – and whilst they prepared the supper in the kitchen Fiona surprised her friend by saying that she intended to tell the women the truth about the story that was circulating in the parish.

Joan looked at her in some astonishment. 'Are you sure about this?' she asked. 'And is it necessary? Perhaps some of the ladies here tonight have heard about it, but we all know you well enough to sympathize rather than condemn. The fact that they're here tonight proves it, doesn't it?'

'Not everyone's here,' answered Fiona. 'There are four missing, and they've never missed before.'

'Oh well… yes, I know, but they are… Maybe I shouldn't say this, but they've never really seemed part of it, have they, not like the rest of us?'

'But I want everyone to feel that they belong. I don't know why they've stayed away, but it seems too much of a coincidence to me. And I have a feeling that the one called Anna lives near Ethel Bayliss. Anyway, I don't want anyone looking at me curiously all evening, as though they're trying to assess how I'm feeling. No, Joan, I'm going to take the bull by the horns.'

'Very well then; you know whatever you do that I'll be right behind you. You're a brave lass.' Joan grinned at her. 'Come along then; I'll carry the tray, and you bring the rest of the stuff in.'

They handed round the cups of tea, small plates and serviettes, and the plate of Joan's home-made fairy cakes and iced buns. When they were all supplied Fiona broke into the chatter.

'Listen, ladies, please, if you will… I've got something to say.' There was a sudden hush as they all looked at her expectantly. 'I'm sure you must all have heard…' she began. 'What I mean is… well… there's a story going round the parish about… about something that happened to me quite a while ago – fourteen years ago, actually – and… I want to put the record straight.'

Some of them looked down at their plates, a little discomfited, but several of the ladies looked her in the eye, nodding and half smiling, all, it seemed, in sympathy with her.

'I had a baby,' she said, 'a baby girl. I was seventeen years old when I discovered I was pregnant.'

'Well, join the club then!' said Sandra Jarvis. The women all looked at her, and the ice was broken as they all burst out laughing.

'Yes, it happened to me an' all,' Sandra went on. 'My mam and dad played hell with me… Whoops, sorry!' She put a hand to her mouth. 'They were very annoyed, I mean, but Gary and me, well, we got married. Then little Gareth came along, then Kim, then Kelly, and Mum and Dad think the world of 'em all now. Sorry, Fiona. I've interrupted your story, haven't I? But I just wanted to say – well – it happens, doesn't it? And I dare say there might be a few more here who were… well… not exactly whiter than white when they got married.'

There was a slight ripple of amusement, more subdued this time, and one or two of the women looked down at the floor, a little embarrassed.

'Well, thank you for that, Sandra,' said Fiona. 'Don't worry about what she's just said, ladies,' she added with a sly grin. 'I'm not going to ask you to put your hands up.'

'Oh, what a pity!' said Karen, Sandra's friend.

'That's enough now,' said Fiona, laughing. 'To get back to what I was saying… I'm aware that people are talking, so I'd like to tell you the truth about it.' She told them, as briefly as she could, about Dave and the church holiday, the lack of understanding and support from her parents, and her banishment to the home for unmarried mothers.

'Actually, it wasn't all that bad,' she said. 'You hear such grim tales about such places, but all the staff there were very kind, provided that we toed the line. But it seems that I made an enemy there – as well as a very good friend – and I think she was out to cause trouble for me when she recognized me again, recently. Hence the story, which seems to have circulated like wildfire.'

'Yes, I must admit I'd heard about it,' said Gillian.

'So had I,' said Sylvia, and a few more nodded in agreement.

'I'm not going to say who told me, though,' said Gillian.

'Nor do I want you to,' said Fiona. 'I'm not quite sure what the would-be troublemakers want to happen. Joan thinks – and I'm inclined to agree with her – that they want Simon to be suspicious about me, and to find out, eventually, that his wife has a guilty secret. But, of course, Simon already knows, and I've had nothing but love and support from my husband.' There was no need to tell them that he had only recently found out the truth.

'That's no more than we would expect of Simon,' said Sylvia, 'and may I say on behalf of everyone here, that our rector has got himself an excellent wife.'

'Hear, hear...' It seemed to Fiona that all the women were in agreement.

'And we are all highly delighted about the forthcoming baby,' added Gillian. 'That story is far more important to us all.'

'Thank you, all of you,' said Fiona, moved almost to tears by the support she was receiving. She blinked and brushed away the incipient moisture in her eyes. 'Now, I think we've said enough on that subject, haven't we? Just stay and chat, ladies, for as long as you like.'

The gathering broke into three or four little groups chatting together. A few moments later Fiona was surprised to see Ruth Makepeace and her friend, Heather, join herself and Joan on the settee. Ruth, a little self-consciously, bent down and kissed Fiona on the cheek. 'I admire you so much for saying all that,' she told her. 'And... for everything. There's something I want to tell you myself.'

'Thank you, Ruth,' said Fiona, moving along to make room for her. 'Everyone is being very kind, but it took a lot of courage, I can tell you.'

'Well, so will this,' said Ruth quietly. 'You see, I resented you at first, Fiona, quite a lot. Then when I got to know you better I realized what a good wife you are for Simon. Far better than I would have been...'

'Oh dear!' said Fiona. 'You really don't need to tell me all this, Ruth.'

'But I do,' Ruth answered. 'You see… I was a little bit in love with Simon, and I thought – mistakenly – that he might feel the same way about me. I don't know if you realized…'

Fiona laughed, a little embarrassedly. 'I'm not so green as I'm cabbage looking; That's something my old gran used to say. Yes, I gather there were a few hopeful ladies in the parish when Simon's first wife died. And who could blame them? My husband was quite a catch! I couldn't believe it myself when he asked me to marry him. I'm sorry, Ruth. It must have been awful for you. A newcomer like me, and I know you'd done such a lot to help Simon.'

'But that was all, wasn't it? We worked together on committees and things, and I imagined something that wasn't there. I know Simon's a clergyman, but he's a bit of a live wire as well, isn't he? And you're so vivacious and outgoing; you're just right for him. I'm rather quiet, and… well, I know now that it wouldn't have been right.'

'Go on, tell them the rest of it,' said her friend, Heather, who, along with Joan, had been listening to the conversation. 'I know you're dying to tell them.'

'Well, I've met somebody,' said Ruth, smiling shyly. 'We get on well together, and I think… well, I know that I love him.'

'And he loves you too,' said Heather.

'Yes, he does,' said Ruth. 'In fact we're getting engaged next week, when it's my birthday. You're the first to know, apart from Heather, of course.'

'And the rest of the staff,' added Heather, 'who must be blind if they haven't put two and two together by now. He's our new headmaster,' she smiled. 'It was love at first sight for those two… well, almost.'

'Oh yes; he came last September didn't he?' said Fiona. 'I remember Simon telling me; he was on the board of governors who appointed him. Ian Saunders; that's his name, isn't it? Well, fancy that! I'm really delighted for you, Ruth, and I know that Simon will be, too.'

'Ian's a widower,' Ruth explained. 'His wife died about five years ago, and he has two children – a boy and a girl – in their early teens. He's the same age as me; well, just a year older. And I get on very well with the children.'

'I'm so happy for you,' said Fiona. 'And I'm so pleased that we are going to be friends from now on… as I'm sure we are.'

'Yes, I'm pleased too,' said Ruth. 'I've felt for a while that I wanted to get to know you better. I lost my husband, Ralph, as you probably know, during the war, and I didn't think there would ever be anyone else.'

'Until you fell for Simon,' said Fiona with a twinkle in her eye. 'And who could blame you, eh?'

Ruth grinned. 'Let's put it all behind us and look forward to the future. I'm so thrilled for you both, about the baby. Perhaps you would like a little girl, would you, after… you know, what you were telling us?'

Fiona smiled, a little sadly. 'Yes maybe I would. But that first little baby girl… she was such a treasure, so beautiful. I could never feel that it was wrong, giving birth to her. I just hope she's having a happy life. I don't really mind about the baby, so long as it's all right. That's what all expectant parents say, don't they? I've a feeling Simon might like a boy; men always want a son, don't they? But I'm sure he'll feel as I do; a boy or a girl would be equally loved.'

'You were very brave, saying all that tonight,' said Ruth. 'And I hope these gossip-mongers are forced to skulk away with their tails between their legs. Their little plan didn't work, did it? I hope they're thoroughly ashamed of themselves...'

Simon was astounded when Fiona told him about what she had said to the Young Wives' group. 'Jolly good for you!' he said. 'That took some pluck, but I know you're not short of that, darling. So maybe the gossip will stop when they find they're not getting the support they wanted.'

'Well, the Young Wives are all supporting me at least,' said Fiona. 'No, not quite all of them; there were four missing. But if I know Joan I think she'll go and have a talk to them. It was wonderful, Simon, the way they all rallied round me. And there's another item of news... Ruth Makepeace is getting engaged, to the new headmaster. I know you'll be pleased to hear that.'

'Indeed I am,' said Simon. 'That's great news! She's been a widow a long time. Such a very nice person...'

'Yes, I like her,' replied Fiona. 'I feel I got to know her better tonight. She and Heather were very supportive.' She didn't feel it was necessary to say any more. And Simon quickly changed the subject.

'With regard to our problem, I don't really know what this group of tittle-tattling women hoped to gain by spreading their malicious gossip.'

'To discredit me in your eyes, I suppose,' said Fiona. 'To point out — to anyone who would listen — that I'm not a suitable wife for a rector, which is what some of them have thought all along; I'm well aware of that.'

'It hasn't worked then, has it? They may find now that nobody wants to listen... That's a pity in a way,' he mused. 'I wanted them to realize that I knew what their game was; to preach a sermon, perhaps, about hypocrisy. I really abhor that "holier than thou" attitude that some folk adopt, as though they have never done anything wrong. We have all fallen short of God's standards at one time or another, and I do mean all… myself included. But perhaps it might be better, under the circumstances, to leave well alone. They may have learnt their lesson.'

Twenty-Eight

There was a good congregation on the following Sunday morning. It was a bright and sunny April day and the sun glinted through the stained-glass windows casting rainbow coloured lights on the heads of the choir members. Simon noticed especially his wife's golden hair glowing in the diffused sunlight, and his heart warmed anew with his love for her. It had been a trying couple of weeks, but he felt that their love would be even stronger because of it.

The women whom he guessed to be at the root of the gossip were all there, but none of them, it seemed, wanted to meet his eye as he glanced round the congregation. Arthur Bayliss, one of his churchwardens, the husband of Ethel – whom he suspected of being the leader of the pack – had appeared a little ill at ease with him for the last couple of weeks, although nothing pertinent to the matter had been said so far.

From his high position in the pulpit – six feet above contradiction, as his former vicar used to call it – he looked round at the congregation. There were a few strangers there; a young couple halfway back, and two girls in anoraks on the row behind them. The first of the visitors were already appearing in Aberthwaite, which was a popular venue for walkers, and lovers of the countryside in general. On the back row there was a young man who looked, somehow, vaguely familiar, although Simon didn't think he had met him before. He always tried to speak to all newcomers at the end of the service and to invite them to come again, if they so wished.

After the final hymn had been sung Simon said the blessing, then made his way to the door at the rear of the church to shake hands with each member of the congregation. The young couple he had noticed told him that they were spending a week touring in the northern dales, and the two girls, as he had guessed, were keen hikers, walking some sixteen miles each day but having an easier day on the Sunday. The young man he had noticed was nowhere to be seen, and Simon supposed that he had made a quick exit, for whatever reason.

Mrs Bayliss, to his surprise, did not seem at all ill at ease now, but then she was not the sort of woman to climb down from her high horse. She actually looked him in the eye and said, 'Very good sermon, rector; thank you so much.' It was a term of address that he disliked. He preferred to be called Simon, but old habits died hard with the older generation. Her minions were less effusive, shuffling past him a little self-consciously, he thought; but he made a point of speaking to them in his usual friendly manner.

When he returned to the vestry to disrobe, Arthur Bayliss approached him, with the other warden, Jonas Fowler, close behind him. 'We'd like a word with you, Simon,' said Arthur. He used the rector's Christian name now, although it had taken him a while to do so. 'Jonas and I,' he began, 'well, first of all we'd like to say that we're very pleased to hear your good news. We're so pleased for you and Fiona, about the baby.'

'Yes, indeed we are,' echoed Jonas.

'And I'm sorry,' Arthur continued, 'that my wife – with others – has been trying to make trouble. For once in my life I spoke to her quite sternly when I got wind of what was happening. A very self-righteous woman, my wife, but – well – she's had a good talking to. I'm so ashamed that they tried to make trouble for a lovely young lady like Fiona.'

'My Blanche has been very upset by it all,' said Jonas Fowler. 'She didn't want to have any part in it. And she's thrilled about the baby, just as if it were our own grand-child; we've got four, you know. She's started knitting already.'

'That's very kind of her,' said Simon, touched by both their comments. He had guessed that Blanche Fowler, a much more gentle and sympathetic person, though dominated at times by Ethel Bayliss, would have tried to keep her own counsel. 'Fiona made a mistake; haven't we all, in one way or another? It's only human nature to go astray, just as it's human nature to want to condemn. Thank you, both of you, for your support. Let's hope we can put it behind us now and look forward to the good times ahead.'

Simon told Fiona about the comments of the two men. 'I feel sure you have nothing more to worry about now,' he said.

'Yes, it seems that it's been a nine-day wonder,' she agreed. 'I think Joan has been doing her best to put things right; and people are more ready to listen to her than to some of the others. Things will settle down now, Simon; I feel sure of it. And… thank you for being so under-standing, about everything.'

He smiled, a little ruefully. 'I've made mistakes myself,' he said. 'But what is important is that it's all in the past.

We found each other, didn't we? And that's a miracle if ever there was one. Or... was it part of God's plan for us? I don't know all the answers, darling, but I know there's not a man in the whole world who is more blessed than I am.'

Sunday was a busy day for all clergymen, none more so than for Simon, who was in sole charge of his church and parish. It was not considered large enough to warrant the services of a curate; neither was there a qualified lay reader, as there was in some parishes. From time to time there were visiting preachers, but for most of the time Simon coped single-handedly with the morning and evening services, plus the service of Holy Communion either at eight o'clock, or at the close of the evening worship.

That particular Sunday was a busy one, with the Communion taking place at the end of the evening service. Simon was interested to see that the young man whom he had noticed in the morning was there again. He didn't stay, however, for the Holy Communion; there were always some who, for one reason or another, did not do so.

Simon was mildly curious, but not avidly so. He was puzzled by the feeling that he had seen him somewhere before, but for the life of him he couldn't remember where. He dismissed the matter from his mind; maybe the identity of the mysterious young man would come to him later.

–

He did not have long to wait. He was alone in the rectory on Monday morning. Fiona was still working part-time at the library, and intended to do so for several months. It was mid-morning – Simon was thinking it was about time for his 'elevenses' – when there was a ring at the doorbell. When he answered it, there was the young man who had been at the services the previous day.

'Oh, hello there,' said Simon. 'I saw you in church yesterday, didn't I? Good to see you again. So... what can I do for you?'

His visitor hesitated. 'It's a little difficult really,' he said. 'May I come in? I'd like to have a chat with you.'

'By all means,' said Simon. 'Come along in...' He ushered him into the sitting room. 'I was just about to make myself a cup of coffee – my wife's at work this morning – so I'd be pleased if you would join me.'

'Yes... thank you. That would be very nice.' The newcomer seemed a little ill at ease. 'I'm Gregory by the way; Gregory Challinor; I'm usually known as Greg.'

Simon nodded, still very puzzled. 'Pleased to meet you then, Greg.' The two of them shook hands. 'And I'm the Reverend Simon Norwood, rector of St Peter's, as I'm sure you know. But I prefer to be known as Simon... Just make yourself at home, Greg. I won't be long.'

He returned with two china beakers of coffee, serviettes, and a plate of chocolate digestive biscuits. The young man helped himself, slowly, to sugar and a biscuit, then put his beaker on the small table at the side of him before starting to speak. His nervousness was more apparent now. He leaned forward, looking at Simon intently.

'There is no easy way to say this...' he began.

'Go on,' said Simon, trying to show encouragement. 'I've heard all sorts, believe me.'

'I'm sure you have.' Greg Challinor grinned fleetingly, before looking anxious again. 'You won't have heard this, though. You see… I have reason to believe that you are… my father.'

Simon gasped as he stared, shocked beyond belief, at his visitor. There was no reason to disbelieve him, though. He knew now why the young man looked so familiar. It was almost like seeing a younger version of himself, as he had been when he was in the RAF. Gregory was dark-haired, though, and there was a look in his brown eyes that reminded Simon of someone else – the young woman he had known quite well, all those years ago.

'Go on… Greg,' said Simon. His voice was husky with emotion. 'Tell me…'

'My mother is called Yvonne,' Greg began. 'She was Yvonne Stevenson when you knew her. You did know her, didn't you?'

'Yes… I knew her,' replied Simon quietly. 'But… I had no idea. We lost touch. She just disappeared, suddenly, and I couldn't understand it. Was that why she left the camp, because she knew…? Oh, how dreadful! Poor Yvonne! I'm so sorry…'

'There's no need to be,' said Greg. 'You mustn't feel guilty. Mum never wanted that. She guessed she might be pregnant, and so she decided it would be best for her to… just go away. And it all worked out very well in the end. I didn't know anything about it, though, not for ages. Mum and Dad were so happy together, and I had no idea that Keith was not my real father. Mum said she'd never wanted to tell me because Keith had cared for me as though I were his own son. I have a younger brother and sister, but it never made the slightest difference to Dad. He loved us all so much. He died, two years ago… and then Mum decided that I ought to know the truth.'

'It must have been a great shock for you, finding out,' said Simon. 'Your... father – was he in the Merchant Navy?' He remembered that Yvonne had told him about her boyfriend.

'No; that fizzled out, apparently. Mum left the WAAF, of course, when she knew she was expecting me. I was born in July, 1944. It wasn't easy for Mum, being on her own; there was such a stigma about it then, wasn't there? But my grandparents were very good and they took care of her. Then just after the war ended Mum met Keith – he was a doctor – and they got married. As I said, I didn't know any of this until quite recently. But when I knew, I had to come and find you. I've been plucking up courage for several months. I hope you don't mind... I know I must have given you quite a shock.'

'That's rather an understatement!' Simon shook his head in bewilderment. He was mesmerized by the revelations. For once in his life he felt at a loss for words. 'No, of course I don't mind. Your mother... how is she?' he faltered. 'I'm so sorry... about her husband. But I'm pleased to hear they were happy together.'

'Mum's a survivor,' said Greg with a smile. 'She'll be all right. Dad was several years older than Mum. Actually, she's friendly with someone she works with now, and we're very glad about it, myself and my brother and sister. She went back to work, in an insurance office, when we'd all left school.'

'So... what did you do when you left school, Greg?' asked Simon. 'Let me see; you must be – what? – twenty-two, now?'

Greg nodded. 'Yes, that's right. Just a minute... I'd better drink my coffee; it'll be going cold.' He quickly ate his biscuit and took a good gulp of the coffee. He seemed much more at ease now that he had told the salient parts of his story, although Simon knew there was still a lot more to hear. He, Simon, now that he had recovered a little from the initial shock, was anxious to know more. Greg – his son, although it was hard to take it in – seemed a pleasant young man, quite mature for his age, and he clearly bore no animosity towards Simon, his natural father.

Greg put down his beaker. 'Yes, I'll be twenty-two in July. When I left school – Manchester Grammar School – I spent three years at university in Durham, reading Law. It was during that time that my father died, and I found out… all this. I'm a junior partner with a firm of solicitors in Manchester now. I was fortunate to find a position near home. I'm still at home with Mum, although I hope to have my own place before too long.'

'You've done well,' said Simon. 'I'm sure your mum is very proud of you, isn't she?'

'I think so,' said Greg, modestly. 'We've all done quite well. My younger brother and sister are both at college now; Graham's at Leeds Uni, and Wendy's at a teacher training college in Bingley.'

'And you're in Manchester? Yes, I remember Yvonne saying that she came from there. I can't remember exactly where.'

'Mum was brought up in Moston, but my father's practice was in Didsbury; that's where we still live.'

There was a moment's silence as the two men regarded one another. Simon spoke first. 'So how did you find out about me; where I live and… everything?'

'It wasn't so difficult,' replied Greg, 'with you being a clergyman.' He smiled. 'You were rather easier to trace than if you'd been one of the hoi polloi.'

Simon laughed. 'Wearing our collars the wrong way round doesn't make us any different from what you think of as ordinary people.'

'No, I can see that,' said Greg. 'You were a curate in Hull, weren't you, before you moved here?'

'Yes, that's right,' agreed Simon.

'Well, my mother had a friend who had been in the WAAF with her. She was called Eileen, and she lived in Hull.'

'Eileen... Yes, I think I remember her,' said Simon. 'There were a few of them who went around together. I asked them about Yvonne, but they didn't know where she had disappeared to.'

'Eileen was the one that Mum knew best, and after a while she contacted her and told her what had happened. Mum said she'd felt guilty at just vanishing the way she did. So they kept in touch after that. Then Eileen saw a photo of you in the *Hull Gazette*...'

'Notorious, eh?' smiled Simon. 'No, it was most likely a report of a church function.'

'Something of the sort. Anyway, Eileen recognized you, and she told Mum. I don't know why; perhaps she just couldn't keep it to herself.'

'She'd be surprised, no doubt, to find out I'd become a "man of the cloth",' said Simon, smiling. 'I dare say Yvonne was surprised, wasn't she?'

'I don't know,' said Greg. 'As I've told you, I didn't know anything about all this until fairly recently. I don't think she was all that surprised. She said you were a very nice young man; very respectable and... honourable.'

'I might have been, if I'd known about it,' said Simon, ruefully. 'But I didn't know. It was wartime, and what happened with your mother was... well, it was just one of those things. I know it's easy to say that, but I did think a great deal about her.'

'She understood all that,' said Greg, 'and it was her decision to do what she did. Anyhow, as I say, you were not difficult to trace. My mum's friend, Eileen, she's a great one for ferreting things out. So… here I am.'

'Yes, here you are,' echoed Simon. 'I can't pretend it's not been a shock, but it's been a very pleasant one. It's not every day that you discover a long-lost son! You must call me Simon, though; I wouldn't expect anything else. I'm so pleased you were all happy together as a family. Your father… I'm sure he must have been a remarkable man.'

'Yes, so he was,' agreed Greg. 'We all miss him very much, but time moves on and we must do the same.'

'Are you staying in Aberthwaite, then?' asked Simon.

'Yes, I've got a week's leave. I came on Saturday, and booked into a bed and breakfast place near the station. They do evening meals as well, and it's very comfortable. I intend to do some walking. I've not been to this neck of the woods before, and I've got my hiking gear with me; I do a little from time to time.'

'I expect you know quite a lot about me then, don't you?' asked Simon.

'A little,' Greg admitted. 'I know you got married last year.'

'Fiona's my second wife,' said Simon. 'My first wife died several years ago. Fiona and I are expecting our first child.' In reality, the second child, for both of us, he thought, in what was turning out to be a remarkably ironic coincidence.

'That's great,' said Greg. 'Congratulations!'

'You must meet Fiona,' said Simon, eagerly. But Greg looked a trifle fazed at the idea.

'What's the matter?' asked Simon. 'Now we've found one another, you're not going to disappear again, are you?'

'Well, no…' said Greg. 'But I don't want to be an embarrassment to you. To your wife, I mean, and… with you being a vicar. I'm sure you won't want stories going round. People gossip so much, don't they?'

Simon laughed. 'Oh yes; we're well used to gossip here. But I can tell you, without any hesitation, that my wife will be delighted to meet you. And as for the folk in my congregation… I might as well give them something really worthwhile to gossip about!'

Twenty-Nine

Fiona came home at midday for a snack lunch that Simon had prepared, as he always did when she was working for the whole day. It was whilst they were eating their sandwiches of roast beef – cut cold from the joint they had had the previous day – that he broke the news to her.

'I've had a visitor this morning, darling,' he began.

'Oh, a welcome one, I hope? I know you don't like being disturbed when you're working.'

'Very welcome, as it turned out,' he answered, just a little hesitantly. He wasn't quite sure how Fiona would react to the news, despite his telling Greg that all would be well. 'It was the young man that I noticed in church yesterday; he was there for both services.'

'Yes, I think you mentioned it,' said Fiona, concentrating more on her beef sandwich than on what her husband was saying. She was finding she was always hungry these days. 'What did he want?'

'Well, he came to tell me he has discovered that… that I am his father.' Simon felt it was better to come to the crux of the matter straight away, rather than hedge around it. There was a moment's silence whilst Fiona looked at him in amazement.

Then, 'What!' she said. 'Who is he, then? Some sort of prankster, trying to cause trouble?'

'Oh no, not at all,' replied Simon. 'It's true, although I had no idea about it, of course. There's no disputing it. He is... my son.'

'But when... who? I don't understand.' Fiona shook her head in a bewildered manner. 'You never said anything about it.'

'Because I didn't know,' said Simon. 'When I was in the RAF I met a girl called Yvonne; she was a WAAF. We had a brief relationship. We didn't intend to; we started off as good friends, neither of us really wanted to get too involved, but... it was inevitable, I suppose.'

'Yes, I can understand that,' said Fiona. 'I didn't imagine you were completely without experience when you got married – to Millicent, I mean. You told me that you'd... well, that you hadn't always been a clergyman, and I knew what you meant.' She smiled. 'Tit for tat, I suppose. What a coincidence, though, to find out about it just now. Are you going to tell me all about it?'

'Of course I am, darling. I didn't mention Yvonne before because it was all so long ago, and I had no idea that there had been any outcome. If I had known that I had a son I would have told you.'

'Would you? I wonder...' said Fiona. 'I didn't tell you, did I, about my daughter?'

'That's true,' Simon agreed. 'No, to be honest, who knows what I would have done? If I'd known in the first place that Yvonne was expecting a child, things might have turned out very differently. I hope I was the sort of young man who would have faced up to his responsibilities. As it happened, Yvonne got married, and they were very happy. She's a widow now, but her husband was a very good father to Greg. He believed Keith was his real father until recently, when Yvonne decided she should tell him the truth.'

'If…' said Fiona. 'Such a little word. The smallest in the English language – apart from "I" – but it's one of the most significant. "If this, if that, if only." We all say it, but it's futile, isn't it? We can't go back, not for all the "ifs" in the world.'

Simon was thoughtful. 'What would I have done, I wonder? And why didn't she tell me? I suppose I can understand why she didn't… As I told you, we didn't intend to get involved, but I was growing very fond of Yvonne. She was a really nice, decent sort of young woman. You told me the same about your boyfriend, Dave, didn't you?'

Fiona nodded. 'Yes; he was a decent well-brought-up lad. But we *can't* go into the ifs and the what might have beens.'

'It was 1943,' Simon went on. 'It seemed as though the war would never end. The bombing raids over Germany… I've told you a little about them, haven't I? Wondering how long I could go on with the meaningless destruction, or so it seemed to me, but we could never say so. It would have been called defeatist talk. Then we lost our skipper, our chief pilot. I saw the plane burst into flames with him inside it. That was when it happened, the next night, with Yvonne and me. I suppose it was inevitable. We comforted one another. It only happened a couple of times…'

'That's all it takes,' said Fiona, quietly. 'I found that out, to my cost.'

'Then I was injured myself,' Simon continued. 'I told you, didn't I, how I could hardly believe my good fortune when I was told I was to be taken off operational duties to become an instructor. It seemed like an answer to my prayers, although I hadn't dared to pray for such a selfish request. I went home on leave... and when I went back to the camp I found that Yvonne had left, very suddenly. I never saw her again. Now, of course, I know why.'

'Things worked out well for her, though, didn't they?' said Fiona. 'Just as they did for me, in the end.'

'Yes; "all things work together for good,"' said Simon. 'A favourite text of mine. It's sometimes hard to see, though, how things will work out.'

'So... what about Greg?' asked Fiona. 'You'll be seeing him again, won't you?'

'Yes; he's staying till next weekend. He's taken a week's leave from his work – he's a junior solicitor in Manchester – and he intends to do some walking whilst he's here.'

'Why don't you take a day off and go with him?' suggested Fiona. 'Get to know him. It sounds as though you got on quite well together?'

'Yes, so we did. It's all very strange... I asked him if he'd like to meet you, darling, and he said he would. He was worried it might cause trouble, though; not so much with you but with the folk in the congregation. I told him not to worry; I'm well able to cope with the gossip. And I don't intend to keep it a secret.'

'You mean... you're going to tell them about Greg?' asked Fiona. 'Surely there's no need to do that. What business is it of anybody's, except for you and me, and Greg and his mother? And you know how they gossiped about me and tried to make trouble. Some of them are probably still talking, although it does seem to have died down.'

'That's precisely why I'm going to tell them about my son,' said Simon. 'You know how gossip starts. Someone may see us together this week, and put two and two together. Greg does, actually, look very much like me. I'm surprised I didn't realize straight away when I saw him; I just thought he reminded me of someone.'

'Yourself,' smiled Fiona.

'Yes; myself when younger. He's a good-looking lad, though I say it myself.' He laughed. 'Anyway, I shall tell them the truth, straight from the horse's mouth, as they say. And let them make of it whatever they will.'

'Hmm… if you're sure,' said Fiona, doubtfully.

'Perfectly sure,' replied Simon. 'Come on now; you're going to be late back for work. We'll have a chat tonight about when to invite Greg to come here. He's calling again in the morning, because I asked him if he'd like me to show him around the area – go walking, maybe, as you suggested – and he seemed very keen. Anyway… off you go now, darling. I'll do the washing up!'

-

Simon and his new-found son spent a couple of pleasant days together that week. Simon dug out his hiking gear – he had not done much of late – and they walked in the foothills of Wensleydale and Swaledale. Another day they drove to Richmond in Simon's car and walked the pathway around the eleventh-century castle, from where there was a magnificent view across the dales as far as the Vale of York.

They agreed that Greg should call Simon by his Christian name. He was really more of a newly discovered friend than a father. They found that they had much in common and conversation between them was easy and companionable. Simon learnt that his son loved books, theatre going and football; he supported Manchester City. He loved sports cars as well, which he could not yet afford, but hoped to do so before very long. Simon was also pleased to learn that Greg attended the local Church of England, having been encouraged to do so by his parents. He had a girlfriend whom he had known only for a few weeks. He assured Simon that he wanted to be sure of his feelings before he committed himself, but he felt that this might well be the right girl for him.

Fiona cooked an evening meal for them after they had spent the day walking. She was very impressed by the young man, and he seemed to be captivated by Fiona. Simon felt it all boded well for the future.

They met him at the station on Saturday morning to see him off on his journey back to Manchester.

'I'm so pleased that you decided to come and find me, Greg,' said Simon. 'It took a lot of courage, I know, and… well, it's been great. We will see you again, won't we?'

'Sure thing!' said Greg. 'Thank you, both of you, for making me so welcome.' The two men shook hands, then Simon put his arms around his son, giving him a brief manly hug.

'You're a grand young man,' he said. 'Tell your mother I said so. And do please give her my best wishes.' Simon didn't add that he would like to meet her again, but he felt it might be possible, sometime in the not too distant future.

Greg shook hands with Fiona, then kissed her gently on the cheek. 'Simon's a lucky chap!' he said, with a sly wink as he boarded the train.

'I think Greg has taken rather a shine to you,' said Simon as they walked back to the rectory. 'I shall have to watch out, won't I?'

'No fear of that,' smiled Fiona. 'He's a very personable young man, though. I'm sure he'll turn out to be almost as good as his father.'

Simon shook his head confusedly. 'It's still hard to take it all in. But I can't say I have any regrets. It's just added another dimension to life, one that I was totally unaware of.'

'Yvonne must have been a very nice person,' said Fiona quietly. 'I'm sure she still is.'

'Yes, she was,' agreed Simon. 'I'm pleased she was happy in her marriage, and has the chance to be happy again. And you and I, my darling, have so much to look forward to.'

Thirty

'Let he who is without sin among you cast the first stone.'

The members of the congregation who had been looking forward to a few minutes' peace and quiet alone with their thoughts, whilst the rector preached his sermon – although he was, admittedly, worth listening to if one felt inclined – were brought back to reality, arrested by his opening words. Did the Reverend Simon intend to take them to task about the stories that had been circulating concerning his wife? If so, then it was no more than some of them deserved, thought the ones who had always liked Fiona and had sympathized with her over the revelations. Others, like Ethel Bayliss and Mabel Thorpe and their cronies, stirred a little uneasily in their pews, looking down at the floor.

'The text is from chapter eight of John's gospel,' Simon continued. 'It is a story that I am sure you are all familiar with, where Jesus comes upon a crowd of people who are about to stone to death a woman whom they believe to be guilty of adultery. I know that such an extreme punishment is not acceptable in our country although, regrettably, it still takes place occasionally elsewhere. But we live in a Christian country, don't we? We understand that folk can stray away from the straight and narrow pathway – fall into sin, some might say – and do things that are considered wrong. None of us is perfect. There is a text that says that all of us have sinned – and I do mean each and every one of us – and have fallen short of the standards that God wants from us. There is another quotation, not a biblical one, which says that the person who never made a mistake never made anything.'

He paused for a moment, looking round at the members of the congregation – a goodly number as was usual on a Sunday morning – many of whom were looking at him with great interest, but others whose heads were bowed. 'There has been a good deal of talk recently,' he said. 'My wife and I are well aware of that, but I have the feeling now that common sense has prevailed. The gossip has been nipped in the bud and, I trust, has died down. We all like to point the finger at times, don't we? To feel that we are in the right and that others are wrong, for whatever reason. My wife, Fiona, made what is sometimes called the oldest mistake in the world; a very human one, I might add. And I trust that by now you have forgiven her, although it is not really our concern, is it? Forgiveness, in a matter like this, comes from God.

'However, I don't want to talk about my wife this morning. I'm sorry if I've embarrassed her...' He smiled in the direction of the choir stalls where Fiona was sitting, and she smiled back encouragingly at him. 'She did have some idea, though, of what I was going to say.' He paused. 'I want to tell you another story this morning...

'Some of you may have noticed that there was a strange young man in the congregation last Sunday; he was there at both services. By strange I don't mean that there was anything odd about him. What I mean is that we hadn't seen him before. As you know, we do try, here at St Peter's, to make strangers – newcomers is a better word – to make them feel welcome. But this young man had gone before I had a chance to speak to him. If you saw him you might have noticed that he bore quite a resemblance to me.' Simon smiled. 'I thought he looked somewhat familiar, but that was all.' He paused again, aware that every eye was upon him now.

'Anyway, the next morning this young man – his name is Gregory, known as Greg – called at the rectory with some surprising news for me. Yes, some of you may have already guessed what I am about to tell you. Gregory is my son, and until that moment I had no idea of his existence.'

There were a few quiet gasps and surprised looks on faces, more on those of the women than the men. 'You are no doubt wondering who, when and how? Well, not so much how; it happened in the usual way, of course.' He smiled to introduce a touch of levity, and many of them smiled back at him. 'I was in the RAF during the war, as many of you know. I was part of an aircrew, the navigator, and I took part in many bombing raids over Germany. I met a young woman who was a WAAF, as so many young airmen did. Life was lived at fever pitch, as those of you who also served in the forces will remember. You can guess the rest. The inevitable happened, although it was not what we intended when we became friendly. I'm not trying to make excuses, but this happens sometimes… doesn't it? Then as some of you know, I was injured during a bombing raid, not seriously, but I was granted a period of leave.

'And when I returned to the camp to take up my new position as an instructor, I found that my lady friend had gone; suddenly, quite unexpectedly, to another posting I was told. I never saw her again. I never heard of her again until on Monday I met her son… hers and mine.'

The silence in the church was profound. Simon felt, however, that the faces looking up at him seemed to be sympathetic rather than condemning or disapproving.

'I expect you're flabbergasted,' he laughed. 'So was I! It doesn't matter how Greg managed to trace me. Suffice it to say that he did, and I am very pleased that he did so. He's a fine young man. He has had a good upbringing with his mother and stepfather, in a happy family and, may I say, none of us have any regrets. For Fiona and myself the future is full of promise, and now we are delighted to have a new family member, one of whom we were unaware until a week ago.

'You may be surprised, shocked even, inclined to think that this is not fitting behaviour for your rector. I have no idea how you will react to this, but, as I told Fiona when I married her, I hadn't always been a clergyman. I think she knew what I meant.'

For once, but for by no means the first time, Simon felt that he had the congregation in the palm of his hand. The rest of the sermon — not a long one — was about looking honestly at yourself and recognizing your own shortcomings instead of being ready to condemn others. In the Bible story about the woman accused of adultery there was not one person who had not done wrong — sinned against God or against another human being — at some time or another; no one who could, in all honesty, 'cast the first stone'. So it was in our own time and circumstances. And it was only God who could see into the hearts and minds of men and women and know the truth about them.

'Your rector, you see, is only human,' said Simon in conclusion. 'My wife and I trust that we will continue to have your support in all that we try to do… and your understanding of our human frailty.'

The final hymn was 'Now thank we all, our God', which was sung enthusiastically. Fiona stood with him at the door to say farewell to the people, as he had asked her to do.

Those members of the congregation who came, maybe, once a month rather than every week made no comment about Simon's surprising sermon. They just shook hands with him and Fiona, all, however, with a smile and an understanding glance. There appeared to be no feeling of reproach.

Others, including Mrs Bayliss and Miss Thorpe, shook hands and said good morning quite civilly, but without any real warmth. Simon knew he could expect no other than that. Women like Ethel Bayliss would not climb down immediately from their high horse, but he had the feeling that they had got the message and that there would be no more unpleasantness for Fiona. After their failed attempt at stirring up trouble, he doubted that they would attempt to treat him in the same way.

Many of the folk smiled readily at their rector and his wife, saying how pleased they were about the forthcoming 'happy event', and hoping that all would go well for Fiona during her pregnancy.

'You look positively radiant, my dear,' said one of the ladies who attended each Sunday but who usually had little to say. 'God bless you, and your lovely husband,' she added, kissing Fiona rather shyly on the cheek. 'We think the world of him,' she whispered, 'and of you, too.'

'Thank you so much,' said Fiona, humbly. She felt that this middle-aged woman, whose name she had to admit she didn't know, was typical of most of the congregation.

She began to believe that she and Simon would have the support and understanding of most, if not quite all, of the church folk. Simon's brave admission might prove to have done far more good than harm, although she had wondered at first if he was making the right decision.

There were a few who were more outspoken, those who knew Simon and Fiona rather better than most people did.

'My goodness, Simon – what a story!' laughed Joan Tweedale. 'You're a dark horse, aren't you?'

'Yes… Be sure your sins will find you out! It's tit for tat, as my wife says,' he smiled. 'It was a shock,' he added, 'but it turned out to be a very pleasant one. He's a grand young man. I hope that sometime – though maybe not just yet – I might be able to introduce him to all our friends at St Peter's.'

—

'Do you know,' Simon said to his wife later that day, 'so many people have asked me whether we want a boy or a girl; and I always say we don't mind…'

'So long as he or she is all right,' added Fiona. 'And it's true, isn't it? We don't mind.'

'I suppose, if I'm absolutely honest, I would have hoped for a boy,' said Simon. 'But I would never have said so, especially not to you, my love. But now… well… it's turned out that I've got a good deal more than I bargained for. A grown-up son of twenty-one! I always thought that God had a sense of humour!'

Epilogue

Fiona gave birth to a baby girl on the Sunday evening of December eleventh, which was the third Sunday in the season of Advent. Simon took her to the hospital in the early hours of the morning. She knew that he must, of course, preach at both services as there was no visiting preacher that day.

He dashed to the hospital after the morning service, hoping to see his wife and, possibly, the new arrival. He was told, however, that she was in the labour ward, and that it would be better for him to go back home.

He was inundated with good wishes for Fiona at the evening service. He said a prayer for her safe delivery, knowing that every member of the congregation was praying with him.

He lost no time in driving, for the third time that day, to the hospital.

'Mr Norwood, you have a baby daughter,' said the smiling nurse who led him into the single room, where Fiona was sitting up in bed with the newborn child in her arms. She smiled radiantly at him. 'It's a girl, Simon!' He could tell by the elation in her voice that it was what she had, secretly, been hoping for.

He kissed her lovingly before gently moving the soft woollen shawl aside to look at his little daughter. She was sleeping, but as he gazed at her in wonder she opened her eyes – a bluey-grey indeterminate colour – seeming to look straight at him. Her hair was a feathery golden down, the same shade as Fiona's, on her perfectly shaped little head. Her mouth was a tiny rosebud and her cheeks tinged with the palest pink. Simon was sure there could never have been a more beautiful baby.

'She's so lovely, darling,' he whispered.

There was a window opposite Fiona's bed, and the curtains were not fully closed. In the dark-blue velvety sky a single star was shining, brighter than all the others.

'The evening star…' mused Fiona. 'It might not be, of course, but it seems like it to me.' She turned to her husband. 'I think I'd like to call her Stella,' she said. 'That is… if you agree.'

'I think that's perfect,' said Simon. 'Our very own little star. Thank you, my love… for everything.'

He was aware, though, of just a glimmer of sadness in his wife's demeanour, together with the joy. He sensed, rather than saw it in her face. He knew she must be remembering the first little girl to whom she had given birth.

He had found his son, although Gregory had been unknown to him. Simon made up his mind, in that instant, that one day, if it was his wife's desire, they would try to find her daughter.